The Wrong Side of Night
By Patti Davis

In any given moment we have two options – to step forward into growth or to step back into safety.

Abraham Maslow

1.

On the first day of autumn rain my mother died. I'll always wonder if she planned it that way. Maybe when she heard rain pummel the roof she decided, Now would be a good time to go, and then through sheer force of will, commanded her heart to stop beating. I will, of course, never know for certain. It's just that so much of her life took shape from decisions constructed in the deep caverns of her brain. Decisions that almost always – mysteriously and predictably – came to fruition.

My mother hated rain. She said it depressed her and made her hair frizz. It was never entirely clear if those two complaints were intertwined or completely unrelated. She was certainly capable of blaming her depression on the inconsiderate weather system that didn't have the decency to just rain in the middle of the night when most people were in bed... so that in the morning everyone could have a good hair day. Especially her. She took the weather very personally. She frequently said, "Well, when am I going to get the weather I want? I realize we need rain, but enough already. I want sun!"

"Talk to God about it," I would always reply. I can't be sure, but I doubt my mother ever talked to God about anything.

The storm began just after dawn -- a drenching one, steady and hard. A leave-the-lamps-on-all-day kind of storm. It was early for rain -- only a few days into the month of October. But then how can you predict anything these days? Hurricanes and ferocious storms sweep across the country at unpredictable times, leveling entire communities. Droughts descend on Colorado that are so bad people can't feed their horses and have to send them to rescue organizations. Louisiana is buried beneath floodwaters while California is running out of water as drought stretches from one year into the next. This rain was a blessing to us Californians, the thirsty earth drinking it in. Although not everyone was rejoicing.

Halloween decorations had just started to appear on front lawns, and children in the neighborhood moaned that the ghosts and assorted skeletons had gotten soggy and didn't look scary anymore. I heard Elliot, two houses away, yelling that the ghosts looked like old paper towels. That morning – hours before my phone rang – I listened to my next-door neighbor explain to Chloe, her six-year old daughter, that she simply could not bring the hairdryer outside and blow-dry the witches. The witches would have to dry out on their own when the rain stopped. Which it would, she said. It always does.

The day before my mother died, I arrived just past noon with my dog Lola, and found her day nurse, Julia, standing outside the
room.

"She shooed me out," Julia said quietly. "She just woke up a little while ago and let Rosario bring her tea but then she told us both to get out."

My mother had round-the-clock care, but since I only visited during the day, I'd only met Julia and a couple of other caregivers. I had no idea who was on duty during the long nights when my mother sometimes slept but often didn't. Julia was slender and pale, quietly deferential to my mother and smart enough to stay out of the way when she sensed a storm brewing.

The sky outside was pebbled with white clouds, like a scrim over the sun. The air had a milky hue. When I went into my mother's room, the bedside lamps were on and the drapes were closed. She was sitting up in bed reading the morning paper.

My mother recently went through six weeks of chemo for lung cancer. She'd never smoked in her life, so it was a mystery how she got it, but it was in both lungs. Too advanced for surgery, they told her, but we can possibly give you some more time with a "drug regimen." That's the phrase they used, which my mother repeated to me. As if it were a new exercise program or diet instead of what it actually is – a holocaust of chemical weapons unleashed on the body to indiscriminately kill everything, bad and good, with the hope that some good cells might survive the carnage.

"Don't you want some daylight in here?" I asked, pulling the cord on the green and gold brocade curtains. I remembered how, as children, my brother and I would go around opening drapes at dawn, anxious for light to spill into the rooms of our apartment.

"I guess."

She peered over the top of her reading glasses. As I drew the drapes, her eyes seemed to match the dullness of the day outside. It was startling to see my mother wither under the assault of the medicines they syphoned into her body. She was wearing a pink bathrobe stained with food, which seemed like a clue to something. My mother was usually so fastidious she wouldn't wear a sweater with an unraveled thread or a broken button on it. Her wig was slightly askew, as if it didn't fit her properly anymore. As if her head had grown thinner too.

As a child, I believed she must have been held in high esteem by God and all the angels, who had bestowed upon her a beauty and an elegance that made heads turn wherever she went. I assumed she woke up in the morning looking perfect. I used to shut my eyes when I brushed my teeth, not wanting to look in the mirror at my own reflection, since I clearly had not received the same blessings. When I knelt to say my bedtime prayers, the words I uttered by rote concealed my true prayer. Silently, I asked God to let me become as pretty as my mother. That prayer went unanswered. I grew tall and long-legged, a girl quickly chosen when teams were being divided up for soccer because I could run faster than most of my classmates. I had my father's dark hair and angular features; my body could best be described as "athletic." Beauty was not to be my destiny, at least not the kind of beauty my mother possessed. In the place where prayers are born, a feeling of betrayal formed. I was sure God's face tilted away from me to smile brightly upon the woman who gave birth to me. And upon her son, who seemed to glow with a light I didn't possess. When Hale died, she was left with me, the girl in the shadows.

I cranked open the window to let in some fresh air. I felt death on the prowl. It slipped through the screen and drifted across the Persian rug, hunting for prey. The orchids beside the fireplace were sagging and dull, as if they knew what was coming and had surrendered. When I walked over to sit on the narrow sofa that faced my mother's bed, the shadows in the room seemed glacially cold. Stepping through them pricked my skin, like a shower of tiny ice shards.

That's when I noticed a tipped over prescription bottle on her nightstand and pills scattered everywhere. I stood up and approached her bed cautiously, held at bay by the tilt of her eyes over the rim of her reading glasses. I looked down at her – frail and ill but determined to get her way.

"You're not supposed to be taking Ambien anymore," I told her, with no authority in my voice whatsoever. "The doctor was very adamant about it. Your blood pressure is so low."

"I don't remember him saying that," my mother answered.

"Okay, but he did."

"If I don't remember it, he didn't say it."

I straightened my spine, thinking this could be the moment when I finally stood up to her, when I acted like the adult I'm supposed to be. But the moment passed and I didn't say another word. I scooped the pills back into the bottle, secured the cap, and set it back down on her nightstand. It would do no good to talk to the night-time caregiver. No one was going to argue with her.

"I'm tired," she said suddenly, pulling the bathrobe tightly across her chest. "I need to nap."

"Do you want me to stay until you fall asleep?" I asked her. I could hear Lola barking in the garden, a signal that she'd found a squirrel to taunt.

"There's no need for that."

When I leaned over and kissed my mother's cheek, I noticed how stiff her flesh was. And she smelled old – like fallen leaves when they're raked into a pile and left too long. I turned my back on the bottle of pills. I turned my back on my mother without saying goodbye.

When I walked out of the house with Lola trotting beside me, the world felt strangely light, as if the sky had expanded, lifted itself higher, although clouds had thickened and the day was even more muted. If it's possible for molecules of the atmosphere to turn silken, I felt they had. The leafy street seemed wider too and the scent of clean autumn air drifted through the car windows as we drove away.

I left there with one thought cleaved into my brain: I should have flushed her Ambien down the toilet. Or at least taken the pills away from her. I replayed the scene in my mind – how the small tablets trailed across her nightstand. The bottle probably tipped over during the night, the ghost of her hand still curled around it from when she'd reached for it in the quiet black hours while the city slept and the moon shone for no one. She was watching me, daring me to do what we both knew I should do. For those few seconds, I believed I could. But I folded. How meek I was, scooping the pills into my hand and trickling them back into their plastic bottle. I set it down beside the newest issue of Vanity Fair and avoided meeting her eyes. The sky was clouding over, a storm was coming, and I didn't say goodbye to her when I left.

I drove down the long driveway, waited for the gates to open, and watched as a sudden gust of wind shivered leaves from the towering eucalyptus trees onto the well-manicured grounds.

A couple of blocks from my mother's house, a Coroner's van drove past me going the opposite way. I thought of it as a sign, some eerie nudge from beyond. Then, predictably, I felt guilty about that.

Late that night the rain started. I woke up and felt like I was being washed clean. I loved those dark hours, with rain beating on the roof and slashing the windows. I thought about my mother dying. It seemed like a beginning, a birth, but also like uncharted territory. I missed my brother that night, felt the emptiness of not having someone who shared my history, someone who I could call in the dead of night. I wanted to talk to him about the pills, the dim-lit house, the scent of death drifting up from the orchids. I remembered a day in the life we used to have – I was twelve and he was ten – when we sat against the sand dunes in East Hampton and watched the sky and the Atlantic turn gray from an approaching storm. As the air around us darkened, we shared secrets with each other. I told him silly things, like how I'm scared of grasshoppers because they jump, and of people wearing shower caps (I have no idea why). But what I really wanted to tell him was that I was scared of him. I longed for him to like me, and I was always afraid he didn't. His eyes would slant toward me with judgements. In those moments he reminded me of our mother. That day, he told me that he loved bugs and wanted to study them when he grew up, but he thought our parents would have a fit if they learned this was his goal in life.

"No, they wouldn't," I told him. "They like you best. Especially Mom."

"It's just 'cause I'm a boy," he said casually, with the unassuming wisdom that children take for granted. "She likes boys better than girls. Anyway, keep my secret, okay?"

I did. It was the only secret he ever shared with me.

As rain fell, I lay awake for a long time, finally drifting off into a light, uncertain sleep. But at dawn I wasn't the least bit tired. I rolled onto the other side of the bed in the gray light and breathed in Stephen's scent on the pillows. After four years together, we probably should be living together, but we'd settled into a comfortable arrangement of separate residences with sleep-overs on most nights, either at his house or mine. He had slept at his house that night because he had to get up at five, and I told him I was going to curl up in my bed. I wanted to be alone, and even though I knew in time I'd tell him why, I had no words right then, not for him or anyone. There was just empty space where I floated, unmoored.

The storm gathered force throughout the day and occasionally I wondered about what I'd felt in those pre-dawn hours. It was the time of night when strange things happen, when thoughts and dreams collide, so maybe I was in some half-dream state and what seemed like premonitions actually meant nothing.

When the phone rang that afternoon, I ignored it at first because it was my landline and most of the people I want to talk to call my cell. But on the third ring a gust of wind blew the rain sideways against the bay window in my living room and reminded me of the wind that came up as I drove away from my mother's house the day before. I thought it was a divine summons telling me to answer the phone even though the display said 'private caller,' which meant I had no idea who it could be.

"Missus Tilly?" I heard, as soon as I said Hello.

"Hi, Rosario, you sound…different. What's wrong? Is my mother okay?"

"No, ma'am. I don't think okay. Julia is in with her, but Missus Amber no wake up."

"No wake up? What does that mean? Can you be more specific?"

"I don't think so. I call 911 and they… Oh! Oh! They just come now. I must go."

With that, she hung up. I pictured her dropping the receiver and racing across the polished floor to the front door. Rosario had been with my mother for more than five years. Her loyalty ran deep and I imagined her eyes welling with tears.

I looked at Lola, a terrier mix I'd rescued from the pound who had become my nearly constant companion. She was looking through the French doors into the backyard. It was walk time and she knew it.

"Sorry, Lola," I said, grabbing the leash and looking around for an umbrella. "You'll have to pee on the way to the garage. We're going in the car."

As I drove east on Sunset Boulevard, I kept the windshield wipers on high because the rain was coming in waves – first mist, then light rain, then torrents. There were deep puddles across the road, but not much traffic. Lola was in the back, in her elevated car seat which allows her to gaze out the window. She immediately started yipping whenever she saw another dog peering out of a passing car.

"We'll be there in about fifteen minutes, and you can play in the garden," I told her…casually, as if this were just another routine visit to my mother's house. Which it definitely was not.

With each chemo treatment my mother had grown weaker. Sometimes, when the light hit her at a particular angle, her eyes looked gray instead of blue. Her skin seemed almost transparent. I could see tracings of veins across her cheeks. When she finished with the chemo, she was still weak and tired most of the time. I knew she was bald beneath her wig, but she was obsessive about that wig. I assumed she took it off to sleep, but in truth I wasn't sure. I could absolutely imagine her sleeping in it.

I knew she was dead. She had loomed over my life with such force it was hard for me to conceive of her ever dying. But she was mortal after all, and she was gone. Rosario hadn't actually said that, but it was there on the surface of her voice like a layer of frost. I scoured the inside of myself, looking for emotions I knew I was supposed to feel. They might be huddled in corners and crevices; they might need to be coaxed out. I wasn't sure how to do that. The emptiness inside me felt vast and strangely soothing. Maybe I had been anticipating this news. Maybe when I put the pills back in the bottle with the carefully printed label, I made the next step inevitable.

Maybe I'd known, in some inexplicable way, that my mother was leaving. I felt like a criminal for breathing so easily into the space that loosened up inside me when I imagined the world without her in it.

Lola got visibly excited when we turned onto the street that, to her, was a geographical marker. It meant play time on a wide green swath of lawn; it meant squirrels in the towering oak tree that centered the yard, and Rosario giving her a treat from the bag she kept in the kitchen. I envied the simplicity of my dog's thoughts.

The rain had lightened by then, turned to drizzle. My mother lived on a street of tall gates and intercoms mounted on stone posts. There are no sidewalks in that neighborhood, no houses welcoming enough to leave their front doors exposed to strangers. The message is clear: If you aren't invited, go away. The rumor is that Elvis once rented one of these houses in the Sixties, but I've never bothered to verify that.

The gates were open and I saw the blinking lights of the Paramedic truck up ahead. Even with the dull gray day, the brass plaque on the brick column at the entrance glimmered as though it was immune to the weather. CASA DEL SOL it said in engraved, loopy letters.

I remembered the first day I saw that sign as I drove in and how my mouth dropped open.

"You named your house?" I asked my mother when I went upstairs and found her.

The exterior of the house had been re-painted from white to a tawny pink color – a shade my mother used often in her paintings, as if to her artist's eye it was always sunrise or sunset. She was in her studio, working on another of the quaint village scenes that had made her famous. Amber Austin was a star of the commercial art world, a villain of the serious art world, and a very wealthy woman.

"Of course," she said to me. "I think it's important to name the things that matter in your life. It means House of

Sun."

"Yes, I know what it means. I do have a rudimentary knowledge of Spanish. I'm just not sure why you identified your house that way. Are you going to open a tanning salon here?"

Ignoring my last question she said, "It goes along thematically with my name. Do you know the significance of my name? Do you know that amber was made by the sun?" She was holding her paintbrush toward me like a pointer, clearly insinuating that I was ignorant.

"Please, fill me in."

"The legend is that Phaethon, a son of Helios – the sun – asked his father if he could drive the chariot of the sun through the heavens for a day. Well, the foolish boy got too close to the earth and scorched it. To save the earth, Zeus struck Phaethon with a thunderbolt. At which point he died and fell out of the sky. His mother and sister were so grief-stricken they turned into trees, and when their tears were dried by the sun, the tears became amber."

"And to think it all started with a bad driver," I said. "One really must be careful when asking Dad for the keys to the chariot. So, aren't you worried that people might mistake this house for a hotel and ring the buzzer looking for a vacancy?"

"Oh, Tilly, stop being so cynical. People know it's my house. I'm listed on the Star Maps for God's sake. And if I want to name my house, that's my business. I certainly couldn't do that before when we were in New York. The co-op board would have had a fit if I'd tried to name our apartment."

"I'm sure they would have. And with good reason."

I watched my mother closely to see if anything would flicker across her face when she referred to our previous life. But her eyes remained steady and triumphant, as if nothing awful had ever happened to her. She backed up a couple of steps, studied the canvas, and then touched up one of the trees, which in her paintings were always lush and healthy. In the world of Amber Austin's paintings, leaves did not turn brown, streets were never littered, buildings never crumbled, and people never died.

Her wavy red hair was pulled back in a headband. She was always a redhead but over the years the color had gotten some chemical help. I was, at that moment, impressed – as I'd often been – by the striking contrast of my mother's coloring. Between her hair and her eyes, she was a marriage of fire and ice. When I was young, I used to wish my light brown hair would miraculously turn red, and that my hazel eyes would shift along the color spectrum to blue. I'd feel prettier then, and maybe my mother would like me better. But I looked like my father; I even had his broad shoulders and slightly lop-sided smile.

When chemo began killing her hair, my mother paid a king's ransom to have two wigs made that perfectly matched the hair she was losing. Her hairdresser came to the house to wash and style the wig that sat on a plastic head while my mother wore the other one. I was there for several of these rituals and I couldn't shake the feeling that there was something Elizabethan about it. I almost expected the girl to start powdering the wig.

My mother was not always named Amber. Her name used to be Charlotte. She wasn't always a painter either. I used to be the only painter in the family. I'd had two showings of my work at a small New York gallery and was preparing for another when our lives suddenly changed forever.

2.

The sky over Manhattan was bright blue. It was an achingly beautiful morning. I was living in a Tribeca loft and working at a Greenwich Village art gallery, often assessing the work of various artists and recommending their pieces to the owner.

From the windows of my loft I had a full view of the World Trade Center. My father worked at an investment firm in the North Tower, on the 103rd floor. Sometimes in the early morning I would look out and wonder if he was taking the elevator up at that moment, or if he was already behind his desk. So much life bustled behind the grid of the towers, but all I could see were lights from the inside and weather systems reflected on the surface. My friend Janice lived in the loft just above me and had the luxury of dictating her own schedule. She was a feng-shui consultant with a successful book on the subject and a list of high-profile clients who hired her to make sure their homes were properly designed for positive energy flow and an abundance of prosperity. Sometimes we had coffee together in the morning, or wine in the evening, with New York's most impressive architecture right outside the windows.

I had an appointment before work that day, in midtown, to look at a sculptor's work. When I stepped outside and looked at the sky, shiny as glass, I couldn't bear to take the subway. Instead, I hailed a cab, rolled down the window, and was happy to be above ground with the crisp breeze blowing across my face.

We'd gotten as far as SoHo and were stopped at a red light when I saw people on the street stop and look up to a corner of the sky behind us. Through the rear window of the cab I got a glimpse of what they were staring at. Black smoke was billowing up from the World Trade Center. We'd just started moving again. I told the driver to stop, handed him more than enough cash, and got out. I was on Bleeker Street and I went over to the knot of people who were standing motionless, looking up at the blackening corner of the sky. Some were on cell phones. The smoke looked like a mushroom cloud.

"A plane flew right into one of the towers," I heard a man say. "Maybe a commuter plane – I don't know."

I grabbed his arm. "Which tower?"

A woman who was talking to someone on her cell phone said, "The North Tower. My friend can see everything. It's a jet! A commercial jet!"

Suddenly, sirens were screaming from every corner of the city, heading downtown. It was almost deafening. Manhattan is always noisy, but I'd ever heard anything like this before.

I knew my father had taken Hale to work with him that morning. The two of them joked about it when we all gathered for our usual Sunday brunch – our effort at acting like a family, even though we had little idea what that meant.

"Hale is going to get good dose of the shark-filled sea on Tuesday," my father joked, lifting his glass of Mimosa in a mock toast.

"Guess I have to get used to it," Hale said. I caught in his eyes a look I'd seen before – a longing for our father to be proud of him, anoint him with the confidence that fathers are uniquely qualified to bestow upon their sons. I saw the disappointment when our father turned back to his food, oblivious to his son's needs.

Hale would soon graduate from Columbia and was planning to follow our father into the world of exalted finance and sophisticated investments. He'd gone to the firm before, but never for a full day.

I tried my father's office number from my cell phone as flames burst through the smoke.

Katherine, my father's assistant, answered with a choked, "Hello…"

"Katherine, it's Tilly."

"Your father's talking to your mother. I don't know where Hale is. Your father said to find him." She coughed, and I could hear chaos in the background – voices falling over each other, the sound of pounding and then shattering glass. "The smoke…" she said and coughed again. "It hit below us – the whole building rocked."

"You need to get out. You need to find a way out!"

"Someone called 911 and they said to stay where we are, they'd come for us."

I knew what it looked like below them. All of us outside knew more than those trapped inside.

"No! Katherine, you need to get out!"

She didn't hear me. The phone cut out then. I tried Hale's cell phone and it went to voicemail.

I moved half a block over, craned my neck and saw that the billows of smoke were growing bigger, the flames were deep orange. Even from that distance, the air was changing, smelling like burning wire and metal and things I couldn't identify.

I called Janice and she picked up on the first ring. "Oh God, Tilly – are you seeing this?"

"I'm not home. I'm in SoHo. I can see smoke and flames. This can't be happening – they'll get people out, right? That's what they do, they rescue people…Could it maybe look worse than it is?"

"It's bad, Tilly. A jet just flew right into the building. I don't know how people are going to get out. Have you spoken to your father?"

"I got through to the office. He was on the phone with my mother, but then the line went dead."

I could hear her crying. She took a deep breath and said, "Let me call you back, okay?"

Everyone on the street seemed to be moving in slow motion. People would stop to ask questions of strangers, exchange information. Then they'd shake their heads in disbelief and look up again. We all kept looking up. As chaos swirled around me, there was a part of me deep inside that was numb, frozen. There was a voice in me that kept saying, It can't be real. Even though it was.

The word "terrorism" floated in the air, uttered again and again, so quickly, an endless loop.

We could see, reflected by sunlight, papers fluttering down – thousands of papers like severed white wings. There was a gracefulness to their flight. A woman screamed that people were jumping, but I'm not sure how she knew that, we were too far away to see. She was holding a cell phone – did someone tell her they saw people jumping? She held the phone to her ear, then moved it away from her and yelled, "Oh God! Please save them!" We kept turning to the inferno that bloomed in the sky as if Hell was rising up to devour Heaven. Sirens were still racing across the city from every direction. I remember wondering if Janice got off the phone because she saw people jumping from the tower. She would be able to see everything from her windows. At moments sunlight glazed the smoke.

Sixteen minutes passed – I knew because I kept looking at my cell phone, hoping either Hale or my father would call -- and then a sound shattered the morning.

All around me, people began screaming and pointing. Smoke engulfed the North Tower, and now a gaping hole yawned in the South Tower. The minutes were both endless and quick as lightning. A man ran out of a cigar shop and screamed, "Another plane hit the second tower! It's gotta be a terrorist attack!" Panic erupted. People bolted, not knowing where they wanted to go, but needing to run somewhere. That's how it is with fear – you just run. One woman's voice rose above the others, or maybe I was just closer to her. Caught between confusion and fear, she screamed out, "Why are they doing this?"

I tried to run back toward downtown but by then cops were there, yelling at us to head uptown. I wanted to find my father. I wanted to see him and my brother fleeing from the building. I wanted to throw my arms around them and wipe chalky dust and soot from their clothes and know that we would have tomorrow. But I was herded in the opposite direction along with everyone else. Smoke blurred the day and an acrid bitter smell snaked through the streets.

I called Janice back and could barely make out what she was saying through her sobs. But I heard the word "jumping." Then I lost the connection and couldn't get her back; I figured all the cell towers were probably overloaded. Traffic lights were out and I realized that stores had no lights on. The electricity was out.

The day was turning smoky and thick, but there was still that impossibly blue sky up there. I was afraid I'd get knocked down, trampled. I ducked into a Dry Cleaner's and tried to still the shaking in my hands so I could try calling my father again.

I got nothing when I called his office number. I tried his cell and got half of his voicemail before the connection was lost. I tried Hale again and couldn't get through at all. Just dead air. Some of the people outside the Dry Cleaner's were screaming that the whole city might be a target, that this was just the beginning. I went back outside and the stampede had slowed a little so I went into a small Deli and asked, Do you know anything? The woman behind the counter was crying. She was Indian, and she was wearing a beautiful blue sari, like the color of the sky when the day began.

"Planes into both towers," she said through her tears. "Big planes. Commercial planes. My friend works there. I'm so scared he might be trapped."

A woman in a disheveled business suit and running shoes came in. She'd probably been on her way to work. "They've sealed off the whole city," she said.

I went to the back of the store, near the freezer, and called my mother on her land line. I was surprised I got through.

This is what I remember: My mother's voice began as a hoarse whisper, but rose quickly into a wail, primal and wild. When she began talking in broken phrases, I remember hearing the word 'jump' and somewhere in that tumble of words she told me my father had said 'we.' Was he talking about himself and Hale? She was rambling, stringing together fragments. "He said the fire was everywhere and they had to choose. No way out. Then he said goodbye. He said I'm sorry and I love you and then all I could hear..."

My cell phone cut off in the middle of her sentence and I couldn't get her back. I thought of how I'd planned to call Hale that evening, ask him how his first full day at the firm went. We didn't often check in with each other or make casual how-are-you-doing calls. There were too many broken highways between us. But there were times when we each tried, and I'd decided days before that I would call him and be a supportive sister.

I started walking again – uptown, folded into a tide of people too stunned to cry. But when the South Tower started to fall, we all stopped and turned to the place in the sky that wasn't supposed to be hollow but now was. I must have screamed because suddenly strangers were trying to soothe me. If my father and brother had made it out of the North Tower, and were still in that area, they were gone. Is that what I screamed out, that they were gone? Did I shriek their names? I remember a man with dusty glasses saying, "You don't know anything yet, hold onto that."

We all just stood there, staring, for what seemed like an hour but was barely twenty minutes. When the North Tower crumbled it seemed like slow motion. It buckled from somewhere lower down and then it collapsed onto itself. I heard gasps around me, but no screams. The shock had stolen our voices. All I could see was the blank spot on the skyline with smoke rushing across it. And the blank sweep of my life -- all the days and years I had left, but they didn't.

People were covered in white ash, their clothes torn and spotted with blood walking uptown. They looked like mummies, or ghosts, or Halloween revelers who got an early start on the holiday. I saw a man with a briefcase, his jacket torn and bloodstained, limping, one leg stiff but buckling at the knee. Something about the set of his shoulders looked like my father and my breath caught. But then he turned and his face, even through the ash, was young and round. A woman in a business suit with running shoes – she must have just gotten to work – was soaked through with water. She was walking with her arms outstretched in front of her. Is that how she got out? Feeling her way through the rubble and the crumbling walls? Her body didn't yet realize she was out. She was still feeling her way. The sprinklers, I thought, seeing other people who were soaking wet – of course, the sprinklers must have gone off.

All we could do was walk north and east. We didn't feel like strangers to each other, even though we were. I told a man my father and my brother were in the North Tower, and he began to cry. I still couldn't. I felt dry as the ash falling over the city. Ash like gray snow. Like the end of everything. Like a nightmare on the wrong side of night. I walked to Bleeker and Lafayette to get the 6 train. But all the trains were stopped. I started walking north and east, blue sky and clear air ahead of me in the distance, as if it was all just a bad dream I could walk away from. My legs were feeling weak and I waved my arms at an SUV that was driving slowly in the right lane. It pulled over and I climbed in beside a man in gym clothes with tears streaking his face.

My Tribeca loft was both my home and my work space. I'd set up my painting studio in front of a wall of windows, the spot where someone else would certainly have put a couch and coffee table. Janice assured me that there was nothing negative in the arrangement, by feng-shui standards. "It's just quirky," she said. There was no way of getting home that day, not that I'd have chosen to anyway. I had one splinter of gratitude – that I had no pets, no children – nothing alive in that wide open space. Not even a houseplant. I asked the stranger if he could take me to Park Avenue, where my mother lived. He said, Sure -- I have nowhere else to go.

As we headed uptown, the air got clearer but the smell followed us. Once we were close to the upper east side, it was almost as if nothing had happened. People were out on the sidewalks, but no one seemed panicked. Except for the corner of the sky where black smoke bloomed, everything looked like it always did.

When we got to my mother's building, the doorman shuffled over to let me in. It looked like his legs had turned to lead; his face was pale and drawn. He shook his head slowly and said, "I never thought I'd see anything like this." He knew my father worked at the World Trade Center, but he didn't ask anything, and I didn't offer.

Later, once he found out that my father and brother had vanished, he couldn't look at me without tearing up.

My mother was drinking Vodka, standing at the window and looking down at Central Park. The television was on; over and over the planes ripped through the buildings, the towers crumbled, plumes of smoke and dust rose up. The phone rang a few minutes after I walked in and my mother moved slowly across the floor to answer it. In a voice flat as cardboard she said into the phone, "No, I haven't heard anything." When she hung up she stared at me and I wondered if she was even seeing me. Her eyes didn't seem to focus.

"There was no way for them to get out," she said. "103 floors up. They were trapped. The news said the plane hit between the 92nd and 98th floors."

I thought about Katherine telling me they were waiting to be rescued. No one could get to them. Rescue wasn't possible. I saw sunlight bouncing off something gold on the mantle and realized it was my father's wedding ring. My hand reached for it, cool metal against my fingertips. I wanted to ask why it was there and not on his hand, but I said nothing.

My mother returned to the window and faced the glass, looking down as if she expected to see her husband and son strolling across the park, heading home. I saw her shoulders shaking and knew she was crying, but my mother was proud and stoic, and I wasn't sure if my touch would be welcome.

Even in the early days of my childhood, when there was tenderness between us, the language of motherhood eluded her. The soft ministrations, the embraces, words meant to soothe a child's hot tears were a foreign language to her. Predictably, I never learned how to turn the tables and speak in comforting tones to her. In that moment, with her back to me and her tears hidden, I did the only thing I knew how to do – I stayed on my side of the room.

I sat down on the couch in front of the television, and when the newscaster said something about people jumping, I leaned closer to the screen.

They looked so tiny. I had to squint to make them out and before I realized it, I was on my knees, inches from the screen. Against the huge face of the towers, lives fluttered down like dark leaves. People who thought they'd have tomorrow, next month, next year, holidays, their kids' graduations, weddings, birthdays, more of life…climbed out windows and jumped into the free-fall of forever. I watched them tumble through the air – away from the flames, down the checkerboard of buildings that would soon buckle. I looked through the smoke and tried to find my father and my brother. I knew I would be looking for the rest of my days.

3.

In the stretched-out days that followed I learned more about my parents' last conversation – an echo strung through phone lines. I learned that they fought that morning, and my father flung his wedding ring through the air. My mother had knelt down, picked it up, and placed it on the mantle as the door slammed behind him. I thought about the bitter taste that words can leave on the tongue. But I didn't know what the words were. What did they fight about? My mother would always leave gaps in the story. I knew the ending, but not the beginning. I asked her if my father put Hale on the phone when he called her after the plane hit, and she said no, he was still looking for Hale. There was so much smoke, she said, and so many people in panic.

The towers smoldered like fallen mountains. The Manhattan skyline looked like an amputee. Everywhere around the wreckage that some were calling "the pile" were burned cars and twisted lamp posts, broken steel and huge chunks of cement. Billows of ash and smoke rose up. Shoes dangled from tree branches. The fire had burned at 2,000 degrees, one news report said. Portions of the towers' facades looked like cathedrals. So many lives cut short and buried, so many prayers unanswered. People had lined up to give blood, hospitals had sent stretchers, prepared themselves for an onslaught of critically injured people. But there was just ash and smoke and ghosts. There was no one to give blood to, no one to load onto stretchers. Hospital workers waited by entrances for ambulances that never came. White pages still rose and fluttered with every gust of breeze. Like tiny flags of peace.

People jumped from the North Tower until it fell. The estimates ranged from fifty people to two hundred. They jumped from all four sides of the building. They jumped to escape walls of flame. They jumped to pull air into their lungs one last time before they crashed to earth.

Silence seemed to descend on the city; everyone walked around with the same blank look in their eyes. No one knew how they were going to count the dead or comfort the living. It was warm for the next two days. At times, I found myself longing for rain, as if a storm could wash away what happened. Or maybe I just wanted the heavens to cry along with the rest of us. In those days of empty skies, the smells of smoke and death burrowed into our pores and psyches. People spoke softly, hesitantly, if they spoke at all. I posted photos of my father and Hale, like so many others who clung to hope. Strangers sat outside together as if they'd been friends for years, on benches and front steps, afraid to have walls around them and ceilings above. The open air felt safer.

Then on the third day, a rainstorm moved through. Photographs of the missing, the dead, the vanished sagged and folded in on themselves. What are we to do, I wondered, standing on the street with rain falling on me – put more photographs up tomorrow? How long will we fool ourselves that anyone will be coming back? That any of them lived?

I couldn't go home – Tribeca was in the "frozen zone." No one was allowed in, with the exception of some people who had to retrieve their pets. Janice left and moved in with her boyfriend on West 64th street. She came across town with her cat and two small suitcases, one of them packed with some of my clothes.

The days ran together. In the evenings I'd meet Janice, her boyfriend Edward, and other friends for wine and food. Sometimes we stumbled into conversations that felt almost normal; other times we fell silent. I was the only one who had lost people in the towers. My grief stretched between us like an ever-widening field. I think I knew already that in time none of us would know how to cross that field.

I slept in my old room at my mother's apartment, sometimes waking in the late hours of night certain I heard Hale on the other side of the wall. He'd continued to live at home while he was attending Columbia, and his scent wafted from his room into the hall. But it was just a dream, an echo, a whisper from the past that traveled across time to punish my heart for hoping. Late one afternoon, my mother and I sat together by the windows as evening moved across the sky. She told me many things that day – both with her words and her eyes. At first, she went so far back in time – to how she and my father met on a subway, which I'd heard a hundred times – that I was annoyed and impatient. I wanted to know why his wedding ring was on the mantle. What happened that morning? She grazed the subject, only telling me that things happen in a marriage, that someday when I got married I would understand. She told me that my father had said he wanted a divorce, but then she brushed it aside as if threats like that were a common occurrence between them. Maybe they were – who really knows what goes on inside someone else's marriage? I let her talk on and on, waiting for her confession, waiting for the truth about that morning, but then I'd catch a soft, faraway look in her eyes that made me feel guilty for my impatience. She reminisced about bringing Hale home from the hospital after he was born and laughed gently about how curious I was. At two years old, I seemed to be unsure about this new tiny being. Was he real or just a doll who cried and pooped?

I remember, when I was a little older, how tiny Hale's hand felt in mine, and how protective I felt about him. We grew up as part of the privileged class in Manhattan – children who would never be mistaken as wanting for anything. We wore uniforms to school and brought our own shiny ice-skates to Wolman rink – no rental skates for us. In black town cars, we passed the homeless, the struggling, the squeegee men, the newspaper vendors. We "summered" in the Hamptons and had a team of professionals decorate the apartment for Christmas. We never took the subway, although a baby-sitter once took us on the 79th Street bus.

After college I moved downtown – as far down as Tribeca -- because on the Upper East Side I felt like I was suffocating. Hale stayed because he breathed just fine in that world.

I didn't know how to grieve for both my father and my brother; there didn't seem to be enough room in me for both of them. I would focus on one, then the other. My grief finally took the shape of twin rivers flowing alongside each other, although Hale's river was deeper and wider, pulled by dangerous currents. I'd spent so much of my life reaching for him but time and again I would graze the empty air of his absence. I had, too often, imagined that Hale and I would be the united members of our family. Away from my mother's steely gaze, and my father's good-natured remove, I imagined I would turn to Hale and find someone who felt like home. Maybe we would even have a secret language, or at least a secret handshake. But Hale basked in the glow of our mother's adoration for him, which meant he had to turn away from me.

My mother used to speak about the storm that was raging when she was in labor with me, and how thunder and lightning heralded my birth. But Hale was born on a bright Spring afternoon when the air smelled like blossoms and the days were growing long. I was the child of storm. Hale was sunlight.

Now he'd vanished into smoke and ash. My heart kept stumbling out into a wasteland, still looking for him, unable to believe he was gone forever. I became acutely aware of the wishes I still held onto, even as an adult -- the fantasies I'd kept hidden in my heart – that one day my brother would let me get close to him, that we would have the easy familiarity I'd seen between other siblings. Those wishes had weight and I didn't know how to let them die now that he had.

His girlfriend Tara came over twice. Tara was one of those effortlessly beautiful girls, blonde and smooth, but the brutality of the loss had torn at her too, scarred her more deeply than she probably knew. I felt like she was looking for a place to belong when everything in her life had shattered. But my mother's suffering filled the apartment. It bounced off the walls and demanded supremacy. I think Tara decided there was no room there for her grief so after the second visit she never returned. She had never really understood that my mother resented her from the start for taking her precious son from her. She hadn't wanted Tara to lay claim to Hale when he was alive; she certainly wasn't going to share him in death.

For many days in a row, I made my way downtown and wrapped a scarf around my face to keep out the dust and the stench. I put up photographs of my father and Hale at St. James Cathedral. I put up more after the brief rainstorm. So many pictures were posted there – smiling faces of people who never imagined their lives would end like that. I looked for tears on other faces but on most of them I saw the same dry shock that I saw in my own reflection.

At Trinity Church, they hosed ash off the gravestones every day, as if in that one corner of the city, death could be kept clean, simple, undisturbed. At Chelsea Piers, on the skating rink side, a makeshift morgue had been set up. At first, I imagined them finding my father's body, or Hale's – parts of them at least. But in my heart, I knew there was nothing left of them.

I had just turned twenty-two a few weeks earlier, but I felt like I'd aged decades in one day.

Several times, my mother would say in a low whisper, "How are we going to go on, Matilda?"

I never could come up with an answer for that question. The future looked like a maze of broken off roads, jagged as the broken buildings.

My birth certificate reads Matilda Austin. My mother gave me that name because when she was in labor, she got through the pain by singing the Australian ballad, Waltzing Matilda, over and over. The song is about a peasant man (a 'swagman') traveling on foot with a bag, called a Matilda, slung over his back. He steals a sheep to eat, gets caught and is facing death by hanging. To avoid that fate, he drowns himself in a watering hole and then haunts the site forever. I could never figure out what would possess anyone to sing such a song during childbirth, and eventually I concluded that my mother must have harbored a deep resentment toward me for putting her through twelve hours of labor and, as a punitive gesture, she decided to name me after a peasant's knapsack.

On my ninth birthday, over a pancake breakfast that the housekeeper had prepared in celebration, I announced that my name from that point on was going to be Tilly. I would answer to nothing else.

"Well, that's a cute name," my father said, looking at my mother for confirmation that she felt the same.

"I guess," she said dismissively. "Although I don't know why someone would rebel against their name."

My father waved his hand as if that one gesture could brush away the tension that often simmered between me and my mother. "It's a very happy sounding name," he said. "And we will honor the birthday girl's wishes. Right Hale?"

Hale responded by opening his mouth as wide as he could to display the masticated mound of pancake on his tongue. My mother patted his arm tenderly, "Honey, that's not good manners," she told him, and stroked his wrist soothingly.

There was a time when I knew my mother's touch. I have splinters of memory, from when I was too young to retain very much, but my memories of her are indelible. Her fingers, light as fog, caressed my shoulders, my wrists. The weight of her hand on my back kept me upright, made me confident I wouldn't fall. She left ghost-trails on my skin. Still, to this day, I could tell you where they are. I can point to them as the invisible markers of a life extinguished by time, although I've never been sure why. Was it Hale's birth? She was clearly smitten with him, but she had seemed so with me once upon a time. Perhaps it was his cheerfulness. Hale, even as a baby, was brightly lit, as if something inside him was always on high beam. This was in stark contrast to me, the child who loved shadows, whose eyes seemed to turn inward when they weren't staring off into space. I have an early memory of my father saying to me on a shiny yellow morning, "Matilda, you can't possibly be sad. You're five years old and it's your birthday! You have friends coming over! The sun's out!" For some reason, that memory is clear as polished silver. I felt the downturn of my mouth and was afraid I'd disappointed my father, so I made a point of laughing and smiling for the rest of the day. When I went to bed that night, my face hurt.

Now my mother and I were bound together by the red cords of loss and the yawning emptiness of having no one to bury. A man I worked with at the gallery – nearly three weeks after the towers fell, when I'd gone back to work -- said, "Even if they find remains, your father and brother are still gone. So, does it really matter?" I wanted to spit in his face, but I ignored him instead. There is supposed to be tangible evidence of death – someone to touch, weep over, even if it's just a part of them. To have nothing means that death is a vast cloud – air and wind and mystery -- nothing to help your senses comprehend the loss. Nothing to let you say, "There – see that hand? That hand touched me, left fingerprints on my skin, my soul. Those arms carried me when I fell off my bike and bloodied my knees." Nothingness is a terrible reality – it haunts and punishes and holds you prisoner forever.

4.

The turn-around at the end of my mother's driveway was bordered by tall ficus trees and beds of azaleas that never had a dead flower on them. Her gardener came five days a week and made sure the grounds looked like one of her paintings. The back of the paramedic van was open and empty – a dim tunnel waiting for a body. When I let Lola out of the car, she bounded ahead of me through the open front door, nearly colliding with a paramedic who had a cell phone at his ear and was speaking quietly but in clipped, professional phrases.

"No vitals when we arrived. The housekeeper said her name is Amber Austin. Hold on a sec." He glanced at Lola racing past him and then looked at me. "Are you the daughter?"

"Yes."

I walked through the entryway and opened the sliding glass door to the backyard to let Lola out.

"I'm very sorry," he said. "There was nothing we could do. I'm talking to the coroner's office now. A police officer should be here momentarily. He'll stay until the coroner arrives."

I heard another man's voice upstairs in my mother's bedroom, and Rosario apparently answering his questions. But behind everything I heard miles of silence. It wrapped itself around me and made me shiver. The rain had paused -- just flat gray light outside -- as if the sky was holding its breath. Then there was the sound of another car speeding up the driveway – the ivory-colored Mercedes I'd half expected to see when I arrived.

Ellen, highlighted auburn hair blowing across her face, LuluLemon workout clothes and hundred dollar Nikes, ran through the front door and stopped abruptly in front of me. Her mascara was smudged under her eyes and black rivulets of tears snaked down her cheeks.

"Is it true?" she said to me, and then noticed the paramedic who had just gotten off the phone. "Is it true?" she asked again, this time in his direction.

He nodded. "Mrs. Austin was deceased when we arrived."

With that Ellen bounded up the stairs, taking them two at a time. The paramedic looked as if he expected me to follow her but when I didn't, he said, "Is she a family member?"

"Not technically," I told him. "She was my mother's personal assistant. My mother bought her that car, confided in her, relied on her, and probably did secretly wish that Ellen had been her daughter. So... if my mother were here to speak to the situation, she would probably call Ellen family."

He looked down and wore one foot into the oak floor. I'd made him uncomfortable.

"Sorry," I said. "TMI. I guess I should go up there."

I looked into the backyard and saw Lola sitting under the oak tree staring up at a squirrel. It was just an ordinary day for her. Rosario, weeping into a paper towel, was coming downstairs behind the other paramedic. She looked at me as we passed each other and she opened her mouth to speak, but whatever she was going to say got smothered by a sob. My cell phone rang and I turned off the volume without looking at who it was. I needed to stand over my mother's body – something I never got to do with my father and brother. They were ash and dust and empty air.

The room smelled musty and stale, as if no window had been opened for days, even though I'd opened one the day before. It was closed now. I noticed my mother's hands, the skin a bluish yellow color, which I knew happens fairly quickly when someone dies, although I'd never actually seen a dead body before. Ellen was bending over her, cradling her head and lifting it off the pillow. It took a moment before I realized she was removing the gold chain from around my mother's neck – the chain that had my father's wedding ring on it.

"Ellen! What the hell are you doing?"

Ellen closed the chain into the curve of her palm and lowered my mother's head back onto the pillow with her other hand. She didn't look at me when she spoke, as if her words had to bounce off my mother's body first in order to make sense.

"Your mother wants to be buried with this around her neck, Tilly. It's all in writing. I can give you a copy of the document. She listed all her wishes. But I don't want someone to steal this when they're preparing her body. I'll put it back on her before the viewing." Ellen stood up straight and took a deep breath. She kissed her own index finger and touched it to my mother's forehead. "Would you like a few minutes alone with her?" She still hadn't looked at me.

It struck me at that moment how alike Ellen and my mother were. They both had the ability to make other people wilt in their presence. I stared at Ellen's hand, closed tightly around my father's gold ring – the ring he'd removed that Tuesday morning in anger, the ring that wasn't on his finger when he died. I felt helpless, which was how I usually felt in my mother's presence.

"Tilly? Do you want some time alone with her?" Ellen asked again, annoyance bristling in her voice. She'd finally turned toward me.

"Yeah, I would. And Ellen? What viewing?"

"Your mother requested an open casket."

I looked at my mother's body – her cheekbones sharp as carved wood, her temples caved in, the dark blue veins of her hands. "Aren't they going to have to do an autopsy? Determine how she died?" I noticed then that the bottle of Ambien was gone. Did Rosario remove it? Or one of the nurses?

"I don't think so, unless her doctor requests it. Or you do." She paused, waiting for me to respond. I didn't. "Amber was quite ill, Tilly. But even if there is an autopsy, people still have open caskets after that. Morticians are very adept at – you know – making bodies presentable."

With that she wheeled around and walked out of the

room. I felt silence rise up from the floor like dry ice. I looked at my mother's open mouth, slack and drooping to the right, no breath coming from it. I'll never again hear her voice, I thought. I'll never again dial her phone number and wonder if her hello will be friendly or cold. I stretched my mind around the realization that it was Ellen, not I, who knew my mother's last wishes. Even in her death she'd managed to make me feel like an interloper – some lowly peasant who had wandered into a house of royalty, unannounced and unwelcome. Tyranny is a strange thing – it can be passed down from one person to another – an unimpeachable legacy. Ellen was already ordering Rosario around. I could hear her downstairs, acting like the new lady of the house.

Tyranny can also outlive death. As I moved closer to my mother's body, I imagined her eyes snapping open to stare me down one last time. I looked at her neck – no throb of pulse, no gold chain with my father's ring sliding back and forth on it. She had worn it constantly since he vanished.

I touched the right side of my mother's neck where the jugular vein lay flat as a ribbon, no blood moving through it. There is also a vein on the left side of the neck, but it isn't as large. The one on the right, its pulse so visible when someone is alive, rests alongside the carotid artery at the base of the neck, one of the intricate tapestries of the human body. I knew this because my boyfriend Stephen, while not an actual doctor, plays a cardiologist on a television series, and plays it so well I've often teased him that if someone in a crowd called out for a doctor, he'd probably offer up his services.

I wondered where the blood was now that it wasn't chugging along through my mother's body. Did it just turn to red lakes inside, stagnant and still? Stephen would probably know, I thought. I'll have to ask him.

I thought about how, within hours after the towers fell, people lined up to donate blood for the victims. But there were no victims to give the blood to. Strange how the thing that transports oxygen and life, that's so vital, can suddenly be useless, sloshing in caverns of the body with no reason to be there, or stored in vials with no one needing it.

I remembered then that my cell had rung, and I thought it might be Stephen. I glanced at the screen and saw I was right. I pulled my hand away from my mother, feeling the cold of her skin linger on my fingertips like invisible ink. Just as I was about to call Stephen, there were footsteps on the stairs and Ellen came back in.

"Tilly, a police officer is here. He's going to stay with Amber until the coroner arrives."

He came in slowly behind her, uniformed and armed, which struck me as amusing given the circumstances. The bed springs creaked a little when I stood up.

"Sure, Ellen. That makes sense. Wouldn't want to risk anyone stealing something from her."

I slipped past them to the stairs, hoping to make a fast getaway. I wanted to grab Lola and leave. I wanted to run like an Olympian sprinter from that house, that neighborhood. I wanted to escape the smell of death and the echo of rattling swords. Except I knew that we can never outrun our history; it's attached to our ankles like Christopher Robbin's shadow.

"Tilly," Ellen said, bouncing down the stairs after me. "There's no need to be so snappish. I am following Amber's instructions. She *will* be buried with your father's ring around her neck, and it's my responsibility to make sure of that. I didn't *steal* anything."

"Actually, I think you kind of did, Ellen. As damaged as my relationship with my mother was, she was my only family. You pretty much stole that." I hated the fact that I had just shown Ellen some vulnerability, especially when I caught the glint of victory in her eyes.

"I'm not responsible for your lack of self-esteem, Tilly."

I was determined to change the look in her eyes. "No, but you are responsible for kissing my mother's ass so proficiently that it lulled her into thinking she'd found her true daughter at long last. Congratulations. Although now you're going to have to go look for another broken family to invade. I mean, you're so good at it, your talents shouldn't be wasted."

Ellen flipped her hair back and narrowed her eyes. Some of the glint was gone. "That was uncalled for," she said.

"Yes, it probably was. But it felt really good."

I left her standing on the stairs of the house that she might – for all I knew – inherit.

Outside in the garden Lola was engaged in conversation with a very chatty squirrel. She had some leaves stuck to her head because the squirrel was ripping them from branches and throwing them down on her with impressive accuracy. Life goes on, I thought. The rain was holding back, just mist and fine drizzle washing down like a veil. I called Stephen back and was surprised when he picked up on the first ring.

"Hey, I saw you called, but I didn't listen to the message. Wait, did you leave a message?"

"Yeah. It went out on Twitter that something happened to your mother."

"And the person tweeting this would know about it how?"

"An ambulance drove onto your mother's estate with sirens blaring. Someone saw it. What happened, Tilly?"

What happened…what happened? One life ended and another life was wrestling with what kind of beginning this might be.

"She's dead, Stephen. She's gone. The coroner should be here soon. I'm going home. There's no reason to wait here for him. Rosario's here. And Ellen – of course. It's a bit uncomfortable in this house."

"Oh, God, Tilly. I'm so sorry. I should be home in about an hour. We're almost ready to wrap. I'll come over as soon as I get back."

As I put Lola's leash on, I heard sirens; they sounded like they were moving closer, but I didn't think the coroner would arrive with a siren blaring. In my mother's hilly neighborhood, with sharply curving streets and dead ends, sound echoed. As I listened though, I was pretty sure they were heading east, away from Casa del Sol.

In the days after September 11th, there were few sirens. In Manhattan, the sound of sirens is an almost constant backdrop. Like traffic. But in those aftermath days, when people sat on front steps and lingered on sidewalks, the city felt haunted and quiet. And papers kept fluttering through the streets. Human beings had vanished, but white pages survived to float on the breeze. Severed wings of the birds we once thought we were.

I kept going downtown, at least as close as I could get. I had to, even though I knew my father and brother were gone. I put up pictures of my father and brother not because I actually thought they might be found. I did it hoping I might find the thread of a story. My father had told my mother he couldn't die in the flames. He made a choice. He'd rather fall through the sky, through thousands of feet, picking up speed as he went instead of being immolated.

It used to be -- in the time before -- that whenever anyone came near the World Trade Center they instinctively looked up. It was so impressive, so monumental. There were days when the upper floors of the towers were buried in cloud. You could travel through different weather systems just by taking the elevator up to those floors. Afterward, it seemed no one could bear to look up again, only down.

The most I could hope for was that the rescuers would find a piece of bone, a tooth maybe, something with DNA. People were taking items with DNA on them to the family service center on Pier 94, so I took my father's toothbrush and a comb of Hale's because I found only a new toothbrush, still in its package, in his bathroom. Thousands of us collected and handed over anything that could identify DNA from whatever fragments might be found. No one ever expects to think like that. No one imagines that they'll be praying for someone in rescue gear to dig up a hand or a foot or a piece of bone. That they'll be waiting for a phone call telling them a body part was found that belonged to a relative, a friend, a spouse. But so many people were waiting for just that. Pieces of flesh and bone. Sometimes, in those long days, I would stop on the sidewalk and feel as if I could hear the echo of prayers floating on the acrid air – mine included. Please God, let them find something.

I heard from someone – I can't remember who – that huge trucks were hauling body parts to where the medical examiners worked around the clock to identify victims. I tried to shut the image out of my mind, but every time I fell asleep it was waiting for me. Latex-gloved hands plunging into piles of body parts. I would wake up with a gasp, my heart racing.

One afternoon I returned to my mother's apartment and found Ian McBride sitting with her. They were drinking tea from delicate flowered cups and sitting close together, sorrow floating around them. Ian ran the company my father worked for; he had lured my father from another firm decades ago and they had become good friends. Ian had been a fixture in our lives for as long as I could remember. When Hale and I were kids, we called him Uncle Ian. He and my father used to play golf sometimes on the weekends. He and his wife would bring presents over for us on Christmas Eve. After he divorced his wife, Ian continued the practice alone.

He stood up and walked over to me, holding his arms out and folding me into them.

"Tilly. I don't know what to say."

"None of us know what to say," I told him. He smelled like aftershave and tears.

He backed up and shook his head slowly. "I was telling your mother that I took a personal day on the eleventh. Some family thing that seems so trivial now. I should have been there."

"Except if you were, you wouldn't be here."

Ian and my mother looked like they could be brother and sister. His hair was a paler shade of red, flecked with gray, but his blue eyes matched hers and freckles dotted his cheeks. He nodded slowly and went back to sit beside her on the sofa.

"Did anyone survive from the firm?" I asked him. I hadn't thought to ask about that before, maybe because I was afraid of the answer.

"Twelve of us. Some were off that day, like me. Some were late getting to work, two had gone out to pick up some breakfast."

"Ian's going to go downtown with me to get the death certificates," my mother said. "They've set up a new system in light of…everything. If you'd like to go with us, you can. We thought we'd go day after tomorrow."

I'd heard about this. A decision had been made that, in order to get a death certificate immediately, people could bring in two affidavits, one from an employer saying that the person worked there and another from a family member saying they went to work that day. The city was in uncharted territory. The normal wait time for a death certificate when there was no body was long, and that wasn't going to work in this circumstance. I wasn't sure if my mother's invitation to accompany them was just politeness, or if she really wanted me to go along. But I said yes.

Two days later, Ian arrived for us in a Lincoln Town Car. The day was cloudy and pale gray, as if rain was an unformed thought in the mind of God. I gave the two of them the back seat and sat up front with the driver for our journey to the New York Law Department. Ian had set up an appointment for us, a courtesy that my mother thanked him for several times during the drive.

The building was crowded, obviously with people who were there for the same reason we were. I looked around at them and thought, I have no idea who you are but I know the most significant thing about you -- I know where your heart is shattered and I know how nothing seems to make sense anymore. By the time we got to a small cramped office where a Mr. Lawson stood up briefly and asked us to please sit, tears were streaming down my face. They came from a place so deep inside me I had no control over them. My mother reached past Ian and grabbed my wrist.

"Tilly, get hold of yourself," she said in a hard whisper.

No matter what the circumstances, appearances were important to my mother; she would tolerate no open displays of emotion. Once, when I was about seven she took me shopping and as we walked out of the department store, a man in the crosswalk was hit by a car. I screamed and began crying. She bent down, held my shoulders firmly in her hands and said, "Stop that right now. You're making a spectacle of yourself."

Giles Lawson handed a form to Ian and another one to my mother. "If you could fill these out," he said. "We just need to document that your husband and son, Mrs. Austin, were in fact there that day."

My mother nodded and filled out the form with nothing showing on her face. Her mouth was set in a straight line, her eyes barely blinked, and her penmanship was, as usual, impeccable. I sat silently, forcing back the tears I wasn't supposed to cry in public, feeling them collect in some deep reservoir below my heart. My tears were for everyone in that building being led into offices just like this one, and for people like Giles Lawson who had to tick off deaths on sheets of paper. I wept for our wounded city, driven to its knees and broken in places that would never fully heal. And for the men and women whose exit from this world was one of horror and fear. A window into the heart of darkness. My tears fell also for the people sifting through an avalanche of rubble and death.

I barely said goodbye when we got back to my mother's building and the doorman rushed out to open the car doors. I just turned and headed down the sidewalk. Ian came after me, calling my name.

"Tilly, your mother is just trying to keep some semblance of control – that's why she snapped at you like that. She didn't mean to be unkind."

I couldn't help it -- I laughed. "Yes, she did."

He shook his head slowly. "No, I don't think so. I'm sorry it happened, though. Take care, Tilly. If you need anything you call me, okay?"

As I watched him walk away with the dull white day around him, I had the strangest feeling that he knew something I didn't.

5

When I got to the end of my mother's long driveway, I noticed more than a dozen people milling around on the street just outside the gate. Two police cars were there -- I assumed some of the neighbors had called for them -- and several officers were warning the grieving fans to not block driveways or impede traffic. A girl with tears streaming down her face pointed as I pulled out onto the street. A couple of people lifted their cell phones and snapped my picture.

Amber Austin's fans would stay there long into the night. When darkness fell, they would light candles; more would arrive with bundles of flowers. The vigil would be featured on all the news stations. My mother was an artist with such a wide following it bordered on cult worship. Prints and lithographs of her paintings sold so well, she'd begun storing some of her original paintings in a locked vault, on the assumption that they would eventually approach the value of Picassos.

I thought about the vault as I turned onto Sunset Boulevard, heading home, and the rain began again, steady and calm, no wind to change its vertical pattern. I had no idea where the vault was located, or where the key to it was. Of course, I had no doubt that Ellen knew every detail.

Legions of fans believed they knew my mother through her paintings. She had shown me some of her fan mail – the women who gushed that she revealed so much of herself in her art, the "mature" men who wrote their phone numbers and e-mail addresses in carefully slanted script. Her fans couldn't get enough of her light-infused skies and the images of clean sidewalks, well-dressed pedestrians, not a tossed-out beer can or a homeless person anywhere. Their affection for her work stood in stark contrast to the sarcastic dismissal of the serious art world. She was called a Hallmark card painter who knew how to successfully market herself. Someone from MOCA snipped, "Amber Austin's work should be in shopping malls, not in Art Galleries." If she weren't my mother, I'd having been saying the same about her work.

It was all so strange to me – especially the intimate missives from strangers, since I didn't feel I really knew my mother at all. There was the mother I remembered from early in my childhood, who created pen and ink drawings of thatch-roofed cottages and barns, taping them to the refrigerator. Later she used charcoal. I would stare at them, asking her to add animals and birds, which she always did. She taught me to draw, standing close behind me, telling me to close my eyes and imagine whatever scene I wanted to create, and then saying to open my eyes and trust that my hand would figure out how to do it. She was both teacher and mystic. She handed me charcoal instead of crayons and told me my dreams could flow out from my fingertips and become art.

I don't think, in those years, my mother had any ambitions to turn her art into a career. Her career was being Keith Austin's wife – a Manhattan socialite who gave parties that were written about in the New York Post. She was content to nurture my abilities. Somehow, she knew when to guide my hand and when to let it go.

I don't know when the change occurred. I don't think there was a definitive breaking away from me; more like a drifting off. She was enchanted by Hale as he grew into a bubbly little boy, full of confidence and swagger, erupting with laughter at the slightest thing, coming up with clever phrases that my parents would repeat to their friends. For a short while, when he was about six, Hale spoke about himself in third person, entertaining whoever was in the room. Was that when I began composing pictures full of shadow? Because I felt like I was sinking into the darker corners of our home? Becoming invisible? My life has more questions in it than answers. I only know that my drawings, as they became darker, pushed my mother farther away. She would shake her head and say that she didn't understand my compositions – why was everything so hidden and dark? At some point during those young years, she stopped smiling over my shoulder and I stopped turning around to find her.

In the days after the towers fell, my mother was, at first, softer with me than she had been before. Sometimes I had the feeling she wasn't even aware it was me – she was just grateful that another human being occupied the now-empty spaces of the home where my father's scent still lingered, where the coffee-maker still went on at 5:30, the time he had set it for, where folders still sat on his desk in the study – folders that no one would open now, that would ultimately be given to Ian so he could deal with them. She talked to me because she needed to talk, not because she intended to let me into her private citadel of suffering.

After nearly a week, she finally turned off the television, at least during the day. I still couldn't go back to my home, but I'd managed to locate friends who also couldn't get to their homes and were scattered around the city. We sat at Starbucks and drank too much coffee, went downtown and stood looking up at the empty skyline. The air still smelled acrid and metallic, and at times I thought it smelled of death. Foolishly, I kept imagining I would see my father or Hale, numb with amnesia, walking the streets looking for who they once were. I would snap myself back to the truth of this new life – they were gone, with no trace left behind.

All of us who couldn't get home needed clothes. My friend Alicia and I went to Bloomingdale's and were shocked by how normal everything felt in there. As if nothing had happened. Perfectly made-up women shopped for handbags and blazers, opened tubes of lipstick and tried the colors on their hands. We quickly scooped up some jeans and sweaters without even trying them on; we couldn't wait to get out of the fragrant, temperature-controlled interior of a world that felt so false.

On a day when mist gloved the sky and rain fell intermittently, I came back to my mother's apartment around noon and found her sitting at the window, her eyes red and a tissue wadded up in her hands. I noticed something glinting around her neck and realized it was my father's wedding ring. She'd put it on a long gold chain; the ring was at the level of her heart and I wondered if that was deliberate.

"I have to figure out how to live now – differently," she said. "I'm not sure I know how. How can I not be Keith Austin's wife anymore? Who am I if not that? You just assume you know who you are, and then something like this happens, something catastrophic and then you're just lost…"

She was rambling, and I wasn't sure what to say. I didn't have a clear sense of my parents' marriage. They never argued in front of us, but neither were they sweetly affectionate. I think I said something like, "I don't know what to tell you. I don't know how to remove the hurt. Thousands of people are going to have to figure out how to go on differently. It's a sad club we're all in."

I should never have underestimated my mother's capacity for transformation.

At some point after the towers fell my mother made the decision to reinvent herself, including choosing a new first name. Charlotte was dead; Amber would be born, although she didn't announce the name-change to me until more than a year later. She might have decided all this in the first raw days when the pain and loneliness were unbearable, or in the months after when we got no news of my father and Hale, not even proof that they were dead. I'm not sure. As with most things, she kept her plans and agendas to herself. If there were early practice drawings of the art that would eventually make her famous, she hid them from me. She let me into her grief, but the rest of her life was a series of closed doors.

The absence of our family was a black hole we kept falling into. My father could fill up a room just by walking into it – not arrogantly, like some men do, but with a quiet confidence, a charming remoteness that lured people to him. I was as drawn to his mystery as others were. He was my father, but he was always just out of reach. Hale seemed mature beyond his years. People frequently thought he was my older brother and were surprised to learn that he was two years younger. He had a sharp wit and even sharper judgments. As much as I longed to be closer to him, he intimidated me as we got older and left childhood behind. I came to mistrust him. Something complicated and harsh lurked behind his eyes, and his smile, which was still bright and infectious, often looked like lies to me. My memories of us somersaulting through the seasons, taking laughter for granted, often seemed like scenes from a dream. Were we ever those children?

One afternoon, shortly after planes began flying again, making us tremble at each sound, my mother looked at me and said, "They're never going to find any part of them, you know. They're dust now. Just dust and memories."

I have an image of her standing alone in her empty bedroom, peeling off layers of sorrow, trying to banish the picture of her husband and son falling through miles of air. Whenever it happened, this much is indisputable: My mother would step out of her widow's skin and emerge as a painter who created quaint city streets and bucolic gardens where nothing ever died.

I had no idea what was truly going on all the times she looked at my paintings – commenting on what she saw as my obsession with dark streets, the streetlamps offering only cold blades of light. She was critical of my work for its bleakness, its gray corners concealing secrets. Things nestle and hide in my paintings, things that aren't always visible at first glance. I had no clue that she was not simply a critic, she was also a student. When she took up painting, she knew exactly what canvases to get, which brushes and paints. She chose to work in acrylic, just as I do. But she made it a point to become a painter of glowing sunsets and silky pink dawns. No shadowy streets for her, no black-ink skies. She became more successful than I will ever be, and I'll always believe that was part of her plan, too.

She finally told me that on the last day of his life, my father said he wanted a divorce. He hurled his wedding ring at her and she bent down and picked it up, put it on the mantle as if that one gesture could make him change his mind. Those were the only details she gave me. I asked her why so many times – why did he want to divorce you? What did you tell him to upset him so? But she would never answer me. Finally, I stopped asking. I assumed it was some kind of dalliance, an affair that they might have been able to get beyond, but I gave up trying to find out. One night I had a ghoulish dream in which they found my father's left hand – his bare sad hand with a pale line around his ring finger. The vapor trail of his marriage.

They never found any piece of him in the rubble. Or of Hale. But at some point, in the midst of a wounded city, my mother swept up the rubble of her marriage, disposed of it in some secret grave, and bought clean white canvases upon which she would create an entirely new life.

6

It was referred to as "pink mist" – the gruesome vapor that rose up when the bodies of those who jumped from the North Tower landed. Some people were on fire as they fell. Others lost clothes on the way down because of the velocity. The thud of bodies echoed against the buildings, reverberated in people's souls, creating an audible memory that would haunt everyone who heard it, probably for the rest of their lives. Photographs were published in the days immediately after. The Falling Man, as he came to be known – his body straight as an arrow, one knee bent, almost casual in his demeanor. The man and woman holding hands, until the ferocity of the air pulled them apart.

No one landed as we saw them in those photographs, though. At terminal velocity the body is forced into a V-position so that when the person lands, the pelvis hits first. The bones shatter and splinter, ligaments are torn apart, there is an explosion of blood. The body is obliterated. How do I know this? I researched it. I asked doctors, paramedics, anyone who would talk to me. I needed to know. As awful as it was, I needed to know.

The fall took roughly ten seconds. People plunged toward earth at 150 miles an hour – not fast enough to render them unconscious on the way down, but fast enough to destroy their bodies once they hit. My brother had pale skin and red hair; he took after our mother. If I picture him in shattered pieces I imagine fine porcelain and fiery red hair. And then, after the towers crumbled and fell, I see him as a cloud of dust. This is what I have left of him. My father had brown eyes, like mine. I imagine his eyes scanning the sky on the way down, memorizing the last sight of his son.

My mother gave an interview to The New York Times, telling them that her husband jumped, that she spoke to him after the first plane hit and he knew no one would be able to rescue them. He was choking, he didn't want to die in the fire and the unbearable smoke. She told the reporter that she was certain her son had jumped as well, along with his father. Keith Austin was her soul mate, she said, and his last words would haunt her forever. He said 'I love you,' she told the journalist. And then he said, 'I don't understand why.' I had never heard that from her, and part of me wondered if it was true, or if she had invented it because she was being recorded. But it didn't matter. He was gone.

Our lives were altered after that interview. For reasons I didn't fully understand, and still don't, a shift in attitude took place in Manhattan. Suddenly it was shameful to speak of people jumping. There was an emerging feeling that for them to have made that choice they were somehow cowardly. As if waiting for the flames – or the collapse of the towers – would have represented bravery. Within days, there were no more photographs of The Falling Man. No one came forward to identify him. The other photographs of people falling that had briefly made an appearance were also no longer seen. Fewer people called my mother, and there were very few invitations to lunch or dinner. Her days and nights were spent in the apartment, adding another layer of loneliness to her already devastated life.

I saw the change in my friends also. There was an undercurrent of awkwardness, a sense that they didn't know what to say, now that they couldn't issue platitudes about how my father and brother must have fought hard to survive. It was as if an entire city of survivors had written a movie about the burning inferno of the towers in which men and women battled nobly against the flames, the smoke, the falling ceilings, the shattered walls, to get out and go home to their families. When the truth was, they had no idea what it was like in there, what people were faced with, nor did they have any idea what they would do if they'd been the ones trapped.

One night in late September Janice and I met for dinner on Columbus Avenue. It had rained that afternoon and the sidewalks were still wet. The smell of rain hung in the air, competing with the acrid stench that still wafted up from downtown.

Janice has long auburn hair that drapes over her shoulders in shiny waves and makes jealous women insist that she must have hair extensions. She doesn't, she just drew a lucky card in the genetic deck. On this evening, she had her hair tied back in a ponytail and hadn't bothered to put on eye make-up, which was unusual for her.

"You feeling okay?" I asked her when the waiter brought our wine and we toasted to nothing. We'd started doing that, just as a gesture, clinking glasses without saying anything. Maybe we were toasting life with all its fragility.

"I think I'm going to move back into my place in a few days," she said. "I can't keep crashing at Edward's. The only reason we stay together as a couple is that we don't live together. He's so disorganized, it makes me crazy, and then we fight. They're letting people back in now."

"I hear a but in there…"

"Yeah, the but is… I'm scared, I guess." She stared into the candle flame. "Every day, seeing the wreckage. That awful hole. I don't want to live so close to it. What are you going to do, Tilly? Are you going to move back?"

I shook my head no. "I have to get out of my mother's apartment, but I don't think I can move back to our building. How would I look out at that empty piece of sky every day and be able to live? To function? I had this horrible thought the other day, that by breathing in the air down there…maybe you're breathing in particles of human beings. I mean they turned to dust and ash, right? Sorry, that's gruesome, I know."

Janice reached across the table and took my hand. "No, it's okay. I don't know how you move through each day the way you do. I think you're really brave."

"I don't have a choice. I'm here and they're gone. I'm never going to make sense of it, but I'll have to fold it into my life somehow."

I looked past her then to try and coax tears back into my eyes, and that's when I saw Martin a few tables away.

"Janice, look over your left shoulder – subtly. Martin Sterling is over there with a bunch of people."

Janice pretended to be looking for something she may have dropped on the floor behind her, and then swiveled back around to me. "Mr. Morality, who thinks sex on the first date is treasonous, but keeps a condom in his shoe just in case he might get lucky? Please tell me you aren't going to go over there."

"I think I might."

Janice rolled her eyes and took a long sip of wine. "Because the sex was so great you're forgiving the aftermath?"

"No. Because Hale was one of his best friends and he's grieving too." I pushed my chair back and started to get up. "But the sex was pretty amazing."

He saw me squeezing between tables and brushed his hair off his forehead – a gesture that always made me melt even when he was practically calling me a slut for sleeping with him on our first date. He stood up and kissed me on the cheek.

"Hey, you," he said. "I've wanted to call you but I didn't know if I should. I mean, I wanted to call you about Hale and just talk to you, see how you're holding up, but I wasn't sure if you'd even want to hear my voice…"

I could have let him squirm some more, but it seemed pointless. I knew he had spent nights staring into the empty darkness thinking about Hale, asking God why. I gave him a quick hug and kissed his cheek.

"You were a good friend to Hale. I know he really cared about you."

Martin glanced at the table. "I'm here with co-workers. So, I can call you?"

"Yeah."

I felt him watching me as I walked back to my table.

"And if he calls, what then?" Janice asked me later when we were leaving the restaurant.

"Don't know. I don't know much of anything these days except that life never happens the way you think it will."

I wasn't thinking about life the next day when Martin called me. I was thinking about fucking him. Actually, at the exact moment he called, that's where my thoughts were. I'd gone for a run in Central Park and some of the leaves were just starting to turn. I was on the sidewalk outside my mother's building when my cell phone rang and I recognized his number.

I first met Martin a year earlier, on a chilly Fall day when Hale and I had decided to take a walk in Central Park. We'd gone to our parents' apartment for Sunday lunch -- our usual commitment -- and when our mother began describing in detail a dinner party they'd attended the night before, Hale gave me a look that said, "Let's bolt." So, we did.

Orange leaves swirled around our feet and the wind was sharp and cold. A black Lab with a tennis ball in his mouth came up to us and dropped it at Hale's feet. His owner, a girl with waist-length dark hair and flushed red cheeks, ran up behind the dog and said, "Sorry, he tries to recruit everyone."

"No problem," Hale told her, throwing the ball and laughing at the dog's impressive speed.

"I'm really bored at college," he said to me as we walked on. "I'd like to quit and just go to work but I think Dad would kill me."

"Don't you need a degree to work in an investment firm?"

He kicked a pile of leaves that lifted and hung on the wind before falling. "Yep. Pretty sure that's the case. That's where you're lucky. No one would say that an artist has to have a degree."

"Is this really what you want to do? Be in finance?" I asked him. It was rare that Hale seemed open enough to me that I felt entitled to ask him questions about his life; this was one of those moments. "I remember a kid telling me how much he liked bugs. Sort of thought you'd be one of those weird science guys with crawly things in jars."

Hale laughed and looked up at leaves floating down from the trees. "I can't say being on Wall Street is my passion, but I want to be closer to Dad, and he's all about work. So, I guess part of me feels like, if we're working together, we'll get to know each other better."

A few minutes later a tall sandy haired man came jogging toward us, waving and smiling.

"Hey, Martin!" Hale called out.

He looked like he'd run a marathon. His face was beaded with sweat and his gray sweatshirt was damp. He was also undeniably handsome. "How you doing, man?" He looked from Hale to me. "You must be Tilly. I'd shake your hand but I'm really sweaty."

"I can see that. Nice to meet you. How far did you run?"

"Today's a 4 miler. Just an easy Sunday run. And I'm not done yet, so I don't want to stop for too long. See you, Hale."

I'm not sure why Hale decided to play match-maker, but he did – talking to me about Martin, and to Martin about me. He assured me that Martin was unattached and reminded me that I'd broken up with my last boyfriend months earlier so it was time to jump back in the water. After a couple of phone conversations, Martin asked me to dinner and even came down to Tribeca from his Upper West Side home turf. I felt like there were two conversations going on at dinner – one with our words and another through the current burning between us, making it seem inevitable that I was going to ask him up to my loft when he walked me home. I was never sure how anyone would react to my living room/art studio, or, for that matter, to my art. Martin stood in front of the canvas I was working on – a late night street with a shadowy figure standing beneath a streetlamp, cold light drizzling around him. I had my first showing booked and was working long hours to get more paintings finished.

"You're really good," he said. "This looks so sad, though. The guy looks lonely."

"He might be. He's whatever you think he is. And whoever you think he is."

I had moved up beside him, close enough to feel the heat of his skin under his shirt, and he turned into me, slipped his hands under my hair and kissed me. It felt like a continuation of the silent conversation we'd been having all evening. We moved to the couch, and when it was clear there was no turning back, I said, "Ugh, not to break the spell here, but I don't have any condoms."

He laughed, took off one of his shoes and withdrew two plastic-wrapped condoms.

"Came prepared, huh?"

He brushed my hair off my face. "Well, I hoped…"

"In the remake of The Thomas Crown Affair, Rene Russo says, 'I hate being a foregone conclusion.' I like that line. I wish I'd invented it. But I'll settle for borrowing it."

Martin stood up, took my hand and pulled me to my feet. "That's not how I see you. Like I said, I was just hoping. Where's your bedroom?"

Making love with Martin was like coming home to someone I didn't remember but knew intimately. I didn't think about love, or tomorrow, or whether we were right for each other. I didn't think at all. Every cell in my body was lit up and we moved in some mysterious choreography that felt both ancient and new. The edges of me fell away. I breathed him in, wanting to get drunk off his scent. I heard myself moan and thought, Oh right – that's me. We slept easily against each other, waking long before dawn to make love again and then dozing off until gray light edged into the room. He left quickly after that, which should have told me something. He claimed he had to be at work early.

"At work early? He's a real estate agent, not a Wall Street guy," Janice said later, when I shared coffee with her, thinking it should have been Martin looking at me through the steam and the hard orange sunlight angling across the room. "What would he be doing at this hour of the morning?"

"So, you're saying I blew it by sleeping with him?"

She shrugged and stared into her coffee.

"He had condoms in his shoe, Janice. It's not like he hadn't thought about it also."

Janice laughed and shook her head. "Tilly, he's a guy. He's always thinking about it. He probably puts those in his shoe every day."

I decided he was never going to call me again, so I might as well put him out of my mind. Which was hard because my bed sheets smelled like him, but once I did laundry, I felt like I had a handle on it. Then two days later on a Saturday afternoon he called and said he was nearby showing an apartment and could he come over. The day had just darkened with a thunderstorm that had suddenly blown in. Rain slashed against the windows. I turned on lamps and cleaned the paint off my hands. Coincidentally, I was working on a painting of rain streaming down a city street and two children in yellow slickers holding hands as they navigated their way through the water. I painted them from an angle so the hoods of their slickers obscured their faces.

"Do you ever paint people's faces?" Martin said when he stood in front of it, tilting his head to one side, then the other. He'd left his umbrella out in the hallway and his shoes by the door. His hair was damp and raindrops had spotted his shirt.

"Nope. It's sort of become my signature. I never felt comfortable painting faces so I decided to go for the mystery. I don't want people to figure things out by looking at the expression on someone's face. I think it's more interesting to use your imagination to fill in that detail."

He turned toward me and slipped his hands around my waist, moving them up beneath my shirt. "Are those two kids in the painting happy?" he said, his mouth breathing warm against my neck.

"Do you want them to be?"

His answer was to kiss me, and my response was to forget that he hadn't called me for two days and to sink once again into the rushing waters of wanting him. We didn't make it to the bedroom. We made love on the couch with only half our clothes removed. This time he had condoms in his shirt pocket and I did register how facile he was putting one on while his mouth was busy driving me crazy.

It was over quickly and he rolled off me and stood up. I pulled the chenille throw from the couch across me and watched him get dressed.

"So, that's all you came over for, huh?" I said. "A quickie?"

He looked surprise. "Well, yeah. I thought this was okay with you. This kind of arrangement."

"Arrangement?"

He pulled a comb from his pocket and ran it through his hair. "You know what I mean. Sex buddies. Friends with benefits. Tilly, you slept with me on the first date. What else would I think?"

"So, because of that, you put me in a category of just-for-sex?"

"I thought it was the category you'd decided on."

"I don't remember deciding on a category, Martin. That one's on you. Have a great rest of your day."

I walked across the floor as gracefully as I could with the chenille throw wrapped around me and closed myself in the bathroom until I heard him leave.

Martin told Hale everything – how I was not relationship material because of my loose morals (that was actually the phrase Hale said he used.) I didn't see Martin again, but the real wound was how my brother looked me from then on – with judgment brushing the edges of his eyes.

That was before the world changed. Before the towers crumbled. Before people vanished completely. Before white papers floated down. Standing outside my mother's building, with the smell of ash still in the air, I made plans with Martin for that evening, knowing I wouldn't be sleeping in my childhood bedroom that night. I told my mother I was going to stay with Janice so not to worry about me. Strange how easily we can feel like we're sixteen again.

I met him at Café des Artistes. In the soft light, with paintings of naked women surrounding us, the past seemed no more consequential than a swift-moving tide that had deposited us on this shore – with our tears and loss and questions that could never be answered. I spent that night with Martin, and many more after that. I never questioned if we were in a relationship, and he never offered a definition of what we had become. We were entwined by a common grief; Hale circled around us, whispered past the window shades when the moon was full. Sometimes after we made love tears leaked from my eyes and stained Martin's skin. "I know," he'd say, stroking my hair, but he wasn't really trying to quiet my sorrow. He just felt like he had to say something.

I tried going back to Tribeca, to my loft. I stood in front of the windows, in front of my easel, and imagined painting there again. I knew I couldn't do it. The empty sky and the pervasive shadow of death held me hostage. Martin found me a sublet on the eighth floor in the Café des Artistes building. The apartment was dark and cramped compared to my loft. I had to turn lights on all the time, even on sunny days. The kitchen was a shadowy corner that I occasionally shared with cockroaches who scattered when I turned on the lights. But there was space in the living room for me to paint and after a few weeks I got used to it.

"You know how women get rid of the cockroaches in their apartments?" Janice asked the first time she came to visit me.

"Enlighten me."

"Ask them for a commitment."

The next year drifted over me, through me, the past that would never again be real often tugging me backwards. But this new world – without my brother and father, without the city as it had once been -- pulled me in as if to say, 'You can't escape this, you might as well live it.' Janice moved to Greenwich Village; she couldn't endure the view outside her windows and the constant reminder of a day that would always ache inside her. My mother and I fell into a gentle truce. She wore my father's wedding ring around her neck always, and she sought out my company – for lunches, for shopping, sometimes just for sitting with her in late afternoons sipping tea. Ian was there a lot, filling in for the friends who had drifted away from her. She was now a single woman, a widow. I guess that messed up their seating arrangements at dinner parties.

"Are you and Martin a couple?" she asked me one rainy day when she'd invited me to have lunch with her at Cipriani's. It wasn't my usual choice of restaurant, but it was a fixture in her life. There was nothing steely in her voice, so I opened my life a crack and let her peek in.

"Not really. I'm not sure what we are. I think we just need each other right now. We share the same grief."

She nodded and sipped her white wine. "That's nice," she said, without meeting my eyes.

I'd noticed sketches around her apartment – cottages and city streets, like the drawings she did when I was growing up. Most were still in charcoal, but some were in pencil. One day I smelled paint when I came in.

"Are you taking up painting?" I asked her. "Instead of charcoal sketches?"

"Just dabbling." The way she said it was like a door closing. Weeks later, she carefully asked me about brushes and where to get the best paints. "I'm just trying to fill up my time," she told me, with a casual shrug that I didn't buy for a minute.

Midway through that year, I sold a painting that would be featured in the Arts section of The New York Times. It was of two tall buildings – clearly the towers – and the sky around them was gray and billowing with clouds. Or maybe smoke. It wasn't clear. A flock of birds was diving down toward the earth, dark wings folded, beaks pointed at the ground. The windows of the buildings were orange, as if there were flames inside, and when you looked closely you could see, in a few windows, people staring out. The painting was both reality and illusion, sorrow and promise. The flames were contained, the towers were intact, birds were diving downward but people were still on the other side of the glass. A wealthy Wall Street investor, who lost many friends on 9/11, bought the painting at a small showing I had of my work. In the Times piece, he was quoted as saying the painting "grabbed onto his heart the moment he saw it and wouldn't let go."

My mother came to that showing, arriving quite late and working the room as if she were hosting a cocktail party. I overheard her telling a few people that she taught me how to draw when I was a child. At the end of the evening she congratulated me, said how proud she was, but in her eyes lurked a more ominous message. It would take more than a year for me to decipher what it was. One of my flaws was that I always underestimated my mother. I clung to the naïve belief that, while she could bristle with jealousy toward other women who she suspected were more fortunate than she, this unattractive tendency would never be turned on me, her daughter. I was wrong. When Charlotte Austin was relegated to the past and Amber was born, no power on earth could stop her from becoming a more successful painter than me. Her air of victory was a constant reminder that I was in a lower class – the downtown girl with a small, eclectic following. It didn't matter to her that the art world dismissed her. She had legions of fans who decorated the walls of their homes with lithographs of her paintings, who asked for Amber Austin paintings as wedding gifts, and who lined up around the block and waited for hours whenever she did a showing. I retreated from her dark gaze and her light-filled paintings into the shadows of my own work. And into the shadows of a small, diminished version of myself. I could never beat my mother at her own game.

7.

I live in a two-story wood shingled house near the Pacific Ocean. The house has seen better days. Apparently when it was built, insulation wasn't a popular concept. Some days, when the wind is strong and sweeps in from the sea, I can smell salt and brine. The rooms feel damp on those days and the furnace argues with the wind leaking in. Evening falls early in this house. The rooms sink into shadow a good hour before lamps go on in other homes – houses with bigger windows, more open floor plans where sunlight has a chance to linger and flirt with encroaching night before finally surrendering. The cold is stubborn in this place. It creeps through walls, rises up through the floorboards. When I chose to rent the house, I wanted it because of its shadows. They fit me. There is a loneliness here, a web of darkness that's evident more in winter than in summer. I recognized it the first time I saw it. I set up my painting studio in one of the upstairs bedrooms and watched the play of shadows both outside and in. It's where I belong, I thought. Let my mother bask in her sunlit mansion, painting her absurdly joyful canvases. I prefer the dark side of the moon.

Three years after 9/11, when my mother and I moved out of New York and came to Los Angeles, we lived in a suite of rooms at a fashionable beachside hotel. She worked with a real estate agent to find a house to buy. I looked at rental ads.

"Why?" my friends in Manhattan asked me when I was packing to leave. "Why are you moving to the west coast with her? You have a life here."

"Do I?" I said.

I wasn't sure I did anymore. My father and Hale were everywhere and nowhere. I couldn't walk in Central Park without seeing my father up ahead, holding onto the back of my bike when I was small, teaching me to ride without training wheels. I couldn't go by Wolman Rink without seeing

Hale and me learning to ice-skate, holding onto each other, falling down together. I was two years older than him, but he was a robust kid, and I could never hold him up when he stumbled on the ice. He always took me down with him.

In the end, he took me down with him again. In the late stillness of so many nights, I have stepped through broken glass into wide open air. I've been inches from him as the sky whistled between us, pulling us apart. I've stretched my arm to hold onto his hand and in that quiet corridor of darkness, long after midnight and long before dawn, I swore I could feel his fingers curl around mine.

Manhattan started to feel unbearably lonely to me. Janice was still my friend – she had stood at her window and watched people jump. Only once did I ask her if she thought she might have seen my father and Hale. She shut her eyes against the tears and whispered, "I don't know." I never asked again. She would always be a witness. She couldn't alter that piece of her own history even if she wanted to. But she never backed away from me, even though seeing me inevitably took her back to the images of that day. Other friends drifted, turned away, saw me as a reminder of what we were not supposed to acknowledge – that people just like them had stepped out into nothingness to escape burning jet fuel and falling ceilings. My mother was the only family I had left. That's what I told myself as I prepared to re-locate to the opposite coast. Was that why I followed her lead and left New York? Or was I clinging to a threadbare hope that we could finally learn to be a family?

On the day of my mother's death, I remembered reading a quote from some unknown person. "You're born twice," the quote read. "Once when you're born to your mother and again when she dies."

On that first day of my second birth, I came home and turned on lamps in my house. I cranked up the heat and fed Lola. I resisted the temptation to go on line and look at the "breaking news." For that same reason, I didn't turn on the television. I knew Amber Austin's death had become a news story; I even passed some TV trucks on my way out of her neighborhood. I was pouring a glass of wine when I heard Stephen's key in the lock. His footsteps were sturdy and reassuring on the hardwood floor as he came into the kitchen.

"Hey." He opened his arms and pulled me in tight. I felt the tears I still couldn't cry rise up, press into the back of my eyes.

I breathed him in for what seemed like a long time before pulling back and looking at him. He still had his makeup on from the set. I knew he'd raced out of there as soon as the director called it a day.

"Was it a stroke?" he asked me. "Sometimes those transient ischemic attacks are a prelude to a major stroke. You said she'd had several the past couple of months."

"Thank you, doctor. I don't know if the TIAs, as most of us non-medical people call them, had anything to do with it. She just didn't wake up, so it seems like her heart simply stopped. I have no idea if they'll do an autopsy."

He shrugged. "Doubtful. Her doctor will probably attribute it to the chemo, her body just not being able to take that kind of onslaught. I think unless there is obviously foul play, someone has to request an autopsy."

"What she requested was an open casket," I told him. "And she wanted to be buried with my father's ring around her neck. I found Ellen taking it off her. It was creepy, Stephen. She said it was her responsibility to make sure my mother's wishes were followed, so she plans on putting it back on her after her body is prepared. First I heard about any of this."

"I'm so sorry, Tilly. I wish I could wave a wand and change your history with your mother. It's complicated losing a parent who was… challenging."

I couldn't help but laugh a little. "That's such a delicate and diplomatic way of putting it. Challenging. You met her – you know how wily she could be. And how competitive. Her greatest source of pleasure was knowing she'd become a more successful painter than me. But lucky for her, she found a substitute daughter in Ellen, didn't she? Pity I never found a substitute mother. I don't know why I'm getting angry now – I mean, she's gone. Maybe I just don't know how to grieve for her, so anger seems like a good alternative. And since you mentioned foul play, the bottle of Ambien that was there yesterday was noticeably absent today."

"That doesn't really prove anything," Stephen said. "Someone could have removed it so she wouldn't take any more of it. Or they could have removed it after she died so rumors wouldn't start that she overdosed."

I disentangled myself from Stephen and went to pour him a glass of wine. A ribbon of chilly air drifted across me. It's never clear where the chill comes from in my house; it just finds its way in even with the heat on. The rain had started again and Lola was standing at the glass French doors staring out at it.

"I'm going to go upstairs and wash this makeup off my face," Stephen said. "Be back down in a minute."

I watched him as he walked out of my narrow kitchen – a rather uninviting space, with no room for people to hang out while the hostess is cooking. I saw Stephen wrapped boldly into my life, taking up more space than any man before him ever had. I saw him as he was decades ago -- the young kid in framed photographs that grace a shelf in his living room; I saw him as the elderly man he will one day be. I never thought I could love someone as deeply as I love him, and sometimes it scares the hell out of me.

Stephen lives up the street, in an expensive newly built house where cold air never creeps in, all the appliances are impressively shiny, and the rooms have been tastefully decorated by a well-known interior designer. The house was once featured in Architectural Digest. We met nearly four years ago, just after he'd moved in. It was early morning and I was walking Lola past his house. Suddenly the front door opened and he padded out in his pajama bottoms and a sweatshirt to get the paper. Even with bedhead hair and sleepy eyes, he was instantly recognizable. The chestnut haired, handsome star of a weekly medical drama who, miraculously, had stayed out of the tabloids except for "sightings" as he shopped for groceries. By the time we met again, I'd watched several episodes of his TV show and was definitely smitten.

We keep clothes and toiletries at each other's houses, but it's understood that the only sleep-overs are at mine because I won't leave Lola alone for the night, and Stephen has a cat who I'm afraid will gleefully slaughter a canine intruder. I took Lola over there one afternoon and Travis clearly wanted to communicate his tiger heritage. But I know it's more than that – this arrangement we have. The animals would probably learn to get along if given the chance. I still have a wall around me. A wall made of broken concrete and bent steel. It's glued together with shattered glass, ghosts, and the ache that's always lurking inside me.

Stephen has a fifteen-year old daughter, Dylan, who lives with her mother in San Francisco but visits occasionally. Some of her make-up and her more outrageous outfits are stored at my house. I'm the lenient one, who doesn't care if she rings her eyes with black and wears outlandishly skimpy clothes, shredded in odd places. I'd rather see what she's wearing than know she's transforming herself in the backseat of a friend's car. Dylan is impatient for her birthday, anxious for the milestone of sixteen. She's pierced her ears and her nose, was contemplating piercing her tongue but I successfully talked her out of it. "You want to swill Listerine every time you take a bite of food?" I asked her. "Or kiss? Because you'll have to." For some reason that worked, probably because I'm not her parent.

A few minutes later Stephen came downstairs in a gray sweatshirt and jeans. As he slid past me in the kitchen to get his glass of wine, I wanted to tell him about the reservoir of tears I knew were in me but were out of reach. I wanted to tell him how grateful I was to not be alone right then, and that I love him so much it terrifies me. But I told him none of that.

"Stephen?"

He came close and slipped his hand under my hair, his palm warm against the back of my neck. "Yeah…"

"I'm scared. I don't know who to be now. She's defined me for so long, even though I fought so hard against that and never wanted to admit that she'd won in so many ways. I feel like an abstract painting now – all the colors messed up and swirled around."

"For whatever it's worth, I've never seen you as being defined by anyone else. Not even your mother. Maybe now that she's gone, you can see yourself as other people see you. I promise you, no one looks at you through your mother's eyes."

"I guess I do. That's the problem."

I wrapped my arms around his waist and buried my face in his chest. Sometimes the only thing that can save you from yourself is to breathe in the person you love, and breathe deeply. I wanted so badly to walk away from who I had always been and step into a clear green future with Stephen, but I could still feel ghostly fingers around my ankles and wrists, holding me hostage.

Stephen ran his hand through my hair, coaxed my head back and kissed me.

"Let's go in the living room, light a fire, and I'll order something decadent and bad for us for dinner. Pizza with extra cheese sound good?"

"Sounds like very good medicine at the moment."

I glanced at my cell phone. I'd turned off the volume earlier so I wouldn't hear it ringing, and I wasn't surprised that I had twenty-seven messages. Scrolling through them, I saw that Janice had called, and Ian McBride. I had nearly a dozen text messages too.

"Stephen, I have to return two of these calls – Janice and Ian. Everyone else can wait – some forever, since a lot of these texts are from news shows."

Janice asked me if I wanted her to fly out, and I knew if I said yes she'd be on the next plane. I told her I'd call her back and we'd talk about it. Ian was crying and I tried to comfort him but didn't know how. He said he'd just spoken with my mother the day before and she seemed fine. It was very sudden, I told him, as if that could make him feel better, which of course it couldn't. I again felt guilty for the tears I hadn't yet cried.

Later, with firelight flickering around us and Lola snoring softly in front of the hearth, I said to Stephen, "I thought it would be different."

"What?"

"When my mother died. I thought I'd feel sad, but also so free it would be like I was weightless. Like a prisoner who's suddenly been released from jail. I feel a little of that, but not as dramatically as I expected. I assumed I'd be instantly transformed."

Stephen pulled me against him and I curled up under his arm like a child wanting a bedtime story. "Do you know any prisoners who have been freed after a long incarceration?" he asked me.

I shook my head no. "But if you do, I want to know how you know them. Although this is a really weird time to tell me you have a criminal past."

"Nothing of the kind. I don't know a single prisoner. But I bet their re-entry into the world and into freedom isn't all euphoria. I bet there are some tears, and a lot of reflection. I bet there's a lot of fear too."

"I guess. I just wish I could grieve for her. But she made it so difficult."

"Tilly, you've been grieving over your mother for a long time. Your whole life practically. You've grieved for the mother she didn't know how to be, the mother you needed her to be. How could you possibly have any grief left?"

I knew he was right. But I still wished the turmoil inside me would quiet down and lightness would take over. I wished for some sweetness to my grief. A flow of tears. As horrible as my father's death was, there was a tenderness to my longing for him, a sweet ache to the place inside me that missed him.

"I don't want to be like my mother," I told him. "Incapable of crying when tears are called for, when they're the appropriate response. Tears reveal what your heart's feeling, so if you aren't crying, that makes a statement too. I saw her cry one time, standing at the window, on 9/11, late that afternoon when we pretty much knew Hale and my father were gone. That's the only time I ever saw her shed tears about anything."

"You're not your mother, Tilly. You may have her genes, but you don't have her soul."

Lola jumped on the couch and wedged herself against me. I heard a siren far away, cutting through the night. "I caught my reflection today," I said. "And for a second I thought I saw the set of my mother's mouth. It made me think of when her mother died and I kept waiting for her to cry, or at least soften. She never did."

Stephen stroked my hair, my neck. "I remember you telling me about that. But you know what? You don't really know if, when she was by herself, she didn't break down and cry like a baby. I'm just saying to consider the possibility that she had a secret life full of emotion that she never showed to anyone else. If for no other reason, it will stop you from looking for her in every mirror you pass by."

We made love that night, gently and tentatively, as if Stephen thought I might break into pieces – like thin porcelain or blown glass. I loved him for that, but I hated my broken places.

"I'm an orphan now," I whispered later, as a blade of moonlight fell through the window. The storm was over.

He rolled over and folded me in his arms. "I know. It's weird, huh? No matter what your relationship was with your parents, it's strange. Everyone I know who's lost their parents has said the same thing – they feel like an orphan."

"Maybe not everyone. I doubt my mother gave too much thought to her orphan status."

My grandmother died two months after the towers fell, in a narrow bed with chrome railings and dull beige walls around her. I never knew my grandfather. My mother simply said that her parents had divorced when she turned eighteen, the theory being that she'd be able to handle it at that age. Apparently, the marriage had been a battlefield for years, but her mother and father believed in staying together for their daughter's sake. My grandmother lived in New Jersey, in a large drafty house with no photographs of the man who was once her husband. Hale and I were told to call her by her name, Teresa, because 'Grandma' made her feel old. Once, when we visited on a steamy summer day, Hale asked about the grandfather we never knew and she snapped, "He died years ago, the son-of-a-bitch. Good riddance, I say.'

"Mother, please don't use that language around the children," my mother said, eliciting a harsh glare from the woman who raised her but who seemed to have no affection for her.

Whenever we were in the presence of my grandmother, my mother would soften her own countenance, as if she needed to prove that she was not genetically programmed to be rigid and unapproachable. I would get the benefit of my mother's temporary transformation, but only until we said goodbye to Teresa.

In 1998 my grandmother was diagnosed with Alzheimer's. She remained at home for a while with round-the-clock caregivers but the house was too big, too dangerous for someone who no longer knew where she was, and the caregivers complained constantly about her outbursts. She was finally moved into a facility in New Jersey and we rarely visited her.

"She won't understand, but I think we should tell her anyway," my mother said to me many weeks after the towers fell, when the air still smoldered and hope for finding survivors was gone.

We stood at her bedside, the ugly beige walls and the faint smells of Lysol and urine and age filtering into me like a toxic cocktail. My grandmother's eyes were pale blue and empty. I listened to my mother's voice as if it were a radio broadcast.

"Mother, something terrible happened. There was a terrorist attack and the World Trade Center was hit. Two towers collapsed, and thousands of people died. Keith and Hale were at work that day. They didn't make it. I know you probably won't understand this, but I wanted you to know."

Teresa's eyes shifted slightly, her mouth moved, but no words came out. When we left, my mother's mouth was a hard, straight line and the sound of her high heels clicking on the linoleum echoed around us. A little more than a month later Teresa died. There were only a few people at her service, and her tombstone bore no message of love or grief, only the dates that bracketed her life. I looked at my mother's tearless face that day and saw behind her columns of women, going back generations, all with that same brittle countenance. My history terrified me. Was I condemned to grow into that same face? Our parents either anchor us in the earth's sweetest soil, or they toss us, untethered and helpless, into unpredictable seas roiled by ghosts.

Stephen's parents live in Arizona, in a house that sits along the border of a golf course. They fly into Los Angeles for awards shows if Stephen is nominated, and for Christmas. I've met them a few times and am always struck by how normal they seem – none of the hurricane warnings and hidden riptides that characterized my family. Arthur and Paige Bendel owned a Mom-and-Pop Dry Cleaner's until they decided to sell the business, retire, and take up golf.

I've wondered sometimes who I would be if I'd had parents who were that accessible – that normal. My father had big, important goals and my mother basked in the glow of his success. Their children were handed expectations as if they were Christmas presents – we were supposed to grow into proper upper-crust Manhattanites, schooled in which fork to use and which subject matters to avoid in dinner table conversations, polite but distant with those who didn't match our status in life. Hale took those expectations willingly, unwrapped them and showed his gratitude by becoming the son he was expected to be. I responded with disdain. I became the downtown girl, the creator of shadowy art – paintings that no one in my parents' world would ever hang on their walls. One of the few boyfriends my parents approved of once told me I must have been born with rebellion in my blood. He said it as he was breaking up with me. I don't know if it's possible for one's bloodstream to have such a personality characteristic, but I do know that my parents gave me a lot to rebel against. The careful, shiny world of upper-crust society begs to be derided, and I was all too happy to fulfill that role.

But there was a past – there is always a past.

8

When I think of my childhood, I think of gray Manhattan days and lamp-lit windows on the faces of buildings. I think of tires splashing through puddles and how Hale and I would laugh if we got wet while we waited to cross the street. I think of our white breath on snowy days and the scrape of our ice skates at Wolman Rink as afternoon slid into early dusk. I think of summers in East Hampton at the house my parents would rent. Before our father would let us go in the ocean, we had to learn to swim in the pool. A tall blonde woman came to give us lessons and, as soon as Hale mastered the crawl, he insisted on racing me. He always won, eliciting praise from our parents. I got used to seeing Hale as the winner. I look back on those days and see myself drifting away from him, putting wide ripples of blue water between us as I floated out in the deep end. I'm not sure if that actually happened, but it's the image emblazoned in my memory.

When we were allowed to go into the ocean, we would duck under a wave and open our eyes, trying to see each other through the murky salt water. Once, Hale reached out and held my hand as the currents moved above us. Our cheeks puffed out with the breath we were holding, and the currents jostled us, but we held on. I think of that day most of all.

For high school, I was sent to a girl's boarding school in Connecticut. My father came quietly into my room to tell me about their decision, and I didn't argue. I didn't even mind. Being sent away to school meant I wouldn't have to figure out my mother's mood every day and determine where the safe zones were.

Whenever I came back for holidays, I felt like an intruder – a foreign exchange student who was magnanimously taken in and allowed to sit at the dinner table. This family who was mine in name and DNA had closed ranks and left me outside. They were a perfect triangle. My parents knew Hale's friends, they discussed current events and projects he was doing in science class. Then they would awkwardly ask me about school and inquire about my interests. But it was clear that I was the unfamiliar guest who would stay for the duration of the Christmas holiday, or for the long summer months, and go away again. We still went to East Hampton in the summers, but Hale and I never swam in the ocean together anymore, never reached out beneath the surface of the water to link fingers. During one of those summers, when as a teenager I took long walks alone along the shore and wandered about town on my own, I walked into an art gallery and knew suddenly what I wanted to do with my life. My mother had taught me to sketch in charcoal when I was very young, and I'd continued to draw, but I kept my art books to myself, never showing my work to anyone. That day, in the air-conditioned space of a white-walled gallery, I allowed myself to imagine my name beneath a painting I had created. For the first time, I discovered what it was like to dream beyond the boundaries I'd accepted in my life.

When I began painting, I tried to paint people. But they never looked real. My first art teacher at boarding school said to me, "What do you really want to paint? What speaks to you? What world do you want to slip into and explore?"

That's how the shadows began. I was comfortable there. Somehow, I understood dark streets and forbidden alleys, even though I had never experienced them for myself. I am never sure, when I begin a painting, if there will be someone lurking in the shadows or if the area will remain just swirls of air and darkness – littered with the detritus that people have left behind -- broken bottles, discarded newspapers, a shoe, an umbrella. In one of my paintings, there is an arm reaching out from the dim murk of a tunnel; the hand is stretching toward a ribbon of daylight, not quite touching it, but the tension is visible. Please let me reach this light, it's saying. In the tunnel are discarded remnants of people's lives – a splintered skateboard, a winter jacket, a stroller with a broken wheel. It was the first painting I ever sold, and it began my soon-to-be-interrupted career in New

York.

Families compose themselves. It happens over generations in a mysterious weaving of history, unrequited emotions, secrets, and unspoken fears. Everyone gets an assigned role, and those roles rarely change. In my family, I was the outsider, the one who didn't fit in, the girl who grudgingly went to college for two years and then quit to devote herself to painting. Hale was the shining star. He was always at the top of his class, destined to follow our father into the glass and steel world of high finance. Our father was the dependable foundation of our family. There were no surprises from him, no outbursts, just a calm reserve and a sense that he was no different with us than he was with everyone else he encountered in his world. There was an evenness about him that was puzzling and slightly unnerving. I never saw him angry or upset; it was as if there were a piece missing. He was kind but distant, measuring out his emotions as if there would always be a predictable outcome. Our mother was a woman of many faces. Her chameleon charms could weaken men and send women into a fast retreat, intimidated by her wiles. She wore her roles in life the way she wore her clothes – elegantly, without a wrinkle or a torn seam. She was the best-dressed mother at school events, smiling perfectly and clapping her manicured hands at exactly the right moments. She was the stylish hostess, arranging business dinners for my father and shooing Hale and me into the kitchen where we wouldn't be seen. When I was a child and found myself alone with her, I sometimes thought she didn't know how to dress for that role. She seemed perplexed, as if her script had been lost in the mail. Mothering a daughter was the one talent that eluded her. With Hale, she resorted to her charms, even when he was a toddler. With me, her eyes went blank, as if I were another species, something left on her doorstep.

I woke up just after three in the morning, with Stephen breathing deeply beside me and Lola snuffling on her dog bed, caught up in some sort of dream. I listened to the quiet of the night, tried to figure out where the North Star was, and I felt something vast and bottomless open up inside me. This is the grief that's been waiting for me, I thought – the grief of a lifetime, the years spent wondering why my mother's eyes never lit up when she saw me, why the bonds that usually anchor parents to children, keeping them safe from storms, never formed between us. I had grabbed onto threads – a look, a word, a gesture – especially after my father and Hale were gone and it was just the two of us. But the threads were fragile as gossamer; I was left with pieces of a dream, a story that had never been real. I was left feeling like a fool.

The moon slipped across the sky and a whisper of silver fell through the window. I thought about my father's wedding ring held tightly in Ellen's hand. I didn't want it to be buried under the earth. I wanted something of his. When I was staying with my mother after the towers fell, I took one of my father's shirts without telling her. It was a white shirt, finely made and infused with his scent. After I moved into the sublet in the des Artistes, I wore it when I worked. I had this crazy idea that my father's spirit would find me through the soft fabric of the shirt and guide my hand as I painted. I kept the shirt until it practically disintegrated, and when it was gone, I once again had nothing of my father's.

"I don't want my mother to be buried with my father's ring," I said to Stephen the next morning. It was just after dawn and we were walking Lola toward his house so he could feed Travis. The storm had moved on, but billowy clouds drifted across the sky.

Stephen gave me a sideways look. "Please tell me you aren't going to jump into the casket and yank it off her neck."

"I can assure you I was not planning on doing that. But I do have a plan."

"Okay…"

"I can just go buy a look-alike ring and chain and switch them out. The thing is, I have to figure out when and where to do it. I'd pretty much have to visit her body before they put her on display, which means getting past Gestapo Ellen."

It was Saturday, Stephen didn't have to work, and I told him when we got up that morning that I had no idea what I was supposed to do with my day. Was I supposed to go back to my mother's house? I didn't know, but Stephen promised me he'd go with me if I decided I should return to Casa del Sol. We were walking up Stephen's path to his front door and he picked up The New York Times that had been tossed onto the boxwood hedge. Lola gave me a look as if to say, "You do know there is a small tiger in that house, right?" In answer, I tightened her leash.

"Going to see your mother in the mortuary probably wouldn't work," Stephen said as he unlocked the front door. "I doubt they'd let you even if you wanted to. Let me give it some thought."

Travis meowed the moment the door opened and came trotting toward us – a determined tabby cat making it clear this was his territory. Lola backed up and took refuge behind my legs.

"Hey Travis," Stephen said, bending down and stroking his back. "Ready for some breakfast? What should we have?"

Travis purred and then walked purposefully over to Lola, who froze, as did I. But rather than hiss, he circled around to Lola's rear end, sniffed under her tail, and rubbed his face on Lola's hind leg. Stephen laughed.

"Well, there you go, Tilly. Your last excuse to not sleep at my house just dissolved. Oh Lord, what are we going to do now?" Still laughing, he headed for the kitchen to open a can of cat food. I guess I hadn't ever fooled him.

Going after him, I said, "Okay, but Travis was mean once before."

"Uh-huh. Just testing to see if Lola would accept that he's alpha cat. It's an annoying habit that the males of all species have in common." He put the can down and came over to me, folding me inside his arms. "I get it, okay? I've always gotten it. You need to have a little bit of a wall up somewhere, just in case the world falls apart again. But you know what? If it does fall apart, you're better off if there aren't any walls around that can tumble down on you. There are safe places in the world, Tilly. There are safe relationships. Maybe now that your mother's gone, you can finally trust that I'm one of them."

"I trust you…"

"I know you do. But only up to my front door." He kissed me and brushed my hair off my forehead. "We'll get there."

Travis was now circling all of us, meowing for his food, and Lola – encouraged by his friendliness – was trying to sniff under his tail. I wondered what it would be like waking up in Stephen's house, a house where sunlight poured in and the floors were polished and new. Where shadows didn't pool in corners and wind didn't leak in. Where our lives would finally be intertwined. I wondered what it was going to feel like to melt completely into the idea of the two of us, with no boundaries and no marked exits. My mother's ghost hand slipped from my wrist and I inched forward into my life without her.

My cell phone rang then and I saw that it was Ellen calling me. I held up my phone to Stephen, showing him the display. "Ugh-oh," I said before answering.

"Tilly, I need you to come to the house today," Ellen said, without bothering to say good morning. "You have to go through some things your mother left you. If they aren't things you want, then they're going into the auction."

"Okay, I'm going to refrain from asking the obvious question – what auction? We'll just see you in about an hour, okay?"

She said okay and hung up abruptly. "I'm feeling a slight sense of dread at imagining what things my mother left me," I said to Stephen. "And why would Ellen want me to go through them? And when did my mother decide to have an auction?"

"I think all I can say is, we'll find out soon enough. But first we need breakfast."

"Somehow I think there isn't enough nutrition in the world to prepare us for what's waiting at the house of sun."

Stephen drove, with Lola in the back seat, her head out the window. I was too slow putting up the passenger side window as we approached my mother's driveway. A horde of reporters and photographers were there, and as soon as someone spotted me they descended on us. But Stephen kept moving forward. The footage on the evening news was of a black Mercedes with a white terrier sticking her head out the rear window, barking at photographers, and a reporter saying, "We believe this was Amber Austin's daughter, Tilly Austin, also a painter."

"I should change my name to 'Also'," I told Stephen when we watched the news broadcast later that evening. "Also Austin – it has a quirky ring to it."

Ellen was frantic when we pulled up to the house. She'd obviously been crying, her mascara had given her raccoon eyes, and she was clutching a yellow pad and her cell phone with white-knuckled hands.

"Thank God you're here," she said, looking from Stephen to me. "The mortuary called. I made a terrible mistake! I didn't realize that we never ordered a casket! We have to choose a casket!"

"Okay," Stephen said calmly. "That shouldn't be too hard. Is there a casket shortage or something?"

"No!" Ellen yelled. "But it has to be the proper casket! I have no idea what Amber would have wanted and I need to get what she'll be with happy with!"

The girl was getting hysterical. I put my hands on her shoulders and forced her to meet my eyes. "Ellen, she's dead. She isn't going to be happy or unhappy with anything…that we know of."

She actually calmed down a bit. "Well, it has to be appropriate. Fitting for who she is. Was."

"Right. So, we'll get an appropriate casket, whatever that means. I've never gone casket shopping before so I don't really know what's appropriate. Do they come in colors?"

I was not prepared for Ellen to insist that I go with her to help her choose the right casket. "It's close by. The mortuary is there at the cemetery," she said. "It shouldn't take long."

I gave Stephen a desperate look, but he said, "I can drive Lola home, and then Ellen you can drive Tilly back when the two of you are finished."

I glared at him, but he didn't seem to care. Traitor, I thought.

"Fine, okay," I said. "But what things did you want me to go through, Ellen?"

She checked her yellow pad. "Right. So…I'm just getting to her closets today. Your mother said whatever clothes of hers you might want you should take. The rest are either being donated to a local charity or they'll be included in the auction."

I tried to conjure up an image of me in my mother's clothes, but it was so absurd it wouldn't even form in my mind. "Ellen, I have no desire to dress myself in my mother's clothes."

"Okay, well then let me get my purse and we'll go."

Lola had already barreled through the house to the backyard. Stephen and I followed Ellen inside and I realized it felt strangely cold. Rosario was putting piles of her belongings at the foot of the stairs, preparing to move out. She had been my mother's live-in housekeeper for years and had apparently transported half her possessions to the house. I looked up the stairs to my mother's bedroom.

"I need to go in there for a minute."

"Do you want me to go with you?" Stephen asked.

"Yes please."

I shivered when I walked in. The bed was made but in my mind I still saw her body in a tangle of sheets and blankets. The stale scent of her illness lingered in the air. The fake head with her spare wig was on the dresser and I saw Stephen staring at it.

"I know. Weird, huh?" I said.

He shrugged. "People have their vanity. They're entitled to it. It is strange seeing it now, though. Hey, Tilly – try to get along with Ellen – it'll make things easier from this point on. She asked you to go with her, so she's reaching out to you."

"Or she regards casket shopping as some kind of bizarre couples therapy," I said. He gave me a look, which made me relent. "Okay, okay, I'll try. Stephen, may I remind you that my mother's bottle of Ambien disappeared, and Ellen seems to control everything around here."

He put a finger across my lips. "You know what? Let's not stir things up, okay? You know she took the pills when she was advised not to. Maybe they contributed to her death, maybe they didn't. She was very ill. Let it go."

Lola gave me a worried look when I got into Ellen's car, as if I was abandoning her. Stephen stroked her neck and talked soothingly to her, but she didn't seem to relax until he promised her a treat when they got home.

I ducked down in the seat when we got to the end of the driveway so that Ellen would be the only one photographed.

"Seriously?" Ellen said when we got past the knot of fans and reporters and I inched back up. "It's that disturbing to have your picture taken?"

"What can I say, Ellen, I'm just a rebel through and through." I was not doing what I'd promised Stephen I would try to do. My behavior definitely did not fall under the heading of trying to get along.

Ellen crossed Sunset and started winding her way through back streets, avoiding the main roads. It was silent in the car until she took a deep breath and exhaled in a long, drawn-out stream of air.

"Look, Tilly, I obviously know you resent me. Your

mother hired me, and she depended on me, and I became very fond of her. My mother died when I was ten, so I really appreciated having a mother figure."

"I didn't know that – about your mother dying when you were so young."

"Of course you didn't," she said. "How would you know? We've never really had a conversation before."

"So, did your father raise you?"

She nodded. "He did. And my sister is three years older, so she grew up fast and sort of raised me too."

There was a night when I was about eight, when I imagined my parents divorcing and my father raising me and Hale by himself. It came about because my father was out of town on business and Ian came over to escort my mother to some black-tie event she really wanted to attend. I decided she must be cheating on my father, and I even imagined testifying in court that I wanted to go live with him. But when he came back, I overheard him cheerfully asking my mother if Ian took good care of her at the gala, so I relinquished my fantasy and never rekindled it.

"Tilly," Ellen said, "I know you had a rough relationship with Amber. But blaming me for it isn't going to help you make sense of it. Or move past it."

I so wanted to come up with a scathing reply. I didn't want to let go of my resentment toward Ellen – my anger was a lifeline keeping me above the deep waters of my mother's death and all the things that had died between us before I was even old enough to process the loss. My father and Hale were in those deep waters, too. What would our lives have been like if they hadn't died on that blue shiny day? Could we have gone on pretending to be a close family? Pretending works sometimes...until it doesn't.

"You're right, Ellen," I told her. "It isn't your fault. When my mother was still Charlotte – long before Amber was created – she let go of my hand and never reached for it again. It's so much easier to blame you than to wrestle with the puzzle of why I wasn't good enough for her."

We'd turned into the cemetery and Ellen looked at me with a softness I hadn't seen before. "I'm sorry things weren't good between the two of you," she told me, and took a deep breath. Exhaling, she said, "Well, here we are. We're going to that building right over there."

I got out of the car and looked around at the sweep of green land dotted with tombstones and monuments. Then I noticed where we'd parked.

"Hey, Ellen? We're parked between Merv Griffin and Farah Fawcett. Should we take a selfie?"

I swear I almost got Ellen to laugh, but she caught herself. "Tilly, that's disrespectful," she said in a hushed voice.

The wind had picked up, shuttling clouds across the sky. I watched the play of shadows and sun on the cemetery and wondered if my paintings would change now, if more light would find its way in.

I had first met Ellen on a sweltering summer day seven years ago. I'd gone to my mother's house to swim in the pool and when Rosario opened the door for me I heard an unfamiliar female voice coming from the living room.

"Tilly?" my mother called out. "Come in here and meet my new assistant."

My flip-flops slapped across the floor, and in my cut-offs and bathing suit top, I suddenly felt self-conscious when a blonde woman in a white sundress, expensive sandals, and delicate gold jewelry strode across the room and held out her hand.

"I'm Ellen Spencer. Nice to meet you, Tilly. Your mother was telling me that you're a painter also."

I didn't have Lola yet – she would have been a good distraction. As it was, I felt uniquely unqualified to be in my mother's elegant home, with the air-conditioning set perfectly, so one could conveniently forget that it was a hundred degrees outside, and with two polished, stylishly dressed women – one young, one older – standing in stark contrast to me, the downtown artist with paint under her fingernails and her hair in a ponytail.

"Nice to meet you too," I said, ignoring the part about "also" being a painter.

I noticed how my mother's eyes were warm and approving when she looked at Ellen. I tried to tell myself that I didn't long for my mother's gaze to turn soft when she looked at me, but I knew I was lying. We never stop wanting our parents' approval, even long after they've let us know it will never come. Over time, I built Ellen into the enemy I needed – the girl who stepped into the daughter role, the girl who embodied the daughter my mother wished she had, the girl who was nothing like me. Stephen once said to me, "Your mother left you long before Ellen came along." And I knew he was right. But it was easier to blame her.

We walked into a room with photographs of caskets and funeral services on the walls. One of the photos showed pallbearers carrying what looked like a canoe.

"I didn't know you could be buried in a canoe," I whispered to Ellen. "Seems like there'd be a law against that."

"It's a casket," a woman's voice said from behind us. "We offer themes for the services. Golf, sailing, fishing, cycling. Even an art theme if you're interested." She held out her hand to Ellen first, then to me. "Monica Barrows. I understand you need a casket for Amber Austin. My condolences on your loss."

"Thank you," Ellen said. "Yes, as I said on the phone, I overlooked that detail. No theme or anything. Just a casket."

Monica had jet black hair cut into a severe shape that grazed her jawline. She wore a black suit and a white silk blouse. Her heels clicked on the marble floor as she walked over to a stack of folders and got one for us. I wondered if her closet had any brightly colored clothes in it or if she always wore black.

"You can look through this," she said, handing the folder to Ellen. "It has all our caskets in it, organized by price." She motioned us over to a bench along the side, right below the picture of the canoe funeral.

"Over sixteen thousand dollars?" I whispered to Ellen when she opened the folder to the first page. "I know my mother was wealthy, but that's ridiculous. It's going in the ground for God's sake."

Ellen flipped to the very back where a casket for $895.00 was advertised. "Well, we can't go to the opposite extreme. That will be the news story. The press will have a field day with that." She flipped open a page in the middle. "This looks very elegant," she said. "For a little over six thousand. Champagne velvet interior – your mother would like that."

I thought about what six thousand dollars could do in the world but decided to keep that to myself. "Yeah – it's shiny and polished. It looks expensive. Kind of like my mother."

Ellen almost smiled but didn't. Turning business-like she stood up and went over to Monica who had taken root behind a desk. "We'll take this one," she said, pointing to the six-thousand-dollar mahogany casket.

While she and Monica arranged everything, I went outside to the acre of grass and the lines of headstones. There is no stone marker for my father or my brother, no gravesite or urn. Their names are on the wall at the 9/11 memorial site, but there is nowhere private I can go to leave flowers or notes or tears. I wondered if I would visit my mother's grave here. I wondered what her tombstone would say – I assumed she had composed her epitaph. And then I realized I didn't even know when her service was going to be.

"This Saturday," Ellen said on the way to Santa Monica where she was going to drop me off at home. "At that big Methodist Church on Wilshire. First there will be a very small gathering of people who were close to her at the funeral home, a chance for some private moments. Then we'll follow the hearse to the church. Then back to the cemetery for the burial."

"My mother was a Methodist?" At that point, I was

prepared for any surprise.

"No. I mean, I don't think so. She liked the architecture of that church. She mentioned it a few times when we passed it on the way to her chemo treatments."

I knew at that moment when I was going to switch out the chain with my father's ring on it. Somehow at the funeral home, I was going to have to convince everyone that I, her only surviving child, wanted a few moments alone with her body. Even though Ellen and I had found neutral ground, she was the one I had to be careful of. I wanted my father's ring, and I was determined to get it.

"Hey, Ellen – what happened to the bottle of Ambien that was beside my mother's bed? It disappeared."

Ellen turned on her blinker and made a left turn onto my street. Her face gave nothing away. "I don't know. Why?"

A flurry of answers went through my mind. Because maybe she took the whole bottle and overdosed. Because she wasn't supposed to be taking them at all. Because maybe if someone had removed the bottle she'd still be alive. Because I turned my back on the half-full bottle and left it beside her bed. But I offered no response.

"No reason. I just wondered."

When we pulled up in front of my house, a familiar car was parked out front. Bryan and Gabe were our closest friends and after they got married Bryan splurged on a bright yellow Range Rover. The first time he drove it over to Stephen's house, I told him he'd never be able to sneak up on anyone again.

"Thanks for going with me, Tilly," Ellen said. I noticed again that she'd dropped some of her brittleness.

"Sure. I can't say that casket shopping was on my bucket list, but it was definitely an interesting experience. I never knew that being buried was so expensive."

I watched her drive off and wondered what her life was like outside the demanding job my mother had created for her. Did she have a boyfriend? Did she have girlfriends she went shopping with? Did she go out at night and sing in

Karaoke bars? Maybe she collected little ceramic figurines or plates with windmills painted on them. I didn't even know where she lived. I only knew her within the boundaries of Amber Austin's carefully constructed world.

I found Bryan and Gabe in the backyard with Stephen, drinking beers and tossing the tennis ball for Lola.

"Hey," Gabe said when he saw me, coming over to put his arms around me. "I'm so sorry about your mother. How're you doing?"

"I'm okay. Thanks."

Bryan threw the ball for Lola and came over to add his arms to the embrace, "Group hug! We brought you an orchid plant. I think it's a far better condolence gift than a casserole or a pie."

Stephen had gone inside and came out with a beer, which he handed to me. "So?" he said. "How did you two get along?"

"Actually, good. I found out that Ellen's mother died when she was ten. It made it more understandable why she would adopt my mother and be so fixated on her. And we chose a casket, although not the canoe one or the golf-themed one you'll be pleased to know."

Lola was standing in front of me with the tennis ball in her mouth. I threw it for her and noticed how alive all the colors in the yard looked to me. The pink camellias, the green lawn. Some snow-white alyssum had popped up after the rain. It was as if the world had been scrubbed clean and everything was more vibrant and pulsing with life.

"Tilly?" Stephen said, in a tone that suggested he'd been trying to get my attention.

"What? Sorry – I was daydreaming."

"I'm assuming you didn't say anything to Ellen about your plan."

"Of course not! I said we got along, I didn't say I'd taken leave of my senses. But I figured out when I'm going to make the switch. At the funeral home. I'll just ask for some private time. It'll seem perfectly reasonable."

Bryan cleared his throat. "I think I speak for Gabe AND myself when I say, What the hell are you talking about? If you're planning on switching bodies, we can't be friends with you anymore. That's just way too gruesome and weird, and besides why would you want to?"

I laughed and looked at Stephen who motioned for me to fill them in.

"Okay, this is top secret, you guys. My mother wanted to be buried with my father's ring on that chain around her neck that she always wore. But I want his ring. So, I'm going to get a duplicate ring and chain and then switch them out."

Bryan put down his beer and gave me a serious look. He was Stephen's co-star on their TV series; Bryan played a neuro-surgeon who was always getting impossible cases with complicated diagnoses, which he somehow miraculously solved. "You know," he said, "the human head weighs about 10 pounds. But the brain only weighs three. So, the skull and the fluids and the flesh make up all that extra weight. I'm just mentioning it, Tilly, because you'll have to lift your mother's head up to carry out your plan – you should know what to expect."

"I think I can handle it," I assured him. "But thanks for the heads up – pardon the pun."

"But then there's the dispute about the weight of the soul," Stephen chimed in. "Do we in fact lose twenty-one grams when we die because the soul leaves the body?"

None of us said anything for a few minutes. The only sounds were the woosh of a car passing on the street out front, Lola panting with the tennis ball in her mouth, and the wind shivering the leaves of the huge ash tree that shaded the yard. I thought about my mother's soul. Did it have weight? And where was it now?

Finally, Gabe said, "I can help you with the ring. I lost my wedding ring about a month after we got married, probably because I lost weight and it was loose. I thought Bryan was going to kill me. So, I got another one, and then I found the original one under the car seat. It must have come off when I was reaching for something. Anyway, you can have it. It's just a plain gold band, but I'm assuming that's what you want, right?"

I nodded yes. My mother would be buried, not with my father's ring, but with my gay friend's extra wedding ring that was once lost, then found, then unnecessary because it had been replaced. I liked the weave of this story; it seemed made up of circles and links.

"Thank you. I accept your donation," I told him.

Bryan and Gabe had brought me a large orchid arrangement in a bowl with bits of sea glass and a few shells at the base of the plants. In my dimly lit living room, the clean white blooms looked like the color of new life, of hope, of a yet-to-be-written-on page. A future that had fluttered away from the past.

9.

At the end of the day, as early evening moved in, I left Stephen at my house studying his script and took Lola for a walk. I also left my cell phone at home, wanting to feel disconnected from the world, at least for a little while. The setting sun streaked the sky with a brilliant palette; the clouds were orange and deep rose, with ribbons of blue-gray. I again wondered if color would now start sneaking into my paintings. More houses had put up Halloween decorations; ghosts and witches watched me from front lawns and porches. A few neighbors passed me with their dogs and said they were sorry about my mother. My acknowledgements were as quick as their condolences. It's strange how awkward people get when death has walked onto the stage. There was one exception. Rachel, who lives up the street, was out walking Dilbert, a male pug who Lola is completely smitten with. Her eight-year-old daughter Nina was with her, obediently holding her mother's hand, until they saw me and then Nina broke free and waved with both hands. They crossed the street and Rachel gave me a hug. While Lola and Dilbert were discussing whatever it is dogs discuss, she said, "How are you? This must be very surreal. I e-mailed you, but I thought I'd give it a couple of days before calling."

"Surreal is a very good description of how I feel. There are a lot of emotions rolling around in me. Colliding sometimes."

"I can imagine. Listen, if you want or need anything – if you want me to run to the store for you, pick up dry cleaning, walk Lola, call me. Or if you want to talk or cry or scream... Or all of the above, I'm available."

"Thanks Rachel. I will. Especially if I want to scream. Stephen hates raised voices."

"I'm going to be an astronaut for Halloween!" Nina said loudly, having waited patiently for us to stop talking.

"Wow, an astronaut – that's very imaginative," I said.

"Is that what you want to be when you grow up?"

"Maybe. I want to be a vet and take care of dogs, but maybe I can go into space too."

Rachel laughed. "I'm just glad she doesn't want to dress up as one of the Kardashians."

"Especially a Kardashian in a space suit – that wouldn't be good. Mars would never be the same."

When Lola and I got back to the house, Stephen said, "Your new BFF called. I answered your phone when I saw it was her in case there was some other emergency."

I unsnapped Lola's leash and reluctantly picked up my cell phone. "Okay, first of all, she is not my BFF. Second, what did she want? I hope not another shopping trip for death accessories."

"She needs to know who you want to invite to the service. And before you make your list, I just found out that Dylan is coming at the end of the week and staying a few days. It wasn't scheduled but she and her mom are having some issues so she wants to come down here. It's up to you, but should we ask if she wants to come to the service?"

Dylan met my mother one Christmas and liked her. Her exact words were "colorful" and "a little bit out there but in kind of a relevant way." I had no idea what that meant.

"Sure, why not?"

I hadn't called Janice back and I'd told her I would. Martin left me a phone message which I hadn't returned. Friends from both coasts had called or texted, and while I didn't have to get back to everyone, there were some who warranted responses. I'd been moving through a strange new world that slowed me down and jumbled time. But there is a business-side to death – part of which is efficiency and manners. I had to step out of the fog I'd settled into and at least take care of some of it.

Janice and I agreed she'd fly in Wednesday, stay at my house, and go with me and Stephen to the service. Martin sounded self-conscious and uncertain, but I assured him it was perfectly appropriate for him to attend. At that moment, I knew more about him than he knew about himself. It was less about my mother and more about Hale. There had been no service for Hale, no burial, no opportunity for Martin to lose himself in a ritual designed to allow people their grief. His best friend had turned to dust, but there was no minister reading from the Scripture, no solemn gesture of laying flowers on a shiny wooden coffin before it was lowered into the earth. My mother was a substitute for Hale. If he couldn't bury his best friend, he could at least help bury his mother.

Just before we were going to hang up, Martin said, "Tilly, this is going to sound really weird but there isn't anyone else I can tell. I had the strangest experience the other day. I was on the upper east side, near where your parents used to live, and I saw a guy who looked so much like Hale. He was about a block away, and this man had his walk, had the same set to his shoulders. His hair was darker...it seemed so crazy that after all this time I'd be imagining seeing him. I mean for a second, I thought, What if?"

"It's not crazy. When you haven't been able to bury someone, when there wasn't even a body, your mind plays tricks on you. For a couple of years, I thought sometimes, What if he survived and has total amnesia? What if both my father and Hale are out there somewhere? And they can't come back to us because they don't remember us. Don't tell yourself you're crazy, Martin. You're just human, like the rest of us. It'll be good to see you. Let me know when you get here."

I had avoided checking my e-mails over the twenty-four hours since my mother died, and when I did, there were 87 messages. Most were from people I didn't know that well, but some I would have to respond to and thank them for their condolences. There was an e-mail from the gallery owner in Venice where I was scheduled to have a showing in November. Jeff wanted to know if I needed to re-schedule in light of my mother's passing. As I typed a reply, telling him I would be fine to do the showing, I thought, He probably has a great relationship with his mother and would be so devastated by her death that he would wipe his schedule clean for weeks to give himself time to mourn. People tend to spill onto others the dynamics of their own family, and then they're surprised to learn there is no similarity.

For the first time in the four years we'd been together, Stephen and I slept at his house that night. I brought a few things with me and, most importantly, I brought Lola's dog bed and put it in the bedroom. She curled up on it contentedly. Travis stretched out at the end of the bed, wedging himself between our feet. The only times I had been in Stephen's bedroom were a few afternoons when we made love and then lay in a tangle of sheets talking until the light outside dulled to blue and I had to go home and walk Lola.

The animals seemed fine with this new sleeping arrangement. I, however, lay awake long after Stephen fell asleep, watching the half-moon outside the window and listening to the muffled sound of traffic in the distance. If I tried, I could pretend it was the ocean. His bed felt bigger than mine, even though it wasn't. The night sky looked smoother, the stars brighter, and the air in his house seemed lighter than the air in mine. But maybe everything was going to feel different to me now. Maybe my mother's death made new cells turn over in my body, shifted my vision and made me hear things in a new way.

My best friend when I was in grade school lived in our building, three floors below us. Kerry had a small poodle named Snickers who used to sleep on her bed and follow her around the apartment. Kerry dutifully took Snickers for daily walks and fed her when she got back from school. Eventually Snickers began slowing down – age and various infirmities were making life difficult for her, so Kerry's parents made the painful decision to put her down. Kerry told me that she held her as she died, and then she said to me, with tears streaking her face, "I wonder if she's on the other side of the moon now."

As I lay in Stephen's bed, the only one awake in the

room, I stared at the moon and wondered if my mother was on the other side of it. I'd never had thoughts like that about my father or Hale, maybe because for nearly a year after 9/11 there was still a flicker of hope buried deep inside me that they'd lived, that they would suddenly remember who they were and come back to us. When those thoughts eventually wilted, grief settled in me, became my new normal, and hope had no place there.

When I finally fell asleep, I dreamed about Hale. I was somewhere in the wilderness, walking along the line of a stream when I saw a cave ahead of me. It was large, scooped into the side of a mountain, and firelight glowed from inside its stone walls. In my dream, I wasn't afraid of what or who I would find there. I went to the entrance of the cave and found Hale sitting beside a small campfire. He smiled as if he'd been expecting me. And I went in as if I'd always known where to find him.

"Fire isn't always a bad thing," he said.

"Why isn't it filled with smoke in here?" I asked him, puzzled by how clear the air was when fire was flickering inside the thick stone cave.

He smiled again. "You just gotta have faith."

I woke up and the moon had moved past the window. Lola was breathing evenly and Travis twisted a little in his sleep, re-settling himself. I slid closer to Stephen, curling around his back; I needed his flesh, his bones, his scent. I needed to know that in the morning I could tell him my dream and maybe he'd be able to make some sense of it. I needed to remind myself that I wasn't traveling through this world alone.

After several years with Stephen I have given up attempting to fix breakfast for us. He's too good at it, and unless we're rushed and it's simply a matter of pouring granola into bowls, when it comes to the morning meal the kitchen is his kingdom. I sipped coffee while he made omelets with goat cheese and tomatoes. I watched the muscles in his back, the calm way he assembled the omelets and slid them from the pan onto plates. I told him once, early on in our relationship, that if the acting thing ever fell apart, he could definitely get a job as a chef.

When he sat down at the table, rich smells floating around us, I told him about my dream.

"What do you think it means?" I asked him.

He shook his head and chewed pensively. Finally, he said, "I've always found dream interpretation to be kind of a bullshit endeavor. Unless you're Carl Jung. He was obviously good at it. I don't know, Tilly. It's interesting about the fire, that in your dream it was almost a nurturing thing. When you think of how he died, it's a curious thing to dream. But as for what it means, I haven't a clue except I'm not surprised you dreamed about him now that your mother's gone. I know you miss him."

"I always missed him. Even when he was alive."

Stephen got up and poured more coffee into his cup. Lola and Travis were both sitting beside the table hoping a morsel of food would drop. We were studiously ignoring them.

"Right. When he was alive, there was still a chance that something could change," Stephen said when he sat back down. "Same with your mother, actually. I know you said you gave up on the notion of having a relationship with her, but I don't know that anyone could stop hoping in some part of their being that their mother would look at them lovingly and adoringly. You're still that little girl who wanted to be the center of her world."

"You're probably right. I hid that particular candle flame under piles of cynicism, but you're right."

"Why don't you paint your dream?" Stephen said. "You're midway through a new painting, aren't you?"

"I am. One that I have to finish before this show that's coming up way too soon."

I had started a painting of dark woods, which was unusual for me since I was known for city scenes – gritty and cold and as far from nature as you can get. I don't know how the woods came to be. Maybe I dreamed them too, I'm not sure, but when I stood at the canvas that day, I just began painting trees – skeletal winter trees, stripped of leaves, with shapes that looked almost human. Like arms that stretched out pleadingly and spines bent with age. As usual, I had no idea where I was going with the painting, or what else would find its way in. Stephen long ago learned to not ask. It's one of the many things I love about him, that he appreciates how I work – each painting is an adventure.

"I have to learn my scenes for tomorrow," he said, taking his plate to the sink. "Are you going back up to your mother's today?"

"I don't know. Ellen texted me back after I told her who I wanted invited to the service, but she didn't say anything about today. It's weird – I wouldn't want the responsibility of organizing my mother's service and whatever else Ellen is organizing, but I definitely feel the sting of being excluded."

I took my plate and cup to the sink, leaned briefly against Stephen before rinsing them and putting them in the dishwasher. Sometimes I just need to rest on him, remind myself of the space he takes up in my life. I got Lola's leash and clipped it on her, still not sure what I was going to do with the day ahead of me. She looked at Travis, then at me, as if to say, Isn't he coming with us?

"I think a cross-species romance might have started," I told Stephen.

He pulled me against him and kissed me. "Let me know if you decide to go up there. I can't go with you – I really have to learn these scenes – but I can chant mantras and light candles for you."

I gave him a look.

"You'll figure it out," he said. "You'll be fine."

"I feel like you're pushing me into a lake and telling me I can swim."

He kissed me again. "No. I don't want you to feel like that. But you are a much better swimmer than you think you are."

Sunlight poured through the front door when I opened it. "If you say something corny like Go with God I'll punch you," I called back to him.

"May the force be with you!"

"Just as bad."

At home, I stood in front of the painting I'd started and imagined a stream winding through the forest – the slender water that ran through my dream. And then I saw, in the dark swirls of night, where the cave would be. The cave with my brother inside, warmed by firelight and waiting for me. That's when the tears began. I sank to the floor and cried for my family, with all its fractures. I cried for my father and Hale, stepping through a broken window into an unforgiving sky. I cried for my mother who thought, right until the end, that she could construct her life according to her will. My flame-haired mother who turned her back on grief and believed she could refurbish her own history just by painting it pretty colors. I cried for the little girl I once was, who didn't understand why her mother didn't like her anymore and took refuge in shadowy places. I sat on the floor for a long time until my tears stopped on their own. Lola waited patiently beside me, occasionally standing up to lick my face and nuzzle me. Finally, I looked at my painting again, saw what I was going to add to it, but decided to go to my mother's house first.

Lola and I arrived to find chaos. Organized chaos, but still… The gates were open, there were about half a dozen cars there, and a security guard. I kept Lola's leash on as we went inside, slipped around strangers moving various pieces of furniture to the edges of the living room, and what looked like a cleaning crew. I found Ellen in the kitchen, sitting at the table with her laptop.

"Hi, Ellen. What's going on out there?"

She blinked at me for a few seconds like she needed to bring me into focus. "Everyone is invited back here after the service for food and drink, so we have to open up the rooms a bit to accommodate them. I added your friends to the list, which brings it to just over 150 people. I think that's going to be it. Your mother wanted the service to be small, and then in a month or so, at the big memorial event, we can have as many people as want to come."

Again, I felt the sting of everything I didn't know about my mother and what her wishes were following her death. It's such an intimate subject, one from which I'd been deliberately excluded.

"And that big memorial event will be where?"

Ellen took a deep breath and exhaled slowly. "I'm not sure at this point. Could be in an auditorium somewhere. We have to get through this first."

The security guard walked in and said, "Miss Spencer, they're here with the paintings."

Ellen shut her laptop and started hurrying out of the kitchen.

"Paintings?" I asked, following her, dragging Lola with me. I felt like a puppy trailing a neglectful human and pulling an exasperated dog along for the ride.

"A few of the originals," Ellen tossed out over her shoulder. "It's a nice touch to have them displayed now, and it will help spread the word about the auction."

I decided to stop asking questions. I hung back and watched the eruptions of activity around me – strangers re-arranging my mother's house. Strangers carrying in her original paintings. But I felt like the stranger. Lola stared at me, confused at being held on leash instead of being allowed to play in the yard.

"Maybe before we leave, Lola, I'll take you out there. There's too much going on right now."

Two of my mother's paintings were set up on easels in the living room. When Ellen moved on to boss around the furniture movers, I stood in front of them and studied Amber Austin's work as I never had before. There were many times I had come into this house and found my mother upstairs working on a painting. I knew she always painted the sky first, as if everything else evolved from that. But I was never curious about her technique – I was too full of resentment that her career had so thoroughly and extravagantly eclipsed mine. On this day, with her death fluttering in the air around me, with the house suddenly feeling both impersonal and safe, I stood inches from the canvases and inspected her brush strokes, her colors, the tiny details of light she'd become known for.

One of the paintings was of a wooden bridge arched over a rippling blue lake. It was in the middle of a bucolic meadow, softly green with lush trees creating pools of shade. A few families were having a picnic near the bridge and a dog was chasing a Frisbee. As usual in my mother's paintings, there wasn't a brown leaf or a dead tree in sight, only wildflowers and long grasses bending with the breeze. White clouds dotted the sky, blotting out half the sun. I saw how tight and deliberate her brush strokes were, how controlled. As if letting loose might have invited in something unpleasant. Some of the criticism from the art world was about her technique, although most of it was about the rosy, Hallmark-card subject matter in all of her paintings. She didn't seem to care about any of that, as long as people lined up to buy her work.

The other canvas was one of her typical city streets, with a golden sunset bathing the buildings and pockets of light shining from some of the windows, as if the residents inside needed to prepare early for night. There were flower boxes and carefully tended trees along the sidewalks, streetlamps that looked like they had been polished by hand. There were well-dressed people on their way to or from someplace.

What always struck me about my mother's paintings was her choice of colors. She mixed shades that hardly ever existed in nature. Trees are never quite that green, sunsets are never that golden, dawns never that shade of pink. The one sky she never painted was a brilliant blue sky like the one over Manhattan on September 11th.

   As I drove away from my mother's house, I saw a man outside the gates walking back to a maroon Honda and getting into the car. There were still fans and a few photographers lingering out on the street, but fewer than the day before. I know what drew my eyes to this man. He walked like Hale, the same slightly off-kilter gait. I thought about Martin imagining that he saw my brother in Manhattan, near our old building. Are these the backwaters of my mother's death? Sightings of ghosts and the flickering-on of memories? Tricks of the eye and wild journeys of the imagination? I had the uneasy feeling that my mother was pulling strings from beyond this world, making sure I would still be hostage to the past.

10.

In order to see the stream that would now meander through my painting, I needed moonlight. In most of my work, the moon – if it's visible at all – is peeking around the edge of a building, or hovering thin and delicate in the sky, weeks away from being full. But in my dream the moon was full; its light flowed silver across the water and guided my way. I needed to paint my dream. I was in the process of smudging out some tree branches, opening up more space for sky and the first full moon of my artistic career when the doorbell rang.

"Shit!"

Lola cocked her head and stared at me. She does that whenever I swear; it's very disconcerting. I considered ignoring whoever was there but decided instead to go downstairs and at least look through the peephole. Rachel was standing on the front step with a Tupperware container. Suddenly I was no longer irritated by the interruption.

"I made a big pot of soup," she said when I opened the door. "Vegetable barley. I had a feeling you might not have enough food here with everything that's going on and I'm making it my mission to nourish you. So, I brought you some." She noticed my paint-spotted shirt. "Oh, you're working. I don't want to disturb you."

"That's okay. Thank you for the soup. I think I do have an embarrassingly empty refrigerator right now. I might not even share this with Stephen – I love your soups. So, I'm about to paint my first full moon. And my first babbling brook. Well, actually it will be a flowing stream, but babbling brook sounds cuter. Want to see?"

Rachel used to have a full-time therapy practice until she had Nina, at which point she decided to keep a few of her patients but devote herself primarily to raising her daughter. Once, when we were talking about my mother, I asked if she'd take me on as a patient. She smiled and said, "We're friends,

Tilly. That wouldn't be entirely proper. But I'm always happy to be a sounding board and give you the best advice I can – for free. So, not being my patient actually works out better."

I led her upstairs to the room that I'd converted to my work space and pointed to where water would meander between the trees.

"The full moon will be in this corner of the sky, so the stream can be illuminated. Down here there'll be a cave with a fire in it."

She looked at the canvas, then at me. "And?" she said. "Who's in the cave tending to the fire?"

"Well, Miss smarty-pants, Hale is in there. I'm painting a dream I had."

After I told her about the dream, Rachel looked around the room and said, "You should paint this room blue, like the sky. I think it would be inspirational."

"I'm shocked that you don't see scuffed Navajo White walls as inspirational."

"Your work is starting to change, Tilly – it might help to have different surroundings while you're working, or at least a different color. It will feel like a bigger space, more open. And also kind of like a new beginning." She glanced at her cell phone. "Hey, I have to go pick up Nina at her friend's house. But think about it. And I can't wait to see what you do with the full moon and the babbling stream."

Later, after I called Ernie, the handyman who frequently mended things in my rattly old house and told him I wanted my work room painted blue, I stretched out on the couch for an afternoon nap. I met Hale again in a dream. I was in Manhattan and the day was gray and drizzly. I was walking by myself on a crowded sidewalk when I smelled roses. It was the scent of our home; my mother always insisted on having vases of cut roses around, even in the dead of winter. I couldn't understand why I was smelling them on a busy New York sidewalk. I rounded a corner and was suddenly at an ice rink. There was a lone skater on the ice –

Hale. He waved to me, beckoning me, and I went out to meet him, mysteriously able to skate on my boots. Then I looked down, and he wasn't wearing skates either, just his street shoes. He twirled me around, looped his arm around my waist as we circled the rink at such a fast speed my eyes began to tear up.

"Don't worry," he said. "I won't let you fall."

The smell of roses hung over us and the wind numbed my face, but I felt safe with him, like nothing bad could happen to us. I couldn't understand, though, how we could do this without blades on our feet.

"Where are your skates?" I asked him, raising my voice over the wind rushing past us.

"You took them," he said.

When I woke up, Lola had dragged her leash over to me and was staring at me.

"Do you have an alarm clock built into you?" I asked her, trying to shake off the dream and return to the real world. I clipped on her leash, found my house key and headed for the sidewalk.

I hadn't thought about Hale's ice skates in years. But now I saw them in my mind – the scuff marks, the always-sharpened blades. A few months after the towers fell I arrived at my mother's apartment to find a box outside in the hallway filled with Hale's clothes. His ice skates were on top.

"I'm giving it all to Goodwill," she said when I asked her what his things were doing out there. I didn't say anything in response, but when I left I took his skates with me. I put them in a box, taped it up, and had mostly forgotten about them, although I did know which closet the box was in.

I walked Lola around the block, letting her jump up on tree trunks every time she sensed a squirrel in the branches. I wasn't sure if I would tell Stephen about yet another dream in which Hale appeared. What if I kept having these dreams? Stephen might justifiably decide I had some serious issues that needed to be addressed. He might think I was losing my grip on reality. There is a strange thing that happens when people in your family disappear – when they die with no trace – and the only remaining family member leaves you stranded in a desert, wondering why you've been exiled from her life. You harbor a suspicion that everyone is just one temptation away from leaving. Or else they'll be stolen by a whim of fate. You go through life seeing exit signs everywhere, clearly marked for whoever was foolish enough to get close to you.

I was hoping to not run into anyone I knew on this walk. I was still caught in my dream; I could hear the scrape of our feet on the ice, and feel the brittle air numbing my skin. I led Lola the opposite way from our usual walk, and luckily we had the street all to ourselves. A cloud bank lined the western edge of the sky. A chain of storms was predicted over the next week, and I wondered if it would rain on the day of my mother's service, which would have a certain irony to it since she hated rain. When we were almost back to the house, I saw a car pull away from the curb – a maroon Honda that looked identical to the one that was outside my mother's house earlier. As it passed me on the other side of the street, I was sure that the same man was driving, the man who looked like Hale. Am I losing my mind? I thought. I'd told Martin that it wasn't crazy to think that he saw Hale, but now I was doubting my own sanity.

In the weeks after 9/11, I would wade into grief thick as mud. Other times, I would stumble into blue pools of nothingness, tasting the residue of my own tears. I would feel hollowed out, as if I were missing some vital organs. But now that my mother had died, there was none of that. Instead I was catapulted into the past through dreams I couldn't explain, distracted by strange sightings which made no sense and could even be hallucinations for all I knew.

That night, Stephen and I went to a sushi restaurant that we frequent so much the waitresses know us by name. Even though it's brightly-lit and loud, it feels private to me because it's so familiar. I described the upheaval at my mother's house and told Stephen I didn't stay long, that I came home to work on my painting instead. But the car I'd seen twice leaned into my thoughts. I remembered what Stephen had said to me about not trusting him completely, and I didn't want that to be true.

Finally, I said, "There was a car outside my mother's gates, a maroon Honda – the man who got back in it and drove off looked so much like Hale, it was really strange. And then when I was walking Lola today, I saw the same car on our street. Driven by the same man. I'm not delusional, I really did see it twice."

Stephen lifted a piece of ginger with his chopsticks but let it dangle there. "Tilly, you've dreamed about Hale, he's obviously front and center in your mind, so it isn't really that surprising that you think you saw him."

"So, I'm imagining him, right? I mean, the guy probably looks nothing like him if I got a good look at him."

"Imagining isn't a crime. It's understandable. But I know you know he's gone. He's been gone for eighteen years."

I gave Stephen a long look, wondering if I dared to ask. "But what if - "

"Don't go there. You'll just torture yourself. If you saw the same car and the same man, it could be some paparazzi guy. You know, trying to get a photo of Amber Austin's grieving daughter."

"Right. That's probably it."

I didn't tell him about my second dream. I told myself I didn't want to sound like a broken record, but I knew the real reason was, I didn't want to sound like an obsessed person who was leaving sanity behind.

We slept at Stephen's house again that night. In a filigree of moonlight, I leaned over him and whispered, "I feel like a bad person for not grieving the way I'm supposed to. I've cried, but not really for my mother. I've cried for my family that was so disjointed and defended we had no clue how to really be a family. But none of my tears have had my mother's initials on them."

He stroked my hair, my face. "When I was in college a girl I'd been dating was killed in a car accident. We'd broken up because she cheated on me with a friend of mine, and then kind of threw it in my face – all the things he was that I wasn't. One thing he was that I wasn't was a heavy drinker. She was out with him one night, he was driving, three sheets to the wind, and he ploughed into a guard rail. The car flipped, and they were both killed. I felt like you do now, like I wasn't properly grieving. I was genuinely sad, there were tears, but I didn't feel like I was suitably devastated. A very wise friend of mine said to me, Grief isn't a one-size-fits-all thing. It arranges itself around who that person was to you in life. So, I'm passing those words on to you. You had a hard journey with your mother, you can maybe lighten up on yourself."

"Easier said than done. Stephen, you never told me before about your girlfriend dying."

"I know. I didn't deliberately keep it from you. I guess we both have pockets of our lives that we kind of seal off. Or maybe everyone does. Things that belong to another time don't always seem relevant...until they do."

Later, when night pressed against the windows and Stephen's breathing let me know how deeply he was sleeping, I lay awake and thought about all the things we don't know about another person, even someone we've been with for years. I pictured Stephen young, college-age, sitting in a dorm room crying but measuring his tears, trying to squeeze out more. I love him not only for the person he is, but for the moments when he has wanted to be different.

My father's parents died in a car accident when I was twelve. A drunk driver broadsided them, and we were told that they died instantly. I remember how my father's eyes turned gray, as if sorrow had set up residence there and turned the inside of him to winter. One day I found him at his desk writing what looked like a letter.

"What are you doing?" I asked him. I was cautious around my father in those days after. I had the sense that his sadness was like blown glass, easily shattered into tears and jagged pieces. I had never seen my father cry, and I didn't know what I would do if he started.

"I'm writing a letter to God," he said.

"How are you going to send it?"

He smiled and shook his head slowly. "I don't need to send it, Tilly. God sees everything. I'm going to put it in a special place, though, so I'll always remember that I wrote it. God won't forget, but I'm afraid with time I might."

I stared down at the thick Persian rug. I wanted to know what he was writing, but I didn't want to ask.

My father's face relaxed, opened up. "I'll read you what I've written so far."

I stood next to him at his desk, breathing in his familiar smells – soap and hair tonic. I have to go on my own memory after all this time, but I recall the letter starting out with anger, with a demand to know why God had allowed his parents to be on the road that night, in the path of a man whose blood alcohol level was more than twice the legal limit, and who recovered from his injuries while his mother and father were so mangled they weren't even recognizable. My parents were good people, my father read, looking down at the white stationery where his careful penmanship slanted delicately across the page. They loved me, and they loved you, God. They lived good lives. But then my father's tone changed. He said he had regrets over things he never got a chance to say to his parents or ask of them. He pleaded with God to keep them close, in the embrace of angels, to whisper to them how much their only son missed them. He said he had faith that they would all be reunited in time.

Then he looked up at me and said, "That's how it should be in families, Tilly – that even death doesn't end the relationships." I remember feeling confused by what he said. Was he telling me that this wasn't true for all families?

He was still working on the letter when I left his study.

I don't know where he put it. It's strange to me that I'd forgotten about it until just now; like Hale's ice skates, the letter had retreated in my memory, waiting for me to look for it. Surely my mother found it when she went through my father's papers, but she never mentioned it to me. Then I wondered if Ellen had ever seen it, and that thought was like a sharp thorn inside me, so I had to banish it from my mind or I'd never get to sleep.

Stephen was up at five for an early call at the studio. He kissed me and tucked the comforter up around my shoulders. "Sleep some more," he said. "And hang out as long as you want. I'll feed Travis his canned food – don't let him tell you he needs more."

It was just getting light when I got up. The rain had started again – fine and steady, a gray veil outside the windows. I bathed in Stephen's white marble and glass shower, with Travis and Lola sitting together on the bathmat staring at me. He had left coffee on for me and I fixed myself a piece of toast before getting one of his umbrellas from the coat closet. As Lola and I walked out into the wet green world, I decided I was going to finish my painting that day. Ernie had texted me that he could be there at nine to paint the room, so I'd have to move my easel into the guest room where Janice was going to stay. The day felt so normal; a seagull's lone cry made me look up as the bird soared under a belly of clouds. Crows were perched in one of the pine trees, quiet and still as death's messengers. But the day wasn't normal. I had no family left now, and Ellen knew so much more about my future than I did. I had no doubt she had seen my mother's will, or at least had been told what it contained. She knew the contents of my mother's house, and the designations that had been made – what was to happen with furniture, artwork, jewelry, the house itself. I had long been on the sidelines of my mother's life; now I was on the sidelines of her death.

While I was thinking about Ellen, my cell rang and there she was. As usual, she didn't bother with greetings or niceties. "Tilly, I wanted you to know the order we're doing the eulogies in. I'm going to go first, then Ian, and then you. I hope you're working on your eulogy."

"Good morning to you too, Ellen. No, I have not worked on a eulogy, but now that I have my marching orders from you, I'll get right on that. I'm actually glad you called -- I have a question for you. I assume my mother kept her personal documents somewhere. I want to look through them for a letter of my father's that I'm hoping she kept."

I could hear a lot of noise in the background. Either Ellen was at Starbucks or she'd ordered work crews up to my mother's house at the crack of dawn. "Sure, sure. That kind of stuff is in the closet in her painting studio. I'll be at the house all day."

"I knew you would be."

By midday, I had the full moon painted and most of the stream. I'd taken Hale's ice-skates out of their box and set them in a corner of the room where I was working. They remained in my peripheral vision and I let myself toy with the idea of hiding them somewhere in the painting. Maybe they had been left in the woods...

Ernie was busy turning the other room into a representation of the sky, and I had all the windows open upstairs to let out the paint smell even though it meant that mist drifted in. Ernie is in his late sixties; he has grandchildren who he dotes on, and he loves his work. He's always saying, "I was put on this earth to fix things! It's very satisfying, I tell you. Important to do what you love." He probably doesn't remember that he's said this to me dozens of times, so I act as if I've never heard it before each time he repeats it. On his way downstairs to get the lunch he brought with him, he peeked in and noticed Hale's ice skates.

"You gonna go skating, Tilly?"

"No. They belonged to my brother."

Ernie nodded and kept looking at the skates. "I grew up in Illinois. Starting in about October we'd wait and wait for this nearby lake to freeze and once it did, you couldn't get us off it. We'd grab our skates when we got home from school and be out there 'till dark. Probably woulda missed dinner if our mother hadn't called us in."

I knew then that the figure in the fire-lit cave was going to be wearing ice-skates, and the title of my painting would be "Waiting for Winter." I didn't always title my paintings; only occasionally did a title come to me, but this one drifted in with the mist that smelled faintly of roses, and with the strange aftermath of my mother's death.

Before finishing the cave and the man inside it, I decided to take Lola up to my mother's house. "Want to go chase some Bel Air squirrels?" I asked her. Her ears perked up and she headed for the stairs. I'm ninety percent certain it's the word "squirrel" that makes her react, but maybe I just don't want to believe she could get that excited about Bel Air.

There were still some workmen at Casa del Sol, although less than before. The garage was open and boxes were stacked in one half of it next to my mother's white Mercedes. The rain had moved on, leaving a gauzy sky behind. I let Lola into the backyard and went through the house looking for Ellen. Finally, I asked one of the workmen where she was, and he said he'd seen her go upstairs.

The sound of her crying gave away her location. My mother's bedroom door was ajar and I found Ellen sitting on her bed, a box of Kleenex beside her, weeping the way children do – in blubbery, breathless waves. My first instinct was to run. I don't do well with people crying; I don't even do well with my own tears. But I remembered the day Ellen and I went to the funeral home and how vulnerable she seemed. I thought of the girl who lost her own mother at such a young age, who eventually found a home with my mother, and I sat down on the bed beside her.

"I just miss her so much," Ellen managed to say before coughing and nearly choking on a new round of tears.

"What do you miss about her?"

Ellen pulled some more Kleenex from the box. "We had the greatest conversations," she said. "I felt like I could tell her anything. She was just so wise and fair-minded. She helped me so much in my life with…everything. And she could be very funny."

"She could? I mean – yes, she could. Of course. I know that." In truth I knew nothing of the kind. My mother apparently had an alternate persona when she was around other people. "A sense of humor is such a gift. Good that she had that." I tried to imagine my mother and Ellen sitting cross-legged on the floor chatting like girlfriends, laughing at each other's jokes. It was an almost impossible image to get my mind around. "So, Ellen, I'm going to go in the closet where she kept her papers and look for that letter of my father's."

Ellen nodded and pulled more Kleenex from the box. She wasn't finished crying yet. I closed the door softly behind me, knowing the echo of Ellen's emotions would trail out into the hallway and follow me through the house, reminding me of what was missing in my life.

There would never come a day when I would sit and weep for my mother as she was doing. The woman I knew was different. She peered down at me from high castle walls, she waved her hands dismissively at my dreams and goals, and she thought nothing of pulling up draw bridges and blocking roads if I was inconveniencing her. There was a gentler mother hidden in the folds and shadows of the past, but she vanished decades ago. I was left with the woman my mother chose to become, and that was not a woman who inspired tears.

11

Whether she was Charlotte or Amber, my mother was impeccably organized. The closet in her painting room looked like an ad for one of those companies that comes and puts your life in order. There were file boxes marked 'Taxes,' 'Investment Statements,' 'Receipts,' 'Charity,' 'Household.' And one for 'Letters.' It was one of those laminated flowery boxes that designers put their names on and sell at Staples or Target. Inside were a few anniversary cards from my father, a couple of fan letters that had apparently impressed my mother. Then I came across a letter from Ian. It was dated September 20, 2001 and it was handwritten. He wrote about the "exquisite sorrow" that now defined her life, and his admiration for the way she was handling it. He said spending the day with her had meant so much to him, and he thanked her for sharing her sadness with him. "Such a loss," he wrote, "is unfathomable. Yet here we are. Of all the things we have gone through together, we never would have imagined this." He mentioned their "complicated past" and assured her that he was there for her in whatever ways she needed him to be. The phrase "complicated past" rattled me; I had no idea what that could mean. As far as I knew, Ian had come into my parents' lives through my father, so my mother couldn't have had a history with him prior to that. But then so many things in my family were not what they appeared to be.

I had seen my mother and Ian downtown one day – I'm not sure, but it could have been sometime around the 20th of September, less than ten days after the towers fell, when ash was still thick in the air, the towers still smoldered, and people were putting up photographs and pleas for information. Was that the day he referred to in his letter? There had been a light rain during the night and I'd gone downtown to see if the photos of my father and Hale were still up. I was near Saint James Cathedral when I spotted my mother's red hair. She and Ian had gotten out of a town car and they were just standing there, staring. I don't know why I didn't go over to them. I don't know why I never told her I'd seen them. Maybe it was the way Ian had his arm tight around her shoulders, or the way she covered her face with her hands and turned into his chest as if her grief shouldn't be witnessed. You could drown in the tears that were being shed along those streets in those long days after, but my mother always held herself to a different standard, even in the throes of unimaginable loss. She never mentioned to me that she had gone down there; she let me believe she sat at home every day waiting for some kind of news.

Now, rifling through the box, I found an undated letter from my father to my mother, apologizing for an argument they'd had, but saying that he often felt like he just couldn't do anything right in her eyes. I was starting to feel uncomfortable – like a voyeur who had found an open window and was taking in all the private details of someone else's life. I was almost going to give up when I decided to look at the back end of the box, and that's where I found my father's letter to God. The pages were slightly discolored, softened by time, but his distinctively slanted handwriting was still so familiar to me that tears caught in my throat. I looked at the second page, wanting to see what he'd written after I left the room that day.

'Lord, I know, if Life's wheel turns the way it's supposed to, my children will have to deal with my death. I hope it's not for many years, but when that time comes maybe they'll have fewer regrets than I do. I hope they know how much I love them and believe in them. I hope they have faith that we'll be together on the other side. My parents did the best they could. I wish I'd told them that instead of blaming them and resenting them for everything they didn't get right.'

He wrote something else about his parents being with God, in Heaven for eternity, but my eyes were swimming with tears and I could barely make out the words.

"Tilly? Tilly, are you in here?" Ellen was clearly over

her tears.

I wiped my face on my sleeve, put the letter in the back pocket of my jeans and came out of the closet into the room which, for a painting studio, was also unusually orderly.

"Tilly – have you been crying?"

I wiped my face again. "I'm fine. What's up?"

"Since you're here, can you go through your mother's jewelry and take whatever you want? The rest is going in the auction of her things. She didn't really say anything specific about any pieces of her jewelry to give you, I just thought there might be something you'd want."

Of course, there was only one piece of jewelry I wanted – my father's wedding ring – and her instructions were to bury that along with her body, so she obviously didn't consider that I might want that. But to avoid suspicion, I followed Ellen into my mother's bedroom where the wall safe had been opened and several black velvet jewelry cases were laid out on the bed. There were garish looking necklaces and clip-on earrings; my mother never pierced her ears, calling the practice barbaric. Rubies glinted up at me – a bracelet my father had given to my mother one Christmas. I remembered the morning, a thick white sky outside the windows, snow drifting down, and light coming from the stones as if they carried it with them, needing nothing to reflect off of. One of the legends of rubies is that people in India believed the gem would enable them to live in peace with their enemies. As I picked up the ruby bracelet, I suddenly wondered where my mother's wedding ring was. She'd removed it years ago, barely a year after the towers fell, but I never knew what she did with it. I assumed she kept it, though.

"Where is her wedding ring?" I asked Ellen, who was standing by the window looking out at the yard below. I could hear Lola barking at a squirrel.

"I never saw her wedding ring. Only your father's."

I raked my hand across the jewelry in the cases, as if her diamond ring would suddenly emerge from a tangle of gold and pearls and huge rings – some of them fake. But I knew this was going to be yet another mystery in the life of Amber Austin, the woman who left Charlotte Austin behind, the woman whose greatest talent was re-inventing herself. She allowed things to fall away from her life – people, events, chunks of her own history. She reserved the right to re-configure herself whenever she saw fit, never being accountable for anything, never being the bearer of wounds or scars. Her diamond wedding ring was just another casualty.

When Lola and I left, I looked up and down the street for the maroon Honda. Something sank inside me when I didn't see it. But maybe Stephen was right – it could have been some reporter from a tabloid trying to get a compromising photo of Amber Austin's grieving – or not so grieving – daughter. I drove home with rubies and my father's letter to God, holding tight to a whispered prayer that the legend of rubies was true, that they would help me live in peace, and that my father's vision of Heaven was also true, and he would be waiting for me on the other side.

Stephen and I had an early dinner of take-out Chinese food and wine. He brought me Gabe's gold wedding ring and I realized I was going to have to match the chain that hung around my mother's neck. I'd always focused more on the ring, but I had memorized the sound the ring made as it slid across the chain. To me it was the sound of secrets and immeasurable loss. In finding the right chain, I'd have to duplicate not only the appearance but the sound.

"I have to write a eulogy for my mother," I told Stephen as we finished off our wine, the gold wedding ring sitting on the coffee table, glinting at us.

"Oh, right. I hadn't thought about that. It's too bad we don't have a friend with a spare eulogy sitting around. So, what are you going to say, do you know yet?"

"I have no idea. I'm going to put it off a little while longer. Maybe I could just find a good poem to read."

Stephen gave me a sideways look. "This is just my opinion, but I think when people do that, it says quite obviously that they didn't like the person who died, they have nothing positive to say about them, so they figured a Wordsworth poem would fill the gap. If that's the impression you want to give, well then, have at it. But I just think you can transcend the past and give a real eulogy that will be poignant and honest and moving. I have faith that you'll come up with something brilliant, Tilly. Don't go the easy poetry route."

"Okay." I had no witty comeback. I knew he was right; I'd have to reach down into myself and compose a suitable eulogy for my mother.

I wanted to finish my painting, and Stephen needed to learn his scenes for the next day, so he went back to his house. Both of us tried to ignore Lola's disappointed expression when she realized she and I were staying put and she wouldn't be spending the night with her feline companion.

In my new blue room, I conjured up the dream in my mind and mixed the colors of firelight. There are always shadows marbled into flames and those were easy for me, but finding the right colors for the warmth, the glow that would bounce off the stone walls of the cave, took some trial and error. Finally, I knew I had it. I created firelight that glowed orange and gold from the hollow of the cave, shining out into the woods, where the moon's cool light fell through bare trees. The figure inside the cave was only partially seen. He was sitting against one wall of the cave, but all that was visible were his bent legs, arms circling his knees, and ice skates on his feet. I wrote delicately in the bottom corner, Waiting for Winter, and then stood back and took in what I had done. Something lit up inside me – a confidence that I had just done some of my best work.

The last showing I had was at the same gallery where I was scheduled in November. It was a few months before my mother was diagnosed with cancer. I had, by that point, stopped talking to her about my work because she vacillated between disdain and nonchalance. Both wounded me. My solution was to stay silent about showings, or mentions in the press, or sales of my paintings. I made a decent living from my art, although compared to my mother it was a pittance. She never asked about any of it. For all I knew she assumed I had given up on art and was working in a flower shop. But I always use social media to promote my work and my gallery events. Ellen, being the meticulous person she is, dutifully monitored my Twitter and Facebook sites. She found out about my show.

Stephen went with me that night. The gallery was packed, and I wasn't sure if my face was flushed from the wine or the accolades I was getting. It was one of those evenings when everything feels perfect, when success and joy twirl around together on the dance floor and time seems to stand still. Then the noise level in the room suddenly dropped and everyone turned toward the doorway. A ripple of whispers went through the room and people parted like the Red Sea for Moses. Except it wasn't Moses, it was my mother. I saw Ellen behind her and knew that's how she found out. Amber Austin, with a cult-like following and an industry built around her artwork, showed up unexpectedly at a small Venice gallery, ostensibly to see her daughter's work. But I knew better. She was there to upstage me. She made her way over to me only after drinking in the adulation of people who never thought they'd be meeting her. I saw her glance around when she got to me, making sure that everyone was riveted and watching her every move. She spotted the two press photographers and angled her face toward them. She glanced around at the countless cellphones aimed in our direction. Only then did she kiss me on the cheek and said, "Hello, dear. Congratulations." She lingered beside me long enough to ensure that everyone got several pictures of us, and then she walked away from me and allowed herself to be fawned over. Amber Austin, painter of light-filled cottages and impossibly happy street scenes, creator of pink sunsets and houses ringed by meadows, the famous artist willing to interact with her fans had lowered herself to come to a small beachside gallery and pose with her daughter. She stayed for less than thirty minutes, holding court, and then swept out as dramatically as she had entered.

I cried in Stephen's arms that night. I felt broken and humiliated. Nothing he said could close the wounds she had opened. He told me that no one else there knew her true motives, and I had sold most of my paintings that night. The rest would remain in the gallery and most likely sell. You were a success, he told me, drying my tears as quickly as they fell. But it made no difference. My mother had reached into the center of me, twisted her hand until I couldn't catch my breath, until I couldn't find in the acreage of my heart the still small place where belief in myself resided. I told myself, in the days following her invasion, that I would confront her, that I would at least tell her how I felt. But I didn't. Like so many times before, I retreated, intimidated by the fire and ice of her, by her success, by her uncanny ability to always come out the winner. She never mentioned my show to me, except to say, tossing the comment over her shoulder, "That's a quaint little gallery. It's very cute."

It was getting late and I was starting to look at the canvas through sleepy eyes. I took Lola out in the backyard so she could pee before we went to bed and I hoped I would dream about Hale again. Maybe I could do a series of paintings based on my dreams, if they kept coming.

A little before three in the morning I woke up. The moon was shining through the window and leaving a silvery pool of light on the bed. Just at the edge of the mattress, Lola was curled up, breathing deeply. I hadn't felt her get on the bed – I must have been sleeping too soundly, and it had been a dreamless sleep. I don't know what made me get up and go to the window that faces the street, but when I looked down, I saw the maroon Honda parked beneath a streetlamp.

I moved slowly around the room, got a sweater, put on flip-flops, and went downstairs, opening the front door carefully as if too sudden a movement might frighten him away. Chilly air brushed my cheeks. I knew who was going to be in the car. I don't know why I didn't feel any anxiety or desperation to get to him. Everything inside me was calm, as if this moment had been pre-ordained, as if I'd been waiting for it. Maybe I'm dreaming, I thought. Or maybe, in some locked-away corner of my heart, I always knew he was still here.

I bent down and looked through the passenger side window and stared into my brother's face. Hale switched on the interior lights and watched me open the door and get in. His hair was dark now, no longer red. It was definitely a dye job. There were lines around his mouth and eyes. I couldn't read his expression – it was flat, giving me nothing. I reached out and touched his arm. He was wearing a black sweatshirt and jeans, but I could feel the warmth of his skin through the sleeve.

"Are you a ghost?" I asked him.

He shook his head slowly. "No."

"So…you didn't die. Did you have amnesia?"

He switched off the interior lights; the amber glow of the streetlamps feathered us. "I didn't have amnesia, Tilly. I wanted Hale Austin to die so I could begin a new life as someone else. Someone with no history."

I felt anger surge through me. It started gradually and then overtook me. "Jesus! Why?"

Hale looked at me calmly, as if I should know the answer, which made me even more angry.

"You fake your death! And now, after eighteen years you show up after our mother has died to say hi, big fake-out, I didn't really die on 9/11? What am I supposed to do with this, Hale? Why did you do that? What was so awful about your life?"

I felt like I was the crazy person right then. Wasn't I supposed to be flooded with joy at discovering my brother was actually alive? Instead I was enraged – at the magnitude of the lie, at the lost years.

Hale shook his head slowly. "My name's Richard now. Richard Buchanan."

"Is that someone who is actually dead whose identity

you took?"

"Something like that."

I noticed a pack of cigarettes on the dashboard. "You smoke now?"

"Sometimes. I do a lot of different things now. I've made a new life, Tilly. I live in Santa Barbara, a little outside of it actually. I help run a vineyard with the woman I've been living with for the past twelve years."

"Does she know? Did you tell her who you used to be?"

"She knows," he said quietly.

He took a deep breath and closed his eyes, tilting his head back. His face was etched into my memory with such deep marks, no amount of time could have dulled the image. I was nine again, looking at his profile as we skated at Wolman Rink. For most of my life I'd been trying to cross the gulf that seemed to separate me from my brother – the sunlit, easy-going child who basked in our mother's love and usually turned away from me. Now I was going to have to try again.

"How did you get out?" I asked him.

"I'd gone down to the fourth floor just before the plane hit," he said. "I'd met a guy who worked at an insurance company on that floor. It sounds so frivolous now – but he was a runner and I went downstairs to see if he wanted to go for a run after work. After I spoke to him I was going to go out for coffee. When it happened it was deafening. The building swayed. Everything went dark, all the lights went out, the sprinklers came on, and there was smoke everywhere. And the smell of fuel…it was overwhelming. So many of us were trying to get to the stairs, I was afraid I was going to be trampled. Maybe some people were, I don't know. It took so long to get down those four flights, it was dark and walls were breaking around us. We just inched along. There are things I'm not ready to tell you about – what I saw, what we all saw – all of us who made it out. But when we got out and I looked up, I knew no one from the 103rd floor was going to make it." My brother opened his eyes and looked into mine. "I talked to Dad. He called my cell and somehow it got through. He said the flames and smoke were everywhere and they'd broken out the windows. He asked me where I was and I told him I got out. I felt like a traitor, like I'd abandoned him but there was nothing I could do. He started to say something else to me – about not wanting to die in the flames -- and the line went dead."

He stopped talking and I saw tears streaking his face.

"Do you know he jumped?" I asked Hale. "Or at least that's what was assumed. They never found any remains."

Hale nodded. "I even thought maybe I saw him falling, but it's impossible to know. I read the interview our mother gave to the paper. Tilly, things happened in this family that you don't know about. I wish I didn't know about them." He looked out at the darkness, the quiet night outside, the moon floating between pine branches, and then he said, "There's so much more to tell you but I don't want to talk anymore right now. You just have to let me do this in my own time. I'll see you again." He turned the key in the ignition.

"Wait, you're leaving? When are we going to see each other again?"

"You found me tonight. You'll find me again. Go back in and get some sleep. And I want this to stay between us. The only other person who knows is Lisa, my girlfriend – I had to explain to her why it would be risky for us to get married. They might find out my birth certificate wasn't real. I have more to tell you, Tilly. But not tonight."

My footsteps felt slow and unreal as I walked back up the brick path. Lola was waiting for me on the other side of the door and whined as I opened it. I dropped to my knees and circled her with my arms. She nuzzled me and licked my face. Suddenly I was so tired I could barely keep my eyes open. I knew as we went back upstairs that there would be no room in my sleep for dreams. Secrets are heavy things. They set down roots in your bones, change how you walk through the world.

12.

I got up before dawn. Clouds were moving into the sky. The forecast was for rain and I could smell it hovering on the wind. My flip-flops were in a corner of the bedroom and my sweater was tossed on a chair. I knew I hadn't dreamed Hale's visit, but part of me wished I had. Lola had climbed up on the bed during the night and was watching me studiously.

"I don't know, Lola. What am I supposed to do with this?" I've always thought, if dogs could actually answer us, we'd be so much smarter about our lives.

Stephen called me on his way to the studio, and I said nothing about the night before. Only that I had finished my painting and was anxious for him to see it. The truth that I wasn't telling him felt bitter in my mouth. I had no idea how I was going to keep from him the fact that Hale was alive; he would inevitably see in my eyes that I was hiding something. Of course, if I did tell him, he might not believe me and decide that I needed a psychiatric evaluation.

The rain began later in the morning and I wished I could stay home, put on soothing music, work on my painting, and drink tea. But Janice was flying in the next day and I needed to go to the market. I also needed to buy some new towels, just in case there was some feng-shui warning about towels that were starting to get threadbare. I knew I had to deal with finding a chain for the ring that would end up being buried with my mother. The imposter ring. So, I was not going to have a calm, stay-at-home rainy day. Janice had texted me that Martin was taking the same flight as her and would be staying at a nearby hotel. I realized there would now be two more people I'd be hiding the truth from.

That afternoon, with rain pelting the streets, I stood in a bead shop trying out Gabe's ring on several types of gold chain. I was listening for the sound I'd memorized over the years. I finally found one that matched my memory and I measured the length so it came down just to my heart, which is where it rested on my mother's body. My mother was shorter than me, but I didn't think it would make that much difference, especially since she'd be lying down. I'd taken Lola with me and when she barked at a trash truck going past on the street, I found myself scanning the block for the sight of a maroon Honda. Was this my future – watching for Hale, wondering when he would decide to tip-toe into my life again for another brief visit? Anger flickered in me.

For eighteen years I'd lived with the hollowness of a death that had no tangible proof it had occurred. Hale, like my father, was just air and emptiness. They were stories, not bodies. Maybe because I had accepted my father's elusiveness when he was alive it was a little easier to accept the blank space of his death. But Hale's ghost trailed me. He waited for me around corners and leaned into me at odd times, like when the sun fell at a certain angle and we were children again, running along the sand in the lazy hours of a summer afternoon. He lived inside me too – in the corner of my heart that had always missed him, that wondered if I'd done something wrong or if I just wasn't interesting enough for him to like me. I used to imagine having easy, close conversations with my brother; I would fantasize so intensely that it seemed like they had happened. But my heart knew they hadn't. One day, I made myself stop imagining because it hurt too much. But there was still a filament of hope, that maybe someday Hale would turn to me with different eyes, eyes that didn't look like judgment but instead looked like home. His death severed every dream I had, every hope that things might someday change – that we might have the bond I'd seen between other siblings. In the acrid air of post 9/11 Manhattan I wept for my father, ached with his loss, but it was Hale who commandeered my nights, my dreams.

Years later, even though it made no sense, it was Hale who at times made me angry because he had left me alone with our mother. My life might have been different these past eighteen years if my brother had been part of it. And now I knew he could have been, he just chose not to. What happened in our family that he would make such a cruel decision – pretending to be dead? Did he always plan on waiting until our mother died to find me? Or did he just see the news report and suddenly decide, I think I'll go let Tilly know I'm alive?

That night, when Stephen and I made love, my heart hurt at what I was hiding from him. I wasn't sure how we could go on if I couldn't tell him the truth. I buried my face in his shoulder, held onto him with the wrap of my legs, but inside – far beneath touch and desire and breath – I had never been more frightened. Just after three I woke up and slipped out of bed. Stephen's bedroom is on the back side of the house, so I had to go downstairs to get a view of the street. Lola watched me tip-toe out of the room but didn't get up to follow me. I parted the shades in the living room and looked up and down the street – no maroon Honda, although I couldn't see all the way down to my house without going outside and I wasn't about to do that.

"You okay?" Stephen mumbled in a thick voice when I got back into bed.

"Yeah, I needed a glass of water."

He reached an arm out and pulled me close to him, curving his body against my back. Me, the liar who was concealing from him that my dead brother was in fact alive. People make decisions for their own lives that end up changing the landscape of other lives. I was not normally inclined to feel sorry for my mother, but I did feel sad for her that she had lived all those years without her son, believing he was dead when he was very much alive but under another identity.

Janice called me early in the morning from the airport. She sounded like she'd already had too much caffeine.

"Hey – we're just about to board. Martin's rented a car, so he'll drop me off at your house. I figured I didn't need a car since I'd just be hanging with you – right?"

"Janice, you're talking ninety miles a minute. How many cups of coffee have you had?"

She laughed. "Yeah, we hit Starbucks. God, their coffee is strong. Anyway…I can't wait to see you. You sound distracted. Which is understandable. You okay, though? As much as you can be okay?"

Something grabbed at me inside. Was I okay? "Yeah, I'm good," I told her. "Listen, ask Martin if he wants to have dinner at my house tonight. I'll tell Stephen. He'll be back from the studio by then."

"Hold on." I heard her talking to Martin and then she handed the phone to him.

"Hey you. Sure, dinner sounds good. You cooking?" Martin knew only too well that I'm proficient at only few dishes, and I don't make them too often.

"No, I'm going to rely on the wonderful cooks at Whole Foods to have something I can heat up. I'm very good at heating things up."

"I recall," he said. I wasn't sure we were still talking about food, but I let it go.

"So, I'll see you both later."

Stephen knew all about my history with Martin, who he'd teasingly referred to as my "friend with benefits." When I texted him and told him we were going to have dinner at my house, so he should come over when he got back from the studio, he replied, "Great, I finally get to meet the friend with benefits."

"His name is Martin," I texted back. "He does have a sense of humor but it's probably best if you use his actual name."

"Duly noted," Stephen replied.

By early afternoon the storm had passed. I opened the window in the guest bedroom so I could hear if a car pulled up out front – Janice had texted me that they'd landed on time. I put fresh linens on the bed, vacuumed, put a vase of flowers on the dresser and a scented candle on the nightstand. The last time Janice visited, nearly eight months ago, I made the mistake of moving a large houseplant into the room.

"Tilly, have you forgotten everything I taught you?" she said when she saw the plant. "Plants in the bedroom are bad feng-shui. They give off carbon dioxide, especially at night, which the person sleeping in the room then breathes in."

"Wow, it's amazing there haven't been deaths reported from people who had Boston ferns in their bedroom," I told her as I carried the plant out into the hall.

I was pretty sure that cut flowers were okay, but if they weren't, she would let me know.

I heard a car pull up outside the house and looked down from the second-floor window. Martin had rented a Mercedes, which I knew I'd tease him about – no cheap car for him. I opened the front door before they had a chance to ring the bell, and Janice dropped her suitcase to hug me. Lola was jumping up on us and Janice reached down to stroke her head.

"I'm so glad to see you," she said, holding on tight to me. "Are you holding up?"

"I am, yeah. I'm really glad you guys are here. And so is Lola. She loves company."

Martin had bent down to introduce himself to Lola, and when he stood up I gave him a quick hug and kissed him on the cheek, as if we'd always just been friends, as if we didn't know every inch of each other's bodies. He looked older to me, but I wasn't sure why. I'd seen him less than six months before when I went to New York to stay with Janice for a few days; I didn't think he could change in that amount of time. But it seemed as if gravity was pulling at him. I wondered if he was grieving for my mother more than I was able to.

When I led them into the house, memories drifted in with them. The day the three of us went Christmas shopping on an icy white day in Manhattan, bundled up and laughing as if the planes had never come, as if we were carefree again, free of grief. The summer day Martin took me roller-blading in Central Park and had to hold onto my arm so I wouldn't fall – I'd mistakenly thought roller-blading was exactly like ice-skating and I'd be instantly proficient. The gray afternoon Janice and I wept at the blank sky outside her window, at what she'd seen and what we all had lost. Boxes were stacked around her apartment; she was moving to her new place in the Village the next day.

Martin made a circle, taking in what he could see of my house from the entryway. "This is a nice place, Tilly. Are you going to buy it? I mean, I'm assuming you'll be able to now. Sorry, I hope that didn't sound insensitive."

"We probably shouldn't assume anything yet," I said. "I think I've been designated as the last to know. So, I haven't really thought about what I'm going to do."

Martin walked over and peeked into the kitchen. "Well, if you do buy it, I can do the paperwork for you. I'm licensed in California too."

Janice laughed. "He gave out five business cards at the airport. You can't fault his work ethic."

"Okay," Martin said. "I'm going to go get settled in my hotel and I'll be back for dinner at…"

"6:30."

"See you girls later."

I led Janice upstairs to the guest room, carrying her suitcase for her. I'd lit the lavender candle on the nightstand and the scent found us at the top of the stairs.

"Ah, that smells nice after an airport and a plane and a rental car which, though luxurious, still smells like other people," Janice said, flopping down on the bed. I sat down beside her, feeling the weight of secrets inside me. I wanted desperately to tell her about Hale, but I'd promised him. "Tilly, is it going to be weird for Stephen to be around Martin? You did tell me he knows about the two of you and your slightly odd history, but still…"

"He'll be okay. Just like I'm okay with his ex-wife. Who knows, they might become friends."

Janice looked around the room and suddenly stood up,

went to the wall facing one side of the bed and took down the mirror that Stephen and I had found at a yard sale a few weeks earlier.

"Uh-oh," I said under my breath.

"Tilly, you can't have a mirror in the bedroom. I thought I taught you this. Especially facing the bed like that." Lola jumped onto the bed and looked from the blank wall to Janice holding the mirror in her hands.

"Better put that down, Janice. Lola might think we're moving."

She leaned it against the wall and gave me a stern look. "This is very bad, Tilly. Almost as bad as the foot of the bed facing the door. When we sleep, our soul leaves our body and if it sees itself in the mirror it can get confused. That's why a mirror facing the bed causes nightmares. And then when the soul is returning to the body, it can get confused between the person and the mirror image."

"Well, that explains it. My last houseguest was totally different when she left here. She was normal when she came and after sleeping here for a couple of nights she was like a character on The Walking Dead."

Janice gave me a narrow-eyed look. "Sometimes I don't know when you're joking."

"I'm joking. I haven't had any houseguests. Can I put the mirror in my work room?"

"Yes," she said. "As long as it's not facing the door."

We took the mirror across the hall and Janice stopped abruptly. "Wow, it's blue! This is beautiful. See, you do know a few things about feng-shui. It's very soothing."

"The credit goes to my neighbor Rachel. She suggested it – she's a psychologist."

Janice had moved over to my painting. She stood in front of it for a few minutes without saying anything. Finally, she said, "This is different for you. I like all your paintings, but I think this one is your best." She pointed to the cave. "Is that Hale in there?"

"Yeah. How did you know?"

"The ice-skates. I remember when you took them from your mother's."

I put my arms around Janice and hugged her. The people with whom we have long histories settle inside us. They ground us, remind us of who we have been, who we have become, and how many paths we traveled to get there.

We took Lola for a walk, and I told my best friend about Hale coming into my dreams. I told her about the maroon Honda and the man behind the wheel who resembled my brother, but I went no further. Severing the truth like that felt like cutting off blood supply to a major artery, but I didn't see that I had any choice.

"Have you dreamed about him before?" she asked me. "Before your mother died?"

"Not like that. Scattered, quick, awful dreams after 9/11, but nothing like these dreams. Maybe our mother's death opened up some channel where he can come to me now."

My words had a different meaning for me, and I averted my eyes so she wouldn't see guilt pooled in them.

"Maybe it's you who opened up all on your own," Janice said.

I let Janice prepare the dining room for our guests. She brought in the orchid plant that Gabe and Bryan had given me and placed it as a centerpiece, she lit candles everywhere, she found placemats that I had forgotten I owned, and pulled delicate wine goblets from the back of a cabinet where they were hiding behind the cheaper Pier One glasses. I put the lasagna I'd gotten from Whole Foods into a large baking dish and made a salad, content to let Janice transform my house in whatever ways she wanted. I knew without looking that she was moving some things around on the walls and shifting the placement of furniture. There was a reason her clients paid her a lot of money; I was the lucky one, getting her talents for free.

As we got everything ready, Janice told me about the new man she was dating, who she met through an on-line dating service – her new attempt at finding a relationship.

"He's very nice. Eric. Cute, and he's a chef, so I'm eating well. But he has a lot of ink on his body. It's very distracting."

I had to laugh. "Really? Distracting?"

"Yeah, I'm always reading something on him, or looking at a picture, seeing things in it I didn't see before. And he has angel wings tattooed on his back. The first time I slept with him I felt like I was being blasphemous."

"Blasphemous…"

"Uh-huh," she said. "As in fucking an angel?"

"Somehow I'm thinking angels don't sign up for on-line dating services. Unless maybe they have their own very exclusive site. Tinder Wings, or Celestial Match.com."

"Fine, make jokes. But the only way I can make love with him is in the dark. Otherwise -"

"I know. You get distracted. Or get too busy reading his biceps."

Stephen and Martin arrived within minutes of each other and whatever worries I might have had about any kind of awkwardness between them quickly evaporated. Martin apparently watched Stephen's show a lot and had detailed questions about what research he'd done for the part. We sat in the living room drinking wine, and I breathed easier seeing that Martin and Stephen were getting along like they'd known each other for years. But when Stephen began talking about observing an actual heart surgery, I cut in.

"Okay, no blood and gore tonight, please? Some of us are squeamish."

They both laughed at me, but Martin obediently changed the subject to how different Manhattan was now that Donald Trump was president. "I lost sales on a couple of apartments in Trump Tower," he said. "I mean, who wants to live in the midst of all that insanity?"

The conversation turned to my mother's service, just days away now, and how Ellen was re-arranging her house to be part gathering place, part showcase for Amber Austin's artwork. I told them how strange it was that Ellen knew so much more about my mother than I did, or at least the mother who reincarnated into Amber Austin.

Stephen gave me a mischievous look. "Although... Tilly did have a bonding experience with Ellen. They picked out the casket together."

"Hey, that'll do it," Janice said, laughing. "Nothing like shopping for funeral accoutrements to cement a relationship."

"We do not have a relationship," I said. "We just got along better that day. And it was illuminating to learn that you can have a theme-based funeral. Into fishing? Why not have a boat-shaped coffin with some fish painted on it. Or I guess if you were a chef you could have a coffin that looks like an oven, although we didn't see that one there."

"My uncle was an avid golfer," Martin said. "He was buried with his favorite clubs. I'm sorry, but I found it seriously creepy." I thought again that Martin looked older to me, almost haggard, but I didn't entirely trust my own observations right then. I felt like a traitor. With everything Martin and I had been through, from the early drama of him telling Hale what a loose woman I was, and Hale agreeing, to weeping together over Hale's death, I was hiding from him the fact that his friend was actually alive.

Later, through candlelight and the rich smells of lasagna and garlic bread, I looked at who was gathered around me in my home. My dining table seats eight, but even though four chairs appeared to be empty, to me they were occupied. My parents and Hale whispered around us. The other chair was occupied by death, the shadow that all of us had waltzed with, tried to fathom. Once death visits you, it never really leaves. It comes in with the breeze that drifts through a window in winter; it slips across the floor with evening shadows. It reminds you that it's always waiting and all you can do is open your arms wide to life.

"Hey Tilly," Martin said, "Remember when Hale invited me and a couple of his other buddies to one of your mother's Christmas Eve parties? She'd rented a Santa suit and she was trying to get me to put it on and do a whole Saint Nick thing."

"Right. And you refused. Kudos to you for standing up to my mother. Not many have." For a moment I was back in our old apartment, with the elaborate Christmas decorations and the uniformed caterers bringing drinks on silver trays.

Martin laughed and suddenly he looked younger, not as frail. "Scott, our friend, was sloshed enough to say yes. He came out in the suit and the beard and the hat, sat down and started pulling these socialites onto his lap, asking them what they wanted for Christmas."

Stephen and Janice were laughing too. "Did your mother regret having asked him?" Stephen said.

"Oh yeah," I told him. "She went on for days after about how inappropriate it was, and how she had to call all the women and apologize. Hey, you take a risk when you ask a cute guy who's had a few drinks to play dress-up."

I looked around the dinner table and thought, This is my family. These are the people I'm tied to in this life.

The Austins were more fable than family. The messiness, the chaos, the tumult of love and arguments and hard-won lessons that characterize most families, that root them and hold them fast even when oceans and continents separate them, didn't belong to us. My family was carefully crafted -- molded and lacquered by Manhattan society, restricted to shallow interactions at home by my father's decorum and my mother's steeliness. We were as orderly as her displays of Limoges boxes and other treasures on the perfectly polished antique tables placed around the apartment. And because of that, we never really got to know each other. There was never easy laughter around the dinner table, or memories pulled from the stream of years and recounted in tender stories.

Janice helped me clear the table while Stephen and Martin insisted Lola wanted to go outside and they should accompany her in the backyard.

"Funny how they made that work – getting out of cleaning up," Janice said as we were loading the dishwasher.

"They're probably talking heart surgeries, which Stephen thinks he could actually do, and Martin is strangely interested in."

"Or they're comparing how you are in bed."

I flicked some water at Janice while I was rinsing off a plate. "Hey, is Martin okay? He looks – I don't know – tired, or different somehow."

Janice shrugged. "I don't really know him that well. I run into him sometimes in the city but we don't travel in the same circles. Did you ask him if anything's wrong?"

"I can't quite figure out how to do that in a civilized way. Martin, you look bad, is everything okay? Or how about, Wow, you look so much older and kind of decrepit. Going through a hard time?"

"Point taken."

We were finished loading the dishwasher and they still hadn't come in, so we went out to the yard. They were standing near the ash tree and threads of moonlight slipped through the branches, laced around them. Lola was stretched out on the grass. Stephen smiled at me and reached out an arm to pull me close.

"Uh-oh, did we miss dish duty?"

"No. We saved them for you. Of course you missed it, clever boy."

Martin laughed, and in the shadows and soft yellow of the garden lights, he looked better. But I knew it was just a trick of moonlight and low watt bulbs. "I'm going to head back to the hotel," he said. "I'm going down to San Diego tomorrow to visit a cousin of mine who I haven't seen in years but let me know what time the service is on Saturday."

"I'm going to have Ellen send a limo here for all of us. No reason we can't all go together."

Stephen went back to his house, and Janice and I tried to stay awake talking but we both started dozing off. I liked knowing she was across the hall; she was a bridge between the life that used to be mine and the life I'd traveled across the country to discover.

13.

A little before three I woke up and listened to the silence around me. After all these years in Los Angeles it still surprised me to open my eyes long before dawn and be enveloped with a quiet so deep it seemed I'd moved to another galaxy in my sleep. Manhattan is never quiet; no matter what time of night you stir and wake up, you hear the city outside your windows. Lola was wedged against my legs and I moved them without waking her. I climbed out of bed and went to the window, pulled by a certainty I couldn't explain. Hale's car was there. No lights were on inside it, but I knew he was sitting behind the wheel waiting for me.

As I tip-toed down the stairs I felt like I was edging back into a history that still haunted me. The chill of the night made me shiver as I walked toward his car and reached for the door handle.

"See?" Hale said when I slid into the passenger seat, "I told you you'd find me again."

"Actually, you found me. How did you do that? I rent this house, it isn't like you could look up property records."

"Our mother's house was featured in lots of magazines and newspapers, so she was easy to find. I figured you probably maintained the family tradition of visiting on Sundays. So, one weekend years ago I drove down here and parked near her house on a Sunday. I saw you drive in and I waited. When you left, I followed you."

He smelled like coffee. I wondered where he was staying since he'd told me he lived in Santa Barbara, but that wasn't the most pressing question.

"Why did you do this Hale? Why did you pretend to be dead?"

He took a deep breath and exhaled slowly. The window was down on his side and he leaned his head out for a few seconds, letting the night air feather his skin. "Our parents had a terrible fight that morning. Did you know that?"

"Yes. Dad left his wedding ring there."

Hale nodded. "Do you know what the fight was about?"

"No. I asked a few times, but…no. Were you at the apartment that morning?"

"No. I'd gone out to grab some breakfast. Dad told me later, right before we walked into the North Tower. The fight was about me. It was about a secret our mother had kept for my whole life. Our whole lives."

"I don't understand."

Hale paused and stared out into the night again. "Dad wasn't my father, Tilly."

"That's not true. That can't be true."

"It is true. Ian is my father."

I started to say something, but Hale motioned for me to be quiet.

"She had an affair with him when you were a baby," he said, "and she got pregnant. She just let our father believe I was his. She and Ian – they both kept it from him. Until that morning. I don't know why she decided to tell him on that particular day, but she did, and then he told me. We'd gotten out of the car and we were standing on the sidewalk. He put his hand on my shoulder and maneuvered me away from the door and people going in. Then he told me, really matter-of-factly, that my mother let him know I was Ian's child. My whole life was suddenly a lie. How was I supposed to know who I was? The man I thought was my father wasn't and my mother had lied for decades – I felt like I was going to explode. You know, Dad said all the right things -- how I'd always be his son and he'd always love me, how this didn't change the way he felt about me. It was bullshit. I saw it in his eyes – I was dead to him. I felt so alone, and so betrayed. All I knew was, I was never going to go back to their apartment again. I thought, I'll move in with Tara, or go stay with a friend…anything would be better than going back there. That's why I went down to the fourth floor – I was thinking maybe I could move in with this guy I was sort of friendly with. Then the planes hit, and I was sure I was going to die, but I didn't. There was so much death around me, so much horror. When I got out, I just started walking. The person I always believed I was had died that morning. So, letting everyone think I was actually dead suddenly made perfect sense to me."

Hale wasn't looking at me. He was staring straight ahead through the windshield into darkness. I thought about the days after the towers fell when Ian came to visit my mother; I thought about the day we drove downtown to get death certificates for my father and brother. In a few days, I'd see Ian at my mother's service. I saw him now in Hale's face, in his features. I tried to remember exactly when Ian and his wife divorced – I knew it was sometime after 9/11, but I couldn't pinpoint when my mother told me about it.

"I don't know what to say," I told him. I was used to my mother shaving off layers of truth to create realities that were more to her liking, but this was something I could never have imagined.

He looked at me then and tears spilled from his eyes. This man who I had never seen cry had now wept twice. I opened my arms in what felt like such an awkward gesture – Hale and I had never comforted each other, never embraced or tried to soothe each other's wounds. Hale fell against me crying, and I let my arms form a circle around him. I felt tears behind my eyes but I was too stunned to cry, too thrown by all I had just heard. If I had discovered that I was adopted, or that I'd been left on my parents' doorstep by a stranger, it would have been less upsetting. It would have made sense to me. I was always the one who didn't fit in. But Hale was the perfect son, a blend of both our parents. Except he wasn't. He never had been.

There was a knock on the passenger side window and I turned to see Janice standing there, a sweater wrapped tightly around her. I reached past Hale, turned the ignition key so I could put down the window. She glanced at me and then stared past me.

"Hale…" she said, her tone balanced between a question and a declaration.

He sat up and wiped his face with the palms of his hands. I got out of the car and faced Janice -- my best friend, who I had lied to and now needed to confide in. I couldn't read her eyes, couldn't decipher if she was angry or just shocked. Night air floated between us. Suddenly Hale reached over and closed the passenger side door. He started the car and drove off without even glancing in the rearview mirror. I slipped my arm through hers and led her back toward the house.

"I wanted to tell you," I said. "I only just found out a few nights ago, and Hale swore me to secrecy. But now that doesn't matter. I'll tell you everything I know."

Lola was, once again, waiting on the other side of the door, her eyes wide and concerned. The three of us went into the kitchen and I filled up the kettle to make tea. Lola stared at us, absorbing the fact that we were not going back to bed, we were staying in the kitchen at this quiet hour long before dawn. She turned and walked away; I heard her climb onto the couch in the living room. One night a few years ago, when Janice flew out to stay with me for a week, we sat in my kitchen with a bottle of wine late into the night talking about men. She had just broken up with Edward, and my romance with Stephen was still new. We were at opposite ends of the relationship spectrum, and we had probably the most intimate conversation we'd ever had – about our deepest wants and fears, about the best lovers we'd had, and the worst. We laughed, shed tears, and finished off the bottle of wine. But this was different.

I had to explain to Janice what I didn't fully understand myself. For eighteen years I had believed Hale was dead. I'd imagined him drifting toward a heaven where evil doesn't exist and death is just a change of clothes. I had needed to make the aftermath – the afterlife -- pretty and soothing, because the horror of that day was almost unfathomable. I didn't know how to feel about him now that he was here, in the flesh, and had been all this time. How was I supposed to deal with the betrayal of him faking his own death? Part of me died too on that September day, in the smoke and ash – the part of me that imagined we could someday figure out how to be a family.

"He asked me not to tell anyone," I said to Janice as I put steaming cups of tea on the table and sat down next to her. She still hadn't said a word. "I don't know how I would have kept it to myself for much longer, so I'm glad you came out there. He probably isn't. I don't know why he came back now. Did our mother's death somehow release him to tell the truth?"

She took a sip of tea. "Lola woke me. She was whimpering at my door and when I opened it she walked back into your bedroom and then barked at me. I called for you and then I looked outside. I don't know what I thought at first – maybe you were cheating on Stephen? But I couldn't really wrap my head around that. Especially not with a guy who drives a crappy Honda."

"He just showed up – sitting out there in his car at the same time of night. But I'd spotted him before that – I wasn't sure, but it looked like him. Once I saw him outside my mother's house, another time on this street. I thought my imagination was playing tricks on me. That's what I told myself. And then I woke up the other night and something drew me to the window. I saw the car with lights on inside and I just knew."

"Why?" Janice asked. "Why would he leave you alone all these years, letting you think he was dead? And your mother too – she lost all that time with her son. I know your mother was a hard woman to feel sympathy for, but I do feel sorry for her."

"Me too. I found out the reason tonight. It had to do with the fight my parents had the morning of 9/11."

"I remember that," Janice said. "The wedding ring your father left behind."

"The fight was about Hale. My mother made a confession. After keeping it to herself for more than twenty years, she decided for some reason to come clean." I took a deep breath and exhaled slowly. The words felt so strange to me. "Hale is really Ian's son. They were having an affair when I was a baby. She could have gone on just keeping the secret. I don't know why she told him. I'll probably never know. God, this family is one deep well of secrets, that's for sure."

Janice put her cup down hard on the table. "So, your father was betrayed by two people incredibly close to him – his wife and his boss who was also his friend. And Hale was betrayed by your mother and the family friend who, if memory serves, you guys used to call Uncle Ian when you were kids. Man, that's brutal. Tilly, I know this is going to sound crazy, but then again we're knee-deep in crazy-land at the moment – do you think your father could be alive?"

"No. Hale talked to him after he got out – he'd gone down the fourth floor and he made it out. Our father was still on the 103rd floor. No one up there could get out. The plane hit below them. He said something to Hale about jumping, just like he did to my mother. Janice, I'm so wracked with guilt over all the things I don't feel. I should feel happy that Hale is actually alive. I'm supposed to be relieved, I'm supposed to be excited about the future we can have together. But I don't feel any of those things. I just feel numb. I feel like he pulled a cord and everything that held my life together into a shape I recognized just came tumbling down."

Janice sipped her tea and gave me the look that always let me know she was peeling back my words and looking underneath them. "I don't think there's a manual for how someone is supposed to feel in a situation like this," she said. "But maybe what seems like numbness isn't really. Maybe it's just all the emotions of a lifetime that are surfacing and making you feel overwhelmed. And kind of paralyzed. You were safe from those feelings when Hale was dead, right? I mean, you could tell yourself they died along with him – the longing for a closeness that you didn't have, the hurt over how much he judged you. All of those complications came back from the dead with him."

I stared into my cup as if looking for tea leaves to tell me the future. Somewhere in me, I thought, emotions must be gathering, readying themselves for an onslaught. But right then there was only a dull ache in the center of my body.

"In a way it was easier," I told her, "when I believed he was dead. It was an absolute, something unchangeable and non-negotiable. I had my grief to get through. But I didn't have the questions that had tortured me all my life, like how can I get closer to Hale, how can I get him to like me...I didn't feel that desperation to have a relationship with my brother -- obviously, since my brother was gone. Does that sound awful?"

"No," Janice said. "It sounds honest. Painfully so. Are you going to tell Stephen?"

My tea was getting cold. I swallowed a gulp of it and pictured Stephen's face, his eyes. "I have to. I can't keep something like this from him, especially not now – now that you know. I've hated the last couple of days when every time I was with him I was lying to him by what I wasn't saying."

Janice nodded. "I know the feeling. That's what happened with me and Edward – that holding back on the truth. Not that it was anything like this, but still it was toxic."

"What did you hold back from him?"

"That I didn't love him anymore. I didn't even really like him anymore." She laughed softly. "Like I said, it was nothing like this. I started hating the way he brushed his teeth, like he was trying to destroy them. His laugh started to bother me. Anyway, Tilly, it's after four. Maybe we should try and get a little bit of sleep before the sun comes up?"

As we walked back upstairs, Lola leading the way, I remembered a day in New York many months after 9/11 when the wind was fierce. I was walking on Columbus Avenue and, even though there were people all around me, I felt like I was alone in my own wind tunnel, trying to navigate my way without toppling over. I felt the same now, sitting in my house – as if I were alone in a wind tunnel, struggling for balance. At the top of the stairs, Janice gave me a tight hug.

"Get some sleep, okay?" she said. "I love you and I'm here for you."

It's the friends who belong in our lives who reach through raging winds to grab onto us, who remind us that we're never as alone as we might think we are. I hoped for Hale that he had that with the woman he lived with – Lisa. And I wondered if my mother found that kind of solace with Ian after my father died.

14.

After drifting in and out of restless, shallow sleep, I stared at the clock and waited for five o'clock when I knew Stephen would be getting up. He answered on the first ring.

"Tilly, you okay?"

"Yes, I just…I was wondering if you can stop by here on your way to the studio. I need to tell you something."

There was a long moment of silence. I knew I shouldn't have said it like that, it sounded so ominous, but I wasn't feeling terribly creative after no sleep.

"Um, sure. Are you pregnant? Or breaking up with me?" Stephen said.

"God no! Neither. It's not even about me, exactly. Well, it is, but…it's more about Hale. He's alive, Stephen."

There was another quick interlude of silence before Stephen said, "I'll be right over."

Lola was watching me through half-lidded eyes. "He thinks I'm insane," I told her.

I barely had time to make coffee before I heard his key in the lock and he came into the kitchen, holding a cup of steaming coffee. He hadn't shaved or combed his hair, but at least he hadn't padded down the street in his pajamas. I stood up and wrapped my arms around his neck, gave him a long deep kiss. "I love you," I whispered. "And I hated keeping a secret from you for the last couple of days. But now I don't have to, because Janice found out last night when he came over here. At three in the morning. That seems to be his hour of choice. Maybe he was always an insomniac and I never knew it. That would be yet another thing I never knew about my brother."

We sat down at the breakfast table and I could tell from the look in Stephen's eyes that he still wasn't sure I was in control of my faculties. I told him everything I knew. How Hale had walked away from the flames and the crumbling towers -- away from the life he had known. How he forged a new life.

When I finished, he shook his head slowly and said, "I heard about a woman who pretended she was in one of the towers and escaped, went on a whole publicity tour about this story that never happened. But I haven't heard of anyone who pretended they died. Although I didn't exactly google that sort of thing. It's called pseudocide, by the way – faking your own death. I guess I can understand his reasoning, but I'd have thought after so many years he would want to go back to his family. I mean, he went to your mother's house, but just lingered there and then followed you home. I wonder if he ever thought about ringing the bell."

"I don't know. It's one of about fifty thousand things I can ask him next time he shows up. If he shows up again."

Lola came padding into the kitchen. Janice was close behind her; she had a sweater on over her pajamas and her eyes were heavy with lack of sleep.

"This sure is a busy house," she said. "Do you guys ever sleep around here? 'Morning Stephen."

Stephen laughed and got up to pour her some coffee. "It isn't always like this," he said. He glanced at the clock on the stove. "Listen, I gotta get to work. But there's something I need to tell you about too."

Janice almost choked on her coffee. "If this is about another dead person who really isn't, I'm going back to bed."

"No," Stephen said. "It's about Martin. He has a leaky valve in his heart. Bad enough that he's looking at surgery. That's what we were talking about outside. He'll have to decide between having it repaired or replaced. Repairing the valve is preferable because he can avoid the risk of endocarditis."

"Okay, Dr. Oz," I said. "We have no idea what that is, but it sounds bad. So, what's he going to do?"

"Well, I gave him the name of the cardiologist I talk to for research – he's a really well-respected doctor. Martin should get a few opinions before he does anything. I think he's going to tell you himself, so you might want to let him do that." He leaned down and kissed me. "I'm sorry to run, but I can't be late for my pretend doctor job."

"Save lots of lives," Janice called after him as he left.

"I knew Martin looked different," I told her.

"Well, we can't tell him we know. Let him fill us in. Or fill you in. I'm not sure I qualify as someone in the need-to-know category."

A familiar fear bloomed inside me. "People get surgery on their hearts and then they're okay, right?" I asked her. "I mean, it's pretty common, isn't it? And he's young."

She sat down beside me and took my hands. "Honey, don't go there. I know what you're thinking. Martin's going to be fine. He's not going to die, okay? Just don't let yourself spin out on that thought. And if you get nervous, Stephen can give you a detailed explanation of what goes on in the surgery and how it's all routine. It might gross you out, but it should make you feel better."

"Yes, he will happily describe surgical procedures to me. I can't say it's ever made me feel better, but maybe this time will be different. As you can see, though, there's a whole language that goes along with these situations that's baffling at best. Sometimes I just sit there glassy-eyed listening to Stephen rattle off medical jargon, having no idea what he's talking about. Anyway, I guess we'll wait to see what Martin tells us. Janice, did you know there's a word for faking your own death? Pseudocide."

"Stephen knew that, right?"

"Yep. He's very curious, so he ends up with information on things that other people don't even think about."

Janice got a faraway look in her eyes. "I need a smart man. Someone who knows stuff. No tattoos, a mind like Google and please God, let him have a job. Or better yet a career. I'm going to meditate on this, try and draw a man like that into my orbit."

"You do that," I told her. "Let me know how it works out."

Later that morning Lola, Janice and I headed up to my mother's house. I wanted Janice to see for herself how Ellen had taken command of the premises and had basically become the ruler of the house. Clouds hovered at the edges of the sky, a reminder of the storms that were predicted over the next few days. I didn't call Ellen to tell her we were coming and when I mentioned that to Janice she said, "Tilly, it's your mother's house. You shouldn't have to ask Ellen's permission to go up there."

I laughed. "There's a lot that shouldn't have been true in my family but was. After I moved into Tribeca, I always called before I went to my parents' apartment. It was just understood that it wasn't a drop-in kind of place. And you know what? It still isn't."

Janice reached over into the backseat and scratched Lola's head. "Do you think Hale will show up at the funeral?"

"I can't predict anything at this point. Not even if he and I will finally figure out how to have some kind of relationship. He broke down and cried in my arms, but I'm not sure that reveals anything beyond the fact that he needed to cry and I was the one sitting beside him. There was only one time – a very long time ago – when I feel like we might have created a bond between us, and I blew it. I didn't open the door, literally and figuratively."

It happened on Christmas morning when I was thirteen, and Hale was eleven. New York was piled with snow and more was falling. The windows in our apartment were flecked with frost on the outside and foggy on the inside with the heat from the furnace and sweet-smelling steam from the kitchen where our housekeeper was preparing Christmas dinner. The four of us were gathered around the tree for our ritual opening of presents. Hale was gleefully ripping open boxes with new ice-skates, a new winter parka.

"You're growing so fast," my father said. "You'll probably outgrow those in a few months."

I opened a large flat box from my parents and

withdrew a shiny silver party dress with a poufy skirt, a high neckline and small capped sleeves. It was the ugliest dress I'd ever seen. It looked like tin foil. But I smiled and said thank you, folding it back into the box.

"Go try it on," my mother said. "You're always dressing like a tom-boy, let's see you in your new dress."

"I don't want to put it on now," I told her. Actually, I didn't ever want to put it on. I wanted to slip it into the trash chute.

"Tilly, go put on your new dress." She had a serrated tone to her voice that always frightened me.

I went into my bedroom and wriggled myself into the tin foil dress, managing to zip it up in the back, at which point I could barely breathe. My still-developing breasts were flattened against my rib cage and the fabric scratched my skin. I had no choice but to go back out to the living room. Tears burned behind my eyes, but I clenched my teeth and told myself, Don't you dare cry. My father looked up from a gift he was unwrapping and then looked down again. Hale's mouth dropped open but he didn't say anything. Only my mother spoke.

"That's lovely!" she said. "Finally, you look like a girl. We'll have to figure out where you're going to wear that – maybe one of your friends' birthday parties or something."

The idea of going out into the world in that dress was so horrifying to me that I took a deep breath and said, "I don't like it. And it doesn't fit me. It hurts."

My mother stood up, crossed the floor that was littered with gifts and wrapping, grabbed my arm roughly and said, "Are you incapable of being grateful? I bought you an expensive dress, and you will wear it."

Her fingers dug into my arm and her eyes drilled deep into my bones. I broke away, ran back to my room where I ripped off the dress, put my jeans and sweatshirt on again and then locked the door so I could cry in peace. I felt like a prisoner, unjustly convicted of a crime I knew nothing about. There was a soft knock on the door and Hale said, in almost a whisper, "Tilly? You okay? Let me in."

"Go away," I told him, through my tears. I didn't want anyone to see me broken.

A minute or two passed. I heard him breathing, felt his presence on the other side of the door, waiting…and then I heard him walk away. He never came to my door again, never tried to tend to my tears or my upset. That was my one chance, and I sent him away.

When I finished the story, Janice said, "But he has come to your door again, Tilly. Now. More than once. Can you see that?"

We were almost to my mother's house. "Maybe. I guess. So much is different now, though."

Casa del Sol was still a bustling scene, but the interior of the house had been dramatically re-arranged to accommodate over a hundred people and showcase my mother's paintings. Ellen spotted us when we walked in and came over with an expression on her face that reminded me of my mother – an air of superiority mixed with the tactical determination of an army general.

"Hi," she said, directing herself to me. "I didn't know you were coming." Then she turned to Janice, held out her hand and said, "I'm Ellen. And you are?"

Janice shook her hand and smiled politely. "Janice. Nice to meet you. Tilly's told me so much about you."

Ellen started to say something but a man carrying boxes approached us and asked her if he should put them in the garage. "Yes, I'll show you where," she said, and she was off, leading the way.

Janice leaned in to me and said in a low voice, "God, she's an awful lot like your mother."

"I know. It adds credence to the theory that we were switched at birth and the whole moving to Los Angeles thing was just a ruse so my mother could reunite with her birth daughter."

I still had Lola on her leash but it seemed safe enough

to let her out in the yard. As we crossed the room that now looked more like a ballroom than a living room and stepped outside, Janice said, "I don't think you're going to get off that easy, Tilly – with the jokes about being switched at birth or what you used to say about being left on the doorstep. Somehow you're going to have to make peace with the fact that she was your mother."

Lola happily jumped up against a tree trunk, confident there was a squirrel lurking about somewhere. "I know you're right," I told her. "So where does Ellen fit in to the equation?"

"Haven't a clue. Maybe she doesn't. Maybe she's just a mosquito on the surface of your life at the moment."

The mosquito came to the French doors and said, "I have the stairs cordoned off, but you can go upstairs if you want."

I turned toward her, prepared to say something sarcastic, but at that moment I didn't see a clone of my mother. I saw the girl whose own mother died way too young, the girl who learned how to paint over her emotions until they were invisible to everyone beneath her shiny, practiced surface. I saw the woman who finally broke down and wept – for my mother – maybe in ways she had never wept for her own.

"Thanks, Ellen," I said.

We left Lola to her squirrel quest and went upstairs, past the rope that looked like it had been borrowed from a museum. I had the same feeling as before – that the air got colder as we ascended. When we walked into my mother's room, I shivered.

"Are you cold?" Janice asked me.

"Yeah. Don't you think it's cold up here?"

She shook her head no. "I think it's just your reaction to being in this room."

"Or maybe her ghost is still in here and is blowing arctic air only in my direction. It would be perfectly in character for my mother to defy whatever the decorum is for those who leave this world and decide to keep crashing in. If there are any rules of decorum in the ghost world."

I sat down on the edge of her bed, carefully made up and smoothed as if it hadn't held the messiness of illness for months, as if a dead body hadn't laid there for hours. I looked at the pillows, saw my mother's wan face, her ill-fitting wig. I smelled again the musty bitterness of a body that doesn't have much time left in this world and heard the gravelly sound of her voice. I imagined her lying there in the dark on the last night of her life. Did it get cold when death moved closer, opening its long arms and folding her into them? Or was there a sense of peace, of release from pain?

Janice was standing at the window looking down at the garden. I could hear Lola yipping and barking. I reached my hand out to the nightstand as I suddenly imagined my mother did – for what though? Her pills? The lamp? The buzzer for the nurse? To this day, I don't know why, but I slid my hand beneath the mattress and my index finger touched the hard plastic of a pill bottle. I pulled it out and saw that it was her Ambien. There were still a fair number of pills in the bottle, so I could set aside one nagging thought I'd had, that she had either deliberately or accidentally died from an overdose.

"Look what I found," I said to Janice.

She came over and sat down beside me. "You told me you were thinking someone had removed these."

"That's one of the scenarios I was playing with. But now I think she put this under the mattress. I don't know why – I just sort of see it in my head. Weird, huh? Maybe she was afraid someone was going to try and take them away from her again. The nurses did try before, but she would find the pills and then yell at everyone. They finally gave up."

"So what are you going to do with them?" Janice asked.

I stood up and walked into the bathroom. "What I should have done the last day I saw her." I poured the pills into the toilet bowl and flushed them down. Then I slipped the bottle into the pocket of my sweater. "I'll throw this away at home."

I had the strangest sense that I'd been given the

opportunity to step back in time, to do what I should have done days ago, and even though my mother was no longer there, it mattered. That one small act mattered. I looked around my mother's room – at the stack of magazines by her bed, the end tables by the small couch arranged perfectly with a silver framed photo of her parents, and another of Hale and me when we were babies. There were a few antique snuff bottles and shallow dishes meant for nothing except decoration. There were no pictures of my father. The room could have belonged to anyone. To me, there was nothing personal there, nothing that hooked onto a thread inside me and tugged on emotions resting beneath the surface, waiting to be awakened.

Janice was watching me silently. "I just realized," I told her, "that the home my parents created in Manhattan and the home my mother created here never felt like they were homes. They were pretty and stylish, and utterly impersonal."

Janice nodded and looked around. "And don't get me started on the bad feng-shui."

"Please," I laughed. "Don't get started on that." I felt a chill go through me again and I picked up my mother's scent still lingering in the air. "The only times I've felt at home were when I had my own place. Kids should feel like they know what a home is. But I never did. I wonder if it was the same for Hale."

"Ask him," Janice said. "You've been given another chance to have a brother, Tilly. He's the only one who shared your childhood with you."

"I'm not sure we shared it. I think we were just in the same place."

We walked downstairs, through the chaos that Ellen had created in the house, to the garden where the only conversation going on was between Lola and a squirrel. I looked up at the arching branches of the oak tree that had seen generations of humans pass beneath it.

"I wish I had a treehouse I could hide in," I said. "Just for a week or so until all this is over. Oh God, Janice, I have to write a eulogy. What am I going to say?"

Lola raced over to us, barked once as if to say, Pay attention to me, and then returned to the tree and the squirrel.

"Well," Janice said. "There were some nice moments between you and your mother when you were really young, right? She taught you to draw, she encouraged you to imagine what you wanted to draw."

"True…"

"So, talk about those. You only need a few of those moments to fill up a eulogy."

Clouds were moving in. I had a day to figure out what I was going to say about my mother – not Amber, but Charlotte. And a day to plan how I was going to switch the chain around her neck with the one that held my friend's wedding ring, so I could finally have something that belonged to my father.

15.

Hale didn't come that night. I wondered if he knew that Stephen was at my house, and was staying away because of him, or if he had confessed more than he wanted to and made the decision never to show up again. I didn't want to sleep alone, so I asked Stephen to stay over, and we ended up making love soundlessly, acutely aware that Janice was across the hall. My house is hardly sound-proof, so we let our breath stifle our voices. When we fell asleep, clouds were blanketing the stars and when I woke up just after three, I could smell mist drifting through the open window. I got out of bed and tip-toed to the window to look down at the street. There was no car out front.

"Is he there?" Stephen mumbled in a sleepy voice.

"No. Sorry. I tried not to wake you."

The glow of the streetlamps looked shapeless and watery. I slid back into bed beside Stephen and nestled against him.

"I wonder if he'll ever come back," I whispered to him.

"I doubt he'd have gone to all this trouble if he was going to disappear again. I looked up 9/11 and how many fake deaths there were – the more I thought about it, I had a feeling a lot of people probably saw an opportunity to cash in."

"But Hale didn't cash in."

"I know," Stephen said. "His situation is different, but I was curious. So, it turns out there were hundreds, maybe even thousands of attempts to fictionalize someone's death so a supposedly grieving family member could get money. Most commonly, they invented a sibling or a spouse who never even existed. They pretty much always got caught. One guy actually filled out his own death certificate and said he was the brother – there was no brother. But he sat there and put his own information on his death certificate. He was trying to escape a conviction for fraud – for using a fake social security number – and he got caught committing more fraud."

I hadn't thought about the logistics of Hale's new life. "So, if Hale has a new social security number, he's guilty of fraud, right?"

"He is. Pseudocide isn't illegal on its own. But what you have to do to create a new life leads you into illegal acts. He made his choices, Tilly – you can't make it your burden. This is going to unfold however it unfolds."

"Is this where you tell me to take it one day at a time?"

He yawned and wedged the pillow under his head. "Something like that."

I had the pre-dawn hours to myself after Stephen left for the studio; Janice wasn't up yet and Lola was still stretched out on my bed. I walked out into the yard, into an envelope of thick mist, and tried to imagine what the following day was going to be like. People would be weeping over my mother's death, but I still couldn't unearth any tears for her. Would I be regarded as cold or just stoic? And did it really matter anyway? I had to write a suitable eulogy and stand in a church – a house of God – to deliver it. To my knowledge, no one had ever been struck by lightning while giving a eulogy that edited down the complete truth about their relationship with the departed, so I was probably on moderately safe ground if I chose only bright, polished stones from the war-torn fields of our history. I would have to reach back into my oldest memories, when my mother's hands were soft and her eyes didn't turn away.

The last time I set foot in a church was September 14, 2001. President Bush had designated that Friday – three days after the towers crumbled – a National Day of Prayer and Remembrance. Across the country, church bells tolled, and people made their way to places of worship so they could pray and weep and ask God why. In Washington D.C., the president, ex-presidents, cabinet members, Billy Graham, and hundreds of others arrived at the National Cathedral in a rainstorm. A gathering of important people, dressed in black and huddled under umbrellas had come to mourn, just as everyone around the country was doing. I watched some of it on television with my mother before heading out to a service with Janice and her boyfriend Edward. I asked my mother if she wanted to come with me, but she shook her head no and stared at the television screen.

"We are in the middle hour of our grief," President Bush said to the assembled mourners.

My mother made a scoffing sound, "That implies there is an end to it," she said. "It doesn't feel like there is."

I closed the door softly behind me when I left. I was meeting Janice and Edward at a church on 65th and Central Park West; Edward had gone there a few times and liked the minister. The sky was gloved and gray, but no rain fell. Unlike the service in Washington D.C., the New Yorkers who came here hadn't pulled out their best funeral attire. I suppose, by comparison, we were a motley group, but we were bonded by loss and the ragged threads of grief. To look into other people's eyes was to look into my own.

When we stepped into the soft light of the church, into organ music and pieces of daylight through stained glass, I felt tears loosen inside me. By the time we sat down in a pew, I was wiping them from my face. Janice reached over and clutched my hand. Her eyes mirrored mine. Edward had his head bowed, his eyes closed, either deep in prayer or wrestling with sadness.

The minister, in a lilting Irish brogue, spoke gently but powerfully, telling us, "For America this has been a time of fire and ashes and death. It has been a time of horror and unfathomable sorrow. It's also been a time of bravery and heart-wrenching love. So many of those who died called home in their last moments to say, I love you. So many acted courageously, either on the planes or in the towers, trying to prevent more deaths. Now they have been called home to God, leaving us with a loss that can't be filled and grief that can't be calmed. It is in dark times such as this when our faith is tested, when we are asked to look beyond this world for the peace that can't be found here."

I looked around the church as he was speaking and thought that New York felt like one huge heartbroken family. It wouldn't have seemed strange to put my arms around anyone there or to accept an embrace from one of them. I wondered, fleetingly, how long it would last. How long would it take for us to slip back into who we were accustomed to being, and start being strangers to each other again?

The minister spoke of the salve of prayer and the strength of love. He said the thousands who died were now cradled in the arms of God. We bowed our heads in prayer and joined our voices in singing Amazing Grace. And then we walked out into the pale, muted day to a life that would never be what it once was.

When I came back to my mother's apartment later that afternoon, I had the feeling that someone else had been there. There were two coffee cups in the kitchen sink and an unrecognizable scent in the air. Her housekeeper was off for the day, so my mother was the sole source of information, but when I asked her if she'd had any visitors, she said, "No," and then turned back to the television where President Bush was speaking through a bullhorn in the wreckage of the World Trade Center. He had flown into the city that afternoon. I didn't believe her, but I couldn't figure out why she would lie to me about such a simple thing. Now I think Ian probably came by and she wanted to keep it to herself.

Janice got up just after the sky lightened. After I made us some breakfast we walked Lola in mist so thick we had to blow-dry all three of us when we came back to the house. Rain was forecast for the following day, and I couldn't help but be amused that a storm was blowing in on the day of my mother's funeral. The woman who hated rain would be laid to rest as it fell, proving I think that God has a sense of humor. The day folded around us, white and timeless. Janice worked on her laptop; she was designing some rooms for a new client. I retreated to my work room, did some touch-ups on my painting, and finally sat down to work on my eulogy.

What I wanted to say came to me when I was brightening the moon in my painting. There was a full moon the night my mother took on the role of Tooth Fairy after I lost my first tooth. I'd almost swallowed it. I bit into a piece of chicken at the dinner table and one of my lower front teeth came out. It had been loose, so it wasn't a complete surprise, but it scared me, and I remembered how my father came over to my chair and stroked my hair, explaining to me that big girl teeth were pushing out the baby teeth.

"The Tooth Fairy will put money under your pillow every time you lose a tooth," he told me.

That night, with moonlight slicing past the window shades, I woke up when I heard my door open. But I kept my eyes mostly closed except for a slit because I wanted to see the Tooth Fairy. I saw instead my mother, a pale blue satin robe wrapped around her and a dollar bill in her hand, which she gently slipped under my pillow. Then she blew me a kiss and tip-toed out. I didn't care about the dollar, or about learning there wasn't really a Tooth Fairy. I cared that my mother loved me enough to tip-toe into my room in the dead of night and blow me a kiss. Hale was three years old then; already, there were moments when I'd felt my mother leaving me – waving her hand for me to go away while she was cooing over Hale. But that night, in moonlight and magic, she told me she still loved me.

Janice was right – there were other moments. Wintry afternoons when it was too cold to go outside so my mother sat me at the dining room table with paper and nubby pieces of charcoal; she would tell me to close my eyes, see what pictures sprang up in my mind, and then draw them. There were summer days on the beach in the Hamptons when Hale was still a toddler and my mother held my hand, leading me into the shallow waves, both of us laughing when we got splashed.

I was on the second draft of my eulogy when the doorbell rang. Janice came in and asked if she should get the door.

"That's okay. I'll get it," I told her.

I was thinking it might be Martin but when I looked through the peephole, I saw Dylan standing there. Stephen had told me she was coming in that evening, and it was a little before noon.

"Dylan! This is a surprise – I thought you were coming in tonight."

Dylan has Stephen's coloring – sandy hair and hazel eyes. Her hair was still sandy on top, but she'd died the bottom half of her tresses a bright shade of blue. She was wearing ripped jeans and a baggy sweater that did nothing to conceal a bandage across her collarbone. A small suitcase was beside her feet.

"I took an earlier flight," she said. "I had to get away from my mom. Dad said he was going to call you and tell you. He told me to come over here 'cause I don't have a key to his house."

I suddenly realized I hadn't checked my phone in hours. I wasn't even sure what room it was in. "I spaced out," I said. "I was working and my phone's somewhere around here, obviously not near me. Come in – it's good to see you. What's with the bandage?"

Lola was trotting down the stairs, followed by Janice, who stopped in her tracks when Dylan said, "I got a tattoo. That's what made my mom explode. Want to see it?" She lifted the bandage gingerly to reveal the lacy shape of a spider web hugging her collarbone.

"Oh God, I can't get away from them!" Janice said.

"She has a current boyfriend with lots of ink," I explained. "It's sort of an issue."

Janice extended her hand to Dylan. "Hi, I'm Janice,"

"Right. Tilly's friend from New York. She's talked about you."

Lola wasn't getting enough attention so she jumped up on Dylan and licked her arm. Dylan laughed and bent down to pet her. She suddenly looked younger – much younger than she thought she was.

I motioned Dylan toward the kitchen. "Why don't we fix some lunch and we can catch up. Janice can tell you why she doesn't like tattoos, which is probably an entirely different set of reasons than your mother has. But first, I have to find my phone."

Stephen had called twice and texted me too. I texted him back, apologized for being away from my phone and told him his daughter had arrived safely and was at my house. Ellen had also left several messages – about what time the limo was coming the next day, had I written my eulogy, how we would go directly from the service to the burial, and then to the house. Suddenly the day that felt slow and dreamy had gotten awfully busy.

Janice and I fixed soup and sandwiches, and Dylan filled us in on her act of rebellion. "My friend who's a little older than me already has her driver's license, so we went to a tattoo place her brother knew about and we both got one. She got an eel and I got this spider web. Then my mother blew her top. She said I was going to look like I belonged in a gang and I'd have trouble getting a job when I was older. She made it sound like the Apocalypse."

"Your friend got a tattoo of an eel?" Janice said. "Who wants an eel on them?"

"She's going to be a marine biologist."

"See?" I said to Janice. "There's an explanation for everything. Okay, Dylan, maybe your mom was being a tad dramatic, but you are young to be doing something this permanent. If you want it removed down the line, it's going to leave marks, so it is kind of permanent."

"I like ink. I want more," she said. "I want one arm covered. Maybe not completely, but like half a sleeve."

I thought Janice was going to implode. "Honey! Think about when you want to go somewhere really dressy and you have a beautiful evening gown on. Maybe some hot actor invites you to the Oscars. And there you are in your elegant dress all inked up like a motorcycle chic."

"She definitely does not like tattoos," I told Dylan. "But, pursuing another version of that scenario, what about a somber occasion like – I don't know – a funeral. It could look out of place. So, did you bring a dress for tomorrow or do we have to go shopping?"

"I brought one. A black dress. Like Dad told me to."

"Is it sleeveless?"

Dylan nodded, clearly wondering where I was going with this.

"Perfect! Okay then, I have an idea," I told them. "Everyone get your stuff, we're driving over to Venice. Lola, you're coming too."

I went upstairs to get shoes and a sweater, and Janice bounded after me, grabbing my arm and hissing, "Please tell me we are not going to a tattoo parlor."

"Not a real one. I know a girl who does henna tattoos. She does piercings too, but we won't tell Dylan that. Anyway, she can get an idea of what it's like to be as inked up as she's describing. It might cure her of the notion. Or, cement it further, but I can't control the outcome. I can just try this method."

"Stephen's going to be so mad at you."

"Not if it works."

As we got closer to the ocean the mist was so thick I had to turn on the windshield wipers. Lola started whining excitedly when she smelled the sea, probably thinking we were going to go play on the sand. She gave me a puzzled look when we parked on a narrow street and headed for a storefront with 'Montana Sky's' painted above the doorway.

"That's her name," I told Janice and Dylan – Montana Sky."

"Seriously?" Janice said.

"Well, I'm sure it wasn't her birth name." In a low voice I added, "Weird how many people in my life have altered their identities, huh?"

Wind chimes sounded our entrance into the small

space that smelled like Patchouli and was filled with shelves of essential oils, some Buddha figures and New Age books. There was a display of earrings and necklaces that immediately got Dylan's attention. Montana was bent over a man in khakis and an Oxford shirt, piercing his ear. She glanced up.

"Hey, Tilly – I'm almost done here. Be right with you."

Montana Sky is one of those women who could morph into anything. She looks like a bohemian version of Marla Maples. If you took her out of her faded jeans and loose velvet top, removed the dozen bracelets from her arm and blow-dried her hair smooth, then put her in a designer dress and heels, she'd look like she was to the manner born. I never asked her what her background was, but I had suspicions that she came from tea parties and holidays in Switzerland. I also had the sense that she'd gone through a few other identities – maybe a biker groupie or a Goth girl.

The man in khakis stood up and looked in the mirror. "Perfect," he said as he took out his wallet. "Thanks Montana."

After he paid her and walked out, I said, "He doesn't look like a guy who'd get pierced."

Montana laughed. "He's a stockbroker by day but he has a wilder life at night. Trust me, he has other piercings you don't want to know about. So, what brings you in?"

Dylan was still looking at the necklaces, and I was hoping she hadn't heard the conversation about hidden piercings. "Well, Dylan over there is my boyfriend's daughter. She just got a tattoo – a real one – and before she follows her bliss and inks up the rest of her body, I thought she should get a henna tattoo – you know, just to see how she feels about it, and see what other people's reactions will be."

"Sure, we can do that."

Dylan had walked over and Montana said, "Hey Dylan, I'm Montana. So, do you have an idea of what kind of tattoo you want? I can do a henna version, that way you can see if it's really what you want."

"I want a half sleeve," Dylan told her. "Over my shoulder and down to my elbow. And I'd like vines and foliage and a tiger face peering out."

"At least she isn't getting a sea urchin or a puffer fish," Janice said.

"Or a spider to go in the web that's already there," I added. "Okay, Dylan, this is my treat. Go for it."

Janice and I walked Lola up the street toward the ocean while Dylan was getting decorated. I called Ellen back and tried to answer her questions as briefly as I could. Then I called Rachel and asked if she could walk Lola for me the next day, as it was going to be a long time before I could get home.

"I think I've taken care of everything now," I said to Janice.

"Yeah? Have you taken care of yourself?"

"Not sure. I'm having trouble defining what that means. I was just starting to grapple with all the dimensions of my mother dying when Hale showed up...undead. You know, they have rehab for everything, but I don't think there's anything for this."

We ducked into shops, got coffees to go, killing time. When we returned, Montana was putting the finishing touches on a Bengal tiger looking out from a tangle of green vines.

"Wow," I said. "That definitely makes a statement. It's beautiful, Montana. I'm not sure her father will think so, but we'll see."

"Don't get it wet for a few hours," Montana told Dylan as she rang up my credit card.

Dylan was smiling like she'd just gotten a new car. "Absolutely not. I'll take good care of this."

My plan could backfire, I thought. I might have unearthed an addict to ink who would end up covering half her body before she turned twenty-one. On the other hand, she might feel uncomfortable the next day in her black dress, one of many mourners at a funeral, but the only one with a tiger emblazoned on her arm.

16.

Stephen hugged Dylan before noticing that her bare shoulder, revealed above her slouchy sweater, was covered in vines. He was already prepared for the spider web – his ex-wife had told him – but he was visibly confused by the extensive artwork on her left arm.

"It's fake," I told him, rushing in to save the day before he could say anything. He'd come straight from the studio and we were in my backyard where Dylan had been throwing a tennis ball for Lola. "It's a henna tattoo."

He stared at me, still trying to piece this together. "Okay…Cindy only told me about the real one."

"That's because I just got it today," Dylan said, tugging her sweater down on that side so he could see the tiger.

Janice gave me an I-told-you-so look and retreated into the house.

"Stephen," I said, "she had this set in her mind. I figured, better to have a fake one so she can get a taste of what it might be like to be inked up like that. It might not seem so desirable after all. You know? She might miss seeing her skin."

He slipped his arm through mine and led me into the house, leaving Dylan to play with Lola, safely out of hearing range. Once inside, he said, "Is this your idea of aversion therapy?"

"Well, that is a commonly used practice for breaking people of certain addictions, so it could work. Not that she's an addict, but then again, we don't really know if she is. Look, she's going to be at the funeral tomorrow and people are going to react however they react – I imagine it's going to be a fairly conservative gathering. So, my thought was – my hope is – that she'll decide that much ink is too extreme. She'd obviously been thinking about it for a while, Stephen, she knew exactly what she wanted. I mean, she didn't even hesitate. If it's any consolation, her friend – her tattoo buddy – got an eel inked on her. So, at least a tiger is more appealing…aesthetically speaking."

"I'm not sure comparing images of wildlife is an effective argument, Tilly."

"It's a creative one."

I knew Janice was lurking in the kitchen listening to us. It's what I would have done.

"I just wish you'd asked me," Stephen said, clearly growing tired of the conversation.

"You'd have said no."

"Probably."

"Well, that's why I didn't ask you," I told him.

He didn't actually roll his eyes, but I knew he wanted to.

We all agreed to spend the night at Stephen's house. He had enough bedrooms for everyone, and none of us wanted to be separated – especially me, the night before I was about to say a final goodbye to my mother, the woman who had commandeered my life so effectively that I was never able to imagine her dying. I kind of assumed she'd live forever.

We had dinner delivered from a nearby restaurant and Stephen discovered something else new about his daughter – she'd become a vegetarian.

"I don't eat anything that thinks and dreams," Dylan told us.

"Wow," Janice said. "What a beautiful way of putting it. God, I hope they don't discover that broccoli has a brain."

Janice had dimmed the lights in Stephen's dining room and put candles on the table. One of the things I love about her is that she transforms every place she's in -- softening it, melting the edges with candlelight and subtle rearrangements of décor, angling furniture to create spaces for conversation. Stephen opened an expensive bottle of wine, Lola and Travis circled the table hoping for dropped food, and it didn't feel as if Death's echo was waiting outside. But I knew it was. The next day, I would touch my mother one last time. I would lift her head up and remove my father's wedding ring, replacing it with an imitation. My last gesture would be one of dishonesty. My fingerprints would be on the back of her head and my guess was that no tears would fall from me onto her frozen expression. So far I felt no guilt, but I wondered if it would bloom inside me once my hand closed around the cool gold of my father's ring.

Through soft light I watched how Stephen interacted with Dylan – how his love for her infused each moment between them. When she reached over playfully and took a sip of his wine, he watched her calmly, taking note of how her mouth turned down and puckered at the taste.

"Like it?" he asked.

"Not really," she said.

"Good, 'cause you're cut off. One sip's the limit. You can have another sip when you turn twenty-one."

There was an easiness between them that I had never known with my father. Our dinner table never felt like this. The lights were brighter, the air stiff with uncertainty. My father would talk about big, important things like the economy of the country, and my mother would talk about who she had lunch with, who was getting divorced, a charity she had lent her name to and wanted them to give money to. Hale would sometimes make them laugh and I would push food around on my plate, feeling invisible.

Martin called while we were eating to ask what time he should be at my house in the morning. I told him the limo was coming at 9:30, but I urged him to come earlier, have breakfast or at least coffee. I was hoping he'd confide in me, tell me about his diagnosis.

It was late when we went to bed. The night was thick with the coming storm, and damp air drifted through the window that Stephen always kept open in his bedroom, except for those times when rain slanted in. I tried to not think about Hale, and whether or not he would come by my house in the still hours after midnight, but it was hard to push him out of my mind. He was always there at the edge of darkness.

I was lying close to Stephen, my cheek against his shoulder, when he stirred a little and said, "I have a theory about why you wanted to help Dylan get all painted up with a fake tattoo."

I lifted myself up on my elbow and squinted through the dark at Stephen, trying to read his face. "And that would be?"

"I think you're taking a perverse delight in having her go to your mother's funeral with a tattooed arm that no one is going to miss seeing. It's sort of your last act of rebellion."

I slid back down to his shoulder and thought about what he was saying. "You're probably right. Ellen is definitely not going to be happy, which will, of course, make me happy. Even though I do have more sympathy for her now that I know her story, but she's still a pain in the ass, and she'll probably end up writing a book about her years with Amber Austin. Then we'll have to endure seeing her do interviews on TV. Anyway, your diagnosis is spot on, Dr. Freud. Although I do also think it might make Dylan re-consider the whole tattoo thing."

"I actually prefer to be Carl Jung. I'm not really in the Freud camp," Stephen said. His voice was getting sleepy.

"Noted. Goodnight, Carl. And by the way, I'm not sure it's my LAST act of rebellion, but it's a good one. One I'll look back on years from now when I need something to smile about."

I wasn't surprised when my eyes opened a few minutes after three – it had become a habit. I slipped out of bed and looked out the window to the dampening street below. I didn't expect to see Hale, but I knew this ritual had folded itself into my nights. As I got back into bed, I had an image of Hale observing my mother's funeral from across a field of tombstones and monuments, scared to come closer but unable to stay away.

I fell into a dream in which I was running up a dark

stairway filled with smoke and crowded with people running down. I was the only one heading up the stairs and I was trying to find Hale; I was yelling his name, but my voice could barely be heard over the sound of the building coming apart at the seams. Then I saw him right ahead of me, running down. He got close to me, I yelled out his name again and reached for him, but he only glanced at me and kept going. His eyes were those of a stranger and for a moment, in my dream, I wondered if it was really him, or just a man who resembled him.

It was just past five when I woke up. The dream had left me nervous and thready. I heard the tapping of rain outside, the edge of the storm that was moving in. Lola and Travis were wedged against each other, asleep at Stephen's feet. None of them woke up when I slid out of bed and tip-toed through the dark to the stairs. I needed to sit in the quiet kitchen with a cup of tea and work some more on my eulogy. I had only made a brief mention of 9/11, but after my dream that didn't seem right. That one day, inked in blue memories -- its terror, its canyon of loss, its uncaring sky -- was a dividing line in my mother's life. It marked the end of her days as Charlotte Austin and allowed Amber to whisper in - a phantom who she would breathe life into, a character she composed, who she would embellish with light and pretty colors. Amber was her way out of the ashes. Thousands of people had their lives cleaved into Before and After. But I don't know how many of them decided to become a different person.

17.

We gathered at my house to have breakfast, drink coffee, and wait for Martin and the limo. Rain was falling steadily, and the gun-metal sky let us know the storm was going to get worse. Rachel came over with a raincoat for Dylan – I'd called her earlier with that particular fashion emergency -- and she decided to stay until we left so that she could walk Lola. Ellen called me three times in the space of an hour to remind me of everything I already knew – the pickup time, the fact that we were going back to my mother's house after the burial, and a reminder that there would be press at the service but not at the gravesite or at her house. I had the gold chain with Gabe's ring on it in my purse along with my printed eulogy, and I told Stephen I was going to ask for a few minutes alone with my mother's body to switch the ring.

"You don't want me to stay with you?" he asked me.

"No, I think this is a crime I have to do solo."

Martin arrived with the first clap of thunder. "Hey, what an entrance," Stephen joked, giving him a quick man-hug. I introduced him to Angela and Dylan and then steered him into the kitchen, hoping for some time alone with him.

"Want some coffee?" I asked him.

"No, I quit caffeine. Doctor's orders." He was giving me a serious look. "Did Stephen tell you about my diagnosis?"

Lying to him felt remarkably easy. "No. He didn't tell me about anything like that. What diagnosis?"

"I have a leaky valve in my heart and I'm going to have to get it fixed one way or the other – replaced, repaired – there are different opinions on which is best apparently. I'm scared, Tilly. Not just of the surgery. My dad died of a heart attack at sixty-seven."

I closed the distance between us and wrapped my arms around him. "You're going to be fine, Martin. I think this is pretty common and they'll fix it. Don't be scared, okay? Fear's probably worse for your heart than caffeine. I know Stephen obviously isn't a real doctor, but he has done a lot of research. He's pretty knowledgeable, so he might know the questions you should ask – when you do see a real doctor again."

"Yeah, we talked about that. I'm sorry, Tilly – this isn't the time to dump my problems on you. It's the day of your mother's funeral for God's sake, and here I am talking about myself."

Janice called out that the limo had just pulled up. I gave Martin another hug. "You can talk to me anytime about anything, Martin."

We grabbed umbrellas, put on our raincoats, and as Dylan was putting on the coat Rachel had loaned her, Martin noticed the Bengal tiger emblazoned on her arm.

"Impressive ink," he said.

Dylan's face lit up. "Thanks. It's actually henna but maybe someday it'll be a real one."

Stephen nudged me and I did my best to ignore him.

The driver was standing outside the car beneath a huge umbrella. He was a tall, muscular black man who looked as if he used to play football. "My name's Albert," he said in a resonant voice. "I'm very sorry for your loss, Ms. Austin. There's water in the back, and if you need the temperature changed, let me know."

Once we were in the limo, Martin said to Dylan, "If you were in New Zealand, and were part of the Maori culture, you'd have tattoos done with chisels made from albatross bone and then filled in with colored dyes. It's called Ta Moko. But unless you're Maori, you can't get one, it's considered disrespectful."

"How do you know this?" Janice asked. I know she was probably wondering if Martin had some forbidden chisel marks on his body somewhere.

"I went to New Zealand years ago. It's magical. There is a Kauri tree that's three thousand years old. The Maori believe huge trunks of the Kauri trees hold up the sky. I gotta tell you, I had a little culture shock when I came back to Manhattan. I kept wishing I was back in the rainforest there."

Martin and I had come together years ago on a ruined landscape. We both felt hollowed out by loss. We held onto each other until we felt healed enough to walk on our own. I thought I knew him. I thought I had let him know me. But maybe it was only a relationship of wounds – of need and loneliness – and maybe that was enough at the time. The image of him in a rainforest standing in awe of an ancient tree that was worshipped by a culture so different from his own was one I struggled to understand. It made me realize that I didn't really know him at all. The world we had shared was narrow, framed by ghost towers and littered with ash and rubble. It was a world where voices echoed, where the lives we once thought were ours fluttered away like the white pages brushing across collapsed buildings, drifting down empty streets. Now I had a chance to get to know Martin in the clean air of another world -- not as lovers, not as wounded veterans of a war we didn't ask for, but as friends.

"Dylan's a cool name," Martin said. "I like that name for a girl."

Stephen smiled and Dylan rolled her eyes conspicuously.

"According to my mother," she said, "I'm named after Dylan Thomas – she liked his poetry. I'm not crazy about being named after a drunk guy who died in the gutter choking on his own vomit."

Janice leaned forward. "Actually," she said to Dylan, "that's been debunked. Not the drinking part – he did drink quite a bit – but how he died. It's basically accepted now that he died of a heart attack."

"In a gutter?" Dylan asked, unwilling to let go of her resentment.

"Don't think so. Possibly on the sidewalk, but not in the gutter. Honey, he was brilliant. You should read A Child's Christmas in Wales. You'd like it, I think. Everyone has something wrong with them. So, he liked to drink a little too much, that doesn't mean he wasn't an incredible writer. It's an honor to be named after him."

Rain slashed the car windows and no one spoke for a long time, each of us lost in our own thoughts. I felt time slipping past me, in the sound of tires on the wet road, in the pressure of Stephen's arm against mine, in the ending of lives and the return of my brother whose death I had once accepted, made peace with. I would bury my mother on this day, and I would keep waking long before dawn to look for Hale. Time is often measured by the tears we cry, by laughter that lingers on the wind, and by the echo of goodbyes. We walk with people – family, friends, lovers – through shadows and sunlight. Seasons wash over us, and it's only when they're gone that we realize how brief those times were.

We pulled up to the chapel-like building on the cemetery grounds and I saw Ellen standing beside Ian under the overhang beside the door. A hearse was waiting to transport my mother's casket to the church, and another limo was behind it, I assumed for Ellen and Ian. There was no press there, no crowd of on-lookers. I knew they were all at the church. But suddenly the loneliness of what I was seeing hit me. I was the only family member, and it would be a funeral procession of only three cars, one of them the hearse. Each of my parents had died alone – one falling to his death through miles of air as buildings burned behind him, and the other slipping away in the folds of night. My mother had a lot of social friends, most of whom would probably attend her funeral, but no one came to visit her when she was ill, when chemo stole her beauty, her hair, and her hope. I looked at the small band of people around me – maybe I could break the chain of loneliness that had linked generations of my family. Rain fell around us as we huddled beneath umbrellas and hurried into the chapel.

Once inside, I made the appropriate introductions to Ellen and Ian, feeling something catch in me when I introduced Ian as a "family friend." Is there a name for the man who had an affair with your mother and fathered your brother? There should be. I wondered, if we weren't there to bury my mother, would I say something to Ian about what I now knew? Would I confront him? I didn't know, but I was pretty sure that whatever he might say to me wouldn't change a thing.

Ellen led us through a room, where larger families probably gather, to a small back room. The lighting was low and warm, coating the dark wood-paneled walls with a soft glow. My mother's casket was on a stand and placed against the back wall. A man in a shiny black suit was standing near it; I assumed he worked at the funeral home.

"There's time for everyone to pay their respects," Ellen said. "And then we'll go to the church."

"Would you like me to open the casket now?" the man asked.

Ellen and Ian turned to me. Apparently as the only family member I actually did have a say in things. "Sure. Okay."

My mother's skin was pale and plumped up, no more blue veins and deep lines. Her wig was perfect, as was her make-up. She looked ten years younger. I suddenly remembered an interview with Whoopi Goldberg, who talked about how, in her younger years, she worked at a mortuary putting makeup on dead bodies. "How was that?" the interviewer asked. "Quiet," she answered.

Ellen had chosen for my mother a coral pink dress, the color of many of the skies in her paintings. And there, resting on her chest, was the gold chain with my father's ring on it. Everyone seemed to be waiting for me, so I moved up beside the casket and Stephen fell into line behind me. I was starting to get nervous, knowing I'd have to be convincing, after everyone had filed by, in saying that I wanted a few moments alone with her. I leaned over her body, as if I were saying something to her, but the truth was I had nothing to say. As I moved away, letting the others file past, I noticed tears spilling from Ellen's eyes.

When it was her turn at the casket, she touched the pale, unreal looking hand that rested on my mother's abdomen, leaned over so far that her hair brushed my mother's face, and said, "Thank you, Amber, for taking me into your life and your heart. I'll always love you."

I glanced at Stephen who gave me a warning look in response – a look that said, Hold your tongue and behave.

Ian was the last in line. He didn't touch her, but bent over slightly and said, "I'll miss you, my friend."

Ellen put her shoulders back, cleared her throat, and was about to move us out. This was my moment; it would be my only chance. Before she could speak, I said, "I'd just like a moment or two alone with my mother, please." I looked straight at Ellen and added, "I'm sure you understand."

"Of course," she said, and made a motion toward the door for everyone to file out. The man in the black suit was the last to leave.

Quickly, I got the chain with Gabe's ring from my purse and returned to my mother's body – her embalmed, unreal looking body. I needed both hands to remove the chain she was wearing, so I set the replacement on her chest. I had to somehow disengage from the fact that I was handling a dead body – my mother's dead body. I tried to only focus on small parts of her – the piece of fabric where I set Gabe's ring, the side of her neck where my hand would have to travel to lift her head. I half imagined her eyes snapping open, even though I knew they couldn't. They were glued shut – Stephen told me that's what they do in the embalming process. And she was, after all, gone. I had to remind myself of that, and I knew that for the rest of my life there would be moments when I'd have to tell myself again that my mother was no longer here.

I slipped my hand under her neck, trying to be careful about her wig, and lifted her head enough for me to maneuver the chain off of her. Bryan was right – her head was heavier than I anticipated. I set her head back down and put the chain with my father's ring on it into my jacket pocket. Then I lifted her again to decorate her with Gabe's wedding ring. I accidentally jostled her wig a little and was just straightening it when the door opened and Ellen said, "Tilly, we have to go in a few minutes."

My breath wouldn't go all the way down, it seemed to catch just below my throat. I tried to level out my voice, conceal the fact that I was terrified. "Okay. I'm done. I just needed these last few minutes with her."

I was so grateful when the black-suited man bustled in and closed the lid of the casket, I could have kissed him. Then three other men came in and they began wheeling her toward the door. I lingered, thinking that it would look more appropriate if I followed behind.

When I came out of the room I collided with Stephen. His eyes were brimming with questions. I gave him a quick nod and took his arm as we followed behind the casket and got our umbrellas. As we were getting into the limo he whispered, "Everything go okay?"

"It did." I was so aware of the chain and ring in my pocket, it almost seemed like they were weighing down that side of my body. I slipped my hand into my pocket, ran the chain through my fingers, and touched the smooth surface of my father's ring. The metal was cold; even my touch couldn't warm it.

I wasn't expecting the trembling that began deep inside me as we sat silently in the limo, waiting for them to load the casket into the hearse. It started in my stomach and within seconds my hands were visibly shaking. Stephen put his hands over mine and Janice looped her arm around my shoulders.

"Hey honey, it's okay. That was hard, huh, being alone with her like that?" she said to me.

I nodded, trying to breathe away the trembling. "I'll be fine," I managed to say. I had told Janice about my plan to switch the chain – I couldn't keep it from her -- but she was being careful to not say anything in front of Dylan and Martin.

My hand remembered the feel of my mother's head, and my eyes had seen more than I wanted them to. The way the makeup on her chest was so thick there were fine cracks in it. The narrow edge of a white bra strap showing at the neckline of her dress. It seemed so strange to me, that they would put lingerie on a corpse. I looked out the window at rain streaking the glass, like the tears I couldn't cry, and remembered, years ago, when I trembled just like this and Stephen had managed to soothe me. We were walking Lola on a Saturday afternoon when she suddenly lunged at a squirrel. She caught me off-guard and I fell, slicing my thigh on a tree root. When we got home, Stephen cleaned it and said we had to have it looked at, because I probably needed stitches.

"No!" I wailed. "I don't want to go to a hospital! I don't care if I have a scar."

"We'll go to Urgent Care. It's less scary," he said, completely calm in the face of my mild hysteria.

At Urgent Care, they numbed the area and put five stitches in the wound, but even though I couldn't feel anything, I began trembling. Stephen held me, stroked my face and arms until the shaking subsided.

"The body knows it's being invaded," he explained to me as we drove home. "Even though you can't actually feel it, the body still knows."

So, although I had tried to focus only on what I was doing in the mortuary – replacing the chain around my mother's neck with an imposter – something deeper and achingly unresolved rose up inside me and refused to be ignored. My mother frightened me, even in death. Her ability to make me feel unmoored, unimportant, unmemorable, lived on even though she lay dead in a mahogany casket, dressed in a sunset-pink dress and a perfectly coifed wig.

The Methodist Church was alive with press vans and on-lookers standing on the other side of a stretched-out rope. They were in raincoats and slickers, holding umbrellas, undoubtedly uncomfortable with the rain pouring down, but determined to watch Amber Austin's coffin be unloaded and carried into the church.

Martin and Dylan were sitting in the jump seats and Martin leaned forward, looking out at the contained chaos outside the safe confines of the limo. "I guess it's show time, folks."

Dylan laughed a little, but it was a nervous laugh. Stephen reached across and squeezed her wrist. "You'll be fine. Stick with us."

Janice took hold of my arm and said, "Before we get out, I'm going to help you with this shaking." She put one hand on the right side of my neck and the other on my left arm and squeezed just hard enough that I felt pulses beneath the pressure of her hands. "Tell me when the pulses match up and feel like one," she said. Everyone, even Albert, was staring. After about a minute I did feel them unite into one pulse. And at that instant, I stopped trembling.

Stephen's eyes got wide, and he stared at Janice. "What did you just do?" he asked her.

"It's called Jin-Shin. You should look it up. Maybe you could slip it into one of your episodes."

"Can it cure Dylan of her love for tattoos?"

"Nice try, Dad," Dylan said.

I started to laugh, but Albert was opening our door, Ellen was waiting for us, and cameras were going off. I was suddenly aware that every facial expression was going to be witnessed and laughing as I arrived at my mother's funeral would not be a good idea. Stephen's hand was on the small of my back, they were unloading the casket from the back of the hearse, and Ellen was talking way too fast.

"You're going to follow the casket into the church, down the aisle, and then take your seats to the right, in the first row – Tilly, are you listening to me?"

"Yes. Right side, first row."

The storm had darkened the day, and the sea of umbrellas between the church and the parking lot looked like something I'd want to paint. Very few faces were visible, just bodies in rain gear and umbrellas scraping against each other in the thick air. As I stared in that direction, I saw a flash of maroon as a car entered the parking lot. Would Hale show up here? Nothing seemed impossible to me now.

Stephen's hand nudged me as we filed into the church

behind my mother's casket. The church was large and modern, and completely filled. I thought I recognized a few people from my mother's Christmas Eve parties, but other than Ian, I didn't really know anyone. A minister in robes was at the front of the church, positioned between a huge Crucifix, complete with Jesus' wounded body, and my mother's casket, which had now been opened. Dylan leaned across Stephen and gave me a wide-eyed look.

"I thought that was just for back there. Opening it, I mean," she whispered.

"She wanted an open casket," I whispered back.

Dylan sat back and then took off her raincoat, letting the tiger on her arm have its time in the spotlight. I glanced at Ellen, who was sitting on the end of the opposite pew and saw her do a very subtle double-take. Stephen kept his eyes focused straight ahead; I assumed he'd probably decided to just remove himself from the tattoo debate.

The minister spoke about Amber Austin as if he had known her, mentioning her talent, her graciousness, and what he called her "incredible bravery" in the face of cancer. Maybe he did know her – I had no idea. My attention slipped away from him and I remembered going into Saint Patrick's cathedral with my father after his parents died. My mother didn't come, neither did Hale; it was just the two of us. My father held my hand and led me into a pew where he knelt and closed his eyes.

"I need to pray for my parents' souls," he told me, letting go of my hand.

I remember feeling like he was leaving me, he was so deep inside himself, and my hand felt the absence of his – a rush of cold air across my palm emphasizing that his hands had a more important duty, to fold together in prayer. My history with my family was littered with moments of loneliness, some when my parents were right beside me. I could smell my father's cologne as he spoke silently to God, but I knew he was far away. By that time in our lives my mother's eyes would brush across me, never lingering, moving quickly to wherever Hale was and seeming to memorize every angle of him.

I'd heard people talk about feeling like they were in a movie, like whatever was going on around them wasn't real and any minute the set would be dismantled and they would return to their ordinary life. For the first time, I knew what they were talking about. I heard people sniffling behind me, I stood up and dutifully sang the hymn we were asked to sing, I listened to Ellen's tearful eulogy detailing how much of a mother my mother was to her, but none of it seemed real. It wasn't until Ian walked up to give his eulogy that the fog lifted and I inhabited the space I'd been given in this odd setting. My mother was dead, her body was on public display, my father's wedding ring was in my pocket, and the man who fathered my brother was speaking about my mother as if they were merely close friends who had shared years of companionship and had waded through a season of grief together.

"On that awful day of 9/11," Ian was saying, his voice cracking slightly, "I came over to wait with her for news of Keith and Hale. News that never came. On that day and the days that followed, I stood in admiration of her strength and her willingness to go on, even though the path ahead was lonely and seemed very dark."

I glanced at Janice. So, he did go over to the apartment that day – yet another thing I didn't know. Hale's name slipped so easily from his mouth, as if he had forgotten that Hale was his son. Did my mother tell him what had happened that morning? That she had finally disclosed their affair, that my father now knew that Hale was really Ian's son? There wasn't just a body in that polished mahogany casket, there were unanswered questions that would probably haunt me forever. I took my printed eulogy out of my purse. The paper felt warm to me and I suddenly caught the scent of roses, even though I saw none in the church. It was the scent of my childhood – the aromatic ghost of our stately, fashionable apartment.

Ian and I brushed past each other as I made my way to the front but I couldn't look at him. I also knew I could not look down at my mother's waxen form. I unfolded the paper and surveyed the sea of strangers in front of me. The only people I recognized were in the front rows. I hadn't shared my eulogy with anyone – not Stephen, not Janice. I had written it alone, in the gray light of a rainy day and in the darkness of a pre-dawn world. My last words about my mother were composed from the solitariness I had inherited from my years as her daughter.

"I'm Charlotte Austin's daughter," I began. "Charlotte Austin is how I will remember my mother and it's Charlotte I want to tell you about. We lived on the Upper Eastside in Manhattan, on the fifteenth floor. When I was a child and it was too rainy to go to Central Park, my mother would sit me at the kitchen table with a large artists' pad and a piece of charcoal – no crayons for me. She told me to close my eyes and imagine a picture I wanted to see. Imagine it, she said, and then let your hand draw it. Her own charcoal drawings of cottages and gardens were often pinned to the refrigerator with magnets. She would usually stand behind me with her hand resting on my shoulder as I drew, whispering encouragement. I hung onto her words as my hand found its way and as I learned to create images on paper. I felt the weight of her hand long after she stopped reaching for me.

"I wish I could tell you I knew my mother well, but I can't. There were moments when I thought maybe I might be able to – moments when we moved closer to each other. In the long weeks and months after the towers fell on that horrible September day, when the loss of my father and brother was like a cold wind blowing across us, we sometimes came together for warmth, for comfort. In those arctic days, we shared an unbearable loss, one that words couldn't capture. Although at times my mother tried -- by unspooling chapters of her history with my father, her memories of Hale when he was a baby. I was more than a witness to her grief, I was her companion on a road no one ever wants to travel down.

Manhattan was filled with people trapped in their own private corridors of grief, their own stories. We were one of those stories." I glanced over at Janice and Martin.

"At some point in those ragged days after," I continued, "with loss still defining every hour, every moment, Charlotte decided to become Amber. I realized I didn't have a prayer of getting close to Amber Austin. She protected herself with pretty colors and cheerful paintings. She defended herself against the past by painting a lovely future for herself. We never again spoke of the family we once were, the family members we lost. We traveled across the country and settled on a cordial relationship, far away from the life we once lived. But what I will always have are the memories of winter days when frost glazed the windows, and my mother taught me to believe that what my imagination created, my hands could duplicate. I will always have the memory of her tiptoeing into my room late at night, pretending to be the Tooth Fairy and slipping a dollar bill under my pillow for the tooth I'd just lost. I pretended to be sleeping but I saw her linger and smile down at me. I nourished myself on that image for weeks after.

"Maybe what's true, for all of us, is that the moments we have shared with others remain in the corners and vestibules of our souls. And when death comes, it loosens the boundaries of life and time, setting free everything we'd been forgetting to look at. Even things we forgot happened. I have more memories than I realized, and I will treasure them. I hope my mother is at peace now. And I hope God welcomed her as Charlotte."

I kept my eyes on Stephen as I descended the steps and returned to the pew. The tears in his eyes were a lifeline pulling me away from the past – from the quicksand of my history and the scent of roses, from careful rooms and unspoken words – into a wide green field where being free seemed possible.

18.

We waited in the limo for them to load the casket into the hearse, and then the procession of three cars headed through the rain back to the cemetery. Janice slipped her arm across my shoulders and said, "I'm so proud of you – that was really powerful."

"It definitely brought me to tears," Martin said.

Stephen was holding my hand and he squeezed it as he gave me a long look that said more than words could. My other hand was in my pocket, holding onto my father's wedding ring, trying to warm the cold metal. Trying to bring life to the chill of death.

"That must have been really hard," Dylan said, "not being able to get close to your mother."

"It was ...challenging," I told her.

She gave Stephen a long look. "I should be nicer to Mom, huh? I mean, I know she tries really hard."

"Yes, you should," Stephen answered. "You might not get along all the time, but you're really lucky to have a mother who's so invested in your life, and who thinks about you all the time." He turned to me then. "Look at that. An unexpected benefit of your eulogy."

Dylan nodded slowly; her brow was furrowed and her face was a study in seriousness.

I saw a flash of lightning in a far corner of the sky and within a few seconds thunder rumbled behind the clouds. I wondered how it would feel to know that your mother thought about you all the time. It was like wondering what it would be like to be Russian, or Portuguese – it was that foreign to me.

Dylan was still deep in thought. "So, you must have felt kind of alone, huh?" she asked me. "I mean if your mother was so distant and everything."

"It's a little like living in a house with no foundation," I told her. "You don't feel very secure. But you know what,

Dylan? People have come into my life and built a foundation under me. Three of them are right here in this car. So, love still came to me, I just had to wait a little while for it."

"Were you a sad kid?" she asked.

"Yeah. I was."

We drove into the cemetery grounds, our small funeral procession. Ellen had told me that it would be only us at the burial, and I saw up ahead that metal posts and a tarp had been erected over a freshly turned plot of earth; a small grouping of chairs had been placed beneath the tarp.

The rain had turned light and steady as we huddled there; the coffin was poised above the section of broken ground. The minister, who had ridden with Ellen and Ian, said a prayer, and Ellen placed a white rose on top of the coffin. For a moment, I felt self-conscious – should I have brought a flower, a memento, or maybe an olive branch and sent it into the earth with my mother's body? I knew Stephen would tell me to stop dwelling on things like that, so I stopped. I watched as the polished mahogany casket was lowered into the ground. A small shovel was nearby for the ritual of tossing dirt onto the coffin. Ian went first, and I was trying to read his face, but he was as impenetrable as he had been all morning. The shovel felt warm in my hands when it was my turn. Dirt clattered onto the wood.

It was the second time in my life I had participated in this ritual. At my grandmother's service, my mother passed the shovel to me, and the image of her dry eyes and her straight-lined mouth floated into my mind. There is something primitive about spilling dirt onto the lid of a coffin, a testament to returning that person to the earth, where their remains will not endure, but will eventually decay. The earth has its way with all of us. My father's parents were cremated, and I recall thinking that it was a more civilized choice. The messiness is handled ahead of time; the goodbye feels cleaner somehow.

Outside my mother's gates, a private security vehicle

was parked, and as our two cars approached, a man got out and, holding an umbrella over himself, hit the opener and allowed the gates to part for us. We were following Ellen and Ian's car, and just as we were about to drive through, I saw Hale's car about ten yards away from the gates, parked along the shoulder of the road.

"Wait – stop!" I said sharply.

Albert hit the brakes, and everyone looked at me. Stephen followed my gaze and saw what I was looking at. As I was reaching for an umbrella, I suddenly remembered that Martin didn't know about Hale.

"I need to get out of the car," I said, my words coming so fast there was little room for breath. "But Martin, I have to tell you this and I'm so sorry to drop this on you right now, but he said to not tell anyone, so I didn't, but then Janice came downstairs…"

"Tilly," Martin snapped, as if I'd lost my mind, "what the hell are you talking about?"

"Hale's alive – I'm sorry, we'll talk more about it, but I have to get out."

I scrambled over Stephen's legs, opened the car door, and stepped out into the slant of rain. I walked as quickly as I could on the wet asphalt, trying not to trip in the heels I hardly ever wore, and when I got to Hale's car, he stepped out and stood facing me in the rain.

"I want to come in there," he said. "I want to speak to my father."

"Right. Okay. Well, that makes sense – I mean as much sense as anything can make right now. Hale, Martin's with us."

He got under the umbrella with me. "I know. I was outside the church. I saw him."

Just as we turned to go back to the limo, Martin came racing toward us, knocked Hale to the ground and punched him. He was pulling his arm back to hit him again when Albert appeared, swooped down on Martin and pulled him off Hale as if he were a rag doll who weighed nothing. Blood streamed from Hale's nose, mixed with rain and ran down his face, soaking into his blue shirt. He struggled to his feet just as Martin, who was still being held by Albert, screamed, "You mother-fucker! Pretending to be dead all these years! I was your best friend!" His voice was breaking. Tears streamed from his eyes.

Stephen, Janice and Dylan had now raced over to us and none of them had grabbed an umbrella. Mine was the only one and it seemed like I should put it over Hale since he was bleeding. Albert had his arms locked around Martin's chest.

"Calm down, man," he said, and miraculously Martin did.

"I'm going to let you go now," Albert told him, "but if you throw another punch I'm gonna grab you again. Trust me, it will not work out well for you."

Martin nodded yes and Albert released him. We were all drenched with rain now. Stephen took a handkerchief from his pocket and put it against Hale's nose. "I don't think it's broken," he said. "Doesn't look like it anyway. But it'll be swollen. And sore."

"Good thing he hits like a girl," Hale said.

Which could have caused another fight, but Martin was still crying. "Why?" he managed to say. "Why'd you do it?"

Before Hale could answer, Albert said, "Listen -- all of you get back in the car. It's raining in case you didn't notice. And I just ruined my brand-new suit. I think the only rag I have in there is what I use to wipe off the windshield, and I'm using it for myself. You all have to find some towels inside."

I let Hale take my umbrella and steered Janice under it -- her mascara was starting to run down her face. It didn't really cover all three of us, but we were already soaked anyway. I felt awful for Albert as we piled back into the limo – not only had he ruined his suit but the back of the car looked like a wave had crashed through the windows, there was so much water inside. Martin was still crying.

"I don't get it, Hale. How could you do something like

that? I'm sorry I hit you – really. But I don't understand."

Hale lifted the handkerchief from his nose, checked to see if it was still bleeding, which it was, although it had lessened. "Martin, my life had fallen apart that morning. I found out that my dad wasn't really my dad."

"What the fuck are you talking about, man?"

"My father wasn't really my father. Ian is my father. My mother told Dad that morning and then he told me. I survived when the plane hit because I was on a lower floor, but I didn't want to survive. I couldn't be Hale Austin anymore. I just kept walking…"

Martin froze, as if he had to play this over in his mind a few times. Finally, he said, "So who are you now?"

"Richard Buchanan."

Dylan shook her head dramatically. "Wow dude, that is seriously fucked up," she said.

"Language, Dylan," Stephen told her.

"Sorry. But it is."

When we pulled up to the house, I saw that six or seven cars had already driven in. "Listen, you guys," I said to them, "we need to go upstairs and find some towels. So that we can at least try to look presentable. And we need to clean some of that blood off your face, Hale."

Albert opened the car door and stood there under his huge umbrella, but the damage to his suit was already done. Stephen put his hand on Albert's arm and said, "I want to get your contact information. I'm going to buy you a new suit."

I imagined Albert going home that night and saying to his family, 'Man, I drove these crazy white people today. They were out there punching it out in the rain, and one of them was supposed to be dead all these years but he isn't. And they're at the funeral for someone else who really is dead. All that drama, with none of 'em having the sense God gave 'em to get out of the rain.'

Luckily, no one was manning the front door, so the minute we stepped in, I pointed to the stairs. We had to duck under the rope Ellen had strung across and I was too nervous to turn back and see if anyone had noticed us. At the top of the stairs I turned my group of water-logged guests down the hall to the linen closet.

"Let's hope Ellen hasn't cleaned this out yet."

She hadn't. There were three shelves stacked with expensive Turkish towels, which I handed out. The closed door to our left was my mother's room. OUR mother's room, I reminded myself. I had a brother again. It was also the closest bathroom.

"Hale – or Richard – or whatever I'm supposed to call you -- come in here with me," I told him. "I'll clean the blood off your face."

The room still held her scent. He followed me into the bathroom where her perfume bottles were still on the counter. I soaked a washcloth with water and started dabbing at the blood on his face. I saw in my brother's body language the coil of anger deep beneath his skin, and I thought it might have always been there. I'd assumed, my whole life, that Hale had it easier than I did, that as the favored child his life had been free of wound, but maybe our mother's adoration of him did damage that I hadn't recognized.

"This was our mother's bedroom," I said. "She died in her bed in there."

"I know."

I stopped wiping away his blood and stared at him. "What do you mean, you know?"

Janice stuck her head in. "Tilly, I need to fix my face in the mirror."

"Yeah, come in. Hale was just telling me that he knows this was our mother's room."

As Janice brushed past me to get to the sink, she said, "Your family has more secrets than King Tut's tomb."

"Out with it, Hale," I snapped. I couldn't adjust to calling him Richard.

"I visited her that evening. The night she died. Earlier, around five. I'd been thinking about it since I read months ago that she was being treated for cancer. It took me all that time to decide if I wanted to let her know I was alive. When I buzzed the gate, I told the housekeeper that I was an old friend from New York, and I pulled out the name of someone from her social circle in Manhattan so she'd say to let me in. It worked. I sat right here and talked with her for a little while – maybe half an hour. She didn't look well. I didn't know how sick she'd been – the press stories hadn't really given details, you know? Anyway, I was afraid the shock had worn her out, so I left."

"Well, it definitely may have worn her out since she died that night." I said. I regretted my words as soon as they left my mouth, but before I could apologize, hard high-heeled steps came toward the bathroom door and flung it open.

Ellen's face was red with anger and her eyes were narrowed into slits. "Tilly, what the hell are all of you doing up here? And what the hell happened to you? Did the limo break down and you had to walk here in the rain? My God, you look like a bunch of drowned rats!" She seemed to just notice Hale then and said, "And who are you?"

"I'm Amber's son. Tilly's brother."

Ellen took two deep breaths and then rolled her eyes. "Amber's son. The son who died on 9/11? Do you think I'm a fucking idiot?"

"I can't answer that," Hale said. "I don't really know you well enough."

"I'm afraid he's telling the truth, Ellen," I told her. "About who he is. I just found out recently. And I didn't know he was going to show up today. So, big surprise all the way around!"

Stephen, Martin and Dylan were now crowded just outside the bathroom door, an audience for Ellen's imminent explosion.

"Tilly, you just have to ruin everything, don't you? You can't even memorialize your own mother without making a scene! You bring in some bloodied guy who says he's your brother who isn't dead after all, and a girl with tattoos all over her! What is the matter with you? You're not normal!"

I don't know why I suddenly felt calm, but with no tension in my voice I said, "To be clear, Ellen, we are memorializing my mother. In the most appropriate way possible. You knew Amber. You did not know my mother."

Ellen began taking big heaving breaths and her face crumpled as she burst into tears. Stephen moved toward her and put his arm around her shoulders. "Ellen, come sit down, you're going to hyperventilate." He led her out of the bathroom over to the bed where he made her sit. I wondered if the sound of her sobbing would travel all the way downstairs.

Hale walked past all of us and said, "I'm going to go down there and talk to my father."

"Your father?" Ellen screamed. "Are you telling me he's alive too?"

I leaned down close to Ellen. "No. His father is a different father than mine. My mother's husband – my father – did die on 9/11."

Ellen looked at me with the most pathetic face – streaked with tears, red with anger and upset and confusion. "What? I can't even understand what you just said. God, you can't even explain things in a logical way!"

I thought of Hale going down to confront Ian with black-clad mourners standing around. "I should go downstairs. I have no idea what's going to happen. Janice, maybe you can try your – thing -- on her. The jen whatever it is."

"Jin-shin," Janice said, moving to the other side of Ellen. "I can try."

"I'll stay here with her until she calms down," Stephen said.

"Okay then." I hooked my arm through Dylan's and motioned to Martin. "You two are coming with me. And, Dylan, if you want a sip of wine, you can have one."

Hale hadn't gotten far. He was half-concealed behind a tall potted Palm in the entryway.

"Having second thoughts?" I asked him.

He shook his head. "Just trying to get up the nerve."

"Well, I'll go with you. This kind of affects me too." I realized how odd it must sound to Dylan that I felt I had to justify standing by my brother's side.

Hale didn't acknowledge what I'd said; he started moving through the clusters of guests – more people had arrived while we were upstairs. I followed, with Dylan beside me and Martin trailing us. There were sideways looks at the disheveled man with blood spots on his shirt, but no one stopped him. Ian was at the far end of what had been my mother's well-appointed living room, but which now resembled a ballroom. I saw him notice Hale from the corner of his eye, and then turn toward him. I saw his face grow pale and his eyes sink to the floor, as if not looking might make his son disappear. Hale stopped in front of him. A tall blonde woman in a perfectly tailored black suit who had been talking with Ian slipped away quickly, wanting nothing to do with whatever this was.

"Surprised to see me, Ian?" Hale said. "Or should I call you Dad?"

19.

Ian's mouth opened and then closed, as if speaking were an errant thought that quickly fled. Hale filled the silence between them.

"You look like you're seeing a ghost, Ian," Hale said in a low voice. Other conversations buzzed around us, seemingly oblivious to the unfolding drama. "I know how that feels. That morning, when Dad told me you were my real father I felt like a ghost. I felt like Hale Austin was some false life I'd been stuffed into and suddenly it had been stripped away and there I was, wondering how I was ever going to make sense of all the lies. I felt like I was dead. I was here, I could see my body, but I wasn't sure who I'd see looking back at me in a mirror. And then the planes hit and there was death all around me, and I decided the only way to figure out how to live was to pretend I died."

Ian took a step forward so that he was less than a foot from Hale's face. "How?" he whispered. "How are you alive?"

"I wasn't on the 103rd floor. I was on the fourth. I got out and kept walking."

"But all these years…And your mother believing you'd died…It broke her heart."

"Hey, you don't get to pull the self-righteous card on me, Ian. Faking my death is trivial compared to what you did."

Tears were balanced in Ian's eyes. "Hale, I'm so sorry. We didn't know what to do once we were sure you were my son. Your mother had your DNA tested and she was emphatic that we keep it a secret. I've never been sure why, after all those years, she suddenly decided Keith should know. Why that morning? Why at all? I just don't know. Maybe it was always her plan to tell the truth when you were an adult."

My mother and her plans, I thought – concocted in some secret cavern of her mind and shared with no one. She was both general and army, strategist and a battalion of one. As much as I disliked Ian for his betrayal of my father, and for his secrecy, I felt sorry for him at that moment. He had a son who he had never acknowledged, who he then believed died in the hell-fires of 9/11. Now, on the day he helped bury the woman who bore his child and bound him in lies, that son was standing in front of him, bloodstained and angry, forever imprisoning him in his past.

"I don't know why I wanted to come here today," Hale said. "I guess I thought maybe one moment of completely raw truth might make all the lies weigh less. Because I still carry them around, even after eighteen years. I try to inhabit this new life – I'm Richard Buchanan now – that's what I wake up as, that's what everyone knows me as. But for twenty years I believed I was someone else. I believed I was Keith Austin's son. I believed I was conceived out of love, that my parents were..." He stopped and I saw tears poised in his eyes. "I don't want to be your son, Ian. What kind of man fucks his best friend's wife and then just keeps showing up for holidays and dinners as if nothing happened? You know what the craziest thing is? Part of me wishes you and my mother had just kept up the lie. I could have been happy being ignorant."

Stephen and Janice had come downstairs and moved in around me like a protective army. Martin was hanging back, as if he didn't know where he belonged in this unexpected drama. I heard behind us a woman say in a low voice to her husband, "That man is probably with the tattooed girl. So disrespectful of them to show up like that, and what is all over his shirt? Is that blood?"

Before Stephen could stop me, I turned to them and said, "Yes – he gave her a tattoo and she removed his tonsils. We always do this at funerals. It's a family ritual."

"Tilly," Stephen said, grabbing my arm. "You're not helping the situation."

Hale and Ian were just staring at each other – father and son from different galaxies. I looked around and saw someone missing.

"Where's Ellen?" I asked.

"She said she needed a drink," Janice said. "I sort of managed to calm her down, but I don't think she really wants to calm down."

I saw her then, walking purposefully toward us, holding a glass in her hand that was half-filled with what I assumed to be Scotch. Rain was falling hard outside the windows and the room had filled with mourners in black who hadn't bothered with my mother when she was ill and dying, but who wouldn't have missed her funeral.

"Tilly," Ellen said, coming close and breathing Scotch on me, "I really think you and your party should leave now. This is very inappropriate. People are going to start noticing."

"Me and my party, Ellen? This isn't a restaurant you own, this is my mother's house." I glanced at Hale. "Our mother's house. But you know what – we'll go. God forbid anyone should figure out that things were not exactly perfect in the Austin household."

I started to reach for Hale, to touch his arm, but he turned abruptly and brushed past us, his eyes focused straight ahead, seeming to see nothing but the door that would close behind him once he stepped out into the rain. Ian's eyes were full of wound. If he had hoped for forgiveness that hope was just killed.

As we made our way across the room, I realized that people had noticed Hale – perhaps not before but definitely as he exited. A woman who I vaguely recognized from my mother's Christmas Eve parties took hold of my arm, her flame-red nails pressing into my bicep.

"I'm so sorry for your loss, dear," she said.

"Thank you."

"Lucille Sykes. We've met at your mother's gatherings." Her blonde chin length hair was so lacquered it didn't move at all when her head turned. "Was that young man with you? He seemed very upset."

I tried to decipher what was going on behind her words and her heavily made-up eyes, but she had a good poker face.

"Well, everyone is upset after a funeral," I said. "Excuse me, but we're heading out. Nice to see you again. Thank you for coming."

Stephen whispered to me, "Do you really remember her?"

"Sort of. But I think she has many clones, or many relatives who look just like her. If I ever do that to my hair when I get old, please euthanize me."

At the front door, we collected our umbrellas. Albert noticed us and stepped out of the limo, opening his oversized umbrella and standing beneath it. Suddenly, Martin yelled, "Hale, wait up!"

Midway down the long driveway, Hale was walking back to the road where he'd left his car. He gave no indication he'd heard Martin.

"I need to talk to him," Martin said as he took off running in Hale's direction, his open umbrella bobbing behind him, doing nothing to keep him dry.

"Are we going to wait for him?" Albert asked in a dry tone. I could read his eyes. He was thinking, Here we go again.

Dylan and Janice had already gotten into the limo. I looked at Stephen who shrugged and let me know it was my call.

"Let's see if he's standing out in the rain when we get up there," I told Albert. "We'll figure it out then. Sorry – you must think we're completely nuts."

"They always give me the crazy ones. I just didn't peg you all for being quite this crazy." He smiled when he said it, but I had no doubt that he meant every word.

As we started up the long driveway, I saw Hale and Martin up ahead, walking together, hunched beneath the umbrella. I memorized the image of Hale and Martin walking away from me in the rain. I knew I'd return to it, on days far away from this one, when questions still haunted me.

188

20.

When we got to the gate, Martin was getting into Hale's car. I suddenly thought, I have no idea when I'll see either of them again.

"I guess we'll be going home without Martin," I said, mostly to Albert.

The sky was pale to the north, as if the storm was thinning out. I felt Martin's absence in the car just as I had always felt Hale's.

"Did he tell you how he accomplished being someone else, all these years?" Janice asked. "I was wondering about that. I mean, he presumably has a driver's license. You need a birth certificate for that."

I shook my head no. "We didn't get around to that."

Dylan pulled her raincoat tight around her, as if she'd suddenly gotten chilled. "So, you have no way of getting in touch with your brother?" she asked me.

"No. If he has a cell-phone he didn't give me the number. So far, he's just been showing up at three in the morning – although not every night, just some nights. The nights of his choosing."

"Was your family always this weird?"

"Dylan!" Stephen said sharply. "That's a rude thing to say."

"Sorry."

"No, it's okay," I said. "The girl knows weird when she sees it. And yes, I would have to say we were always hovering outside of normal. Wouldn't you say so, Janice?"

Janice laughed. "I guess." Then she turned serious. "It just always seemed like you all had been dropped into some play with no script to guide you. Like family was a totally foreign concept."

I felt my own history wash over me. "Well put. And true."

When we got back to my house, Stephen got Albert's information, including his suit size, and said he'd have a new suit delivered to him in a few days. He also tipped him a hundred dollars, even though Ellen told us the tip had been taken care of. Rachel opened the door for us and Lola burst out as if I'd been gone for days.

"I walked her a couple of times between rain showers," Rachel said. "And I brought you guys a pan of homemade eggplant parmesan. It's thawed out, you just need to put it in the oven."

"Thank you," I said, hugging her. "I owe you."

"No, I'm happy to help." She gave me a serious look. "Just take care of yourself, please? Don't let yourself get all shredded by…everything."

That evening, as Janice and I fixed a salad and rich smells floated around us, as Dylan and Stephen's voices trailed into the kitchen from the living room, I wished my house could always have this much life in it. Janice would be going back to New York the next day and Dylan would be leaving as well. I realized that loneliness had yawned inside me throughout my life. Growing up in Manhattan, in our busy east-side life, my parents' social gatherings and holiday events would bustle around me, but I always felt alone, invisible. If I'd slipped out with the caterers and stowed away on their truck, I wasn't sure anyone would have noticed I was gone.

"You okay?" Janice asked me. We were standing at the kitchen counter with lettuce and vegetables piled on cutting boards.

"Yeah. Why?"

"Because you've been scooping out that same avocado for five minutes."

"Oh." I looked down at the empty shell I'd been scraping. "It's just that I'm going to miss you when you leave. When everyone's gone and my house is quiet again. The past few days this place has felt so warm and busy, and full." Tears came without warning and I was helpless to stop them.

Janice put down the paring knife and wrapped her arms around me. "Honey, you do know that you and Stephen sticking to this separate houses thing is silly – right? You've been together for years, and I don't think he's the one who's insisting on this arrangement."

I nodded, trying to squeeze words out of my throat that now felt thick with sobs. "I've just been alone for all my life. Even when it didn't seem like I was alone, I was. Inside me, that's how it's always been. It felt safer that way. And it doesn't make me happy, but I don't think I know how to change."

"No one knows how to change," Janice said. Her voice was low and soothing. "You just do it. You just take a big leap and trust you'll land safely. Tilly, I know how deep your mother's judgements got carved into you – she made you feel like you weren't worth anything. But that was her problem, it really had nothing to do with you. You were just in the line of fire. You buried her today. You need to bury her inside you."

I heard footsteps and Stephen walked in, stopping short when he saw my face. "Oh. Sorry...I'm interrupting something serious."

I wiped my face with my sleeve. "It's okay. I'm okay. Really."

He kissed my forehead and wiped the remaining tears from my cheeks. "Martin called. He's taking an Uber over here. Hale is...well, I don't know actually what Hale is doing, but he isn't with Martin."

I nodded and forced a smile, but I knew it wasn't convincing. Janice grabbed a placemat and silverware and handed them to Stephen. "Can you add another setting to the table?" When he went into the dining room, she gave me a serious look. "You need to really open up to him about how you feel and why this war is going on in you. You need to, Tilly. He deserves that."

"You're right, I know you're right."

I looked at Stephen in the dining room, carefully placing silverware on the table. I looked at his back, imagining how I would feel if he were walking away from me for good, if he no longer had patience for me and the last image I had of him was his back. The thought sent an ache traveling through the center of my body. Maybe he'd thought the same thing I did – that when my mother died, my fears would loosen and the history that had chained me for decades would relax its grip.

When I opened the front door for Martin, I saw stars glinting through the pine trees that line the street. The storm had broken and left drifting clouds behind. The air smelled like wet soil and the sea. I hugged Martin and thought how familiar his body and his scent were to me. My father's ring pressed into my skin; I was wearing it beneath my sweater. Since only Stephen and Janice knew about my piracy I figured it would always be the secret talisman I hid under clothes, out of everyone's sight.

"I know you have a million questions," Martin said, pulling back from my arms and stepping inside the house. "But I need a glass of wine first."

"Absolutely. Follow me."

In the kitchen, Janice playfully inspected his knuckles, making sure he hadn't slugged Hale again, and Stephen gave him a quick man-hug and asked him how he was feeling. I thought again how much life there was inside the walls of my home on this post-funeral night, and how I would miss that when quiet returned.

Over dinner, Martin told us how he and Hale had driven down to the beach, sat in the car while rain fell, and talked about the day that changed everything.

"He was so blind-sided when your father told him," Martin said, his eyes serious and boring into me. "It was like some horrible dream he wasn't sure he'd ever wake up from. He said he felt hatred for your mother – for her infidelity, her lies, but also for revealing the truth to your father after twenty years. He thought, at that point, it would have been kinder for her to have just maintained the lie. So, there he was, looking at the man he always thought was his father and learning that they were not father and son. And probably the biggest wound was seeing in his father's eyes a distance and a rejection that cut him to the bone. Add to that, he was at the company Ian owned, so he was basically working for Ian that day…I don't know if he'd want me to share this, but I'm going to. He said there were times afterward when he wished he really had died in the towers."

Janice shook her head and stared into her wine glass. "He felt like he'd been erased. He wanted to start a new life but how could he do that after two decades of lies? The life he'd lived up to that point must have seemed meaningless to him."

"That's rough," Stephen said.

"So how did he do it?" Dylan asked. "I mean, in a movie he'd go to some shady person and buy a new identity, I guess. But is that really what happens?"

"Basically," Martin told her. "You get the identity of someone who's died. That's when you start breaking the law. Using a false social security number, a false birth certificate. It sounds like Hale has been pretty careful, though. The woman he lives with owns a vineyard in Santa Barbara and he works with her, but he doesn't have a bank account, he isn't technically employed, so he doesn't have to file a tax return. She basically supports him, although he does run the place with her."

"But he has a driver's license, right?" Stephen asked.

"He does. So, he broke the law there. What really surprised me was when he said Tara helped him right after 9/11. Gave him money, helped him get out of Manhattan."

"Tara?" I said. "So, she knew that he hadn't died, but she came over to grieve with us? Wow, that was some act."

I remembered Tara's face etched with tears and sorrow, and how she stayed mostly quiet, as if losing Hale had thrown her world off its axis. Oddly, I recalled her hand delicately resting on my mother's hand as she said that somehow all of us would get through this.

"Maybe it wasn't totally an act," Martin said. "She had

to make a decision about whether or not she'd stay with Hale, live a lie with him. Live in secrecy somewhere other than New York. Ultimately, she couldn't do it. So, she did lose him, just not in the way everyone thought. Anyway, she gave him some money, and she did what he asked – she sold the Rolex his father had given him for his eighteenth birthday. Obviously, he couldn't do it himself. And then she got him to some motel outside the city. From there he took buses across the country."

Hale used to wear that watch every day. He must have suddenly seen it as an emblem of betrayal and dishonesty. I thought back to when he reached the magic age of eighteen. He had a string of parties thrown for him by college friends and one given by our parents, which was the only one I was invited to. I remembered my mother trying to be hip and relevant, talking to Hale's friends about music she knew nothing about and clubs she'd never been to. They were very patient with her, although I suspect there were some laughs at her expense afterward. Late in the evening, my father gave him a small black box and Hale gasped when he opened it and saw the gold Rolex shining up at him. It wasn't just the watch, though, it was the pride he felt his father was bestowing on him. How it must have crushed him to see a different look in Keith Austin's eyes on that clear Fall day just hours before the world around them shattered.

Dylan looked around at everyone, as if she didn't know who to direct her comment to. "It must be awfully isolating and lonely pretending you're dead. I mean, you can't talk to anyone you used to know, so you don't really have anyone in your life. And when you meet new people, you can't share your past with them. Everything you do and say has to be a lie."

Martin nodded. "I think he's still lonely, even though the woman he's with does know and it sounds like they're happy together. Still, he's had to make up a whole life that never happened. He said he went to a therapist for a while and was treated for PTSD."

Dylan, the youngest among us, had extracted a splinter

of truth that went straight into my heart. I found myself wondering how he kept it together, an anonymous person on a bus as America rushed past the windows – highways and farms and lakes, people with lives and families. Did he look out at windows lit up warm in the night and wonder if he would ever have a home? I've spent years painting shadowy figures with no faces while Hale has been living a faceless life. He'd adopted a dead man's name as his own, and presumably invented a past from scraps of other people's stories.

"Did he give you any way of reaching him?" Stephen asked Martin. "A cell number?"

"Nope. He took my number and I gave him yours, Tilly. He just seems so mistrustful, which I guess is understandable, but you'd think after eighteen years he'd have learned to trust a little. Although I don't know if time passing makes a difference in something like this." He paused and gave me a look I couldn't decipher. Then he said, "He told me something that I'm not sure I should be telling you, but I'm going to. The day years ago when he came down here and sat outside your mother's house…it was a Sunday, and you were visiting -"

"He said he followed me home, that's how he figured out where I lived."

"Yeah, but he didn't just mark down the address and leave. He sat in his car for a long time, debating whether or not he wanted to knock on your door. He even got out of the car once. But in the end, he said he felt too guilty. He just couldn't face you. He couldn't face what he'd done. He didn't say it, but I think when your mother died, he was somehow able to move away from some of that guilt. It's like he was freed somehow."

Stephen reached over and squeezed my hand. Janice shook her head slowly and said quietly, "Boy, your mother had such power over both of you."

The last time I was in New York, Martin and I went to the 9/11 Memorial. We stood quietly with the sound of falling water around us, each of us lost in our own thoughts. He had already been to the Memorial and knew where Hale and my father's names were. My fingers traced the letters of their names etched in cold black stone. This is what's left of you, I thought. We started to go downstairs to the Museum, but something inside me panicked and I couldn't do it.

"It's okay," Martin said soothingly. "I understand."

We returned to the trees and water, to a pale sky that had a thin layer of fog over the blue I didn't want to see. We lingered there with the weight of memories and the ache that never really goes away. Maybe another time, I thought, I'll be able to go downstairs to where my father and Hale were on a massive wall with the thousands of people who died that day, but today this is all I can do.

When Martin left my house, he said he'd be back at noon the next day to pick Janice up. The hard reality of everyone leaving hit me again and Stephen noticed my eyes tearing up.

"You're becoming very sentimental these days," he teased.

"I know. This was really fun with everyone here. Which is a weird thing to say when the reason for everyone visiting was a funeral, but still…we had fun."

After Stephen and Dylan went back to his house, Janice and I quietly cleaned up the dinner dishes, each of us lost in our own thoughts. When we took Lola out to the backyard for her night-time pee, the sky was a patchwork of stars.

"The storm's gone," Janice said, her head tilted up to the heavens.

"Yeah. And the rain might not have done much good. The Santa Ana winds are supposed to start blowing soon."

"So, what do I do about Hale, Janice? I have a brother again. He's alive, he came looking for me, but I don't know what he wants. Hell, I don't even know who he is."

"I think you have to let him call the shots, Tilly. You really have no other choice. Maybe you'll get to know who he is now. Or maybe you'll look at the past differently."

"Is there some re-arrangement of furniture that will help me with this?"

Janice laughed softly. "Sadly, no. But don't put that mirror back up in the guest room. Or in any bedroom."

Standing in the clean dark with my best friend and my dog who was pressed affectionately against my legs, I was acutely aware of how unsettled I felt. I was balanced on an edge of memory, and I didn't want to slide down the back of it into a world I had tried to leave behind. But we never really leave the past behind. I will always be the girl who lay awake on long nights and listened for her brother's breathing in the next room. I used to think, if I could match my breathing to his, then perhaps I could be more like him – more outgoing, funnier, a child my parents could love. I was the dark child, the girl whose charcoal drawings were becoming more and more dense, as if in my world it was always night. I was the girl in the shadows long before I began painting shadows. Hale blazed with a light that our parents nurtured and bathed in. He made friends easily and always had stories to share. I used to practice smiling in the mirror, wondering if I could arrange my features to look more like my brother's. Eventually, I claimed the shadows I was drawn to, accepting that they were part of me and, when they became a trademark of my art, I trusted that there were people in the world like me. People who would look at my paintings and say, Ah, someone else who hides from the light.

Now Hale was back from the dead, and there was no more light coming from him. His shadows were even deeper than mine and he seemed imprisoned by them. I didn't know how to figure him out. Worst of all, I didn't know if I wanted to. It was easier to grieve his absence, simpler to have lost my brother in the smoke and ash of crumbled buildings. It was much harder, and more painful, to feel the loss of him when he was right in front of me.

21

The call came a little after seven the next morning. It had just gotten light out and I was going to walk Lola. Janice was sitting in the living room with a cup of tea. I didn't recognize the number, but I answered because I thought it might be Hale.

"Tilly Austin?" a male voice said.

"Yes…"

"Eric Fogelman from TMZ. I'm very sorry about your mother. My condolences. We heard that your brother attended the event after the service. Your brother Hale who was thought to have died on 9/11?"

I walked into the living room and mouthed 'TMZ' to Janice.

Her eyes got wide. "Uh-oh."

"Um. How exactly did you hear that?" I asked. I didn't know what to do and I thought if I stalled, maybe something would come to me.

"From a family friend."

"Whose family?"

"Ms. Austin, is it true? Is your brother alive?"

"You know what, Eric. I'll get back to you on this. I'll check the guest list and get back to you. 'Bye."

When I hung up, I stared at Janice and ignored Lola who was tugging on her leash. I knew the blood had drained from my face.

"Okay," Janice said in her take-charge voice. "You are to do nothing until you talk to Stephen. He's been in the public eye a long time, he'll have an idea how to handle this. Tilly, do you think it was that woman who spoke to you when we were leaving?"

"Maybe. But it doesn't matter now. The word's out." Lola barked at me. "Okay, Lola. We're going. I'll walk her over to Stephen's. He's probably fixing Sunday breakfast for Dylan."

Janice put down her tea. "I want Sunday breakfast."

"Then get dressed and come with us. We'll invade his house."

Stephen's house smelled like pancakes; the scent engulfed us when he opened the front door. Travis came scampering over to Lola, meowing and rubbing against her. Dylan was in pajamas, sleepy eyed and nursing a cup of coffee. A plate of pancakes was sitting in front of her, so far untouched.

"'Morning," she said. "I don't know why my dad has to get up so early even on Sundays."

"It's healthy to maintain the same sleep schedule," Stephen said, pouring pancake batter into a frying pan. "It's good for your immune system, might help prevent dementia, it relieves stress. Not to mention that you have more productive days."

"I'm not even sixteen, Dad. Why should I be worrying about dementia?"

I waited until we were all sitting at the breakfast table to tell Stephen about the latest development in my on-going family drama.

"So, Stephen, TMZ called me this morning. Someone told them that Hale, my deceased brother, is not deceased after all and, in fact, showed up at our mother's funeral, or more precisely after her funeral."

Stephen doesn't usually look stunned, but his expression was as close to shell-shocked as I'd ever seen it. "That's not good," he said. "What did you tell them?"

Janice laughed. "That she'd look into it and get back to them. I believe her exact words were that she'd check the guest list. Great pancakes, by the way."

"Can't you just tell them it's not true?" Dylan asked.

"It doesn't quite work that way," Stephen said. "My guess is that someone there took a picture of him with their cell phone. TMZ probably wouldn't follow up like that without some kind of proof. It's too bizarre of a story and they wouldn't want to waste their time if they didn't have something tangible. You're going to have to say something, Tilly. If you don't, it'll get bigger."

"But I can't just ruin my brother's life like that. Once I open the door they're going to ask me everything – where does he live, what name does he use."

Stephen's cell phone rang and he looked at the display. "This isn't a good sign. It's my publicist calling me before eight on a Sunday morning." He gave me an ominous look as he answered. "Hey, Vanessa. Happy Sunday. I have a feeling I know why you're calling. TMZ wants to know if Tilly's brother is actually alive and they figured I must know something. Right?"

He listened for a long moment and then said, "Okay, I'll tell her. Have a nice rest of your day."

"So, Tilly, Vanessa is going to tell TMZ that I don't have any comment, but she said pretty much what I said – you need to tell them something. The longer you wait, the more they're going to investigate this."

Dylan had started eating her pancakes, and with her fork poised in midair she said, "Why don't you tell them he had amnesia and he's just starting to come out of it. And then do the whole, please give us some privacy at this difficult time thing?"

Janice said, "You have a very smart daughter, Stephen. I like that suggestion."

Stephen nodded. "It might work for a while, at least to slow them down. And then we'll pray for some huge scandal that'll put this on a remote back burner, and maybe they'll never think about it again."

"Yeah, maybe Ivanka Trump'll get busted for drugs," Dylan said.

Janice laughed. "That would do it."

"Okay, fantasies aside," Stephen said, "I think you should call the guy back now, Tilly, and use Dylan's script."

"Right. Amnesia, and privacy at this time. Got it."

He answered on the first ring. "Fogelman."

"Eric, hi. It's Tilly Austin. We spoke a little earlier…well, I'm sure you remember that. Listen, I just want to say that we're going through a difficult time right now with my brother having suffered from amnesia all these years. He's starting to come out of it, slowly. Very slowly. And we'd just like some privacy at this time."

"I see," Eric said, his voice measured and calm. "Does he live here in Los Angeles?"

"Like I said, we'd like some privacy at this time."

"But he has to have been getting by somehow, like with an assumed name?"

"Once again. And for the last time, we'd like some privacy. 'Bye." I hung up before Eric Fogelman could take another breath.

Everyone was staring at me. "What? That's what you told me to say."

"I know," Stephen said. "The delivery was a bit…I don't know, awkward and panicked sounding. But we can pray for that Ivanka Trump scandal. Or another scandal."

I could feel my face forming into a sulk. "I'm a painter, not an actor."

Stephen got up and bent over me, curling his arms around my neck and kissing the top of my head. "You did fine. It's not easy playing things out in the spotlight." He glanced at the time on his cell phone. "Dylan, we have to leave for the airport in two hours. I know how slowly you can move, so start thinking about getting your stuff together."

When we finished breakfast, Janice and I put our arms around Dylan and said goodbye to her. I felt the now-familiar sadness tugging at me. "Come back soon, okay?" I told her. "By the way, with everything else going on I never asked how you feel now about being inked up?"

Dylan laughed. "You mean did your aversion therapy work?"

"Yes, Miss Smarty-pants. Did it?"

"I don't know. There were so many distractions I haven't given it any thought. But this fake one will last a while longer, so I'll have time to figure it out."

"Make sure you tell your mother it's fake," Stephen said. "Like the minute she sees it."

He walked us to the door and told me he'd come over later in the afternoon after he'd worked on his scenes for the next day. The neighborhood was always quiet on Sunday morning; you could almost feel people sleeping in. The sky was deep blue – the after-rain color, but also the color of the sky on that Tuesday morning so long ago. I always felt awkward when people in Los Angeles would gush over a beautiful blue-sky day because I could never fake enthusiasm. Blue sky will always take me back, always make me think of how nature betrayed us that day, giving us such a lovely sky while horror was splitting wind currents on its way to us.

After Martin and Janice left for the airport, and I commanded myself to dry the tears I hadn't wanted to cry, I set up a clean canvas. I wasn't completely finished with the painting I'd been working on – the firelight needed some touch-ups, and the ice-skates weren't quite right. But I needed to start painting what had imprinted itself in my mind – a sea of black umbrellas, a coffin, and a lone man standing in the rain, watching, with nothing to protect him from the storm.

That's where Stephen found me when he let himself in and came upstairs. I knew from the expression on his face that something was wrong.

"Remember what I said about a photo of Hale?" He handed me his cell phone. "Vanessa just sent me this link. Someone at your mother's house yesterday took Hale's photo and gave it to TMZ."

The headline screamed: BACK FROM THE DEAD. The photo, I could tell, had been taken as Hale walked away from Ian. In fact, I could see part of Ian in the background. Beside it, they had found the photo of Hale that was used in 2001 after the towers fell, in the hope of finding him. They didn't have much of a story, other than the photographic proof that this had to be Hale Austin who had showed up after his mother was buried, and an un-named person's claim that he was there.

"It would be a hell of a lot easier if I had a way of reaching Hale. He wouldn't even give his number to Martin – I asked again before they left for the airport, just in case he'd been sworn to secrecy or something. It feels like a betrayal to talk to anyone about this when Hale's made it pretty clear he wants to hide. But then, he's left us with this mess to explain so what are the options?"

"Was he always this difficult?" Stephen asked.

"You know, I'm not sure. Maybe. I think I made so many decisions about him -- who he was, how our parents felt about him, how he was the favored child – that I might never have figured out who he really is."

We took Lola on her end-of-the-day walk and it was obvious without either of us mentioning it that we were both on alert for any unfamiliar cars, or people jumping out of the bushes with cameras. We decided Stephen would sleep at my house, in case Hale made another three in the morning visit, and we agreed to see if Travis would adjust to a sleep-over.

"We'll try it," Stephen said. "If he rebels, I'll take him home and leave him there. He's so smitten with Lola, he just might adjust to new surroundings."

So often, when we were discussing our animals, I had the distinct feeling we were also talking about ourselves.

By 8:30 that night, we looked like a family that had cohabitated for years. Stephen and I were curled up on the couch watching a rerun of Law and Order, a fire was blazing in the hearth, and Lola and Travis were lying in the warmth of firelight inches from each other. Earlier, when Stephen brought Travis in and let him out of his carrier, Lola immediately began leading him through the house, as if she knew instinctively that he had to get a complete idea of where he was and what was around him. We were trying to keep our eyes open until the end of the episode. One of the things that had immediately bonded us was that Stephen and I are both dawn people; staying up late holds no appeal for us. Early on, Stephen commented that he's in the right line of work, with early studio calls that find him driving through quiet dark streets of the city while morning grows from a thin gray line into a new dawn. "Best time of day," he said. It was one of those moments at the beginning of a relationship when you want to look up and thank the Heavens for bringing you someone who shares with you something as vital as the same sleep schedule.

I jumped when the doorbell rang. My first thought was a reporter, and I know Stephen assumed the same thing.

"I'll go," he said.

I lurked behind him at a distance, watched as he looked through the peephole and, after glancing at me, opened the door and said, "Hale. This is a surprise."

I knew I should have held myself in check, but I was angry. He had once again disrupted a peaceful evening -- whether it was me sleeping in the dead of night, or Stephen and I relaxing in front of the fire, Hale's intrusion changed everything. "Were you booked at 3 AM so you had to move me to this time slot?" I said.

Hale didn't react. Stephen gave me a slightly admonishing look, and motioned for Hale to come in.

"I'm sorry," I said. "It's just that you've created chaos while staying remarkably absent from all the chaos -- leaving it to everyone else to deal with. You're a news story now, in case you didn't know."

Hale brushed his hand through his hair. It was his tell. Whenever he was uncomfortable, or didn't know what to say, he resorted to that gesture. Some of my anger left then; I knew I'd hit the mark and I felt badly for him. I watched as my brother moved awkwardly into my home. Lola trotted out from the living room, sniffed him, accepted a pat on her head, and returned to the fire and her feline paramour. I found myself wondering if Hale had any pets, and how he felt about animals. I didn't know this man. I knew versions of him – pieces of memory that seemed to be missing some vital parts.

Hale had always been more mystery than brother.

Still, we were related. The DNA chain that bound us was indestructible. I looked at Hale taking up space in my home and realized how much space he had always occupied in my life – with both his presence and his absence. Sibling or stranger, he lived inside me. He never allowed me to truly forget I had a brother, even though I had tried.

Stephen poured him a glass of wine and we sat in the living room, with dog and cat nestled by the fire and the sound of wind brushing past the windows.

"I was heading back up north," Hale said. "I didn't make it out of L.A. before Lisa called me and said she'd texted me a link to a news story. My photo was there, and the story was that I'd returned from the dead after my mother died." He glanced at me. "Sorry – our mother, I meant to say."

"We saw the story," I told him.

"I don't know, maybe I wanted to get caught. Be exposed. I've made another life for myself, and that's what I set out to do, but I still feel like I'm a hostage – to that one horrible day, to 20 years of lies that went before that day. Lisa, my partner, is really understanding, but sometimes I feel like she deserves more. When I went to see our mother, I stupidly thought she'd give me an answer about what she told Dad that day – why after twenty years? All she said was, 'It was time.' I mean, what the fuck does that mean?"

Stephen leaned forward and searched Hale's face. "How did you get out of the tower that day?"

In the silence, I heard embers crackling in the fireplace and leaves scratching across the patio. It almost seemed like I could hear our heartbeats, or a star falling outside. Finally, Hale started talking. "We didn't know what it was at first. The sound was so loud and the whole building swayed. I'd gone down to the fourth floor, and someone said it must be a bomb or some kind of explosion. When we ran to the elevators, we realized they were plummeting and crashing. We didn't know yet that fireballs were coming down the elevator shafts. I remember a woman shouting that a plane had flown into the tower somewhere on the upper floors, and someone else was yelling that we had to get down the stairs. By then, the lights were out and all the sprinklers were on. The smell of kerosene was overpowering. We ran for the stairs, but it was pitch black in there and parts of the walls were coming off. So, between all the debris and the sprinklers, four flights was going to take a while. We linked hands, and I remember hearing a woman's voice behind me, praying the 23rd Psalm. We had two flights to go when we heard another explosion – or maybe it was more that we felt it reverberate. It was the South Tower being hit, but we didn't know what it was then. When we got to the lobby…" Hale stopped and took a long sip of his wine. "I'd never seen anything like it. No one had. Elevator doors were blown out, there were burnt people inside them. All the windows were gone, the marble walls were breaking off. There was a woman, completely blackened, no hair, a zipper from whatever clothing she'd had on melted into her skin. A man was pouring water on her from a black plastic trash bag. There were other bodies, almost unrecognizable…but we had to get out…we couldn't help them, they were dead. When we got outside, other people had managed to get out but some were burned and wounded. Firemen were helping them. I saw bodies falling. It sounded like a gun going off every time a body landed." Hale looked at me. "That's when Dad got through on my cell. He could barely talk, he was choking. I told him I got out, and I told him I loved him. He didn't say anything. All these years I've wondered if he heard me. I'll always wonder about that."

"I have to ask this," I said. "Did you think about calling our mother? Or me? Or anyone?"

He shook his head slowly. "I think I already knew I wanted to be dead. I let myself be moved along, away from the towers, and when the South Tower started falling we all ran. That's when I knew I was running away from everything I'd known and running into the blank space of a life I'd have to create. My arm was bleeding a lot. I didn't notice it until I was running away while the South Tower was coming down.

I ripped off my sleeve and tied it over the wound, and then I just started walking. I should have felt lucky that I survived, but I didn't. I hitched a ride with this guy driving a bread truck and went to Tara's. When I started telling her everything, I knew what I had to do. For her to stay with me she'd have had to leave everything she knew, and in the end she couldn't do that. She thought about it, but she couldn't."

"So why did you show up now?" I asked.

He shook his head slowly and finished the wine in his glass. "Like I said, maybe I wanted to finally tell the truth. I have nightmares sometimes – a lot of times – and maybe telling the truth will make them stop."

"Well, you might have to tell the truth to a whole lot of people at this point," Stephen said. "I don't think the story is going to go away."

"I know. I'm sorry, Tilly. I'm sorry to have done this to you."

"Just out of curiosity," I said, "did you apologize to our mother when you went to see her?"

"I did. I said the words, but to be honest it wasn't very sincere. I've just never been able to get past my anger, even after all this time. I really wanted her to come clean with me, to tell me the truth not just about that morning but about Ian. I asked her pointblank if she and Ian were in love. She flicked her hand and said, 'No, nothing like that.' So, I guess I was born from a fling she decided to have with her husband's friend. Makes me wonder why I was the one apologizing."

"She liked conquering people," I told him. "That and blowing things apart. It gave her control."

Stephen stood up and said, "I'm afraid I'm going to have to turn in. I have an early call and being sleepy is not going to make for a good work day."

Hale ran his hand through his hair. "It's getting late. I'll go. I just barged in on you – again."

"Are you going to hit the road tonight?" I asked him. "That might not be such a good idea."

"I'll find a motel. I checked out of the place down near

the beach."

I felt Stephen's eyes boring into me and I knew what he was trying to say – Hale's your brother, don't send him out into the night.

"Why don't you just stay here tonight?" I said. "I have a really nice guest room which, thanks to Janice, is now a perfect example of good feng-shui."

Hale nodded and I saw, for a moment, the young boy he used to be – shy, not always sure of himself even though he could put on a good front. I went upstairs ahead of him and found an unwrapped toothbrush, put clean towels in the guest bathroom, and listened to the sound of Stephen and Hale's voices as they approached the stairs. My house was somewhat full again, I thought, remembering how sad I was earlier as everyone departed.

When I got into bed beside Stephen, I maneuvered myself under his arm and listened to his heartbeat against my ear.

"Stephen, remember last year when you brought up the subject of us living together?"

He shifted a little and tilted his head down to look at me. "Uh-huh."

"Janice said I should be clear with you about why I'm so weird."

"Wait, that's what she said?" he asked.

"No, not in those words. Those are my words. She knows about my habit of keeping a little bit of distance between myself and ...well, everyone. It's my survival tool. I decided when I was pretty young that if no one got all the way in, then no one could ever look at me dismissively or judgmentally in any way that would matter because I could always say that they didn't know me that well. And there was less chance of getting hurt. I made myself imagine that I had this huge wall inside me to protect what was the most vulnerable, and my mother could never get over it. It just made sense to apply that rule to everyone, because you never know."

His fingers were laced in my hair and his other hand stroked my shoulder. "I know that, Tilly. But I have to confess, I've been okay with this arrangement. I realize I have my walls too. You know, I didn't tell you before about my ex-girlfriend dying in that car crash because I think that was the moment when I sort of shut parts of myself off and wanted to protect my heart a little bit. I mean, I did bring up the possibility of us living together before, but I was kind of glad you said no. I guess I figured separate houses is kind of like separate bathrooms, only more so."

"Well, you have a point there. So, what now?"

"I'm ready to open this conversation again," Stephen said.

I slid up and kissed him. "Before I met you, I had pretty much wrapped my head around the idea of just being alone for the rest of my life. I'd had a few dates with a man Rachel knew, and I think he was using me as a surrogate therapist. I was so bored listening to his complaints about his ex-wife and his various phobias, I couldn't stand it anymore. And then there was the date with a guy I met at the dog park. We went to dinner at a restaurant and he had to use the bathroom. He pushed back from the table and said, 'Gotta go choke the cobra.' That was it. Last straw. I thought, I am done with men."

Stephen laughed so hard his eyes watered. "I've never heard any guy say that, even in a locker room," he said. "He sure thought a lot of himself. I mean, a cobra is a pretty big snake."

Now I was laughing. "So…I should have kept his number?"

"No, you should have left the restaurant right then and stuck him with the whole check." His laughter wound down and he turned pensive. "You know, I saw you walk past my house a couple of times before we met. You were walking Lola. And I thought, that woman looks very independent and interesting. I asked a neighbor who you were and they told me, so I googled you. I could have cared less who your mother was, I was taken with your art and the uniqueness of your paintings. I definitely wanted to meet you. I wish it hadn't happened so early in the morning when I hadn't even combed my hair."

"You never told me this…"

He kissed me again. "It's a night of confessions. So, our previous conversation about living together is officially re-opened. But right now we need to sleep."

Later, as dark breezes slipped through the window and Stephen breathed beside me, as an owl hooted in my neighbor's tree and the thin sound of a faraway siren sliced through the stillness, I thought of the young girl I once was, listening for my brother on the other side of the wall, wishing there was a magic tunnel through the wall and I could reach for him. We are, always and forever, who we once were. Maybe Hale didn't know that. Maybe he didn't realize that learning who his real father was didn't extinguish the life he'd lived up to that point; it didn't make it irrelevant or untrue. DNA is a powerful thing, but who we become is so much more complex. It's a mysterious alchemy, formed from choices and whims of fate. From deep nights beside lovers we ache for and pale dawns when questions linger in the air. From seasons memorized by the heart and from the people who stay long enough to know us.

22.

After Stephen left, carrying an unhappy Travis away in his cat carrier, I made coffee and called Janice in New York, filling her in on the press story, which she hadn't seen, and Hale's surprise visit.

"It'll be ironic," she said, "if this publicity and this exposure is what brings you and Hale closer. Like finding each other in the brightness of sudden fame."

"That's very poetic," I told her.

"I try."

I heard through the phone a door slamming and a man yelling, "Ok, I'm outa here! Thanks for the mercy fuck!" And then another door slammed.

"Ugh – Janice?"

"Sorry. I broke up with Eric. The tattoo man. He's not taking it well. I tried to let him down easy."

"With a mercy fuck?" I said, not even trying to conceal my amusement.

"It seemed like a good idea at the time. Anyway, more importantly, I was going to call you today because Martin and I talked on the plane the whole way back to New York. The entire flight, and...I don't know how to finesse this, so I'll just say it. I like him, Tilly. I mean, I'm attracted to him. But if that's weird for you, because of your history with him ..."

I couldn't help laughing. As unexpected as it was, I could see the two of them together. "Janice, my thing with Martin was eighteen years ago. And our first not very successful hook-up was a year before that. I think you should go for it. He changed a lot with 9/11. I guess we all did, but he definitely isn't the arrogant guy I first slept with when Hale fixed us up. You have my blessing, seriously."

"Okay. Well, I wouldn't go for it if it bothered you. But I'll let you know how it goes. I think he might feel the same, but we'll see."

After we hung up, I sat at my small kitchen table,

looking out the window at the widening ribbon of dawn. I thought back to when Martin and I fell into each other's lives. We used to listen to old Joni Mitchell albums a lot. 'We are stardust, we are golden…' We were stardust then, I thought; there was something pure and uncomplicated about the easy flow of tears, about our bodies twined together in the black hours of night, needing each other's heartbeats, drinking in each other's breath. It was less about sex and more about reminding ourselves that we were alive. The city smelled like death; ghosts whispered around every corner. You could see shadows veiled across strangers' eyes and you knew they had lost someone too. But in the dark, wound around each other with the city rumbling far below, Martin and I were stardust.

Now he was facing a procedure on his heart. I knew how scared he was. I also knew, if Janice were with him, she would be able to quell some of his fears. She not only made homes more peaceful, she had that effect on people too.

I was still in the kitchen when I heard Hale's footsteps on the stairs. Nervousness fluttered through me; we were teenagers the last time we had breakfast together.

"Morning," Hale said, walking in tentatively, like he wasn't sure what to expect.

"Hi. How'd you sleep?"

"Good. Must be that positive feng-shui in there."

"I made coffee. And I have breakfast stuff. I don't know what you like."

He hesitated, as if he felt uncomfortable asking me for anything. "Maybe just a piece of toast?"

"Sure. Peanut butter? I do remember you used to like peanut better."

He smiled then and I saw a glimpse of who he used to be. "Yeah, peanut butter would be good."

I handed him a cup and he poured himself some coffee. I remembered that he used to load up his coffee with half-and-half, so I handed him the carton from the refrigerator. "Some things don't change, huh?" he said, turning his coffee into something that resembled desert. "Like how people drink their coffee."

The reality of our shared awkwardness made me feel closer to him. He didn't know me any more than I knew him, but if I looked backward to the history we shared, I wasn't sure how it could ever have been different. Our mother's face loomed over the landscape of years. She was the one pulling at our family from different corners, making sure we would never bond together, because if we did she wouldn't have control.

"We have to figure out what to do," I told Hale as we sat at the table drinking coffee and eating peanut butter toast. "But first let's take Lola down to the beach as soon as it gets light out."

"Sure. Are dogs allowed on the beach?"

"Nope. But this time of year no one patrols too much. Our family always got along better by the ocean. Remember?"

Hale nodded, his eyes suddenly far away.

The sky over the ocean was faded blue; smog from the city was already drifting toward the coast as the winds changed direction and turned dry as dust. It was low tide, and the only other person on the beach was a lone runner. On the short drive from my house to the sea, Hale told me about Lisa, the woman he lived with. They had been together for twelve years, she was five years older than him and she had a nineteen-year-old son who was at college in Colorado.

"So, you have a family," I said to him.

"I do. Lisa's husband died of a heart attack about a month after 9/11. Weird, huh? How things keep bouncing off that day in one way or another. They started the vineyard together and she was pretty much running it by herself when we met. I never thought I'd end up learning so much about grapes. And wine – except for drinking it. I knew how to do that before." He gave me a long look. "You have a family too, Tilly. Stephen, his daughter. I saw how happy you look with him. I was glad to see that, really. You were always alone when we were growing up. You never brought friends home or anything."

Hale was right about that. He was the social child, the one with play dates and invitations. I kept to myself. Maybe it's why I don't paint faces – there haven't been that many of them in my life. I wanted to say something profound and deep to him about the two of us being a family – brother and sister, no matter what had happened in the past. But mistrust was a thread woven into every moment between us. I didn't know how to break it; I didn't even know if I wanted to.

Lola ran across the sand down to the edge of the water, sending a flock of seagulls into the air. We took off our shoes and walked north, toward bluish hillsides in the distance. My brother and I used to run across a white sand beach in long ago summers when we had no idea what brutal turns the world could take. Those days were ripe with laughter and blessed with sunlight. And they were only a moment long. I looked at him beside me now, our grown-up footprints marking the sand behind us, our silence revealing how far we had drifted from each other. Or maybe how far apart we had always been. My brother was the place inside me that was colored dark with absence and made heavy with regrets.

Hale stopped and pointed out across the water. A pod of dolphins was swimming in the same direction, keeping pace with us, a few arching and leaping above the shallow whitecaps.

"When we were kids we probably would have tried to swim out to them," I said.

Hale laughed. It was a gentle laugh tinged with sadness. "Probably. Remember that night we snuck out of the house and went out to the beach to look at the moon?"

I hadn't thought of that night in so many years, the memory felt like it had jumped out at me from behind a locked door. That summer, I was thirteen and Hale was eleven. The Hamptons house we usually rented was under renovation, so my parents had rented a house right on the beach. I was restless that summer. Hale had friends he hung out with, but I didn't. The full moon shone through my window that night and spilled light across the room. In the quiet dark, I grabbed a sweater and put it over my pajamas. Carefully, I walked past my parents' bedroom and opened Hale's door.

"Are you awake?" I whispered.

"Yeah."

"Come on," I said and held out my hand.

Together, we tip-toed through the still house and went out through the French doors where miles of beach were silvered by the moon and the only sound was the waves breaking on the shore. We went down to the water's edge and sat down, the vastness of the Atlantic in front of us, silent houses behind. I remember not knowing what to say to Hale but wanting desperately to find a way to him. Sometimes, even when he was inches from me, as he was that night, he seemed like a mirage – something that would vanish the harder I looked. He was the first one to speak.

"Our mother would kill us if she knew we were out here," he said.

"Do you know that's always how we talk about her – we always say 'our mother.' We never call her Mom when we're talking to each other about her. But we say Dad when we're talking about him."

Hale shrugged. "Yeah, I guess. Maybe we're just more comfortable with him. It's easy to call him Dad. She doesn't really seem like a Mom."

Looking at my brother that night, his hair messy, his pajama bottoms too big for him, I wondered if I'd been wrong about how easy it was for him in our family. "She loves you a lot, I don't know why you wouldn't be comfortable around her," I said tentatively, afraid he'd shut me down, maybe get up and walk back to the house.

Hale smiled and shook his head. For a moment, he looked older than his years. "You don't get it, do you? It's hard for me, too, just in a different way. I feel her leaning over me even when she isn't around. It's like I can always feel her thinking about me, needing me to love her."

Now, years later, we were again sitting by the sea, struggling with what to say to each other, struggling to cross the empty miles that seemed to have been woven into our family long before we could make sense of it. The sun settled on our shoulders, bounced off the water, created shadows on the wet sand. Lola was chasing the shadows, spinning in circles and lunging. But so much felt exactly the same – the thin threads of tension between me and Hale, the absence of familiarity even though we grew up together, lived under the same roof with the same parents.

"I might know why our mother decided to come clean about Ian that morning. I've had years to think about it and I'm pretty sure I'm right." Hale said suddenly. "The day before, I told her and Dad that I was going to propose to Tara. Dad was really happy for me. He gave me a big hug, I even thought he had tears in his eyes, but I don't know – I could have just imagined that part. Wishful thinking, you know? Our mother pretended to be happy and, if you didn't know her, it might have been believable. But I knew better. I was leaving her for Tara, that's how she saw it. I wouldn't be her possession anymore. So, she lashed out in the most potent way she could think of. Revealed who really fathered me. She knew Dad would tell me, she was counting on it. You probably don't know this – you were away at college then – but when I was sixteen she had Ian teach me how to drive. She said she didn't want me to be one of those New Yorkers who never learned to drive, so I spent days with Ian. I asked her why Dad couldn't teach me and she laughed and said, 'Well, he knows how to drive, but he's lousy at it.' I wonder what her conversations with Ian were – if she told him he could have a few days with his son? I had so much rage in me that morning when Dad told me – I was just seething. I was angry about everything – her smothering, her manipulations, her deceit. And I felt so helpless. I went upstairs with Dad and started doing the work he gave me, but I was so distracted.

That's why I went downstairs. I thought I'd talk to the guy I knew at this other firm, and maybe clear my head."

Lola had moved up the beach, so we got up and followed her. We were the only people on the shore. The wind was getting stronger, sand was strafing the shore, blowing hard toward us.

"Hale, what was it like with you and our mother? I mean, before. Did you talk like friends? Were you comfortable around her?"

He smiled a little and shook his head. "Not really. Was anyone ever comfortable around her? I think I felt a little cocky in that I knew I could do no wrong in her eyes. But when I got together with Tara, things changed. She was chilly to Tara from the beginning, and at first I tried to pass it off as nothing, but I think Tara figured out the jealousy part of it."

"What did you say to her when you showed up at her house?"

"After it seemed like she had absorbed the fact that it was me standing in her bedroom, she asked me why. Just that one word – 'Why?' And I told her that she'd taken my life away from me. I didn't feel like I knew who I was anymore, the life I'd lived up to that point had been a lie, and when everything was in flames and falling -- when the world blew apart -- the only thing that made sense to me was leaving everything behind and starting a new life as a different person."

We were interrupted by my cell phone ringing. I looked at the display and when I saw Ellen's name, I turned off the volume. "I don't need to get that," I said.

"I wanted to hurt her, Tilly. Even after all those years, I wanted to hurt her. I'm not proud of that, but it's true. It was obvious how ill she was. I mean she was so pale and gaunt. She looked to me like she was dying, and I thought what a horrible person I must be to want her to suffer more."

I put my arm through Hale's, a gesture that felt uncomfortably foreign to me. "Horrible people don't feel guilty about things like that. You wanted to punish her –

that's pretty understandable. It's not horrible, it's human nature. How did you leave it with her?"

"That I didn't know if I'd see her again, and that I was going to keep working on trying to forgive her." He squinted his eyes and looked out across the water. "The first part of that came true. I'm still stumbling on the other part."

The day was getting brighter, the sun rusty with smog. A few people, some with surfboards, were walking across the sand to the water. Hale looked up at the sky.

"The devil winds are here," he said. "We've had a hard time with the drought at the vineyard. I hate to see these winds come up."

"We should probably go before the lifeguards show up and kick us off," I told him. I whistled for Lola and she turned and raced back to us.

"Still got your New York whistle," Hale said.

"Always. Hale, we still need to talk about what to do with this news story."

As we were getting in the car, Hale's cellphone rang and he answered, "Hey, Lisa," without glancing at the display. I wondered if Lisa was the only person who had his cell number.

"Okay, if you can grab the insurance papers, then do," he said after listening for a minute. "But it sounds like you don't have much time. Get Bella in the car and leave. Why don't you drive down here. Everyone we know up there might be in the same situation. Call me from the car once you're on your way."

"What happened?" I asked him.

"A fire just started in Santa Barbara – a big one. The winds are really strong up there right now and Lisa was told to evacuate."

Instinctively I turned to the north and looked at the sky, even though I knew it would take a while for the sky to fill with smoke. For a second I was back in Manhattan, looking up at the towers burning against the sky, praying my father and brother had escaped.

"We have a dog," Hale said. "Bella. She's an eight-year-old Shepherd and sometimes it's hard to get her in the car. Her hips, you know?" I saw the worry etched across his face. The idea of fire shattering his life again must be his worst nightmare.

"Hale, Lisa can come to my house. There's room for both of you to stay there."

He looked at me, his eyes blinking fast as if he was trying to process what I'd said. "Okay. Thanks, that's...that's really nice of you. Bella won't be any trouble. She likes other dogs and she mostly sleeps a lot now."

It's a strange dance, I thought, learning to act like brother and sister when our history was full of echoes and untraveled paths. We'd inherited a wilderness – that was the legacy of the Austin family.

I turned the car radio to a news station, but the only news about the fire was that it had started quickly, was spreading, and some evacuations had been ordered. Hale was clenching his jaw; I could feel his fear.

"It'll be okay," I said, the way people always do when they don't know what else to say.

He took a deep breath and exhaled slowly. "Meanwhile, I guess we have to make a press statement or something. Right?"

"It would be a good idea. If you're up for it, I'll call the TMZ guy back."

23.

Eric Fogelman answered on the first ring again. Either he always kept his phone incredibly close to him or he was really anxious to hear from me. I had no idea how this was going to work. Would we meet him someplace? Was he going to photograph us? Tape us?

"We basically do everything on the phone or, preferably, by Skype," Eric told me.

Which is how Hale and I ended up sitting in front of my computer, on Skype, talking to a man who looked years younger than I'd imagined him to be. He had blonde hair tied back in a ponytail, a smooth unlined face and he was wearing a t-shirt with a picture of Che Guevara on it.

"Che Guevara, huh?" I said to him before we started. I was wondering if he'd learned about him in history class, or if he perhaps knew nothing about the man on his shirt and just liked the picture.

"Yeah, he was an interesting guy. Executed in 1967, a long time before I was born. I got this in a second-hand store. You don't see many of these around anymore. Anyway, let's get started." He smoothed his hair back with his hands and adjusted his posture. "So, Hale, everyone believed you died on 9/11. I'm assuming your name is etched in stone at the memorial site along with thousands of others. Yet, here you are, alive and well. You showed up after your mother, Amber Austin's, funeral and no one – not your sister or anyone else -- had any idea you were alive. Now's your chance to explain."

Despite his youth and his surfer-boy face, Eric had an edge to his voice once he honed in on the subject matter. I looked carefully at Hale, wondering how this was going to go. Hale squared his shoulders and took a deep breath before speaking. His eyes seemed far away, as if he'd traveled back through time and was once again in Manhattan on a warm Fall day with deep blue skies.

"Right. Well, we have to go back to 9/11. I got some

220

news that morning that pretty much devastated me – not too long before the first plane hit. My father told me that I wasn't actually his son. I was twenty years old and was just told that I wasn't who I'd always thought I was. My mother dropped a bombshell on my father that morning, telling him that she'd had an affair with his friend, who was also his boss. I was the result of that. I felt like I'd lost everything – my father, my identity. I'd gone down to the fourth floor of the North Tower and when the first plane hit I was able to get out." I knew from the set of Hale's jaw that he was picturing again the dark, water-logged stairway, the incinerated and mangled bodies in the lobby. He was smelling again the fuel and the fear all around him. "My father was still on the 103rd floor. There was no getting out alive for anyone up there. He jumped, which is what everyone assumed I did. The truth was, I wanted to be dead, so I decided to pretend I was. I won't try to make excuses or justify what I did. Obviously, it was wrong but I -"

"But what about your family?" Eric interrupted. "Your sister Tilly who is sitting here with you? Your mother? Did your mother die not knowing you were alive?"

"No, she knew. I went to see her just before she died. I apologized for what I'd done. Look, as I started to say, I'm not going to make excuses. It's taken me this long to decide I have to come clean and tell the truth -- that I am alive, that I didn't die that day. I believed, all those years ago, that I could create beauty from ashes – that I could walk away from the turn my life had taken earlier that morning, and the horror of what happened later, and I could compose a new life. In some ways, I have. And I like the life I've created. But the past is still there. You don't put it to rest with lies. I realize that now."

My sense was that Eric had wanted to ask some tougher, more pointed questions, but Hale's openness threw him off. He turned to me and said, "Tilly, you have a brother again. A brother you thought had died. What's that like?"

"Ugh...complicated. Eighteen years is a long time, and there's some adjustment that's needed. We're getting to know each other again." I felt like I was walking a narrow line between truth and lies. The word 'again' was a bitter wafer on my tongue. Hale and I hadn't known each other well before that day of fire and death and endless clouds of ash. Maybe it was too late now to change the past.

Eric asked a couple of lightweight questions and then said to Hale, "Your name must be on the wall at the 9/11 Memorial. What happens now with that?"

Hale hesitated. I knew that was something he hadn't thought about. "I suppose it will have to be removed," he said.

I hadn't known what to expect and I was surprised that we weren't asked more questions, but maybe, if we were lucky, that meant this wasn't going to be a big story. When we signed off, Hale dove for his cellphone. We had turned off the volume on our phones, but I'd heard both of them vibrating during our interview.

Ellen had texted me twice and tried calling three times, leaving only one voicemail in which she insisted she must speak to me immediately. Her text was in all caps – CALL ME! It annoyed me more than the phone calls. She had the same worldview as my mother, which was: the world is mine, you're just living in it, and I expect you to be there for me when I want you. I heard Hale talking to Lisa and went out into the yard to call Ellen. Lola trotted behind me; I could tell she was picking up on my tension.

Her phone rang several times and I was hoping I'd be able to simply leave a message, but luck wasn't on my side. Ellen's voice was brittle and abrupt when she answered.

"Tilly, I've been trying to reach you all morning! Where have you been?"

"I see that you've been trying to reach me, which is why I'm calling you back. And it's actually none of your business where I've been. Although, if you must know, I was getting my appendix out and there were some complications, but all is good – they stopped the massive bleeding and recovered the scalpel they inadvertently left inside me."

There was a rather long pause before Ellen said, "I don't appreciate your humor at this time. I'm getting calls from People magazine and CNN about Hale. I am responsible for carrying out your mother's wishes, which is a full-time job right now. I do not have time to be a spokesperson for your family dramas."

"Oh, good to know. Do you think Sean Spicer might be available? I mean, he probably needs a job. And clearly neither Hale nor I can adequately speak for ourselves." I heard Ellen let out a long sigh. "You're off the hook, Ellen – we've done an interview about Hale's return from the dead."

"With whom?"

Ellen should have been a schoolteacher. She could have scared even the most delinquent students into behaving, just with the tone of her voice.

"TMZ."

"You're joking, right? That's your idea of handling this? What's the next stop, The National Enquirer?"

Hale walked out into the yard and Lola went over to him, lifting her head so he'd pet her. It was strange seeing Hale in my backyard, stroking my dog's head, but I couldn't dwell on that because Ellen was chattering on about the auction of my mother's things and how overwhelming her responsibilities were and how she just didn't need this added distraction right now. I forced myself to remember her weeping over my mother's death. Pretending to be my own therapist, I mentally leaned back and thought: Tilly, think of the young girl whose own mother died unexpectedly. She couldn't help herself, she had to fill that space with your mother.

"Ellen, you definitely have a lot on your plate. So, do whatever you need to do and I will handle the other dramas." My father's ring slid on the chain under my sweatshirt and the sound took me back through time.

A crow cawed as it flew overhead and filled the silence that fell over us when I hung up. Hale tilted his head and looked up at the bird. "Do you know it's fairly easy to tell the difference between a crow and a raven?" he said. "Their tail feathers are different. Crows' tail feathers are all one length but ravens have longer middle feathers so they look wedge-shaped when they're open. Their calls are different, too. Crows caw and ravens make a low croaking sound." He looked up at the sky again. "That was a crow."

I remembered then that Hale, as a kid, was always gathering random information about different things. He'd memorize facts he'd heard on television, or things he'd read in science magazines. There was no consistent theme to what he chose to learn; he just seemed drawn to gathering knowledge. Like Stephen, I realized. The man I love bears a resemblance to my brother, I thought, and I hadn't seen it until that moment. It was as if my heart, like a pilgrim, had wandered unknowingly toward the familiar. When I was a kid, I went through a period of trying to get closer to Hale by searching out odd facts that I thought he might appreciate. Once, I proudly told him how owls have to turn their heads all the way around to see because their eyeballs are fixed in the sockets. He nodded as if he already knew that, and I felt – as I often did -- like I was looking at him from miles away.

"Is Lisa on her way?" I asked him.

"Yeah. She should be here in 2 or 3 hours depending on traffic. Okay if I go upstairs and take a shower?"

"Of course."

I wondered how people in normal families speak to each other. Surely, they don't feel it necessary to ask if it's okay to shower when they're visiting a relative. In every moment Hale and I were picking our way across a foreign land. When he turned to go into the house I had the strangest thought: What if he wasn't really here, but had just floated in as a restless ghost seeking to form a connection he'd never known in life? I listened to his footsteps on the oak floor and watched his shadow disappear up the stairs. Lola came over and nuzzled me just as a strong gust of wind rattled leaves from the trees.

"I don't think ghosts have shadows," I whispered to

her, and she cocked her head as if contemplating what I'd said.

Random fact: The distance between the moon and earth changes constantly. With each orbit, the moon will reach a close point to the earth (perigree) and a far point (apogee.) For as long as I can remember, I have circled Hale, orbited around him, trying to move closer. I prayed for our own version of perigree. What we had at the moment seemed like that, but I didn't feel the satisfaction, the joy, that I once – long ago -- imagined I would. Sometime after my disastrous first fling with Martin, when Hale sharpened his already weapon-grade judgements -- I accepted distance as the definition of our relationship; his death on 9/11 put to rest any remnants of longing that were left in me. But now he was back, a presence in my home, my life -- the sound of water through pipes, footsteps on the stairs, dishes placed at strange angles in the dishwasher. I didn't know what to do with any of this.

The rain falling in my new painting was hard and relentless. I've always liked the challenge of painting water, the way it's both shiny and dull. In my night paintings, the glow of streetlamps will create tiny prisms in a puddle on the sidewalk, reflect off of sheets of rain falling from a storefront awning. I was working on the drops ricocheting off black umbrellas when Hale knocked softly on the open door and came in. He walked over to the finished painting of him in the fire-lit cave and stood in front of it, his head cocked to the side and his mouth set hard in concentration.

"Are those my ice-skates?" he said finally.

"They are. And that's you, which you might not have deduced since you don't have a face. I'm still not painting faces – it's become sort of my trademark. How did you know they were your skates? Ice-skates look pretty much the same everywhere."

He pointed to scuff marks on the side. "I always managed to scuff up my skates right there. I kept trying to improve my turns and I'd lean way into them. I'd fall way too often, too." He came over to stand beside me, his eyes following the movement of my hand. "Our mother's funeral, I'm guessing," he said.

"Yeah. That sea of black umbrellas appealed to me. Did you keep up, over the years, with the extent of her fame? The cult following that kept growing?"

Hale laughed a quick, soft laugh. "I did. I wasn't off the grid, Tilly. I knew what was going on. I even googled you sometimes to check up on your career. I know you did a showing out here a while back, and our mother came."

"It wasn't a supportive gesture. She came to upstage me. And she succeeded."

Hale went over to the armchair I'd placed in a corner of windows to serve as my "thinking chair" when I need to visualize a painting in my imagination. It creaked a little when he sat down. I heard Lola padding up the stairs and she walked in, tail wagging, looking at each of us as if she was surprised that Hale was still there.

"Why did you come with her to California?" Hale asked me. "I've always wondered that."

I let my paintbrush play with raindrops before answering him. "Because I had no other family. And because I still had this foolish idea that maybe she and I could actually figure out how to become one. My friend Rachel, who's a therapist, said to me, 'Why do you keep going to the hardware store for bread?' At some point, a while after we got out here, I stopped doing that. But I still visited her every week, especially when she got sick. I didn't want to feel any guilt when she died."

"And? Do you?"

"No. No guilt. Other uncomfortable feelings, but no guilt."

Hale's phoned pinged with a text and he looked at the screen. "Lisa's less than an hour away."

I put my paintbrush in a jar of soapy water and swirled it around before taking it into the bathroom to rinse it off. It was too distracting to try and work with Hale there. My chest felt tight, as if tears and words had collected there and were begging to be acknowledged. If I couldn't talk to Stephen, which I couldn't because I never wanted to bother him when he was working, I needed to talk to Rachel. The day outside had turned windy and uncertain, rife with devil winds that can tear trees from the ground and send loose shutters clattering to the sidewalk. The weather added to the nervousness that had taken up residence in my stomach.

"I'm going to take Lola for a walk," I told Hale. "Help yourself to anything in the fridge. Or if you want to see what news they have on about the fire, the remote is right by the TV downstairs."

The wind pushed against us on the sidewalk and pine needles swirled down from the trees. Last year, when the Santa Anas blew this hard, a huge branch broke off a tree on the next block and crushed a parked car. Lola pulled on the leash as if walking fast might keep us out of danger. I heard the whisper of ghosts on the wind – my mother with her brittle tone that could make 'hello' sound ominous; my father's cautious inquiries into our lives, our days, as if parenting was a chess game requiring meticulous deliberation and well-thought-out moves. And Hale, the veiled one whose bright smile hid dark currents.

Rachel's car was in her driveway, but it was possible that she was in a therapy session with one of her few patients. I knew she wouldn't answer the door if that was the case. She spotted me through the window before I could ring the bell.

"Hey Tilly. How's it going? Come on in. Hi Lola." She bent down and stroked Lola's head, kissed her nose.

Dilbert raced down the hall and almost collided with Lola, who proceeded to smother him with her tongue.

"I made a huge pot of chicken soup when it was rainy and now it's getting hot out so I'm putting most of it in the freezer. Let me give you some to take home."

"Sure. Although what I really need is chicken soup for the soul."

Rachel glanced at me as she was pouring soup into a

Tupperware container. "That bad, huh?"

I sat down at her kitchen table, sliding the newspaper away from me. She'd complain occasionally that her husband kept having the paper delivered but hardly read any of it. "He gets all his information on-line, but there's something about the paper waiting for him each morning…" While she made us tea, I filled her in on Hale being outed as a not-really-dead person, our TMZ interview, and the fire up north that had now resulted my brother and his partner being my houseguests.

"I heard about the fire this morning," Rachel said, carrying two steaming mugs of Chamomile tea to the table. She sat down across from me. "But I missed out on all the other juicy stuff. By the way, Chamomile is good for soothing upset stomachs and upset hearts. So, Hale's return has brought up a lot for you, I'm guessing. Things you thought you didn't have to pay attention to anymore, like the fissures in your family and how much of an outsider you always felt you were. I'm betting with your mother's death, you figured everyone was gone so you didn't have anything left to think about."

"That's a good summary, yeah."

"Except it doesn't work that way. And Hale coming back like this is showing you that. You should thank him."

"I should just go home and tell him thank you?" I said.

"No. I meant inside yourself. You needed this, Tilly. You've kept yourself in this sort of no-man's land, right in between living your life and locking the door on your past. I know you grieved after 9/11, when your father and brother were gone, but you haven't really grieved over your life with your family before that and all the things that weren't there. I'm pretty sure you've been walking around lately with your chest feeling like someone's stepping on it."

"How'd you know that?"

"I'm good at what I do. Here's something I tell my patients fairly often. Whatever emotional baggage seems to be holding you back is usually the emotion that was your survival tool in the past. It was your lifeline. For you, it was your fierce determination to not be hurt by your mother, to keep yourself protected just enough that she couldn't inflict too much damage. There's some anger there too, but it helped you survive her gamesmanship. It's as if you've been in a river holding onto a rope because without it, you'd drown. Then someone comes along and says, 'Hey, did you know you can swim? You don't need to hold onto that rope anymore.' The natural reaction is to not let go, to not believe them. But I'm telling you, Tilly, you don't need that defiance anymore. You don't need to hold yourself at a distance – not from Stephen, not from your past with your family, not from Hale, however things play out with him. You can show up for all of it and be fine. You can swim! You won't drown."

I didn't realize until Rachel stopped talking that tears were running down my cheeks. She got up and came back with a box of Kleenex. Kissing the top of my head, she said, "I'm afraid this is all the chicken soup for the soul I can give you right now. I have to get to Nina's school and help with costumes for a Halloween performance her class is doing. She's going to be Glenda the good witch. Her class decided on a rendition of The Wizard of Oz. She first wanted to be Toto, which would have been a challenge."

Lola and Dilbert had wandered in as if there might be some food available for them. I hugged Rachel goodbye. "Thanks. You've given me a lot to think about. I suddenly feel like I have rope burns on my hands."

"In my experience, those heal," she said. "I'm here whenever you need me."

The wind was blowing hard and smelled like dust. I thought about time and how quickly it can move. Just days ago, it was raining and now we were being scorched by winds and burned by fire. Not that long ago, my brother was dead, a name etched in stone on the 9/11 memorial. Now he was in my house waiting for his girlfriend to arrive.

My phone rang and I saw that it was Stephen. "Hi. You're on a break?"

"I am," he said, and I heard the weight of breath in his voice. "I know you guys talked to TMZ and I know we were all hoping that would be it. But apparently this is amounting to a big story. Vanessa called me -- she's heard from CNN and The New York Times."

"So, what do we do? I mean we as in me and Hale – not me and you."

"I think Hale is going to have to do some more interviews, explain himself. Whether you want to be part of it is up to you. My guess is that this is so unusual, everyone has latched onto it."

"Stephen, Hale is waiting for his girlfriend to come down from up north. There's a big fire up in Santa Barbara and she had to evacuate – with their dog, who Hale says is very nice. She's old. Sleeps a lot. The dog -- not his girlfriend. I said they could stay at my house. So, I'm feeling a little overwhelmed. Can we sleep at your house tonight? Leave them with the run of my place?"

"Of course. Tilly, I have to get back to work. They're calling me. I'll be back before six probably. Love you."

"Love you. Sorry about all this."

I knew I didn't have to apologize to Stephen, but I suddenly felt like my life was a huge cumbersome thing. Death was simpler -- my brother disappeared into smoke and ash and rubble. Mine was one of thousands of stories, and even though the details in each life were different, the stain of loss spread across all of us. But now Hale and I were a news story, a sort of freak show. I had an ominous feeling that the immediate future was not going to be a friendly place. People who are suddenly in the spotlight for questionable actions are either forgiven or decimated. There is no middle ground. Two ravens flew overhead – I knew they were ravens from the sound of their calls and the shape of their tail feathers. I envied their flight.

24.

Lisa looked like an older version of Tara – shoulder length blonde hair tied back in a loose ponytail, chiseled features which I could see from the window as she walked up the path to my door. She walked slowly, keeping pace with a large German Shepherd who ambled, limping slightly. Lisa was wearing jeans and a white shirt, and I didn't notice any jewelry. I could easily imagine her out in the vineyard checking on grape vines. I watched her for a few more seconds before calling upstairs to Hale.

I kept watching as he rushed out to meet her just before she got to the front steps. He wrapped his arms around her and held on tight, breaking away finally to lean down and stroke Bella's head. I couldn't hear what they were saying but the easiness of their body language told me that Hale had found a partner to travel through life with despite the weighty history he carried with him. There were times in our past when I studied Hale from a distance – when he was with a girlfriend or hanging out with his male friends. I was trying to know him better. It was like watching a movie and hoping to get clues about the main character. It never worked, but here I was trying again.

I met them at the front door with Lola close behind me, cautiously watching Bella. Lisa held out her hand and smiled. Her smile was one of those that spread across her face.

"I'm so glad to meet you, Tilly. And I can't thank you enough for taking us in right now. This fire blew up so fast. Everyone around me had to get out. They're saying that, because it just rained, they might be able to contain it fairly quickly, but at the moment the winds are pushing it on." She had a soothing, resonant voice and it didn't surprise me that Hale had fallen in love with her.

Bella decided to lie down at the foot of the steps and Lola immediately went over to her, sniffed her ears and prodded her with her nose.

"Bella's an old girl now," Lisa said.

"I think Lola wants to make sure she's okay," I told her.

I fixed lunch for us – salad and Rachel's chicken soup – while Lisa made calls to neighbors who had also evacuated. So far, no one knew if their properties had burned or were safe. I thought about the endless hours of waiting on 9/11, when hope still lived inside us and every ring of the phone might be my father or Hale, or someone who had spotted them. For a moment, I considered telling Hale about that, but I didn't. Instead, I asked Lisa about her family.

"I have an older brother," she said. "Sam's a year older than me. He lives in New Mexico – he's a high school teacher and he used to teach here in L.A. but he said he needed a more relaxed pace." She smiled and I could see the affection in her eyes. "His wife is a dental hygienist. They love it there. We try to always get together at Christmas either there or in Santa Barbara. They have two teenage daughters who, thankfully, stay out of trouble most of the time. I miss him – I really look forward to the holidays."

Hale nodded. "Yeah, we have a great time at Christmas. Lots of friends and family."

His words wounded me; it was as if, to him, I wasn't family. Before I met Stephen, most of my Christmases were spent alone. My mother continued her tradition of throwing an elaborate Christmas Eve party but made it clear that she "didn't do Christmas" anymore. Rachel included me in her family's Christmas a couple of times but they sometimes went out of town to her husband's parents. Those years, I would pass the day by myself, envying the warm chaos I'd see at houses I walked past, wondering what it would be like to know that your holidays would be spent with family – planning for it, never doubting it.

The fire in Santa Barbara had grown to nearly a thousand acres. A few structures had burned but it was impossible to find out which ones. Hale went into the living room to make some calls and see if he could get more information, and Lisa started clearing the table.

"How did you two meet?" I asked her.

"Richard was working at Whole Foods," she said, and then caught the startled look on my face. "Sorry, that must be weird for you. I've only ever known him as Richard, even though he told me after a while who he really was…or had been."

"Right. I understand. I've only ever known him as Hale, so I don't think I can call him Richard."

She gave me a warm smile. "Well, at this point, he'll probably answer to both names. Anyway, I'd look forward to seeing him whenever I went into the market, and then we started chatting. I thought he'd never ask me out, but finally he did."

"And when did he tell you? About himself – about that day."

"It was a while," Lisa said. "Many months. We were pretty serious by the time he said something. He told me late one night when we were lying in bed. I had the feeling that he needed to tell me in the dark. He needed to not be seen. I had a moment or two of doubt – you know, could I stay with him now that I knew he wasn't really Richard Buchanan? But I'd fallen in love with him. So, no matter what my head came up with, my heart won out."

I heard Hale walking back toward the kitchen. I wondered who he was with other people. Who was the man Lisa fell in love with? And Tara, all those years ago? I felt like I had a better sense of who Lisa was, after only knowing her for a few hours, than I did of who my brother was.

"No one really knows anything yet," Hale said, his cell phone in his hand. "It's chaos there, as you can imagine."

The news reports said that large areas of Santa Barbara were being evacuated. The winds were erratic and it was difficult to predict where the fire would turn next. People were being urged to leave when they were told to and not try to be heroic. I left the downstairs of my house to Hale and Lisa and went upstairs to work on my painting. I could hear the echo of the television, and occasionally the layering over of their voices. I should feel happy, I thought, that my house had more life in it again, but I couldn't shake the nervousness that crawled through my bones. It felt strangely familiar, and I had to admit to myself that, even in the clear air of our childhood, even when we played on white sand beaches and floated over blue waves, I was always nervous around Hale.

The first call came just as I was starting to work on the sea of black umbrellas. I saw that it was a New York number so I answered, thinking that maybe it was either Janice or Martin calling from a different number.

"This is Beth Strobman from The New York Times. I'm trying to reach Tilly Austin." Her voice was clipped and caffeinated.

Several thoughts sped through my brain – I could hang up; I could say, 'Wrong number.' Or I could pretend I didn't speak English. But, racked with indecision, I just said, "Ugh-huh."

"Is this Tilly Austin?"

"Ugh-huh."

"I'm calling about your brother Hale Austin and the report that he didn't actually die on 9/11. Can you speak to me about this?"

My voice felt like taffy. I couldn't seem to get words out. "No, I can't," I told her. "We need privacy right now." And I hung up.

"I'm an idiot," I said to Lola, who had dozed through the call but woke up when she sensed I was addressing her. "I have got to get better at this."

My phone rang three more times with unidentifiable numbers, and I didn't answer. I turned the volume off and tried to concentrate on my rainy funeral scene, but I knew the callers had left voicemails, so I gave into temptation and checked. The calls were all from reporters – the New York Post, the Daily Beast, CNN. I called Janice instead, needing desperately to hear a soothing voice.

"Hey girl," she said. "I was going to call you. I guess you know you and Hale are a pretty big news story."

"Yeah, I thought maybe if we let TMZ interview us, that would be it. They'd have the story and move on to something else. I guess that was foolish notion."

"Not foolish," Janice said. "Maybe just overly imaginative. So, what are you guys going to do?"

I suddenly realized that I didn't have to be inextricably linked to what was now a news item. I could step aside and let Hale deal with it. "Janice, am I being a bitch if I tell Hale he has to make the decisions here? That it's his story? And that I don't feel like I have to be front and center on this with him? I mean, I know I can't escape it entirely, but…"

"I think that's fair. He's made his choices, starting with what he did on 9/11. You don't have to be joined at the hip through this. Did he ask you to be at his side for interviews?"

"We haven't really discussed it, so no."

"Then I think you can just explain to him that you're supportive, but you don't want to be always included in whatever press he does. Hey, I was going to call you about Martin. Things are kind of…moving along. We've been seeing each other, and it feels really good, Tilly. Easy, you know? He's seeing another doctor tomorrow about his heart, so that's going to be kind of scary, but I'll nurse him back to health."

"I have no doubt you will." Other than Stephen, Janice was the one person I'd like caring for me if I was ill or recovering from surgery. "I'm happy for you guys. Now you can get off that dating site."

"Already done. We'll probably be sending you thumbs-up photos from a hospital bed soon."

"I'll be on the lookout for those. And Janice? Stephen and I talked about our weird housing arrangement. Turns out he was kind of a participant in that too. As in, he had own issues with keeping some safe distance. But I think we're working through it. So, we'll see."

"I'll consult on the feng-shui aspect when you combine homes," she said.

"I wouldn't have it any other way."

My signal for when Stephen was unlocking my front door was always the sound of Lola's paws across the floor, trotting to greet him. On his night, there was another set of paws, slower and heavier, following behind. Bella had been paying close attention to Lola for signs of how this house worked, and now she was getting another clue. I was in the kitchen chopping vegetables and putting them in the Wok. Rice Pilaf was simmering on the stove. I heard Stephen introducing himself to Lisa, greeting Hale, and then he came into the kitchen and slipped his arms around me. Arms I'd been waiting for all day. Both dogs were trailing him.

"Smells good," he said. "You're being very industrious."

"Well, I learned that my brother and Lisa are vegetarians, so I figured stir-fry is one thing I know how to cook. Did you save lots of patients today?"

Stephen was already washing his hands in the sink, reaching for another knife to help me chop vegetables. "Unfortunately, I lost a patient. A young housewife who got shot in a drive-by shooting. Her family was devastated. But they've become very friendly this week on-set, so they all went out to dinner together tonight. This is her last day of filming, since she died today."

"What a world you get to live in," I said, laughing. "Death's just a prelude to dinner."

He smiled at me and said in a quiet voice, "You know, I could make a reference to the fact that we're fixing dinner for your brother, who until recently was dead."

"True. My world is definitely stranger than yours at the moment."

We were standing at the counter like an old married couple, chopping vegetables. Something about the image made me feel settled and safe inside.

"Lisa seems nice," Stephen whispered, even though they couldn't have heard us over the sound of the television.

"She is," I whispered back. "Very calm and easy-going. I actually feel more comfortable around her than I do around

Hale…or Richard as he's known to her."

Stephen smiled and scooped some vegetables into the Wok. "I'd forgotten about that. Of course she wouldn't be calling him Hale."

"Yeah, at this point it kind of seems like we're both dancing around calling him anything. I could be imagining that, but I don't think I am. On another subject, under the heading of the world goes on even when California is burning, Janice and Martin are now a couple."

"Wow, that's great!" Stephen's expression changed quickly from elation to concern. "I mean, is it? Are you okay with this?"

"Absolutely. She told me there were sparks flying on the long plane ride home. I think they're kind of perfect for each other and they definitely have my blessing. He's going to deal with his heart problem soon, it looks like, and she'll be there to nurse him. So, they'll get to know each other really well. I have no idea what kind of patient Martin is going to be. He was a big baby whenever he had a cold, but maybe this will be different."

Over dinner, Stephen asked a lot of questions about running a vineyard, growing healthy grape vines, making a good wine. He is the ultimate diplomat, able to engage anyone and make them feel comfortable. But the subject we were avoiding hovered over us. I'd heard earlier, amidst all the news of the fire, Hale's name mentioned by a newscaster. I caught the phrases "faked his own death" and "the chaos of 9/11." I listened to the wind screaming outside, and almost thought I could detect the smell of ash leaking into the house. Maybe I was going to have to broach the subject -- bring up the calls I had gotten and the mounting pressure to get more of Hale's story from him, a story dissected now in the hard light of breaking news. But Lisa surprised me. She took a long sip of wine, put her glass down and looked around the table.

"So, we should probably discuss what to do now with the press. Tilly, you and your brother were one of the top news stories this evening." I noticed how she once again avoided calling her partner by either of his names.

"It's really Hale who is the top story," I said, choosing to not avoid his name. I looked at my brother across candlelight and felt how hard it was for me to stand my ground with him. Our mother drifted through the room, curled herself into the shadows. "I honestly don't feel like I have a responsibility to do interviews with you or be out front in this situation." I said it without flinching, without moving my eyes from my brother's face, but the knot in my stomach stole some of my breath.

Hale met my eyes, and I couldn't decipher what was behind his placid expression. "That's fine," he said after a few seconds. "I chose to come back at a really public time, I chose to walk into our mother's house with all those people there. So, I'll have to face the music."

Stephen leaned forward. "You might want to consult an attorney," he said slowly. "I mean, there are some legal issues here in terms of using another identity, things like that. I wouldn't want you to say something in an interview that could get you in trouble."

"I know someone," Lisa said. "Although he's in Santa Barbara, so now might not be the best time to contact him."

"I'll think about it, and figure something out."

"Good," I said. "I'm going to give you the names and numbers of the media people who contacted me today, and then you can decide who you want to call back."

I noticed how maternal Lisa was with Hale, how she suggested to him that they determine ahead of time what he should and shouldn't say, how she assured him that dealing with this now meant it would fade from public view more quickly – people would move on to another story. I wondered if this was always the dynamic of their relationship, if she protected and nurtured him more in some ways as a mother than a girlfriend. She graciously offered to clear the table and load the dishwasher, and I accepted, taking note of the fact that Hale didn't set foot in the kitchen.

———

238

Stephen and I took Lola and left the house to Hale, Lisa, and Bella, retreating to the familiarity of Travis gluing himself to Lola's side and the quiet of empty, well-appointed rooms. My heart felt tired, as if it had been pushing something heavy uphill again and again – a tiny Sisyphus with my brother's reincarnated life as the boulder. I was acutely aware that a part of my brain rehearsed conversations with Hale prior to engaging him, as if spontaneity and a natural flow of dialogue were impossible between us. Thinking back, I realized that, to some degree, I had always done that with Hale.

When I crawled into bed beside Stephen, I remembered that for the past few nights I'd had busy, elaborate dreams that fled as soon as I started to wake up. I would try to grab onto a thread, pull them back to me so I could examine them, but it was hopeless. All I was certain of was that my mother was in them. They disintegrated so quickly, I couldn't retrieve an image of her, or decipher what her role in the dreams had been. I was left only with the haunted sense that she had slipped back into my life. She'd returned with Hale, staring at me through his eyes at unexpected moments, and at other times, whispering through him. Now she had pirated her way into my sleep. I was about to tell Stephen about this, but his arm was draped across me and his breathing was deep and steady. One of us should sleep peacefully, I thought.

25.

For the next two days, wind scraped across the city. The sidewalks and streets in our neighborhood were thick with pine needles and small branches that had snapped off. The lights flickered sometimes, as if the power was going to go out, but it never did. In Santa Barbara, the winds were even more fierce. The flames had changed directions and it looked like Lisa's vineyard would be spared, but residents still weren't allowed to return because the fire was unpredictable and hadn't yet been contained. Hale plunged himself into doing interviews, both by phone for print media and by satellite for news stations around the country. I tried to stay out of it, but it was hard to miss him; there was some mention of him every time we turned on the news. He spoke about everything – how he used the name Richard Buchanan and had tried to leave his past behind him, buried at Ground Zero. But the ghost of who he once was wouldn't let him go. Stephen warned me to stay off social media, especially Twitter, and I did until Janice called me and said, "Have you seen all the comments on Twitter about Hale?" Abandoning my resolve to remain ignorant, I saw that they were almost equally divided between people who sympathized with him and those who hated him. The most vicious comments were from those who had lost a friend or loved one on 9/11 and resented Hale for faking his death when the person they loved was irretrievably dead. I saw one clip of an interview in which Hale was asked about the vitriol against him. His answer was logical and sympathetic, making me wonder if he'd prepared it before the question was asked.

"My father died that day," he said. "My heart breaks for everyone who lost someone. But my story isn't theirs. If I had died, or if I had continued to live as Hale Austin, those thousands of innocent people would still be gone. It wouldn't have made a difference in the scope of the tragedy."

Each night, Stephen and I relinquished the house to Hale and Lisa. We walked Lola up the street in the whiplash of dark winds and retreated to a place that felt the same as it did before my brother's return. I needed that reminder – that there was a world before everything changed, and a world that would be waiting for us after everything settled down.

"It'll be over soon," Stephen told me as we walked toward his house for the second night. "You know how fast the news cycle is these days. I'm not sure it will be over for Hale, though. There's going to be some kind of consequence for him using a dead person's name and social security number."

"Will he go to jail?" I hadn't let myself think of this before. Suddenly I had an image of visiting my brother in prison and talking to him through thick glass on a phone that smelled like other people's breath.

A gust of wind buffeted us as we went through Stephen's front gate. I smelled traces of smoke in the air. "I doubt it," he said. "But he'll have to work something out. He really needs to talk to an attorney, I don't know why he didn't before doing all these interviews."

Travis met us at the door and meowed loudly. "I have no idea what's in his head, Stephen. I'm painfully aware now of how little I know about my brother. I guess I never really knew him, although I think when we were really young I liked to imagine I did."

The wind entered my dreams that night, turning them chaotic and frightening. My mother was screaming at me, asking me where Hale was, shrieking that it was my job to watch him, that I could never do anything right. In another dream, I was desperately looking for Lola in the streets of Manhattan. Other dogs would come around corners, cross in front of me, but none of them were Lola. Just as my other dreams had, these unraveled the moment I woke up. I was left with scattered images, but no linear memory of the dramas that had played out in my sleep, dramas that caused me to wake up with my fists balled up tight and my breath caught in my throat.

It was still dark when Stephen and I got up. We sat in the kitchen drinking coffee, waiting for dawn.

"I had a dream about my mother and Hale," I told him. "I can't really remember all of it, just the one part where she was screaming at me that it was my job to watch him, and where was he?"

Stephen blinked sleepy eyes at me. "Where were you in the dream?"

"I know we were in New York, but..." I suddenly had a flashback of my dream. "You know what? It just came back to me where we were in the dream. In Central Park, at the carousel. When we were small, Hale did disappear -- only for a few minutes -- but our mother was with us that day and she freaked out. In my dream, we were adults, but it was the same freak-out."

It happened on a bright Saturday in April; the park was crowded. Couples were stretched out on blankets, people were playing Frisbee, or cycling along the road. Our sitter had called in sick, so my mother inherited us for the day. She had no idea how to entertain two young children, one of them still a toddler; after lunch she suggested we go to the carousel in Central Park. We climbed on the horses and rode around and when they stopped, Hale wasn't on his horse. I climbed off and looked around for him but I didn't see him anywhere. That's when my mother realized he was gone and started screaming out his name at the top of her lungs. Other mothers seemed frightened by her hysteria, but a couple of women tried to ask her what he was wearing so they could help look for him. I don't think she ever answered them, she just kept screaming his name. Suddenly he appeared from between two of the horses.

"He climbed down all by hisself!" he said proudly. He was still in the phase of referring to himself in third person.

My mother scooped him up in her arms and smothered him with kisses, as if he had been gone for hours, when it had been less than five minutes. Then she glared at me and said,

"You were supposed to be watching him. What's wrong with you?"

"Wow. I hope your sitter was calmer than that," Stephen said.

"She was. Without her, I think I'd have ended up in Bellevue before eighth grade. You know, I wonder -- if my mother hadn't died hours after Hale visited her -- would she ever have told me about his visit? And if she did, would I have believed her?"

Stephen laughed. "My guess is, you'd have checked the bottle of Ambien to see how much she'd taken."

"Probably true." I listened to silence outside the windows. After days of strafing wind, it was strange to hear nothing. "Is she ever going to vacate my dreams, Stephen?"

He hesitated for a few long seconds before answering. "I don't know. But I have a feeling it depends on how – or if – you resolve your feelings about Hale. There's an answer there somewhere, you just have to find it. Maybe you don't want him in your life at all, or maybe you want to have an occasional relationship with him, just polite interludes in the midst of long absences. Or maybe a miracle will happen and you two will bond in ways you never did before." He caught the look I gave him and shrugged. "Okay, that last one's not the most likely scenario. But the point is, it's this limbo state that's exhausting you, Tilly, and it's probably opening up graves and letting ghosts out. Your mother and Hale are all wrapped up together. It's a theory, anyway."

My coffee was getting cold. Lola was curled up under the breakfast table, snoring softly. Stephen's words crawled through me in slow motion. I knew he was right, and I knew this was my own solitary journey. He could help me, offer advice, but I was alone on this road.

"How come you're so much wiser than me?" I asked him.

"I'm not. It's easy to sound wise when it isn't your own life you're talking about. You'll figure it out, Tilly. And whatever you come up with will be the right answer."

I stayed at Stephen's house for a while after he left for the studio. It was already light out when Lola and I walked home; the air was coppery with smoke residue but there was hardly any wind. When my cellphone rang and I saw it was Ellen, I realized I hadn't thought about her at all for the past few days. Hale had dominated my thoughts and had left room for little else.

"Tilly, your mother's attorney is going to be calling you," she said, forgoing any small talk, which I was now accustomed to from her. "We have to schedule a meeting in his office regarding Amber's will."

"Okay..." I said slowly, suddenly imagining the embarrassment I'd feel if Ellen inherited my mother's entire estate and I was left with a crock-pot.

"Obviously Hale is not included in this meeting, nor was he included in her will, since your mother believed he was dead. I just thought I should mention that in case you decided you should bring him."

Ellen exhausted me more than Hale did. But I reminded myself that she was grieving in ways I couldn't.

"Fine, Ellen"

She seemed surprised that I wasn't snapping at her. "Okay then, so Arlen Deutsch is going to be calling you. I wanted to give you a heads-up."

A slight breeze slipped across my face and I detected some moisture returning to the air. If the Santa Anas were over, then the fire could be contained, and Hale and Lisa would return home. I wanted my house back. I couldn't make myself feel comfortable with Hale there, and I'd tried, but our history stood between us, solid as the Great Wall of China and seemingly just as ancient. Sometimes, when I passed Hale in the house or was in the same room as him, I picked up the scent of roses – the perfume of our childhood traveling down the years to find me. To haunt me. The few times I'd gone into my work room to paint, I smelled it. Had Hale been in there, or had he just unleashed our mother's ghost and sent her billowing through the rooms of my house? I'd made some progress on my new painting -- the sea of black umbrellas and the relentless rain, the man on the outskirts of the crowd. I'd left room to include a casket, but I wasn't sure I wanted it. I kept returning to the hovering figure standing apart from the black-clad mourners, the only one without an umbrella. I knew I was going to attempt to paint his face, but I didn't feel brave enough yet. I couldn't seem to get lost in my work with Hale in the house. Even when he was out, his presence lingered. Lisa left each day to visit some friends she knew in Los Angeles, but her presence in my home was light and calm. She didn't distract me. Hale carried an anger inside him that was like a force-field. He changed the ions in the air, and they didn't immediately change back again when he left the premises.

As I unlocked the front door, I heard Lisa and Hale arguing upstairs.

"I don't need a lawyer!" Hale was saying, his voice sharp as a blade. "I know what I'm doing!"

It was surprising to hear Lisa's voice raised in anger. "Hale, you have no idea what you're doing!" she told him. "This is serious stuff. You're just saying whatever comes into your head, to the whole world! You're probably getting yourself into more trouble than you need to be in. You need someone to guide you through this!"

I closed the door hard so they would know I was back, and they immediately stopped talking. Bella ambled out from the living room and greeted us. The stairs were hard for her, so Lisa had put her dog bed in front of the fireplace. I was in the kitchen staring into the refrigerator when I heard Hale's footsteps.

"'Morning. I have to meet a reporter from the L.A. Times for coffee." He paused as if he was debating what to say next. "Some good news about the fire – they have it fifty percent contained. We should be able to go home soon."

I wasn't sure what to say. The now familiar awkwardness that always bloomed between my brother and me made me choose my words carefully. Finally, I said, "I'm sure you'll be relieved to be back in your home."

"Yeah, we will." He looked like he was searching for words, like something important was forming in his thoughts. But then he just said, "Well, see you later."

Lisa was coming downstairs as I was going up, and I could tell she'd been crying. "You okay?" I asked her, not at all sure if I wanted an answer.

She looked away from me, tried to manage a smile, but failed. "Hale and I just got into an argument. We don't usually argue, so it's kind of upsetting. I guess I'm just seeing another side of him with all this publicity and his open confessions to anyone and everyone. He seems kind of…I don't know…reckless. Is that how you knew your brother?"

"Lisa, I wish I could help you and give you some profound insights into him, but the main currency in our family was distance. Hale and I were never close. There were moments when I thought we were moving in that direction, but they were so fleeting I'd feel foolish afterward for even entertaining the idea."

"It's like he's on some kind of mission," Lisa said. "But I don't know what the mission is. He's talked so openly in interviews about buying another identity, inventing a past for himself that never existed. I mean, it almost seems like he's asking to be charged with a crime."

"Maybe he is. Maybe he wants to be punished. But hey – don't listen to me. I watch way too many episodes of Law and Order. Listen, I'm going to run to the market and then start putting up Halloween decorations, if you feel like assisting with witches and ghosts."

Hale came back as Lisa and I were unpacking frightening looking figures from plastic boxes out on the front lawn. Lola and Bella had curled up together in a pool of sunlight, and wispy clouds were streaking across the sky, a sign that the devil winds were ending. Hale didn't come over to Lisa – he just stopped on the pathway and gave a quick wave. The smile she returned to him seemed forced. I started to wonder if Hale's resurrection would mean the end of them as a couple. I lifted out one of the large witch figures and realized I'd picked up the one in a gauzy wedding dress. Lisa glanced at the witch and then focused on me. Something shadowy moved into the clear blue of her eyes.

"Relationships are hard," she said softly.

"How did your husband die?" I asked her. "If you don't mind my asking."

She lifted a bloodstained ghost from one of the boxes. "He had a heart attack. It was really sudden, totally unexpected. He was out working in the vineyard, up on a ladder, and he fell. The men working with him thought, at first, that he'd just lost his footing, but when they went to him, they realized he wasn't breathing. They ran and got me...he was gone. Just like that. Death is so different when it just snatches someone away in an instant. The shock is paralyzing. But then you know about that, too, don't you?"

"I do. For weeks, I still thought that Hale and my father would show up. I imagined they'd had amnesia and would suddenly remember."

Lisa looked up at the sky and I saw tears pooling in her eyes. "Michael was the love of my life. We'd been together since college. You know, we never argued. We'd have very civilized disagreements sometimes, but we were so in tune with each other. I felt like part of me had been amputated when he died, like I'd never be whole again."

I wondered if she would ever say that Hale was the love of her life. "And now?" I asked.

Before she could answer me, a dark blue sedan pulled up in front of the house, and two men in suits got out. I prayed they were going to another house, but they came to the front gate and pushed it open. One of the men looked like he was in his late forties, with salt and pepper hair and the beginnings of a paunch. The other man, trailing a step behind, was younger – blonde with wide shoulders and posture that radiated confidence as well as hours spent in the gym.

"One of you Tilly Austin?" the older one said.

I stood up and grabbed Lola before she could go over to them. "I am."

"Is your brother here? I'm Detective Greene and this is Detective Ballard. Hale Austin needs to come with us and answer some questions."

Lisa stood up and tool a few steps toward them. "Is he under arrest?"

"No, ma'am. But we need him to come with us. Is he here?"

"I'll get him," Lisa said, and went into the house.

I didn't know what to say to them. Witches and ghosts were spread out between us on the lawn. A thin cloud passed across the sun, changing the color of the day for a few minutes. Finally, I asked, "Why can't you just talk to him here?"

The younger blonde detective answered. "It just doesn't work that way," he said.

"How did you know he was here? And how did you know this is my house?"

The salt-and-pepper man leveled me with a look. "We're detectives, ma'am. That's what we do."

Hale walked out of the house with Lisa and stopped a few feet from the two men.

"Hale Austin, you need to come with us for some questioning. We aren't arresting you, so I'm not going to mirandize you or anything like that. But this isn't optional. You need to come with us."

Hale didn't say a word. He just started moving toward the gate. The two men glanced at each other and walked quickly to get ahead of him. Did they think he was going to make a run for it? They held the gate open for him, and the younger detective opened the back door of their car, motioning Hale to get in. When they drove off, Lisa and I turned to each other with blank stares.

"I'm going to call Stephen," I told her. "If there's anything we can do, he'll know what it is."

She nodded and then picked up the witch in a wedding

dress. A breeze blew the white gauze back across her shoulder and she brushed it off. "I'm going to hang her from the tree, okay?"

"Sure. Sounds like a good place for a witch on her wedding day."

There was something serious and determined in Lisa's demeanor. Gone was the serenity and easy calm that I'd gotten used to from her. It's funny how, when people are battling storms inside them, they turn into impenetrable fortresses. As if they have to keep their storms encased behind walls where no one else can see them, or calm them, or judge them. I'd left my phone in the house, so I went inside, glancing back to see Lisa climb up on the step ladder and start lashing the witch to the tree. Her mouth was set in a hard line and her hands were working quickly, as if there were a danger in slowing down. Lola followed me up the steps into the house and we both paused when we crossed the threshold. My home suddenly felt different this time without Hale in it – lighter, as if a season had changed. I remembered driving away from my mother's house the day before she died, sensing that death was moving close, and how the sky felt bigger. I felt guilty that day for welcoming the feeling, and I felt the same now as I went through the front hallway into the kitchen. My mother and my brother were like twin spirits inside me, both messengers of guilt and uncertainty, both cloaked in the regrets of a lifetime – regrets that I couldn't dismantle because I didn't really believe anything could have been different in our family. Over the years, I had occasionally wondered what my life would be like if my father had lived. He was often a safe port in the storms of our family life, but just as often he was absent, even when he was right there. Pointlessly, I'd asked myself sometimes – usually in the deepest hours of night – if time and age might have opened him up. If he had grown old, would he have been less inclined to turn away and more willing to meet my eyes?

I saw on my phone that Arlen Deutsch had left me a message, but I needed to talk to Stephen. I was about to call him when Lisa came in holding a long string of orange pumpkin lights.

"I found these in one of the boxes," she said. "Okay if I string them up near the front door? You have an outside outlet right there."

"Sure, that's fine. Uh, Lisa, you don't have to do all this yourself. I'll be out to help you in just a minute."

She softened a little; I saw her shoulders drop and her eyes turned sad. "I have this thing I do, when life gets upsetting – I just go into high gear and find stuff to keep me busy. I kind of become a one-person work crew."

"So that you don't have to think?"

"Exactly."

"What happens when you slow down and the thoughts come?" I asked her.

She laughed a little – a laugh dangerously close to tears. "It's usually not pretty. So, I'm going to go hang pumpkin lights because I hate anyone seeing me cry."

Lola gave me a worried look when Lisa walked out as if to say, 'Shouldn't we go after her?'

Stephen answered on the second ring, and I apologized for calling him at the studio even though I knew he was on a break, otherwise he wouldn't have picked up. I told him about the detectives taking Hale away and he interrupted me.

"Did they mirandize him or anything?" he said.

"No, they just said they wanted to question him."

"Okay, well that's a good sign. They aren't arresting him…yet. Maybe now he'll get an attorney. Tilly, we're just going to have to wait and see how they plan to handle this. You can't force an attorney on him…no matter what you see on Law and Order episodes."

I had to laugh. "You know me too well. I was just thinking of those attorneys who show up unexpectedly in the midst of questioning and throw the detectives out of the room."

They were calling Stephen back to the set. I motioned to Lola that we had to go back outside, and as we walked toward the door I imagined Hale in a windowless room being grilled about the last seventeen years of his life. For a moment, I caught the scent of roses. Stephen was right in what he told me before, about how the entanglement of my mother and brother -- like a knot of barbed wire inside me – was the core of my discomfort. I was hostage to both of them, and somehow I had to break free.

For the moment, though, I had to help Lisa put up Halloween decorations. She was busy snaking the pumpkin lights around the front porch banister; pale, bloodied figures keeping watch over her as they swayed from tree branches. As adults, we like Halloween because it lets us revisit a time when fear was more innocent, when it was all make-believe. It gives us a reprieve from the fears that have taken root as we stumble through adulthood.

26

It was late afternoon and Lisa and I were sitting in the front yard with cups of tea, surrounded by tombstones and scary figures. I felt guilty that Lisa had done most of the work, but she'd been adamant about keeping herself busy. A thin veil of clouds was drifting across the sun, muting the day.

"I'm going to head back to Santa Barbara today," she said. "They're letting residents back in – I talked to one of my neighbors earlier."

"Have you talked to Hale? Did he call you since Moe and Joe took him away this morning?" She laughed and I realized it had been a while since I'd even seen her smile. "Sorry," I said. "I don't remember their names and I have a habit of trying to make jokes when things are serious."

"I understand. I haven't heard from Hale, but I have no idea how things work when detectives take you in for questioning. Do they confiscate your phone? Anyway, I did text him to say I was going to go back home and I haven't gotten a reply yet. So, that means whatever it means, I guess. Either he doesn't have his phone, or he didn't check it, or he doesn't want to answer me…"

Lola, who was as usual lying beside Bella, suddenly got up and ran over to a corner of the fence, her tail wagging wildly. Rachel and Nina were coming down the sidewalk with Dilbert. I motioned for them to come in the gate and Lola greeted Dilbert as if she hadn't seen him in years.

"People should greet each other like that," Lisa said softly.

I introduced Rachel and Nina to Lisa, and Rachel looked around at what my yard had become. "Good job," she said. "We have to get our decorations up. You outdid yourself this year, Tilly."

"Not me. Lisa did most of the work, maybe all of it. I didn't even remember I had some of these emaciated figures."

Lisa stood up and said, "Good description. You

definitely don't see a lot of overweight ghosts and witches. Listen, it was nice meeting you, Rachel, and you too Nina. I'm going to get my stuff together so I can hit the road."

When she went inside, I said to Rachel, "I don't think things are going well with her and Hale. And I know things aren't going well for Hale. Two detectives came here this morning and took him in for questioning."

Rachel bent down to talk to Nina. "Honey, why don't you take a closer look at all the witches and goblins? Maybe we'll need to get more decorations. Go see which ones you like." After Nina had skipped across the yard, Rachel said, "I'm so sorry. Does this mean he's going to be arrested?"

"I have no idea. They said they weren't arresting him right then, but I'm guessing that can change once he's sitting in a room answering questions. He hasn't really been communicating much with anyone, except – ironically – the entire world every time he does an interview."

"So, she's leaving and he's still at the police station?"

"Yep. Not a good sign."

The yard had taken on a golden hue, with sunlight splintering through the pine trees. For a moment, I picked up the smell of the ocean. I imagined Lisa driving north as the day faded, the gray ribbon of road crisscrossed with shadows. I imagined her crying the tears she'd been holding onto all day, with Bella sitting obediently beside her, watching in the way dogs do when they know you're sad. Regardless of what unfolded between her and Hale, I didn't want to lose touch with her. Not only had I grown fond of her, but we had something in common – neither of us really knew who Hale was.

Stephen and I decided to stay at my house that evening. I had no idea if Hale was still with the police, but his car was parked in front of my house, some clothes that Lisa had brought down for him were in the guest bedroom, and he had a house key I'd given him. A reasonable assumption would be that he'd come back at some point. Stephen brought

Travis over and we ordered pizza and opened a bottle of wine. I'd spoken to Arlen Deutsch's assistant and agreed to one of the time slots that Ellen had suggested; her schedule was apparently so packed, she had limited availability. When I told Stephen about my fear of being humiliated if my mother left everything to Ellen, he smiled and wrapped his arms around me, holding tight for a few minutes.

"Can you give yourself credit for something?" he said. "Your fear isn't about not getting your mother's money, it's about being embarrassed. That says a lot about you. I would guess that the majority of people would be focused on the fortune that's sitting there. But you're thinking more about the possibility of being humiliated in front of other people if your mother decided to use her last will and testament to knock you down again."

"Well, okay…I guess that's commendable. But then again, I'm doing okay financially. I'm hardly in the one percent, but I don't need to be."

Stephen brushed my hair back from my face. "Give yourself some credit for this, okay? It reveals who you are."

We were debating the last slice of pizza when I heard a key in the front door. Lola barked and ran toward the door but then whined her version of hello when Hale stepped into the house. He walked slowly into the living room.

"Hi," he said, and I noticed how sheepish he seemed.

"Were you with the police all this time?" Stephen asked.

Hale sat down in the arm chair closest to me and let out a long breath. "Yes and no. They questioned me for a long time, but they also just left me sitting in the room for long stretches of time. I drank some bad coffee and waited, and finally they drove me back here. I have to appear in front of a judge early next week. I guess they thought they'd nail me for social security fraud or something, but all I did was use a fake birth certificate to get a driver's license."

Stephen nodded, running through something in his head. Finally, he said, "Seems if they were going to arrest you they'd have done it today. You might get off with a fine. You know, you can take an attorney with you when you go in front of the judge."

"No. I'll just take whatever the judge gives me. Anyway, Lisa texted me, so I know she went back to Santa Barbara. If you want, Tilly, I can go to a hotel. I don't want to overstay my welcome."

I couldn't bring myself to say yes to that, even though there was a part of me that wanted to. "No, it's okay, you can stay here."

"I'll go back up north after my hearing…that is, unless he throws me in jail." He laughed a little, but I didn't believe for a second that he was finding humor in any of this.

Stephen handed him the last slice of pizza, which he devoured. They probably hadn't fed him all day.

I lay awake that night listening to Stephen breathing beside me, and to Lola and Travis lying close together on her dog bed, their inhales and exhales providing a calming rhythm. I imagined Hale breathing in deep sleep down the hall. I heard wind blow through the tree branches outside the window and somewhere, several streets away, a dog was barking. The rest of the night was still, as if nothing else was breathing at this late hour. I wondered what would happen with me and my brother as we moved forward through time. I felt so alone when I was with him. It seemed like the distance that was cultivated in our family had formed itself into a hard shape inside me and Hale's presence made it move and ache. That's how it is with history – it carves out shapes inside us, some smooth and pliable, some painful to the touch. All you can do is memorize the map and breathe past the rough spots.

Lying in the dark, I thought about my father and tried to visualize the cold, detached expression that Hale said hurt him so deeply on the morning of September 11th. I realized I could barely recall my father's eyes. His image was fading; maybe it had been for years and I just didn't know it. There were the brief connections and interludes that I remembered – him writing his letter to his parents, the two of us at church after they died. And there was a night when I was very young and had a nightmare; it was my father who answered my screams. I can picture how lamplight bounced off his eyes as he stroked my face and comforted me back to sleep. But for the most part, my father is a shape drawn with fading ink. He is feelings that still live in me – a longing to engage him, have his full attention, the soft hurt of him turning away to his newspaper, or his desk, or his phone. But the feeling of home, of security, is never there. When I think of him, I think of echoes in hallways and windows smudged with small fingerprints from me looking down at the street, memorizing my father's walk.

It's my mother's eyes I see reflected in Hale's – blue ice and dark judgements. It's why the scent of roses drifts in when Hale is around. It comes in with her ghost.

27.

Arlen Deutsch's office was on the nineteenth floor of a sleek black and marble office building in Century City. As I walked through the lobby, I was mentally calculating what I'd probably have to pay for valet parking, which I'd just indulged in since I didn't want to travel into the underground abyss of the cheaper parking garage.

It was a flat sunlit day, the kind of typical California weather-less day that sometimes made me miss New York and its changing palette of sky. When I left my house, Hale was sitting out in the yard reading a book titled "Get to Know the Real You." I squinted to see who wrote it and saw the name Berenger West. I'd heard of him – he gave lectures and did television appearances on self-transformation. Apparently, he commanded large audiences when he gave a speech.

"That book looks pretty dog-eared," I said to Hale. "You must read it a lot."

He put it down and looked up at me, hesitating before saying, "He's been a big influence on me. I don't think I'd be telling the truth now if I hadn't started reading him and following his teachings. I read in the paper that he's doing a lecture tomorrow night at a church in Venice. I'm going to go...I was thinking, I mean I don't know, but maybe you'd like to go with me?"

It was surprising to hear Hale invite me to something like that, something that had so much meaning to him. "Let me think about it," I told him. "I'll see if Stephen had any plans he didn't tell me about."

It was Friday and Stephen had only a half day of shooting so we'd talked about going on a hike with Lola in the Santa Monica mountains that afternoon. I didn't want Hale to come with us, but I hadn't come up with a polite way of telling him that this was an outing just for the three of us, and now I felt pangs of guilt because of his invitation to me. The awkwardness of having Hale in my home, of not feeling at ease with him, was constantly crawling beneath my skin. I found I couldn't work on my funeral painting while he was there. I wanted to paint his face – the first face of my artistic career -- but I was incapable of starting it while he was still around. It was as if I was waiting for him to leave so I could see him more clearly.

My shoes made a hard sound on the black marble floor. People talking animatedly into cellphones brushed past me.

"Tilly!" Ellen's voice landed on my back and as I started to turn around I thought of how much I didn't want to ride up in the elevator with her. "I pulled in right behind you," she said when she caught up to me.

She was wearing black pants, a conservative looking white blouse and a black cashmere sweater. I was sure her black heels bore the stamp of some famous designer, but I'm not well versed in fashion. Even though I'd chosen an ankle length skirt, suede boots, and a relatively expensive cream-colored sweater, standing next to Ellen I felt like I was outfitted in bargain basement clothes. Just as my usual resentment of her began to surface, I saw in her eyes the same look that was there the day we went casket shopping. The chain with my father's ring on it was hidden beneath my sweater, and as soon as my resentment melted into some version of compassion, the ring got warmer against my skin. Maybe it wasn't just my mother's presence that lingered. Maybe my father could be with me too – not with the scent of roses or the residue of fear, but with a warmer touch, a reminder to be kind.

"You look nice, Ellen," I said.

She gave me a surprised look and thanked me cautiously. I felt my father's ring move against me and for a quick moment, I remembered his eyes.

The waiting room of Arlen Deutsch's office was air-conditioned and professionally decorated with low gray couches, a glass coffee table, and a large bookcase full of law books. A fake potted palm was placed beside the expansive windows, as if to fool people into believing it was real and needed sunlight. His assistant, a tall dark-haired woman in her thirties, wearing a fitted business suit, put bottles of water in front of us on the coffee table and informed us it would be just a few moments. When her phone buzzed, she led us into an office that mirrored the décor of the waiting room. The windows looked out at other office buildings and glimpses of blue sky in between. Arlen Deutsch stood up behind his desk and offered his hand to each of us. I remembered him then from my mother's Christmas Eve parties, although he looked older than my memory of him. He was tall and alarmingly thin, with snow white hair and a long square face, a face that didn't seem accustomed to smiling.

"I'm very sorry for your loss," he said to me when he sat back down. Then he looked at Ellen and added, "And yours. I know how fond you were of Amber."

"Yes," Ellen said softly. "I was." She bent her head down and stared into her lap.

Oh, please don't start crying, I thought, but Ellen shifted in the leather chair, straightened her shoulders, and seemed to compose herself.

For the next twenty minutes, Arlen Deutsch went through my mother's assets, which were considerable – not just the house and its contents, but her paintings, her jewelry, and also her stock portfolio. I was trying to appear as if I was taking it all in but the truth was, I was thinking about my canvas of black rain-soaked umbrellas and the faceless man at the edge of the crowd. I returned to the room when he said, "So, as for Amber's wishes…"

He read from white pages as if it were a legal brief with no emotional consequences, but maybe that's how attorneys are trained to present things. I tried to imagine my mother's tone of voice as she was dictating to him how she wanted things dispersed after her death, but I wasn't sure how she'd have sounded; it would have depended on her mood that day, on our last conversation perhaps, or on whether or not she resented the fact that I and not Ellen shared her DNA.

Amber Austin, being of sound mind and body, instructed her attorney to liquidate her estate – both through outright sales such as the house, and auctions of the contents of the house, as well as her original paintings. There was one exception – a single painting, which she left to me. It was called, "Day at the Lake." I had seen the painting; it was another of her blissful scenes, this one with several families picnicking on the banks of a pristine blue lake, long grasses waving around them and white-winged birds hovering on wind currents. Children were flying kites, playing with dogs, and parents were calmly setting out food. It was quaint and idyllic, a million miles from anything I would ever paint. A million miles from who the Austin family was.

She named two organizations as the recipients of a five hundred thousand dollar sum, to be split equally – Planned Parenthood, and an art school that I'd never heard of but which she apparently had taken an interest in. She also left Rosario fifty thousand dollars. Everything else would be split three ways, between me, Ellen, and Ian.

"Ian?" I said before I could stop myself.

Ellen leveled me with a look full of reprimand. My mother shivered into the room. "Well, Tilly, they did have a history," Ellen said. "For lack of a better term."

"I'm obviously aware of that," I told her. "I'm just wondering what statement my mother was making with this gift to Ian. Did she happen to tell you her reasons, Mr. Deutsch?"

Arlen Deutsch was doing his best to remain placid, but his eyes gave away his discomfort. "No, she simply communicated her wishes. I did ask Mr. McBride to be here today but he is back east and was unable to come. He gave me permission to proceed without him. I should mention, Tilly, that your mother obviously didn't know about Hale being alive, so he isn't provided for in her will."

"I know. Maybe his father will share the wealth." I regretted my words as soon as they left my mouth and I truly had no idea why I said them. I think I was just angry at how the broken places in my family kept coming back, like sharp edges pushing me into an all too familiar abyss. Did other people sit in lawyer's offices listening to wills and trying to de-code them? What was my mother really trying to say by leaving me that one painting? And Ian certainly didn't need money so what was the message behind her gift to him?

This is how the dead haunt the living – by never letting them rest. By forever dropping questions in their path. Questions they will keep stumbling over without ever finding answers.

While Ellen and I were waiting for our cars, I had the sudden urge to give Ellen the painting my mother had left me. Maybe that was the only way to stop wondering about her motives.

"Ellen, you can have that painting. It would mean more to you than it does to me."

Ellen turned to me with a mixture of sorrow and surprise on her face. "That's very generous of you, Tilly. I have a small canvas of your mother's. She gave it to me for my birthday last year. So, you should keep it. You'll figure out what to do with it."

Her last sentence echoed around me as I drove home. Did she know my mother's reasons for choosing that one painting as her posthumous gift to me? Had they discussed it?

When I got home, Hale was tossing a tennis ball for Lola in the backyard. She dropped the ball and ran to me as soon as I stepped outside.

"How'd it go?" Hale asked. "Did she leave you some soup spoons? Maybe a flower vase or two?"

Sunlight was behind him, spilling over his shoulders. I remembered watching him in sunlight as a toddler when our nanny took us for walks in Central Park. He was the kind of child that caught everyone's eye. He made smiles bloom on the faces of strangers.

"Actually, with the exception of some charity donations, she divided her estate between me, Ellen and Ian. I was surprised she included Ian – I mean, it's not like he needs the money."

"She wanted you to wonder about it," Hale said. "She obviously wrote up her will before she knew I was alive, so you knew nothing about Ian. It was her way of keeping you haunted by what you didn't know and couldn't figure out. Or maybe she was setting up Ian so he'd have to decide whether or not he wanted to tell you."

I looked up at the flat blue sky, wishing there were clouds, or fog – anything but all those miles of emptiness. "A lot of families don't have questions and dramas like this," I said, more to myself than to Hale. "A lot of families are – dare I say – kind of normal."

"True. Lisa's family is pretty normal."

I studied my brother's face, trying to read behind his eyes. "How are you and Lisa doing?" I asked tentatively.

He shook his head slowly. "I'm not sure. This is a lot for her to deal with. And, truthfully, she doesn't deserve it."

A text came through on my phone and I knew, before even looking, that it was Stephen. He was home and getting ready for our hike.

"Hale, I have to go. Stephen and I are taking Lola on a hike. We don't get to do things like this too often, with his work schedule."

"Have a great time. I might go take a walk on the beach."

The fire trail that cut into the Santa Monica Mountains was wide and steep. The Pacific Ocean spread out below us on the left and a built-up city shone white and gray on the right. Around us were new green grasses from the recent rains, but they looked fragile, ready to dry up and turn brown if more rain didn't come soon. Lola trotted out ahead of us but kept turning around to make sure we were still close by. Stephen tilted his head up to the sky and took in a long breath, as if there were no sweeter air in the world.

"It's a beautiful day," he said, sliding an arm around me. "Every day's a beautiful day."

I nodded, wondering as I often did why he was attracted to me – a painter of dark streets and shadows, who never said things like that.

I told Stephen about my mother's will, trying to inject some humor into the fact that she left me a painting I would never hang in my home, and one that was impossible for me to relate to, with all those happy families lounging around a lake.

"Do you think part of her wanted you guys to be a family like that? With puppies and kites and picnics?" Stephen asked.

"I don't know. Trying to psychoanalyze my mother is like crawling down a rabbit hole looking for a pony. It's an exercise in futility. I feel so silly for having believed I could leave my family behind once my mother died. I thought, everyone's gone, so I can loosen the chains and be free. But when Hale showed up, I saw how stupid that assumption was. We never leave our families behind."

Stephen held onto my arm when we reached a steep incline with loose rocks on the trail. "You know, under all that anger and turmoil that Hale carries around," he said, picking his way around rocks, "there's a lot of hurt. Have you tried getting him to open up about that?"

"He's given me glimpses, but no – I can't say I've made a real effort. You know that guy Beringer West? The new-age speaker, writer, transformational guru? Hale was reading one of his books today. Apparently West has had a big influence on him, and he invited me to a talk of his tomorrow night."

"Oh, well you should go, don't you think? You might get to know him better. You know what they say – if you want to know someone, get to know their guru."

"What? Who said that?"

Stephen laughed. "No one. I just made it up."

A red-tailed hawk was balanced on a wind current above us. We stopped and stared up at it, prompting Lola to run back to us.

"Good thing you're not a Chihuahua," I told her. "Or I'd be

hiding you under my sweatshirt right now."

We walked to a high spot on a hill and stood staring down at the ocean. All that blue, all the secrets hidden beneath currents and miles of water, life we would never see...it's important to remember how small you are in the balance of nature. Standing up there with the vastness of the Pacific below me, I felt Hale flutter away from me. I felt my mother drift down to the rocky ground at my feet, like dust surrendered by the wind. Stephen, tall and sturdy beside me, was my family. The only family I needed. When my mother and I first moved to Los Angeles, I used to take long walks on the beach. It was before I had Lola, before I'd met Stephen; I was alone. I thought maybe, by the sea, I'd find some trace of my family – stir up memories of the happier times we had in long-ago summers. But all I found was loneliness. One afternoon when storm clouds were moving in, I sat on the sand and cried. I asked God to please let me have someone in my life. I don't want to be this alone, I said to the wind and the first raindrops, and to a God I hoped could hear me. When I met Stephen, I was certain my prayer had been heard.

"Remember the hike we went on when we were first seeing each other?" I asked him.

He smiled and kissed the top of my head. "Yeah. We can't do that here though. Someone would spot us and we'd end up on their Facebook page."

We'd been together for a few months when we went on a hike in Topanga Canyon. It was December and the day was cold and foggy. Looking down from the hillside all we could see were billows of white fog. We went off the trail at one point and found a small open area hidden from view by tall bushes and trees. Stephen used his jacket as a blanket and we made love on the ground as mist dampened our skin and winter leaves crunched beneath us. I was so in love with him, and everything felt so perfect, I thought, If I die right now it will be okay – I've known the absolute best of this life.

"I wasn't suggesting a repeat," I told him. "Just remembering. Besides, it wouldn't be the same without the fog."

Our footsteps kicked up dust clouds as we walked back down the trail. Lola had worn herself out and was staying close to us. "So what are you going to do about Hale's invitation?" Stephen asked as we went from the fire trail to asphalt and walked to his car.

"I think I'll go. Maybe I'll find out who my brother is – you know, behind the curtain."

28.

Saturday afternoon, Janice texted me a photo from the hospital, with Martin lying in a bed, looking pale but cheerful, giving the thumbs-up sign. Janice was beside him, smiling also, her arm outstretched, making it clear this was a hospital selfie. The caption read: 'All done! All better!' I called her as soon as I got it.

"Hey," she said, sounding a little breathless. "I'm just helping Martin get dressed. They're letting him go home…well, to my home so I can take care of him."

"So, everything's okay? He'll be fine?"

"He will. He has to take it easy for about a month. And then kind of ease back into things, but there shouldn't be any more problems."

I could hear the lightness in Janice's voice, something I hadn't heard in a while, certainly not when she was with the tattooed chef. "I'm really happy for you two," I told her. "It's kind of poetic, you helping Martin heal his heart."

"Well, he's helping me heal mine too. Only thank God I didn't need a surgeon's help also."

I showed Hale the photo on my phone and he said he'd call Martin later, but I wasn't sure if he meant it. Even though they had talked, I suspected their friendship had been damaged by Hale's fake death and unexpected return.

Stephen made plans that evening to go to a movie with an actor friend of his, and I googled directions to the church where Beringer West was speaking. I'd already told Hale that I was going to drive. There was no way I was going to ride in his small car that sounded like it needed an engine overhaul. Lola gave me her best mournful look when she realized we were leaving her at home alone, but miraculously I found a dog show on television, so she was happily staring at the screen when we left.

The last time I'd been in a car with Hale was at three in

the morning, when secrets and tears fell between us. Unless we were going to employ the radio as a distraction, or drive in silence, we were going to have to make conversation. I felt my chest tighten as I maneuvered into traffic.

"So, this guy West has helped you, huh?" I said.

"He has. He really emphasizes looking clearly and non-judgmentally at your past so that you can get beyond it and live the life you're meant to live. He talks a lot about God, but not in a denominational way. I guess you'd have to define it as Christian, because Jesus' teachings are part of it, too. But it's absolutely not in the born-again, God-will-punish-you realm."

"Hale, do you think there was ever any chance we could have been a close, happy family? Or even a somewhat normal family? Were the odds just stacked against us?"

He smiled and shook his head. "I don't know. To be honest, I'm not sure why our parents had kids. It didn't seem like parenthood meant that much to them. We were just part of the décor."

"Wow, that's harsh. You weren't part of the décor, Hale. Our mother doted on you."

"That's how it appeared. But appearances are deceiving. Remember that antique chair she bought at an auction one year? It was some ridiculous price that even Dad raised his eyebrows at. She put it in a corner of the living room, by the windows, and told us we were never to sit in it. Then she gave very specific instructions to the housekeeper about how to polish the wood and brush off the fabric on the seat cushion. She was fixated on that chair. I was just another version of the chair, Tilly. An expensive possession. Ultimately, I was going to cost her her marriage, so I was pretty damn expensive."

I didn't know what to say to him. I realized that, at some point, he had reached past childhood and discovered that our mother's eyes were not full of love, but were instead brimming with possession, ownership. And it wounded him as deeply as her disdain had wounded me. None of us got out of this family unscathed, not even our mother. She bore children but never experienced the deluge of helpless, heart-churning love that most mothers feel.

Hale and I began the same way. Each of us floated in our mother's amniotic fluid, getting nutrients and strength from our watery world. The amniotic fluid protects the fetus, cushions it from blows, from being injured. It provides a constant temperature, prevents heat loss. But what else is transmitted to that tiny being who is encased in this protective sack? At fifteen weeks, the developing embryo can see light filtering in from outside the womb, even though its eyelids are shut. Did we see our mother's shape crisscrossed with shadows of anger? Did we inhale her nimbleness with the truth, absorb her deceptive nature? Some women swear that babies in utero can take in their mother's emotions and even be affected by what she listens to. Rachel used to listen to Sarah McLachlin's music when she was pregnant with Nina, and after Nina was born, when she fussed a lot and wouldn't sleep, it was those songs that quieted her. At nineteen weeks, the embryo can hear its mother's heartbeat as well as sounds from outside, like voices. Were we soothed by Charlotte Austin's voice, or frightened by it?

There was no one left now but me and Hale to attest to our mother's dark artistry, her ability to weave distance and mistrust into a family that looked so shiny on the surface. Maybe that was enough of a bond to sustain us. Maybe it was a starting point for a relationship we'd never known how to have.

If the word 'church' were not on the front of the building, no one would ever have pegged it for a church. There was no steeple, no religious symbol. It was a large white building that could easily have housed offices, although it did have lovely French windows in the front. I found a parking spot up the street and as we were walking to the church, I saw that the line of people waiting to get in had grown.

"Looks crowded," I said.

"I got tickets for it," Hale said. "A lot of those people

lined up there probably just showed up hoping to get in."

There were pews inside, but nothing up front that had any religious overtones -- just a podium, and thick purple curtains behind.

"I hope he lets people meet him afterward. I'd love to just shake his hand and thank him for how he's influenced me."

"What kind of church is this?" I asked Hale. "Do you know? I mean, there's nothing denominational anywhere."

"I think it's Christian, but not narrowly so. I'm actually not sure. Remember? I don't live down here."

Berenger West was tall and athletic looking; he strode onto the stage with a confidence and ease that suggested sports were in his background. I guessed him to be in his early sixties. He was wearing dark slacks and a pale blue shirt; his salt-and-pepper hair was thick and just long enough to let people know he didn't fall into the ranks of conservatism. The place erupted in applause when he took his place behind the podium. He led us in a brief prayer about expanding our minds and making peace with our emotions. He asked God for guidance so that every man and woman present could reach their full potential and be everything God intended them to be. I found myself liking him. I understood why Hale was drawn to him.

He was talking about not anchoring ourselves in the toxic emotions of the past, the habit patterns that only serve to keep us stuck and unhappy. He was starting to smile, his hand was just coming up in some kind of gesture. Those will forever be my last images of him. Because when shots peppered the air in a deafening barrage his head exploded in blood and brain matter. Then more bullets ripped through his body as he fell, making it jerk in a horrific dance. I swear there was a second or two of silence before people began screaming and more bullets ripped across the pews, but I could just be imagining that. The shots rang in my ears. I saw people's mouths open in screams but I couldn't hear the screams. I saw the man shooting just for an instant. He was by a side door and he was young and pale, his face partially hidden by a dark green hoodie.

Just before Hale pushed me down, I turned and the blonde woman right behind me had her hands up to her face…then both her hands and her face were gone. Warm blood splattered on my neck. Hale's mouth was shaped around the words 'Get down' but I couldn't hear his voice. He pushed me down on the pew and threw himself on top of me. I smelled blood and smoke and other acrid smells that I couldn't identify. Hale was heavy – his weight was hard against my rib cage and I was struggling to breathe. Then I felt his body bounce. Something warm was pooling on my chest. Hale shifted his weight, rose up enough for me to see his face, grimacing in pain.

"Just my arm," he said, and then managed to push both of us off the pew onto the floor.

The wood above us was splintered and the floor was slick with blood. Hale slid us across the narrow space so that we were wedged under the pew we'd been sitting on moments before.

The shooting stopped suddenly but I didn't move. Hale put his finger across my lips. He mouthed the words, 'Don't scream.' Maybe the shooter is re-loading, I thought. There isn't anywhere else for us to go if he finds us here. I listened for his footsteps but I heard sirens instead – they were getting close. People were moaning, crying, but not that many. The silence made it seem like only a few of us were still alive. Hale's blood was warm against me.

The sirens were right outside. Then more shots rang out, but they weren't inside. All I could hear around me was sobbing and muffled words, someone saying, 'Please help me' in almost a whisper. Men's voices shouted 'Police!' and there were hard footsteps, air moving around us, shadows of people above us, and finally someone's hands reaching down, touching us under the pew.

"We're alive," Hale said.

"It's okay," a man's voice answered. "You can come

out."

We slid out into the moaning and the crying, and the silence behind the sounds. There was blood everywhere – on our clothes, our hands. Hale grabbed his arm and blood seeped through his fingers. So many police were there, and SWAT officers. Paramedics were rushing in. The police officer who was bent over, helping us up, said to Hale, "We gotta get that treated. Both of you come with me."

A few other people were being led out, but so far not many. When we got outside, I looked up at a half moon and the glint of stars. Then I looked down at a body yards from me. SWAT officers were standing over it. A dark green hoodie, pale skin, his body splayed and frozen. The shooter.

The officer led us to an ambulance. Hale was calm, telling the paramedic he'd been shot in the arm, maybe just grazed he said. The paramedic looked at me and I think I told him I wasn't hurt. I poked at myself, though, to make sure. I'd heard about people being in shock and not realizing they were injured. My clothes, my hands, were sticky with blood, but I could find no wounds on my body. Another paramedic came over to me and ran his hands over me, saying to the others, "She's not injured." Some wounds don't show on the flesh, I thought.

My phone – I needed to call Stephen. I felt panic start to flame through me then and my body began shaking uncontrollably. But I managed to stand up and head back through the doors. Paramedics were taking wounded people out on stretchers, but others were motionless, torn apart. There was so much blood, shreds of skin and bone everywhere.

"Miss," a paramedic said, gently taking my arm.

"I need my purse. My phone. I have to call…"

He held my arm as I picked my way to the pew where we'd been sitting, past the blonde woman with no face. My purse was on the floor soaked with blood. My memory is choppy – I remember calling Stephen, and his voice whispering hello. He's in a movie theater, I thought. But then I don't remember what I said. I only remember shaking and my throat closing up as I looked outside where they were loading Hale into an ambulance. The paramedic took the phone from me and calmly told Stephen what had happened and where we were. His hand was strong on my arm as he led me back outside.

"Where are they taking my brother?" I asked him.

"UCLA, in Santa Monica," he said. "He'll be fine. It's not a bad wound."

I'm not sure how long it took for Stephen to get there. I don't think the moon moved across the sky at all, so it couldn't have been long. I just kept staring up – at the night sky, the cream-colored moon, the North Star, looking for a God who seemed to have forgotten us.

I remember Stephen's arms around me. The smells of blood and death were getting stronger. His friend drove him so he could drive my car home. He lifted me into the passenger seat and fastened the belt around me. I guess my legs were too wobbly to get in by myself. Somewhere along the road I asked him to pull over and I got out; I threw up in a patch of ivy outside an apartment building.

My voice came back then. Headlights sped past, and through the open window I tried to breathe in the night air. "Hale saved my life," I told Stephen. "He threw himself on top of me. We have to go to the hospital and see him."

His hand reached for mine, squeezed it tight. He'd have Hale's blood on him now too. "Tilly, we'll call there when we get home. I think it's best that you go home right now," he said.

"I don't want him to be alone." I broke then, tears filming over the lights and the traffic, running fast down my face. I didn't want to wipe them off because my hands were caked with blood.

"They'll let us know how he is. We'll get you cleaned up, and if we can get him tonight we will. You'll be okay, Tilly. I won't leave you alone. You'll be okay."

I hung onto Stephen's voice – a rope keeping me above

waters that could too easily drown me.

Lola backed away from me when we walked in. Her tail drooped and she looked frightened. I knew it was the smell of blood. I started ripping at my clothes as soon as Stephen closed the front door.

"I need to throw these away," I told him, wanting to reach for Lola but knowing I shouldn't.

"Okay. Let's get you upstairs into the shower."

I made him take my clothes back downstairs and put them in a plastic trash bag while I stood naked and trembling in the bathroom waiting for the water to get hot. Lola came to me then, whining and nuzzling my leg even though it was stained with blood that had seeped through my jeans. Maybe dogs can go into shock, too, and now she was edging her way out of it.

Hot water tumbled over me, watery blood swirled around my feet until finally, mercifully, it went down the drain. My father's ring was around my neck, the gold smudged into a rust-color. I watched it turn shiny again, as if it was new, washed clean. But I would never be washed clean, I knew that. The weight of Hale's body would always be on me, pulling me down, saving me. The blood of people I didn't even know had stained my skin, migrated into my bones. Water rivering over me would never take that away. Stephen's hands reached through the water, gently washing me with soap. I tried to breathe in the smell of the soap – anything to counteract the smell of death.

"We have to call Lisa," I told him when I was wrapped in towels and he was drying my hair. "Her number's on my phone."

"Okay, I'll do it."

My cellphone was on a shelf where I kept a stack of towels. It had been in my pocket when I tore my clothes off and I'd set it there without looking at it. Now I saw it was smeared with blood. Wordlessly, Stephen got a cotton ball, some rubbing alcohol, and cleaned it off before looking for Lisa's number. His voice was gentle, telling her carefully, slowly, what had happened. She had heard about the shooting but had no idea Hale had gone to the lecture.

"He'll be fine, Lisa," Stephen told her. "He was shot in the arm. I'm going to call the hospital in a minute. I'll make sure you talk to him tonight."

He got out the blow dryer and handed it to me. "You're still trembling. Let's get you dry. Having a wet head isn't going to help stop the shivering."

A few seconds after he turned on the blow dryer, my cell phone rang. Stephen looked at it, then at me. "It's Hale," he said, handing it to me.

"Hale, are you okay?" I wanted my voice to sound strong, but it was thready and weak.

"Flesh wound," he told me. "A deep one, but still – not too bad. They said I can leave."

"We're coming to get you."

The radio in Stephen's car was tuned to CNN and as soon as he started the ignition, a reporter's voice was saying, "The identity of the shooter is not being released yet..." Stephen reached to turn it off, but I stopped him. I wanted to hear it. "But we do know that he was nineteen years old. Fourteen people are dead and eight are wounded, two critically."

Stephen reached over and gripped my shoulder. I knew he probably wanted to cry, too, but was holding back for my sake.

"The only thought I had while it was going on," I told him, "was if I die, how are you going to find out? Who will tell you? You were the only thing I could hold in my mind."

There were a few news vans outside the hospital. We parked and raced past them, slowing down only when we got through the glass doors of the hospital. Hale was waiting for us in a seating area near the front desk. His arm was bandaged and in a sling; his clothes were caked with dried blood. The blood of strangers, I thought. People he couldn't save. I put my arms around him and said, "We're alive. Because of you, we're alive."

He nodded and I could feel the weight of this night building up in his body, sinking into his bones and muscles. Stephen asked if he'd called Lisa and he said he called while he was waiting for us. A couple of flashbulbs went off as we left the hospital; it was hard to conceal a man covered in bloodied clothes. But we walked quickly to the car and no one followed us.

At first we were silent on the way home – no radio, no attempt at conversation. Then Hale said, "I told Lisa I was happy to be alive. When I got out of the tower that day, I was angry that I was alive. This might be the first time…" His voice broke and he didn't finish the sentence. He didn't need to.

My sleep that night was black and dreamless. Like I was dropped into a cave with thick walls and no sound. At moments I rose out of it, felt Stephen's body against me and Lola's weight on the bed, but then I fell back. When my eyes snapped open and the quiet night settled around me, I looked at the clock. 3:03. Hale's hour. I edged up in the bed and slid my legs out, trying not to disturb Stephen and Lola, and went to the window…I wasn't sure why. I looked down at Hale's car parked in front of my house and felt relief wash through me. I knew then that I'd feared he would leave – disappear again. I tip-toed out of the bedroom, thinking that I wanted to peek in on him, the way a mother would with a child. The way our mother never did. But I saw a lamp on in my work room and I knew I hadn't left it on. Hale was sitting on the floor staring at my unfinished painting of faceless figures in black at a funeral, and the one man standing apart from them, the one who was going to have a face.

"That's me?" he said when I came in and sat down on the floor beside him.

"Yes."

"And I'm going to have a face?"

I actually laughed a little, which shocked me – it felt like I hadn't laughed in a very long time. "You are," I told him. "You will be the first face I've ever painted."

"We're never going to really get past this night, Tilly – what happened in that church. I don't think people can get over something like this. But maybe it helped us get past everything that was keeping us apart. Maybe we can figure out how to be a family. Maybe I can figure out how to be there for Lisa, let her get to know Hale Austin now."

I looked at my brother's face as he said this – the softness in his eyes, a rim of tears balanced there but not falling, his expression open and questioning. That was the face I was going to paint.

Everything would always circle back to this night. I knew that as I walked back down the hallway to the man I loved, the man who would have been the last thought in my mind if I'd died under a strafe of bullets. Years from now, I thought, October winds will bring me back to this one wedge of time. Some memories will have dulled while others will remain sharp as glass. In the still hour of three A.M. I'll stir from sleep, listen to the darkness, look out the window at the scattering of stars. I'll remember again how my brother threw himself on top of me to save my life, and by doing that, saved both of us.

29.

Hale was a news story again, this time as one of the survivors of the most recent mass shooting. The nineteen-year old's name was Franklin Jessup. He was originally from Georgia, and he had decided that Berenger West speaking in a church was somehow contrary to God's law. He'd posted dark, threatening messages on his Facebook page before – posts about false prophets and how they should be killed in the name of God. Before he drove to the church that night he used his Facebook page to rail against a church hosting a messenger of Satan. Then he put an AR-15 in his car, drove to the church, and opened fire. A SWAT officer killed him when he ran outside and aimed his weapon at the police.

Hale's second round of publicity might have helped when he went in front of the judge. He was given a fine and a stern warning to keep the name he was born with and never again take on someone else's identity.

"I think he felt kind of sorry for me," Hale said when he came back to my house that afternoon.

I looked at the sling on his arm and thought about all the news stories of the shooting. "I'm sure he did," I told him. "He probably thought you'd been punished enough lately."

We were in my work room and I had started to paint Hale's face, but it was going slowly. I knew what I wanted to see in the eyes I was painting, but I was new at this face thing so I kept starting over. Hale laughed and said, "Am I that challenging?"

"No. Don't take it personally. This is a big change for me. I've built my career on being the artist who doesn't paint faces."

"Well, I'm honored to be the first. Seriously."

I looked at my brother when he said that and found myself studying his eyes, his face, more than I ever did when we were young. "What thoughts went through your head the other night?" I asked him. "Or did any? Was it just raw survival?"

He looked out the window. Afternoon sunlight slanted through the pine trees and a thin layer of fog was moving in from the ocean. "I just thought I had to save you. You weren't supposed to die like that. You deserve a lot more life."

"Don't you?"

"I wasn't thinking of that then. But now...yeah, I think I do."

I wondered, not for the first time, what other lives and journeys Hale and I might have shared. If this life and all the lives before are one vast river, then we've floated on the same currents, breathed the same air in times outside the boundaries of memory. If we live long enough, and are lucky, we find ourselves reaching for that – the unknown bonds, the invisible threads that survive by faith alone.

Hale stayed for Halloween, and Lisa drove down with Bella. As blue evening gave way to night, and the sidewalks lit up with streams of costumed children and protective parents, Hale, Lisa and I sat on the porch in front of huge bowls of candy. Stephen said he'd stay at his house for the first hour of trick-or-treaters, then leave candy out front and come down the street to my house. It was our usual ritual, but I could tell that this year it was grating on him.

"What?" I asked him earlier, before he left for his house. "You definitely want to say something."

He kissed me quickly. "I do. It would be much nicer if this were all at one house. I want us to talk about that again. About living together."

"We will. I'm not scared of that anymore."

I watched Stephen make his way up the sidewalk, past a few tiny toddlers who were always the first trick-or-treaters to come by. Just days ago, when I thought I was going to die, Stephen's face etched itself in my mind, my heart – on the fear that paralyzed me. Any fears I had before that night were gone. I bent down and kissed Lola, whispering in her ear, "Want to live with Travis?" I'm certain she understood.

278

I brought wine and Nachos out to the porch and we took turns holding out bowls of candy for the kids whose costumes always amazed me. I asked Hale if we were ever that inventive and he shook his head and said, "Not that I remember." Rachel came by with Nina, who had chosen a wig of long shiny black hair and a rather fashionable looking witch costume. It had a little white collar, a cinched in waist, and lace on the sleeves.

Lisa held out the bowl of candy to her and said, "Are you a witch or Kim Kardashian?"

Nina lifted her chin and said, "I'm a witch on the cover of Vogue."

"Well, it's about time," Lisa said.

When Stephen came, Hale and Lisa took a walk up the street, arms laced, their heads close together. "I think they're doing better," I told Stephen.

He gave me a long look and said, "Hale asked me earlier if I thought the two of you should maybe go to New York together for a couple of days. He wants to go to the 9/11 Memorial, and I have the feeling he wants to see Ian. I guess he still isn't sure how you'll react, so he was checking it out with me first."

"It takes time, doesn't it – to get to know someone when you've had a lifetime of distance. He and I should make this trip. On the weekend, so you can take care of Lola, okay?"

Stephen looped his arm around my neck and kissed the top of my head. "Good choice. I'll have all your belongings packed up and moved up the street by the time you get back. And Lola's bed will be placed next to Travis' bed."

"Subtle, Stephen. Very subtle."

"Trick-or-treat!" two skeletons and a pink clad angel yelled.

A light rain was falling when we landed at JFK. The forecast for the next few days was drizzle and low clouds. It seemed appropriate, a blanket of gray, soft rain – as if the sky was being gentle with us. Janice said we could stay at her apartment, since she was staying at Martin's nursing him back to health after his surgery.

We had dinner with them the evening we arrived, and it was like being with a couple who had been together for years. There was an easy familiarity between them, and the kind of love that waits for us if we're lucky, transforms us if we're willing. I'd never seen Janice as happy, and I'd never seen Martin as open. He was still pale, and it seemed like he'd lost some weight, but he looked at Janice as if he'd finally arrived home.

"They each found their other half," I said to Hale as the two of us walked back to Janice's apartment through a veil of misty rain.

"You have too," he said. "With Stephen."

"And you?"

He didn't answer for a few seconds. "Maybe. I think so. It's just that we kind of have to start over now – now that I'm Hale Austin again. Now that I'm not hiding. I know Lisa loved Richard Buchanan. We'll have to see if she loves the guy who disappeared inside Richard Buchanan."

I'd asked Hale a couple of time if he was certain about meeting up with Ian, and when he assured me he was, I made plans for us to meet Ian at the 9/11 Memorial, out front by the pools. Hale was quiet on the cab ride down, looking out at all the construction on the West Side Highway like a tourist who was in New York for the first time. Then it occurred to me that's exactly what it was like for him.

"Looks different, huh?" I said to him.

"Yeah. All this construction. I used to really like this drive, looking out at the water. It's not so pretty anymore."

The mist was light enough that we didn't need umbrellas, but many of the people standing around the pools did have them and I suddenly wondered if we were going to have trouble finding Ian. But as we got closer, he spotted us and walked toward us with fine rain brushing over him – a little stooped, as if his body had taken on the shape of a question mark. When we got to him, he gave me a quick kiss on the cheek and held his hand out to Hale. There was a second's delay, but Hale took it and the two shook hands in that stiff way that men have of not acknowledging the emotions that roil underneath.

"Let's go over to the pools," I said. I wanted water; I wanted the sound and sight of water plummeting down into the depths of everything we'd lost on that horrible day.

Our hands brushed across black stone, names of people who should still be with us engraved there forever. Hale and Ian both started talking at the same time, stopped abruptly, and laughed awkwardly.

"Please," Hale said to Ian. "You first."

Ian looked down at the tumbling water and then met Hale's eyes. "I'm so sorry. I know that sounds so trivial now, but I don't know what else to say. Your mother – she didn't want anyone to know, and I went along with what she wanted. I have no idea why she told your father that morning. He called me when he got to the office. He was crying, he was beside himself. He felt so betrayed – by both of us. And what could I say? I was guilty of everything he was berating me for."

"Why did she decide after twenty years to tell him?" Hale asked.

Ian shook his head. "I don't know. She never spoke to me about it. Never said she was going to do that. I've wondered so many times – what would have happened if she hadn't decided to tell Keith that day, the day the world as we knew it ended. What if she'd told him a week earlier? Would we have been able, all of us, to make some kind of sense of it? To deal with Keith's anger and pain, and with our regrets – maybe have some kind of relationship?"

"If I might interject," I said, "our mother didn't have regrets. Those weren't in her repertoire."

They both looked at me and I saw something shift in both their eyes. Sadness moved aside for a moment and there was a common recognition that we had all been under Charlotte Austin's control, and there was never anything we could have done about it.

"Do you remember when I taught you to drive?" Ian said to Hale.

"I do. We had fun that day."

Ian smiled. "We did. I wanted so badly to tell you that day. Of course, I wouldn't have, but I was so torn apart by the secret I was keeping, and the guilt I lived with."

It occurred to me then that Charlotte Austin, the woman who would become Amber, left barren acreage behind in all the lives she touched. She created distance, and conflict, and when she was really on a roll, regrets that couldn't be lived down.

I looked at Hale and then at Ian – a man who wanted a chance to be his son's father now. Gray mist drifted between them, the sound of water was all around us. "You know what?" I said to them. "She's gone, and we're alive. We all have a chance to live our lives differently."

Ian blinked back the tears that were rising in his eyes. He put his hands on Hale's shoulders. "I'd like to get to know you now. I'd like to be as much of a father as you'll let me be."

"I'd like that," Hale said.

We walked through the entire Memorial, even downstairs, in the room where photos line every wall. Hale and Ian knew so many of those people, I wasn't sure they would be able to go through that room, but they did. Somehow, in the midst of all that death, they were figuring out how to piece together a new life.

The mist had lifted when we said goodbye and hailed cabs. The day was pale and gauzy, but lighter. I remembered how, the day before my mother died, I drove away from her house and suddenly felt that the air had gotten lighter, the sky bigger. Maybe this world, with all that lives and dies, is just a huge puzzle and what we're really doing here is putting the pieces together.

"Are you going to keep in touch with him?" I asked Hale later.

"I am. It would be nice to have a father right now. And

I'm thinking he might like to have a son. So, we'll see what we can do with that."

30.

We are, in the end, the stories we have lived and the stories we leave behind. Hale Austin was once a shiny child who made adults smile and wish their own kids were like him. He grew into the promise that was molded for him by parents who didn't know how to parent but knew how to plant expectations along the road ahead. Charlotte and Keith Austin were champions of reaching high for impressive goals, but somewhere along the line they forgot to look down at their children who waited, as children do, for tenderness. When the towers fell, Hale's story changed, along with thousands of others.

For eighteen years, I believed his story turned into one of nightmare – stepping out into miles of air, smoke and flames at his back, free-falling to an explosive death that obliterated him. It was my nightmare too. For a thousand nights he came to me in dreams, pulling me out with him into empty air. It was only when I fell in love with Stephen that the dreams stopped. I never stepped through broken windows again, never reached for my brother as air whistled past.

Then Hale's story shifted, went backwards and forward at the same time. He was the man who had walked away from death but pretended he hadn't. He was the shadow on the street at three in the morning. He was tears under the glow of streetlights, and confessions pulled from a ragged place of loss and pain. He returned with a different name and a different life – that will always be part of his story, too. And love – he found that with a woman whose heart had navigated grief's rivers, and who chose to accept the altered life of a man who used death as a way to be re-born. Now she's getting to know the man who disappeared. In the chaos of bullets and blood and people being slaughtered, Hale finally got how precious life is. He threw himself on top of me to save my life, and in doing that discovered that his own life mattered too.

That's the strange thing about death -- when it grazes

you, comes so close you memorize its breath – it often ushers in more life.

I have a story too. I was the girl who let her mother's hand guide her own, who learned to create pictures from her imagination. The girl who didn't understand why, one day, her mother turned away and never reached out again. She filled that empty space with shadows, and enough anger to keep her going. When her brother was born, she let herself think that he might fill up that space. And for quick, mercurial moments he did. But trust was too hard for her; the shadows felt more like home. She painted them, made them her motif for art and for life. Love unwrapped some of them – the patience of a man who waited for her to realize that trust isn't a suicide pact.

Stephen understood that shadows and distance had protected me for so long, stepping away from them was like crossing the Rubicon.

Sometimes I try to push my memory back to a time long ago. A younger time, when Hale and I were children. A time when summer felt like forever, when we plunged beneath the waves and held hands, our cheeks puffed out with the breath we were holding. When we raced across white-sand beaches believing we could outrun the wind. Pale afternoons in Manhattan when our skates scraped across the ice and Hale always out-skated me.

I need to remember how I listened for my brother's breathing on the other side of the wall. I need to see again the moonlit night when we snuck out of our summer beach house and sat on the sand. Memories have to be nurtured, preserved, or one day you'll reach for them and find only dust.

Hale and I are making new memories now – getting to know each other by reaching for the stories that litter the roads we've traveled while also looking ahead to the untraveled paths.

My mother doesn't haunt me anymore. The scent of roses never wafts into my home or waits for me around corners. It's as if, when Hale saved my life, she gave up. Or maybe I did – I'm not sure.

I showed my finished painting to Stephen before anyone else. He stood back from it, studied it silently – the sea of black umbrellas, the rain pelting down, part of a coffin visible at the edge of the dark-clad mourners, and a young man wet with rain watching calmly from a distance. His expression is gentle, open, with only a hint of sorrow. Then again, the raindrops on his face could be tears…

"It's really good, Tilly. Amazing, actually – I think it's the best piece you've done. How does it feel to have painted your first face?"

"It feels like everything led up to this. I couldn't have created any version of this painting before now. In a way, painting Hale's face let me get to know him better."

I leaned against Stephen. I had my life with him because of Hale. My painting would be displayed at the gallery in November and, if I was lucky, someone would buy it and hang it in their home. My brother's face would be studied by strangers who would see what they wanted to see in his eyes, in the set of his mouth.

Eventually, they'll impose on him pieces of their own lives. They'll come to think they know him. But they won't know what his breathing sounds like on the other side of the wall. They won't know how his tears look under the glow of streetlamps. And they won't know how walking away from death twice finally made him grab onto life with both hands.

ACKNOWLEDGMENTS

Deep gratitude to Carolyn Leavitt for her brilliant and astute editing.

Thank you also to Judy Melenek, M.D. and Daniel Holstein for answering my research questions, gruesome as some of them were.

Thank you to David Rambo, Nikki Valko, and Ben Press for early reads of the book.

Thank you to Jon Stich for the beautiful cover art and to David Hume Kennerly for the photo. Thank you also to Don Epstein, Sandi Mendelson, and Suzanne Simonetti for support and encouragement. And to Joel Rothman for invaluable computer assistance.